A FOUNDING MOTHER

A NOVEL OF ABIGAIL ADAMS

STEPHANIE DRAY *&* LAURA KAMOIE

wm

WILLIAM MORROW

An Imprint of HarperCollinsPublishers

hc.com

FIRST EDITION

Interior text design by Diahann Sturge-Campbell

Library of Congress Cataloging-in-Publication Data has been applied for.

ISBN 978-0-06-323476-5

26 27 28 29 30 LBC 5 4 3 2 1

PRAISE FOR *A FOUNDING MOTHER*

"*A Founding Mother* is a vivid and meticulously researched portrayal of one of American history's most remarkable women. Dray and Kamoie bring Abigail Adams to life as a fierce intellect, a woman who powerfully defied limits set before her, and whose courage, wisdom, and strength helped shape the nation. This inspirational story of Abigail Adams's incredible life is historical fiction at its absolute finest."

—Madeline Martin, *New York Times* bestselling author of *The Secret Book Society*

"Stephanie Dray and Laura Kamoie are back with another tale of America's founding mothers, this the most famous of all: Abigail Adams herself. America's most famous first lady shines from every page, spiky, clever, and admirable whether holding her family together during the revolution, presiding over the White House during her husband's presidency, or wondering if it was all for naught as she watches her nation's capital burn. The research shines, the prose gleams, the characterization is a delight, and the themes are timelier than ever—on the eve of our nation's 250th anniversary, I can think of no book more necessary than *A Founding Mother*."

—Kate Quinn, *New York Times* bestselling author of *The Briar Club*

"Stephanie Dray and Laura Kamoie's *A Founding Mother* is a must-read for history buffs—or anyone wanting to know more about our country's tumultuous founding. 'Remember the ladies,' Abigail Adams famously wrote, and here we finally remember Abigail, from a young bride and mother, through the upheaval of the revolution, her triumphant turn as wife of the young Republic's ambassador to London, and one of the most memorable first ladies. This is Dray and Kamoie's best work yet!"

—Lauren Willig, *New York Times* bestselling author of *The Girl from Greenwich Street*

"Simply marvelous! Abigail Adams speaks directly to us in an exquisitely told story of her life. And what a life! Wife to one president, mother to another, and a steadfast believer in the promise of the future of our shaky new country. One of the earliest advocates for women, she was a wise counselor and companion to her husband, President John Adams, from his early days as a lawyer in the Boston Massacre trial to his guiding role as president emeritus decades later. In this memoir, she speaks with such honesty and fervor you feel you know her and have been with her for the duration."

—Margaret George, *New York Times* bestselling author of
The Confessions of Young Nero

"Stephanie Dray and Laura Kamoie have long delighted and moved readers with their deeply researched, richly immersive novels of America's early leading ladies. Once again, the hardest-working duo in historical fiction delivers—this time taking on the incomparable life of our most significant founding mother, Abigail Adams. By turns soul-stirring and provocative, and always inspiring and insightful, *A Founding Mother* presents America's origin story as you've never seen it before, beautifully rendered through the voice of a formidably brilliant heroine and deeply thoughtful patriot. This novel is a gift to readers and ought to be required reading as our nation marks its 250th birthday."

—Allison Pataki, *New York Times* bestselling author of
It Girl

To our mothers, who nurtured and shaped us, and all the other mothers struggling to make a better world for their children.

Dear Reader

ABIGAIL ADAMS LEFT more than a thousand letters by which history might judge her thoughts, character, and legacy. In crafting this novel, Abigail's letters were used liberally to allow her to speak for herself whenever possible. To that same end, letters from Abigail's husband, sisters, children, friends, and other correspondents proved useful for inclusion. In those letters, Abigail and her intimates sometimes used language that might be considered impolite or insensitive to a modern ear; occasionally they expressed condescension and bigotry, too. We have adopted that language only when necessary to give a fair and honest portrait of the woman and her times. And for purposes of clarity, we have often mentioned places, titles, or organizations by the name that would be most familiar to the reader even if not the historically correct name at the time. Other choices and changes are explained in the Note from the Authors at the back of the book, which we hope you will enjoy after this story.

Prologue

QUINCY
Massachusetts
August 1814

WAS IT ALL for naught?

Mine has been a life spent bleeding, starving, fighting, and straining to bring six children and a new nation into being. At nearly seventy years of age, I am exhausted by the struggle. My hair is white, my back bent by time, my hands and knees stiff with pain. And as I dig in the dirt to plant a rosemary bush of remembrance by the family tomb, I'm reminded by the mocking song of the cicadas that four of my six children are dead. The other two are lost to me. And our nation's capital is under attack.

For more than four decades—long before we won our independence and long after—the British have menaced our cities, terrorized our coastlines, seized our ships, kidnapped our sailors, and tried to stamp out the flame of our revolution.

Well, this time, they may finally do it.

So I've come to commune with my lost loved ones, fists full of the soil of my country for as long as I may still call it that.

I ignore the approaching carriage on the road—a simple chaise pulled by one horse. I don't wish to be disturbed. I don't wish to put on a brave face as yet another person looks to me for reassurance that this hour is not as dark as it truly is.

But then I hear John call my name and look up with surprise to see my husband in the driver's seat, his aged hands gripping the reins.

At nearly eighty years old, John is still noble in profile. And he still looks the part of the president he once was. But his presidency was more than a decade ago. Now his sight is failing, his teeth are bad, and there is scarcely a hair still left atop his head.

Fortunately, his mind remains active, though that is presently a curse, for he knows that all we have done—and all we have been—stands in peril.

Pulling the carriage to a stop, he motions to me with urgency. He is too frail to get up and down without assistance, so I go to him, brushing dirt and dried grass from my black skirts. Of course, I am also frail, so it takes three tries before I manage to haul my old bones up into the narrow seat beside him. "You have news?" I ask, my voice atremble.

He nods, tears glistening. Then his shoulders slump as he surveys the rolling hills. "Never did our country appear more beautiful than amidst this catastrophe . . ."

I brace for the worst. "Washington has fallen, then? The British have taken it?"

John's mouth flattens to a grim line. "Worse. It is conquered and set ablaze."

I take a pained breath—then another—before I can speak again. "The president's house?"

"Burned," John replies.

I am sent reeling by this news, flooded with memories of those bygone days when I hosted dinners and a grand New Year's party in that lovely white manse as the president's lady. I can still picture the oval room, the red upholstered furniture, the sunny, picturesque view of the Potomac River. I cannot imagine it all devoured by flames at the hand of a tyrant . . .

Nevertheless, John catalogs the destruction. "Both chambers—House and Senate. The Treasury Building. The war department. The naval yard. The Library of Congress. All burned to rubble and ash."

Outrage heats my cheeks. Some would consider it wrong that I grieve more for the books—for all that knowledge lost—than for the mighty edifices so many years' effort took to build. But I do. John once wrote that liberty cannot be preserved without the people desiring and possessing a general knowledge. More than anyone, I know he hasn't been right about everything. But about this, he was correct. "Barbarians," I spit. "This is no superior act of warfare. Just a haughty act of Gothic *vandalism*. And the British still think themselves our betters . . ."

John is silent.

I go silent, too, until I finally summon the courage to ask, "Is the war lost, then?"

My husband's gnarled hands juggle the reins. "The United States has not yet fallen, but I see nothing to prevent the enemy from victory. President Madison has fled and is in hiding. We have no regular army and cannot get one. The militia fight when they please and run when they please. Our revenue is inadequate, our credit has fallen, our dignity lost." He heaves a sigh. "I'm afraid the English have guillotined us."

My breath goes shallow, my hands and scalp prickle, and my heart thuds with despair.

This is the end, then. The end of the American experiment. The death knell of the United States. The destruction of everything we believed in, everything we struggled to build, everything we sacrificed for. I look to the cemetery where my trowel and gardening gloves still lie and imagine a new headstone standing among the others, this one for the United States of America. Perhaps we ought to bury John's copy of the rough draft of the Declaration of Independence. It would make as good a symbolic corpse as anything else, and burying it might safeguard it against British destruction besides.

John senses the tenor of my thoughts and offers one slim hope. "How many states the British will conquer, I know not: but they will not subdue them all."

Will it matter? With Massachusetts threatening to break away and make a separate peace with Britain, my husband—who has gone from traitor, to patriot hero, to president—would likely be deemed traitor again. And he wouldn't be alone.

All the surviving founders of the Union could face the same fate. *Dear God*, the fathers who fought and bled, risking life and property to obtain independence and secure a democratic form of government, are surely asking themselves if they fought and bled in vain.

But what of the mothers of this country?

Fathers might drive the ploughs that till the fields of our future, but mothers provide the water, pull the weeds, and nurture the buds. Because men oversee the harvest, they take the credit for the crop. But without mothers, not one sprout would grow— whether the fruit be a child or a nation. It is mothers who nourish and guide each shoot toward the light without knowing what may blossom and what may wither on the vine. Without knowing which children will live or die. And as one of those mothers, I cannot help now but think back upon the acts of my life that may have brought us to this place.

Part One

Chapter One

W HEN I WAS first with child, revolution was not yet even
a fever dream glistening on the perspiration of my
brow. As the world came into bloom that spring—my
belly as swollen with possibility as the buds on the trees—my worries were decidedly smaller: my mother was being overbearing.

"Lord have mercy," said my sister Elizabeth as she watched me
waddle down the road. "Mother will give me an earful when she
learns I permitted you out and about in your condition, Abigail."

"Permitted me?" I asked with exasperation. My wedding was six
months past—surely enough time to be treated as a grown woman
of twenty who might come and go as she pleased. "I couldn't bear
to miss another market day," I said, huffing and puffing past farmers as they bundled asparagus and radishes in their carts.

"I could've done the shopping for you," Elizabeth chirped, her
lively eyes on the Middle Parish Meeting House, with its plain
white walls and steeple—more modest than the one our father,
Parson Smith, presided over in Weymouth. "Mother sent me to
make sure you rested."

"I don't need rest," I argued, striding a little faster to prove it.
"I need fresh air and exercise."

I'd been too long cooped up at my husband's farm by the lingering snows. Soon enough, I'd be confined by my lying-in until
the child was born. So, I welcomed the muddy half-hour walk to
the town center, past stone walls, smoking chimneys, swaying
willows, and a salt breeze that hinted at the sea.

It was not, of course, the pervasive scent of the ocean I knew from my seaside childhood home. Whereas my native Weymouth was fish and ships, sailors and traders, my husband's native Braintree was more earth and plows, farmers and millers. Nevertheless, I was determined to embrace this place as my own, for it was where my child would soon be born. And I still had much to do to make ready.

On this market day, chickens clucked from nearby cages while pigs snuffled in their pens. Children played chase amongst stalls whilst apron-clad women perused goods at leisure, baskets looped over their arms. But I had a list of rather specific things to buy.

My husband needed paper. We were also in need of candles, soap, tea, sewing pins, and swaddling for our forthcoming child. My mother-in-law had already provided a cradle, not to mention a pap spoon and frilly little caps for the baby's head—all things my own mother protested as bad luck.

As often as not, it ends in tears, my mother had warned, for as a parson's wife she had often prayed with grieving mothers who had lost their babes in childbed. *Which is why you need to be especially careful, Abigail, with your frail constitution . . .*

I was the smallest of my siblings, standing no taller than five feet. My mother had always fretted over me, driving me mad with her prognostications that I might die every time I took a sniffle. She thought me too weak to be out of her sight. And perhaps it was this over-solicitude that made me such a rebellious child.

As a girl with a rambunctious and giddy disposition, I fled my good mother's authority at the slightest provocation, stealing upstairs to my father's library to lose myself in books that described fascinating places across the sea that I longed to visit.

Wanderlust, my mother said, was not fit for a clergyman's daughter.

Nevertheless, I often ran away from the parsonage to take long walks on old trails, my skirts snagging on bayberry bushes, my mood buoyed by the salty scent of the nearby sea. So much did I love nature that friends called me *Diana,* after the maiden goddess of the hunt. And family warned that I risked turning out to be *a very bad woman* unless my parents chose a strict husband to tame me.

Of course, in the end, I chose my own husband: John Adams, a country lawyer nine years my senior, whose money now jingled in my coin purse. And noticing the rare relish with which I intended to spend it, my sister said, "Well, don't blame me if Mama or your Mr. Adams is cross with you for going marketing in your state."

"Never fear," I said, entering the general store. "My good man trusts me to do as I think best."

Which was the reason I married him.

Inside the store, my neighbors gossiped in the rows between barrels of salted fish, jars of spices, and sacks of flour. Some stared too openly at my swollen belly, and under their scrutiny, Elizabeth murmured, "At least let me carry your basket for you."

"I'm perfectly capable of managing on my own," I said airily, never guessing how often I would, in the future, be called upon to prove it.

At present, I was concerned with the dwindling supply of paper behind the counter.

"People are buying it in a panic," the shopkeeper told me. "But once that tax is imposed, they'll need to pay for a stamp on anything official, so it won't help them to hoard paper."

The Stamp Act recently passed by Parliament had been received here in the colonies with such outrage that I could not think they'd really go through with it. So I said, "Well, Mr. Adams hopes it will not be imposed, as he believes the Stamp Act to be unconstitutional."

As the town's foremost rising lawyer, my husband had drafted the so-called *Braintree Instructions*, which registered the sentiments of the town against the tax. My husband was now writing a series of essays for the *Boston Gazette* arguing that the measure was fundamentally different from taxes upon us that Parliament had levied before. Which was why he needed the paper . . .

But before I could buy any, the shop door bell jingled and Dr. Cotton Tufts entered wearing a powdered wig, dark coat, and cravat turned askew.

The good doctor was a kinsman on my mother's wealthy Quincy side—younger at thirty-one years old than he looked— and he set eyes upon us right away. "Abigail! Elizabeth. What a surprise to see you young ladies this afternoon."

"Is it truly a surprise, Cousin Cotton?" I asked, entirely exasperated, for I could think of little reason he'd ride out from Weymouth unless he'd been sent by my mother. "Have you much doctoring business in Braintree?"

Dr. Tufts smirked, turning to Elizabeth. "Oh, your sister is cross. I know it, because when Abigail is in a pleasant mood she calls me Uncle Tufts. And when she's vexed with me it is Cousin Cotton."

"I am not vexed with *you*," I said. I was vexed that my mother had summoned so many physicians, so unnecessarily, while I was in my adolescence. And now it appeared my marriage would not stop her.

But I had always liked Cotton Tufts, because I'd known him as a young man so single-minded in his pursuit of knowledge that he sometimes forgot to remove his fingers from the books he was studying before he closed them. I was fond of teasing him, and with a similar fondness of teasing me he now said, "I'll have you know, Mrs. Adams, that the duties of a country doctor take him sometimes quite far from home. Not unlike your husband, who, if your dear mother is not mistaken, is riding circuit this week to dispense the benevolence of the law."

This was as much of an admission as Cousin Cotton would make that my mother had indeed sent him to find and check on me. I could only wonder how many stops he'd made before finding me here. "So, how are you coming along, Abigail? Any pains or concerns about your pregnancy I ought to know about?"

My younger sister gasped at the audacity and impropriety of such a question posed in public, but I only arched an amused brow. "None I'd discuss in a shop!"

One always had to remind the deceptively severe-looking doctor about convention. There seemed too little room in his big brain for propriety or the trifles of public appearance. Stifling the urge to neaten his messy cravat, I added, "In any case, the midwife would not appreciate your meddling."

"They never do," he admitted. "Nor do I like to meddle in

women's business. Nevertheless, you lack your older sister Mary's wide birthing hips and—"

"*My good sir,*" I interrupted, easily able to imagine my older sister's mortification to have her hips so publicly spoken of.

At this, Dr. Tufts seemed to regain his senses, and now, as if we were still girls under his care, he sought to reward our indulgence with confections. He motioned at some candy jars and purchased sugared orange peels for me and nut brittle for my sister.

When we thanked him, he lowered his voice to say, "As things progress, Abigail, if something should go wrong, promise to send for me."

"I shall," I said, popping a candied orange peel into my mouth. But I wasn't going to send for him. I wasn't going to need to. I reassured myself that I'd come through the forthcoming trial of childbirth and prove to everyone that I was stronger than they knew.

At that moment, I noticed another patron at the other end of the counter. It was my neighbor, the Widow Copeland, with tears in her eyes as she tried to comfort her little five-year-old daughter Patty with a squeeze of the girl's hand.

"I'm sorry, madam," the shopkeeper was saying, offering back her paper currency. "I cannot accept it."

She'd offered old colonial bills—now suspended by Parliament. We could no longer issue money here in Massachusetts, and few businesses now accepted it as legal tender. But the poor woman pleaded. "It was my husband's pay when he fought in the war between His Majesty and the French. It was good enough to induce him to give his life for king and country."

"But it isn't worth—"

"You men start these wars," she interrupted, angrily swiping at her eyes. "Then you leave women to carry the burden alone. I'd starve and die in dignity if I had only myself to think about. But I'm a *mother*. I have to find a way to live for my children, even if it means kneeling in front of all your customers to beg that you take the money my husband earned protecting shops just like yours."

I worried at my lower lip, wondering if I had enough coins to gift her the salt fish and cornmeal she had in her basket. I wondered what my very frugal Mr. Adams would say if I did.

Thankfully, the shopkeeper either took pity on her or wished to avoid a spectacle. "I'll open a line of credit for you. In the meantime, use your old currency to pay provincial taxes; they'll have to take it. At least until Parliament devises some other way to bedevil us."

I left the shop that day rattled by the plight of my poor widowed neighbor. And as we set out on the muddy road for home, I let Elizabeth carry my basket. Because if motherhood meant always finding a way, then despite my pride, I did not wish to do it alone.

I WAS BLESSED with a blue-eyed baby girl who delighted my heart. Where I was dark, she was fair—more like her papa. And though I knew my husband was below stairs pacing by the hearth, eager to meet his child, I decided to keep her to myself a few minutes more.

I had secretly hoped for a daughter and gloried in my triumph. Nestled in childbed, I breathed her in, marveling at her auburn lashes, kissing the pink spot on her head where she was soft and tender. My first child. My first daughter. Would mothering her make me soft and tender, too? Or would it make me stronger?

In the end, I hadn't needed to send for Dr. Tufts. My hips turned out to be wide enough. And now, flooded with maternal bliss, I felt capable of anything.

When I finally sent my sister Elizabeth downstairs to fetch my good man—who had been gloomy and apprehensive during my ordeal—he bounded up the stairs without the gravitas proper for a propertied man of twenty-nine with a growing legal practice.

Upon entering the birthing room, John kissed me with breathless relief.

And I smiled, saying, "I present your daughter, Mr. Adams."

I laughed as my husband's stern expression *melted* at the sight of his newborn peeking up from the folds of the blanket. John Adams was an utter misanthrope, or so I liked to tease, but he had a more tender heart than anyone else knew. And once I discovered that tender heart, I claimed it—and gave him mine in return.

That was why I'd let him whisk me away from my father's parsonage to install me as mistress of this slope-roofed saltbox farmhouse where we set straight to the business of children. A business at which we'd been too efficient!

"Tongues may wag," I told him. "But do not be vexed with our daughter for arriving two weeks early."

"Oh, I'd forgive her anything," John said, reaching as if afraid to break her. "Why, hello, little Miss Adorable . . ."

I gasped in mock offense. "She's already usurped the pet name you bestowed upon me in courtship?"

"Oh, but you are *Mrs.* Adorable now," John said, cradling her. "And I propose to make little *Miss* Adorable your namesake entirely. Our little Abigail."

Though I was delighted by this, it was not the convention. "You don't wish to name her after your mother?"

"*No*," he said, firmly. Very firmly. For relations with his nearby mother and brothers were ofttimes strained.

"You don't fear confusion with two Abigails?"

"She will be *Abigail Amelia*," John pronounced.

I liked the sound of this. I pictured the sort of young lady our daughter might become with such a name. *Abigail Amelia* sounded like a cheerful girl. Elegant, not pretentious. Which pleased me, as I could never abide vanity.

In fact, when, as a coltish fifteen-year-old girl, I first met John as a guest at my father's table, he'd boasted so much that I'd made sport of him. And smarting from my taunts, John gave every impression that he thought me a sharp-tongued shrew. In his enormous pomposity he'd chided me for my unladylike habit of sitting cross-legged with a book. When I shot back that a gentleman had no business to concern himself with the legs of a lady, he'd flushed beet red and fled.

Thankfully he returned at a later date, somewhat humbled, and gifted me a book. I don't know if he'd been advised by one of my sisters that books were the surest way to my heart, but in any case, he was able to apologize and to laugh at himself, which made me welcome his courtship.

My father opposed the match, and my mother's Quincy relations thought John Adams beneath me. None understood my attachment to the short, stout lawyer, whose name was familiar to us primarily because his kin were maltsters in Boston.

But I sensed in him a man of destiny.

And something about Mr. Adams's natural irascibility had appealed to the rebelliousness in me. Perhaps because he courted me by way of bickering, encouraging me to argue with him as if he gave my opinions weight. And because he was a man of words, not the rod.

In John Adams, I'd seen the possibility of freedom. And I'd insisted upon my heart's desire until my parents finally gave their consent.

Never for a moment since had I doubted my choice. And now I hoped our daughter, with her beautiful name, would inherit her father's many wonderful traits. Our little *Abigail Amelia* . . .

WITHIN DAYS OF my daughter's birth, the name *Abigail Amelia* was shortened to *Abigail*, which then became *Abby*, until finally, during the exhaustion of breastfeeding, I murmured *Nabby*, my own childhood nickname, which stuck.

Motherhood was a tiring business. So much so that I swallowed my pride and thanked my mother for sending Elizabeth. Not that my little sister was much help—as often as not, she took a blanket up Penn's Hill to write poetry and lallygag in the sun.

Fortunately my mother also sent my old nurse Phoebe, the enslaved woman who had swaddled me in my infancy. Phoebe was, to me, both friend and second mother. She was also the subject of much childhood rebellion, for I'd determined at a young age that slavery was an evil—and argued unsuccessfully with my father to set Phoebe free.

Thus it was always with feelings of guilt that I accepted Phoebe's help, even when she professed eagerness to assist. "Now you give me that baby to bathe, Miss Abby, before you get too tired and drop her."

Phoebe still called me *Miss Abby*, though everyone else more properly called me *Mrs. Adams* now. Too tired to argue, I let Phoebe take the baby into her arms, bathe her, and rock her to sleep with songs from her native Africa.

When my small breasts threatened to run dry of milk, Phoebe insisted I take fennel and barley water instead of tea, so I could better nurse Nabby. And when I did, she said, "Lord, you were such a wild colt as a child, I could never credit the idea of you as a mother. Never did I think I'd see you contented with a baby at the breast. But here we are."

Taking umbrage, I retorted, "Grandmother Quincy said wild colts make the best horses."

"Well, you're saddled now, Honey. And in mothering this little one, you'll need to be steady."

Steady. I could be steady for Nabby. Especially since I thought her the most special child in creation. Elizabeth claimed she was not often charmed by babes but mine was an exception. Phoebe could not resist pressing kisses on Nabby's chubby cheeks. And John often stared at her in her cradle.

I did, too, for I was fascinated by every movement of her tiny fingers and every hair upon her head. And I didn't want to miss attending to a single one of her needs, whether milk or touch or comforting words. As friends and family paid call to welcome our daughter into the world, I ought to have been embarrassed by my overweening pride! After all, I used to feel so vexed when parents chitchatted about every queer little thing their child did. I'd resolved never to become tiresome by prattling on endlessly about my own children. But now I was proud as a peacock of my baby and eager to show her off.

My parents had already come to coo over their granddaughter. But there were more introductions to be made. "Might we visit Salem?" I asked my husband while we breakfasted. I wanted to see my older sister, Mary Cranch, whose approval I craved. And I knew John would enjoy the trip because Mr. Cranch was John's friend as well as brother-in-law.

In courtship we'd been a gay foursome, and now that we all had wee ones, I longed to see our babies together in a cradle.

Alas, my husband said, "We cannot go to Salem just yet. Farming and the courts are coming too thick upon us. In fact, I'm shortly to argue a case in Martha's Vineyard."

"What sort of case is it?"

"A complicated one," John said.

Giving him a droll stare, I rocked Nabby gently in my arms. "As most are. Do you fear this one might confuse my female brain?"

To our daughter, I whispered, "I *do* hope your papa knows legal talk won't give me the vapors."

"Don't be *saucy*, woman," my husband grumbled, hiding a smirk behind his napkin. "It's a case involving a child. The mother—having fled her drunken husband—arranged to indenture the boy to his grandmother until the age of twelve so that his father would have no claim on him."

"Clever mother," I murmured, stealing a crust of toast from John's plate.

John arched a disapproving brow—either at my words or at my crust thievery—and pulled his plate closer. "When the boy finally did turn twelve, he didn't want to go with his drunken wastrel of a father."

"Smart boy, too, then." Because my own brother was always drowning in rum, I held drunken wastrels in low regard, which my husband had cause to know. "Can you blame the boy for not wanting to go with such a father?"

John scratched at the back of his head in answer. "It isn't the boy's choice. His father has rights to him. But all the womenfolk of his family formed an army of Amazons to keep the father away. And when the lawmen finally came to seize the boy—"

"*Seize* him?" I startled, midbite. "Lawmen seizing a twelve-year-old boy?"

"Came to *escort* him," John corrected. "Into his father's custody."

"You mean, they tore him from the only safe hearth and home he'd ever known."

John pointed with his fork. "Your partiality makes me think it's a good thing women do not serve on juries."

With my daughter in my arms, my whole body shuddered against the idea that anyone should ever be *impartial* about a mother being separated from her child. "I think it would be better if women served on juries so the partiality of human nature did not always go one way—against the woman."

"Must you always champion your sex?" my husband asked, apparently amused by what he took to be this peculiarity of mine.

"Someone has to champion my sex," I replied. "Since your sex won't. Pray tell me you're not arguing before the court that the mother must give up her boy."

John gulped down a forkful of eggs, now a little irritated. "No, I'm arguing in favor of the officers."

"Which officers?"

"The ones who came to get the boy. The women attacked them. The boy's aunt, in particular, being a fearsome shrew, waved two frying pans at the officers with menace. So, they arrested her. She's suing for assault and false imprisonment."

My lips tightened involuntarily.

John noticed. "Do not say she was justified!"

"Very well." I sipped my tea. "I won't say it."

Puffing up as he was prone to do, John began to lecture. "My dear wife, one cannot have civilized society without *the law*."

"Can a society still be called civilized if its laws are so unjust?" I asked, because *the law* always prioritized a father's rights over a mother's.

"An interesting question," John said. "One of frequent debate in taverns these days when it comes to these odious acts of Parliament. But a man scarcely expects to encounter such a quarrel at his breakfast table with wife and infant."

"Are we quarreling?" I asked sweetly.

He bit back a smirk. "We're bickering."

When we bickered, it was playful banter about such trivial matters as his barbaric habit of leaving the shutters open to the night air—when any civilized man, or indeed any barbarian, should know shutters must be shut at night. But this was a serious matter, and he did not want to admit it. So, I merely drank my morning tea—ever a saving grace for a new mother whose babe does not sleep through the night—knowing that my uncharacteristic silence would force my husband to stew.

"The laws might be unjust," my husband finally blustered on. "But by *rebelling*, anarchy follows. This woman and her frying pans unleashed chaos on the whole island. Brawls led to shootings—all because of women's violent passions."

All because of a wastrel father, I wanted to say.

Instead, I gentled my husband's impatience with a kiss on the cheek and a second helping of eggs, consoling myself that though John might be of acerbic temper, he was as good a father and husband as God ever bestowed upon the earth. And I loved him dearly.

. . . even so, I made a silent promise to my baby girl: I'd defend her with frying pan, broomstick, or musket if need be. Even if the price was anarchy.

Chapter Two

BOSTON
Massachusetts Bay Colony
January 1770

T HERE IS NEVER enough time in the haze of nursing and swaddling. In truth, time passes like a quick-fingered thief through a mother's memories and best-laid plans. Nabby was barely two years old when her little brother John Quincy was born, and then came Susanna. Five years had passed in a blink, my husband's legal practice was thriving, and all three of my children were toddling across the floorboards of our new house in Boston. We'd moved to the city so John could be near the courts, and we'd grown comfortable in our lodgings, with a view of the harbor and proximity to Bowes's bookshop.

Boston's air often stank of rotting fish, emptied chamber pots, and other refuse, but I'd grown accustomed to it. That and the clacking coaches, clucking chickens, criers, and chapmen. But the exciting pulse of so much to do and so many people to see compensated for these drawbacks.

The real trouble with Boston was the rising menace of British regimental soldiers and their clashes with colonists over taxes on paper, glass, and tea. Even now, from the window, as I prepared a tray of chocolate for my husband, I could see soldiers banging on my neighbor's door to force their way in. For British soldiers claimed the right to search homes without warrant.

They'd actually attempted it at my door not long ago.

John had come roaring down the stairs, demanding an explanation for the intrusion. Upon seeing him, the officer looked confused. "We're to search the abode of Mr. Adams."

My husband crossed his strong arms, exposed by rolled shirt-sleeves. "I *am* Adams. Mr. John Adams, esquire."

The soldier flushed. "We must've mistaken the address."

John had peered down his nose with the imperiousness of a magistrate. "You were perhaps looking for my cousin Samuel?" When the soldier lingered in embarrassed silence, John could not pass up the opportunity to needle him. "Well, you shouldn't be searching *his* house either. Not without a proper warrant. Unless, of course, you mean to furnish me with yet another profitable legal case."

The soldiers withdrew, for my husband's threat was not idle. Defending colonists against government abuse had become his specialty and now furnished him a good living. Visitors sought him night and day.

But tonight the visitor who occasioned the tray of chocolate was the very same cousin who had occasioned British soldiers to bang upon our door. At that time, I knew Sam Adams only slightly. He was a gaunt figure radiating Puritanical piety whose intense gaze and reflexively contrarian ways sometimes put me ill at ease. It wasn't the contrarian so much—that was an Adams family trait—as it was the aggression accompanying it that jangled my nerves.

As it did now when I overheard Sam say, "All you do is write about British abuses, John. You don't *do* anything about this tyranny."

"That's unfair," my husband snapped. "What I *do* is ensure you and your rabble-rousers have protection of the law. Did I not force the Crown to drop its case against Hancock?"

He meant the Crown's seizure of John Hancock's merchant ship under charges of smuggling—a charge my husband defeated in court, though he believed the man to be guilty as sin. But the prominent and wealthy Hancock had been singled out for punishment because of his political beliefs. Which my husband simply could not abide.

Of course, neither could he abide the tactics of the mob, egged on by Boston's Sons of Liberty.

Five years ago, a group of angry colonists had hanged a tax collector in effigy from the Liberty Tree—a large stately elm on the corner of Essex and Orange Streets where colonists gathered to protest the Stamp Act. Once the effigy was hanged, they stomped it, beheaded it, and held a funeral for it to intimidate that official to resign.

It was rumored that Samuel Adams had instigated this intimidation, and I believed those rumors. One could not argue, however, against the effect. The tax collector did resign. Others followed suit all over the colonies, rendering the Stamp Act unenforceable. But now new taxes on imports like tea had been passed, and Sam wanted my husband to do more with the Sons of Liberty to protest them.

From my place by the entry—not knowing whether I should knock and take the chocolate in—I watched my husband rub at his temples. "I support the boycotts. You won't find a leaf of British tea in this house. But your *methods*, Samuel."

Sam all but crushed his damp tricorn hat in a tightening grip. "I cannot be held to account for what the mob does."

His protest seemed far too glib. His clenched hands might not do the tarring and feathering, but his words often inspired these deeds. And now my husband pointed out, "If they're not your methods, neither do you decry them."

Sam rose to pace by our fire. "What other means do people have to resist unconstitutional acts? We have no representation in Parliament—"

John broke in to say, "Unpropertied men of England have no representation in Parliament either."

Nor the women, I thought.

But Sam simply turned and skewered my husband with that zealot's gaze. "You don't believe that is a justification, John."

"No," my husband admitted. "I believe there should be no taxation without representation, and that if we allow ourselves to be treated as if we have fewer rights than an Englishman in London, we do a great disservice to ourselves and to our children."

On that note, I cleared my throat and brought in the now lukewarm chocolate, interrupting them with cheery talk of friends and family. Sam asked after our youngest, Susanna—little Suky. She'd been sickly, and Sam expressed concern. "I'll pray for you and your little girl, John. May she soon be in better health."

In the weeks to come, Sam continued to rile up Boston against the unfair taxes, yet a tax on our tea remained. And to make sure we paid it, British soldiers ran drills in the snowy streets, shouting:

"Fix Bayonets!"

"Shoulder Firelocks!"

"Present Arms!"

It was dispiriting to see soldiery in our streets. They were not here, as they claimed, to protect the public. They were here to intimidate, subjugate, and force our obedience to unpopular laws at the point of a musket. And their shouts tested my nerves. I had a household to manage and children to care for. How could I do it with this racket—and the threat it was meant to represent—outside my door?

"March! Halt! To the Right! About face!"

On tiptoe, peering out the frosted window, four-and-a-half-year-old Nabby asked, "Mama, shouldn't we tell the soldiers not to wake the babies?"

Nabby fussed over her siblings—two-and-a-half-year-old Johnny and thirteen-month-old Suky. My oldest considered herself too grown now for an afternoon nap but knew her sick little sister needed rest. I, too, feared the soldiers would wake my babies, and abandoning my sewing with a soft thump into the basket, I snapped, "Someone certainly should have a stern word with those lobsterbacks."

I immediately regretted calling them lobsterbacks, because Nabby tended to parrot me, and if her father heard us using that derogatory term, he'd be wroth.

Well, he'd simply have to forgive me, for I was heavy with another one of his children, swollen at the ankles, and in a terrible mood—made worse by the lack of good tea, for I only pretended to enjoy the herbal liberty tea we patriot wives brewed. At our sewing circles—between snippets of gossip and more serious talk of how we might resist British tyranny—we traded satchels of these herb teas around, claiming we no longer missed the real stuff.

But miss it, I did, especially the further my pregnancy progressed. I pinched the bridge of my nose against the headache brewing there when the shouts of the soldiers finally awakened my little Suky, who started to cry.

Rushing to her, I found Suky red in the face, her cry raspy. *Poor sickly child.* The previous summer, upon the advice of Dr. Tufts, I'd taken her back to Braintree to escape the city's foul vapors, but nothing gave her comfort. Now I scooped my wailing littlest girl from her cradle and kissed her forehead, which was warm against my lips. "Fetch me a wet cloth, won't you, Nabby?"

Nabby was already quite dependable, just like my sister Mary had been at her age. Perhaps the oldest child is ever thus . . .

I wanted to send for Dr. Tufts, but he was too far distant in Weymouth. So, reluctantly, I sent for Dr. Joseph Warren. He was reputedly a fine doctor—but personally, I mistrusted that a man so good-looking could also be a serious man of science. Moreover, I preferred a doctor to be a good deal older than Joseph Warren's twenty-eight years.

But with Suky so sick, I had little choice, and I was relieved when the smooth-cheeked Dr. Warren arrived promptly to examine her with both thoroughness and a gentle hand.

Alas, his diagnosis was grave.

"A pleurisy," Dr. Warren declared.

"Is it as dangerous as your expression leads me to fear?" I asked.

He plainly despaired of telling me, "Many children die of this ailment because there is nothing to treat it save a mix of lime, sugar, and distilled cordial water. Failing that, a potion of Maredant's Antiscorbutic Drops, which I do not have and cannot get."

"I have only two withered limes in the larder," I said desperately. "But sugar and cordial water I have aplenty. Will that do?"

He nodded. "I'll mix it for you."

While I rocked my crying baby, the good doctor squeezed the limes into the cordial water with sugar. Then he lowered himself into my rocking chair, took my baby into his arms, and dabbed at her lips with a cloth soaked in the concoction.

How grateful I was to Dr. Warren for trying to ease my child's pain and for the tenderness with which he treated her, staying with us even when he was already late to attend another patient.

When he finally left, Nabby tried to coax her sister to suck the lime cordial from her fingertips. But our hearts sank when little Suky would not take even a drop.

Meanwhile the drilling continued outside my window. *"March! Halt! To the Right! About face!"*

I could take no more and sent our maid to ask the sergeant if he might leave off for another day so my sick baby could rest. But no sooner did my maid poke her head out the door to interrupt the drill than was she accosted by rude hoots and whistles, and propositioned by impertinent British soldiers who offered to bed her for a wage.

"Count yourself fortunate we don't *take* you," a jeering soldier shouted. "And the dinner from the table of your mistress afterward."

I heard their cruel laughter even after my maid slammed the door and pressed her back against it, breathing hard.

Scoundrels! How I burned with offense. "Mr. Adams will hear of this when he returns and will certainly speak to their superior officer."

But when would my good man return? John was not yet a rebel and revolutionist, but he increasingly spent time in taverns discussing the news of the day and was often late in coming home. By dusk I grew frantic, for the baby was listless in my arms. I felt death's grip on her. Oh, how I wished for my mother, whose over-solicitousness for my health I now understood. Mama knew better than I did how to tend to an ailing child. And I now despaired that she was so far away . . .

As the candle burned down, I continued to rock poor Suky in my arms, tears streaking her burning cheeks. Her cries exhausted her, her fingers too weak to grasp mine. Our maid fed the other children and put my little boy to bed. But Nabby stayed at my side, her face pressed to my belly even after sleep carried her away.

She was still with me when John finally shuffled in, snow dripping from his tricorn hat, looking consternated to find his three girls in the dim candlelight of the parlor.

By then Suky no longer cried. Each of her stuttering baby breaths was a struggle. And one look at my grim expression seemed to tell John that we must resign ourselves to the worst.

Wordlessly, he took a sleeping Nabby into his arms and carried her to bed before returning to me with the family Bible. My husband was the son of a deacon, and I was the daughter of a parson, so it was natural that we should look to God for the salvation of our baby girl. We prayed together; we prayed and prayed for baby Susanna until our voices were nothing but hoarse whispers and choked sobs, for the baby's breaths slowed, shallower and shallower each time.

Susanna died in my arms that night.

When she passed, a wild, almost inhuman, sound of agony escaped me. Clutching her lifeless little body to my heart, I felt a madwoman with sobbing grief. I wished to run into the snowy street and rend my garments.

It was only John, holding us both against his chest, who kept me still and sane and anchored with the solid weight of him. "Our other children need us," he whispered tearfully, reminding me with a hand on my pregnant belly that such grief could endanger the life there, too. "They will learn from us how to meet life's most painful misfortunes."

We must bear up for them, he meant.

Soon dawn would break, and we'd have to tell Nabby and Johnny that their sister had gone to heaven. So, I somehow composed myself, letting numbness overtake me as I looked down at my dead child.

Thirteen months. That was all the time that dear little soul lived on this earth. Just long enough to come into an awareness of herself and the love of her parents. The pain of bringing Susanna into this world was infinitely less than the pain of seeing her pass back out of it. It was the wrong order of things, to outlive a child.

But as our house went quiet and still with mourning, the soldiers continued marching outside—muskets at the ready. And that was unnatural, too.

Chapter Three

BOSTON
Massachusetts Bay Colony
March 1770

I WAS STILL MOURNING our baby's death when, before the spring thaw, a new disturbance outside my window brought fresh pain.

Men with torches marched down our street demanding justice for a young boy who had been beaten by redcoats. Seeing a crowd of angry men in the night frightened me. We were firm patriots in this house—but when a mob starts breaking windows and putting houses to the torch, women and children often meet violence no matter what side they take.

Worse, John had not yet returned from a meeting, so I was alone with the children and servants. I wanted to send my husband's hired man to summon him home. But how could I send anyone out into this danger?

Fortunately, the manservant was already grabbing his cap to duck out the door. "I'll discover what's happening, Mrs. Adams, and fetch your husband home."

"You have my gratitude, sir," I said, though words did not seem enough. But almost the moment he was gone out into the icy night, I regretted sending him.

We heard what sounded distinctly like the snap of muskets in the distance. Then screams. And here we were without any man at all in the house to defend us.

Starting on the task myself, I said to the maid, "Bar the windows."

Then I looked for something with which we might protect ourselves. I knew John kept a set of pistols in the house. I was familiar with hunting muskets and fowling pieces, but as a parson's daughter I'd never had cause to learn how to fire a pistol. And I feared I might harm myself or the children if I tried. But remembering my husband's old case from Martha's Vineyard years back, I glanced over the stove, where my cookery hung. A frying pan . . . well, that I could certainly wield.

So I grabbed a cast-iron pan, then hurried up the steps, which now made me breathless, heavily pregnant as I was. I quickly gathered Johnny and Nabby into bed with me fully clothed, in case we might have to flee. And for a second time in months, I worried for the lives of my children. I had been unable to save Susanna. But my fingers curled around the handle of the cooking pan because I knew that however doomed the cause might be, I would *fight* for the children that remained to me.

How long I huddled there, my knuckles going white around the iron handle, I cannot say. My arm was numb, my back cramped. It could've been hours. It felt like a year.

At last, John returned with his servant, bursting into the house. He ran up the stairs, two at a time, shouting, "There has been a slaughter on King Street!"

Only upon reaching our bedroom did he realize our children were present, so he motioned for me to join him in the hall. There, in hushed tones, he explained, "British soldiers fired on a crowd."

My stomach clenched in horror. "You witnessed it?"

"No." John slowly removed hat and wig from his balding pate. "We heard the commotion and thought it was a fire; I grabbed my hat to join the brigade, only to find blood in the snow."

"And people were killed?" I asked, my fingers still frozen around the handle of the pan.

"At least five, perhaps more wounded."

Fearful of further violence, I asked if we ought to pack up the children and retreat to his family farm in Braintree. But John said, "I don't think it necessary just yet. The governor showed some courage; he actually ordered the arrest of the British soldiers who fired on the crowd."

"As well he should," I said, fury mounting. "But what will happen now?"

John gave a noncommittal shrug, sitting down on the top stair to remove his sodden boots. "The Sons of Liberty will mount patrols to keep the peace until these soldiers are tried; but it remains to be seen if they can get a fair-minded jury anywhere in Boston."

I agreed with my husband that the British soldiers—who stood accused in what would eventually come to be known as the Boston Massacre—deserved a fair trial.

But I never expected that my husband would be the one to ensure it . . .

"NO ONE ELSE is willing, Abigail," my husband argued a few days later, after his cousin Sam's most recent visit.

"For good reason no one else is willing to defend these brutes," I replied hotly. "Just the *rumor* that you're considering defending the redcoats has ruffians throwing rotten eggs at our door, and I doubt my beeswax polish can restore it."

Would it matter to them if the mob knew it was their favored son Samuel Adams who asked my husband to defend the soldiers?

Better you than a Tory lawyer, Sam had said. *You can defend these men without casting aspersions on the city of Boston.*

Sam had a political strategy in mind—one shared by my patriot uncle Colonel Quincy, who also wanted John to argue the case.

But my husband had his own reasons.

"Everyone deserves a fair trial," John insisted to me and anyone else who might ask. "A good and zealous defense. If we believe we have the same rights as British citizens, then we need to protect those rights."

"But why must *you* take the case?" I asked.

"Why not me? I have the ability and the will. Why should the duty of protecting liberties fall to anyone else?"

I had no answer for that. Even if I was not still numb with the grief of a mother who had lost her baby, I would not have an answer to it. Because God called us to use our gifts to help others whenever we could.

And in any case, there was no talking John out of it. For all that I was a grieving mother, he was a grieving father looking to turn his mind away from the pain and make meaning of our lives.

The next day, the burly young bookshop clerk at Bowes's handed me a volume amidst shelves boasting of old Roman tomes. "Is it true, Mrs. Adams, that your husband will defend those bloody *redcoats*?"

I thumbed my book while trying to think of a reply that wouldn't get us tarred and feathered.

Tempers were still high in Boston; the five young men who had been shot were Samuel Gray, Samuel Maverick, James Caldwell, Patrick Carr, and Crispus Attucks—a formerly enslaved man who was the first to be shot. All now hailed as martyrs while the redcoats who shot them were condemned as vicious murderers.

So I answered the clerk honestly, but cautiously. "Mr. Adams was asked to represent them at trial, and he feels it is his duty."

Nabby had been worryingly silent since the death of her sister, but now, peeking out from behind my petticoats, she precociously repeated her father's high-minded ideas. "Papa says everyone deserves a fair trial."

Thankfully, the clerk smiled down at Nabby. "Your papa is a brave and honorable man."

Lifting his eyes to me, the clerk added, "Possibly a little foolish, though. You know, I warned Captain Preston not to fire on the crowd that night and I don't believe he *did* give the order."

I startled. "You were there?"

"Oh, aye, I was there," the store clerk replied, folding his meaty arms over his chest. "Tussled with some of them rowdy boys, too, trying to get them to stop provoking the British."

I wilted, because if the redcoats had been *provoked* to fire on the crowd . . . well, that could help my husband get an acquittal.

It was bad enough that John had taken the case. If he *won*, our family might very well be ridden out of Boston on a rail. We'd lose friends, property, income, and our standing in the community—accepted by neither patriots nor loyalists.

By standing on principle, we'd stand alone.

Still, right was right, and holding my daughter's hand, I felt compelled to ask, "Would you be willing to testify, sir?"

Back at home that night, John was far more pleased to hear the answer than I was to tell him.

"He'll testify?" John took up his quill. "What's the clerk's name?"

"Henry Knox. And he says he'll testify *if he must*."

John clapped one hand on the table in satisfaction. "He isn't the only one. Every day, this matter proves itself to be a straight-forward case of self-defense!"

Having agreed to take on the case, he allowed himself the vanity to think he would win. With books open on every surface, scribbled notes piled to one side or crumpled and tossed at the fire, he was a legal force to be reckoned with.

Thankfully, he wasn't blind to the danger.

Late that night, when finally he came to bed and found me still awake, he placed a fond hand upon my belly beneath the covers. "Don't fret, Abigail. Should my work prove too unpopular here in Boston, I am prepared to give up the house and move back to Braintree."

Twining my fingers with his, I said, "On the one hand, I daresay Boston is losing its charm. But I would not like to return to a life where you ride circuit and are gone more days of the week than you're home. Especially not with me so near to my time."

"We can move after the baby is born," John promised, smiling in the candlelight. "A little sister for Nabby, I hope."

Certainly one child could never replace another, but perhaps a little girl would ease our grief over Susanna.

God had other plans.

In May, I was delivered of a boy we named Charles. A delicate little baby with blue eyes and golden curls. Quite the perfect cherub.

A rare joy, for the trial was beginning to consume my husband whole.

"Let justice be done though the heavens fall," John would thunder, quoting Latin to justify taking on such an unpopular cause.

This trial was threatening his ability to keep food on the table. He pretended it did not distress him. Yet, anyone with eyes could see the dreadful toll. He grew thinner, and a sickly pallor washed over his countenance. His temper shortened. And by autumn, I found unpaid bills on the table and my husband clutching his chest, his jaw clenched in a grim line.

"John?" I rushed to him. "What is the matter?"

"Don't scold me for opening the windows at night," he wheezed. "I cannot—I cannot breathe."

Watching my husband fight for breath, I eagerly helped him fling the windows open wide. But it was not enough. John staggered, struggling with the back door. I helped him into the alley, the wet cobblestones littered with oyster shells and a child's hoop and ball.

My husband leaned his weight on me, and as he dragged in desperate breaths, I asked, "What ails you? Congestion in your lungs?"

John shook his head and pointed to his chest as it heaved up and down. "Terrible pain. Tightness."

My father had seen parishioners die of such symptoms. Terrified, I put my hands to my husband's cheeks. "Inhale slowly. With me now."

I breathed with him in the dim light from our kitchen until he was finally calm enough to sit on the stoop. Then I sent for a physician, though I feared Dr. Warren might refuse to come, because the good doctor had openly condemned my husband's clients as murderers.

Thankfully, upon being summoned, Dr. Warren flew to our home. Pressing his ear to John's chest, and gently palpating his neck, the doctor finally declared, "You are working yourself to a nervous exhaustion, my dear Adams. And for undeserving British brutes, I might add. You should quit this trial."

John managed to argue between breaths. "Everyone . . . deserves . . . representation."

"Be that as it may, you must rest," the doctor said, propping my husband up in bed with pillows. "Before this anxiety becomes a genuine threat to your life."

Later, downstairs, with worry on their faces, my older children crowded about the doctor's knees. "Your papa simply gave us all a scare," he said, producing from his medicine bag two pieces of candied fruit—one for Nabby and one for Johnny.

I sputtered a surprised laugh. "Our family physician, Dr. Tufts, always gives confections to his young patients."

"A trick of the profession," Dr. Warren replied.

I was grateful that Dr. Warren had eased my children's worries, because I knew the sight of their strong father brought low would bring nightmares. And I also appreciated Dr. Warren's compassion about our bills. "No payment is necessary, Mrs. Adams. Especially as your husband is not apt to follow my advice to quit this trial."

"No, Dr. Warren," I said. "I don't suppose he shall."

The young doctor smiled with understanding. But in the days that followed, I endured the cold stares of fishwives on the street. Suspicious eyes followed me in the marketplace. Social invitations dried up. I was no longer welcome at patriot sewing circles. And one evening I found myself standing on our doorstep, staring down at a flaming bag of horse manure. I glanced up to see a man across the street spit in my direction, glowering. I wouldn't give him the satisfaction of a flinch. Instead, I kicked the bag into the street to douse the flames, then slammed the door.

But after that I did not often step out of the house.

Oh, it burned to think our neighbors called me a Tory, for I considered myself as fierce a patriot as any. But when the case finally came to trial in October, John pleaded his case to the jury, saying, "Facts are stubborn things. And whatever may be our wishes, our inclinations, or the dictums of our passions, they cannot alter the state of facts and evidence."

Evidence he had aplenty.

John won the case.

Only two of the redcoats were convicted of manslaughter and sentenced to have their thumbs branded. Captain Preston was acquitted of having ordered his men to fire, and because of it, many people were furious with my husband. His remaining clients deserted him in droves, and the newspapers condemned him.

"I did not expect to be rewarded," John admitted, glumly. "But I expected people would be fair-minded. That eventually, they'd see the right of it."

"The jury did," I said. "That makes it worth it. We all want to be *thought* righteous, but to *do* right is the Lord's command."

That did make John smile. "In any case, we are too unpopular here now to stay. In the spring we ought to move back to Braintree."

I agreed, though it felt like exile. And I truly feared we'd live the rest of our lives on that little farm, struggling to make a living in humble obscurity.

Chapter Four

PLYMOUTH
Massachusetts Bay Colony
Summer 1773

IT HAD BEEN a long few years since the infamous trial in which my husband earned his reputation, for good and ill. But our exile in Braintree came to an end when Samuel Adams told the public that his cousin John was just the sort of *legalistic* patriot voice needed to persuade the British of their folly and overreach. And such was Sam's influence that people who once threw rotten eggs at our door promptly elected my husband to the state legislature.

Since then, John had won re-election three times, earning the respect of his constituents by writing petitions to royal officers, by suing officials who abused their authority, and by standing as a firm but reasonable voice for the colonists.

Instead of our world contracting to that little saltbox farmhouse as I'd feared, it was expanding in exciting new ways. We'd moved back to Boston, buying a house on Queen Street, and my husband befriended patriot colleagues in the legislature, including the powerful James Warren—of no relation to the good Dr. Warren of Boston—who had invited us to stay as guests at his house in Plymouth while John attended a session of the County Court.

Now, seated in the carriage next to John with eight-year-old Nabby asleep on my shoulder, I chirped, "I've never been so far as Plymouth before!"

"I fear it won't be the exciting adventure you anticipate." Eyeing his satchel of papers, John explained, "There will be much legal talk."

"There always is," I replied with a grin. "I shall not mind it."
I inhaled the fragrant summer air, my gaze taking in every detail of the landscape as we made our way south. With four children underfoot—Nabby, Johnny, Charlie, and a new little boy we named Thomas—I was desperate for a change of scenery and adult conversation. And having left the boys behind in the care of relatives, I was looking forward to meeting the learned Mrs. Mercy Otis Warren. For our hostess was the rarest creature—an American playwright.

The talented Mrs. Warren had dared to take up her pen and aimed it with satire against the acting British governor. She had published it anonymously, but it was not a secret well-kept. And I thought her patriotic play was *marvelous.*

How could I not, when my own husband featured in a thinly veiled role? In truth, I was nearly breathless with anticipation to make Mrs. Warren's acquaintance. So much so that John poked fun. "You'd think we were on our way to Buckingham House to meet the queen."

I laughed. "I doubt Queen Charlotte would ever welcome me as a guest. I might as well imagine visiting the moon! But I've always felt a great inclination to visit the Mother Country."

John chuckled as we bumped along the road. "We've scarcely traveled thirty miles and already you're dreaming of England? Just what business does a wife and mother have traveling abroad?"

I slanted him a glance from beneath my straw bonnet. "I could hardly have traveled to distant lands *before* I was a wife and mother. Thanks to the many dangers we're subject to from your sex, it's almost impossible for a single lady to travel without injury to her character."

Well, he had no argument to that!

And while he gawped in feigned offense, I added, "Women may be domestic beings, John, but we inherit an equal share of curiosity about the world. If nature had formed me of your sex, I should certainly have been a rover."

"A rover?" John grumbled. "You're a saucy woman." Then, glancing down at Nabby, who had awakened to watch our interplay, John asked, "Did you know what a saucy mother you have?"

"What's *saucy*?" Nabby asked. "Am I saucy?"

"No, you're just as you ought to be," her father said, approvingly. "Soft and biddable as a mewling kitten."

I wasn't so approving. Certainly, no mother wishes for an *impudent* child, but a little willfulness never hurt anybody. Nabby was a dutiful help to me around the house; she fetched eggs without breaking any; she'd learned to churn butter, and how to swaddle her brothers. But I took her with us on this journey because I hoped for her to learn so much more than *housewifery*. And I wanted her to learn it from a woman-intellectual at that . . .

Upon our arrival in front of the gambrel-roofed house on the corner of Main Street, the esteemed Mrs. Warren came to greet us and I felt a renewed surge of anxious excitement. Oh, to meet another woman with whom I could discuss important things!

I'd been trying, for years, to foster intellectual rigor amongst the ladies in my circle—most especially with my sisters. Mary, Elizabeth, and I had practically taught ourselves to read and write, for our parents had not thought a formal education necessary for girls. I was still self-conscious about my spelling and penmanship, hoping that my expression of ideas would overcome my mistakes. Now I'd have the chance to test my wits against an older educated woman, and I was as intimidated as I was eager to make a good impression.

"For you, Mrs. Warren," I said, nervously presenting a jar of my best blueberry preserves. "A token of thanks for hosting us."

"You're most welcome," Mrs. Warren said, eyeing the jar of preserves distractedly, her lips tight, hair pulled back severely, countenance remote as a scholar.

I'd been told she was working on a new play. Perhaps that's why she greeted us with such a distracted air. So I said, "I'm a great admirer of your work."

She only nodded. "Thank you, dear. A servant will take your bags up."

Her demeanor might've set me back on my heels, but as we spent time together that week, I realized that Mrs. Warren simply didn't feel compelled to indulge in the usual petty pleasantries. And I found that refreshing.

After giving a withering criticism of a book we'd both read, she said, "Honesty is far more important than pleasantry. Honesty being the first thing one must teach a child."

She had definite opinions—especially about children's education. And so did I. "Mr. Adams plans to send our boys to Harvard. But I daresay he's given no thought to Nabby's education. It's a fearsome responsibility to entrust to me in our changing world."

"As well-equipped to teach her as I'm sure you are . . ." Mrs. Warren looked me up and down. "I imagine it's difficult with little ones always underfoot."

I flushed, glad for an older and wiser new friend who understood my difficulties as a mother. "It's true. I cannot give Nabby the attention she deserves when I'm forever chasing after little boys."

"I have only boys. I always wished for a girl to educate. Perhaps when Nabby is older, you might leave her with me for some tutoring."

It was commonplace to send one's boys away to learn, but not girls. This was a remarkable opportunity—all the more so because the Warrens were such prominent people. Leaders of the state legislature swept in and out of Mrs. Warren's parlor, where she held court—and held her own—against the greatest patriots of Massachusetts, including her own brother, the formidable lawyer James Otis Jr.

I liked the way Mercy spoke her opinions boldly without ceding an ounce of femininity. And always, it seemed, with an eye toward advancing her husband's career. One evening, when the gentlemen went off to smoke their cigars, she told me, "Mr. Warren is a great and honest man who has exerted every nerve. It is the least I can do to help him in every sphere." And when I nodded, she added, "Your Mr. Adams is also a man on the rise. I liked the speech he gave, in which he said we should 'trust no man living who has the power to endanger public liberty.'"

I smiled a little, for that line was as much about my husband's general misanthropic nature as it was about politics. "People have praised it . . ."

"Indeed, and he may collect more laurels still. But he won't get far without your support, my dear."

"He has it," I insisted.

"Be sure you mean it," she warned. "If you encourage him in his rise, don't imagine that you'll only be called to endure flaming horse offal and angry neighbors in the future. I foresee a struggle ahead that will demand far more sacrifice. Remember the heroic Roman matron Portia. Would we have her courage in a day of trial?"

I blinked, having read all those old Roman stories. "You think we may one day be called upon to follow our husbands into the grave?"

She shook her head. "For myself I dare not boast *that* much courage. I do not mean that we'll be called upon to die by our own hands like Portia. I mean that we'll be called upon to hero-ically struggle with the calamities of life. And to patiently resign ourselves to evils we cannot avoid rather than shrink like cow-ards from the post allotted us by the Great Director of the The-ater of the Universe, before we've finished our part in the drama."

I ruminated upon that for the rest of the evening.

Later, in the privacy of our bed in the guest room, John asked, "Does the educated lady live up to your expectations?"

"Oh yes," I said, still considering her words. "I only hope I've made a good impression on her."

"Abigail, you cannot fail to have made a good impression. You may be younger and less schooled than Mrs. Warren, but I think your mind is sharper."

My eyes widened at this unsought compliment. "Oh, John, that is not true. Do not flatter me."

"I flatter myself," John replied, laying his head down with obvi-ous discomfort on the unfamiliar pillow. "A man of *my* towering intellect needs a wife who can exercise his brain. The smarter I am, the smarter you must be."

I laughed at his pomposity. "Well, then I'm sorry to say Mrs. Warren is not only smarter, but more courageous, too. Do you know she travels alone to see her husband when he works in Wa-tertown? I should like to have such audacity and independence."

"Would you?" John asked, with narrowed, sleepy eyes. "Next you'll tell me she rides astride a horse with a spear like an Ama-zon, visiting lands far and wide to satisfy her wanderlust."

Poking him in the ribs for such teasing, I said, "I'm the one with wanderlust; I think Mrs. Warren is satisfied to experience the world through her books, wielding a pen instead of a spear."

I then shared Mrs. Warren's offer to help educate Nabby, to which John said, "I wouldn't object, since it pleases you to imagine our daughter as a lady scholar."

"Doesn't it please you to imagine it?"

"I'm not much given to imagination," my husband admitted. "But perhaps one day I shall indulge you and we'll travel abroad to slake your wanderlust and encounter marvels like lady scholars."

It was only a dream, but it cheered me to dream of the ways in which my children might come of age in a better world.

Chapter Five

BOSTON
Massachusetts Bay Colony
December 1773

I WRINKLED MY NOSE at the bitter taste of coffee while trying
to ignore the uncomfortable looks from patrons of the Green
Dragon Tavern who were forced to mind their manners because a lady was present.

In truth, I wouldn't have been present if my husband weren't
late in meeting me for our planned excursion to Henry Knox's
new book and stationery store near Pi Alley. It was too cold to
wait for John on the street. And the proprietor of the tavern had
taken pity upon me with a steaming cup of coffee to help me
ward off the chill.

I could not now seem ungrateful by refusing to drink it. But when
my husband finally stomped in, dusting snow from his shoulders,
he noticed my expression and laughed. "You'll get accustomed to
the taste of coffee. And it might even ease your headaches."

In Boston we could no longer get our hands on honestly smug-
gled tea. Which meant either surrendering to Parliament's newest outrages or going without tea for our morning sustenance.

Now, staring down into the steaming coffee that was meant as
a substitute, I whispered, "But it is such a *noxious* drink."

Mirth shone in my husband's eyes. "I quite like it myself.
Certainly better than the witch's brew of chicory and whatever
else you ladies pluck from the meadow to make so-called liberty
tea."

That I could not entirely deny. Nor that *tea* was the topic of conversation all around us as John's friends and colleagues gathered.

I noticed Sam Adams, in an austere black cloak, and Dr. Warren, in a woolen blue coat with wooden buttons. They were at home in this establishment. But John Hancock—an exotic bird of a man whose throat wobbled beneath a lace cravat as he adjusted the embroidered sleeves of his yellow frock coat—was decidedly out of place.

A man of Hancock's stature and fortune wouldn't normally frequent the Green Dragon Tavern, but because it was too cold to meet beneath the Liberty Tree, the tavern now served as a meeting spot for patriots.

Sam was speaking to Dr. Warren and a bespectacled schoolteacher named James Lovell, who asked, "Do they really think they can *force* us to drink only the East India Company's tea?"

Sam's reply was a husky growl beneath his dark tricorn hat. "They may think it, but by what moral authority do they forbid a free people to import tea from anywhere else but Britain?"

Having quite forgotten a lady was present, James Otis Jr. now banged his tankard on the table. Having once been violently struck by a British customs official, Mrs. Warren's brother had been wrong in the head ever since, but sometimes he still spoke eloquently, as he did now. "What of the *legal* authority? Parliament has committed this outrage on hardworking colonists for the sole benefit of the East India Company to rescue it from its debts. If we accept these shipments of tea, then we are accepting the idea that Parliament can tax us without our consent. And I, for one, say *no taxation without representation!*"

As this wasn't the first time they'd had this discussion, the men repeated his slogan as a chant. They were, in some sense, performing for each other and working up their courage to do something about the forced shipments of tea sitting on vessels in our harbor.

That I had myself become all but enslaved to that baneful weed, there could be no doubt. Since quitting it, my throbbing temples told the tale. But so much the worse if a whole people should surrender their rights because of it.

In other colonies the protests had been so vociferous that ships turned around and returned their cargo. But here in Boston, despite thousands gathering in protest, the governor forbade the ships from returning the crates of tea because his sons intended to sell it on consignment.

I hoped sincerely such blatant government corruption would not be placidly endured by Bostonians. And encouraged by the talk in the tavern, I now thought it would not be. Still, I was glad to abandon my coffee when my husband said, "Come, wife. I promised you books."

I wanted a primer for Nabby, who had spent the summer with Mrs. Warren and returned with better prospects of learning before she turned nine. But a few days later, Nabby soured on learning when her six-year-old brother, Johnny, mastered her primer and was hungry for more.

"Your papa says you're a prodigy," I told our oldest son, who was now wearing britches and looked quite the young gentleman.

Meanwhile, Nabby lingered by the window where it seemed that crowds were again swelling in the streets. "What's happening, Mama?"

"No doubt a protest is gathering about the tea," I said. "A tax on the tea must be paid today or it will be confiscated and unloaded anyway."

I thought the crowd was likely to be in the hundreds, but I was wrong. *Thousands* were heading to the Old South Meeting House. Indeed, all manner of humanity moved together, shoulder to shoulder. Through the window, I recognized the local barber, having closed his shop in the middle of the day to make his voice heard. I recognized, too, Paul Revere, a prosperous silversmith, in powdered wig, a hammer dangling from his belt. Close to him, a knot of fishwives marched in their kerchiefs. Shipowners with jeweled walking sticks and cloaks flapping behind them confidently strode past. Next to them walked groups of Black freedmen, mostly sailors and whalers judging by their rough linen shirts, short-waisted jackets, and woolen Monmouth caps. Mud-spattered farmers from nearby towns pushed wagons of cabbages, having been diverted from the market to protest. Millers, rope makers, tanners, and coopers marched in force. Irish dockworkers were there, too, their hands rough and red, fists raised as they shouted, "Boston must not surrender!"

As if called, I went onto the front stoop to better witness the sight. On the street corners, printers hawked pamphlets. Enterprising vendors sold mincemeat pies, hot johnnycakes, and roasted nuts from their carts. Children ran alongside the moving mass as if it were a parade or a festival.

This assemblage of angry citizenry was a sight that might have once repelled my husband, but I did not think it would perturb him now. Three years more of abuses had worn down his refrain *but your methods, Samuel.* We'd grown used to—and even been exhilarated by—some of the unrest.

So even though John was away for the night riding legal circuit, I did not bolt the windows or hide upstairs. Instead, I entrusted my children into the care of servants, donned my coat, and eagerly plunged into the crowd.

I could not get close enough to the front to hear the fiery words of Sam Adams as he whipped up the audience to appeal to the governor. But we did catch word, passed on the cold wind, that the governor had already refused. The royal governor of Massachusetts Bay Colony would not hear the citizens of Boston. He would not allow the ships to turn back.

"You rabble can drink the tea or choke on it," some Tory cried from a window on the street—risking his life in this crowd, I thought. "Either way, you *will* pay."

At that moment I chanced a glance in the direction of my husband's hotheaded cousin. Seldom did Samuel Adams let himself look defeated, but in this moment, he seemed utterly so. He shouted with a ring of true regret, "This meeting can do nothing more to save the country."

With angry muttering, people dispersed. But I did not think that could possibly be the end of it. And indeed it was not. For that night, the Sons of Liberty descended upon Griffin's Wharf with hats pulled low, hoods covering their heads, some even adorned in Mohawk war paint to reject their British roots and pronounce themselves thoroughly *American.*

I knew this because word spread quickly amongst the patriot ladies of Boston that the idea had been Sarah Bradlee Fulton's. She'd helped with the disguises and advised the men on how to conduct themselves.

My neighbor confided, "Once they stole aboard the *Dartmouth* and her sister ships, they dumped more than three hundred crates of tea into the harbor."

"Three hundred crates!" I cried.

"Aye, and they took care to ensure that this act of political protest cannot be dismissed as anything else. Not a ship was damaged; no other cargo destroyed. They even swept the decks clean of spilled tea leaves."

Only a woman would have suggested that, I thought.

It was admirable restraint. Only the tea was destroyed. But that was enough. The damages would be . . . well, nearly incalculable.

When John finally returned, I'd attempted to work out a figure on Nabby's chalk slate. "My God, the expense," I told John, a bit too gleefully. "The destruction of that much tea might be worth nearly ninety thousand pounds!"

"It's the governor's own fault," John said, surprisingly gleeful himself. "If he wasn't afflicted with such stubbornness and greed, this tea might've been saved. Now the East India Company may be bankrupted. Certainly, they will be if other colonies follow our example. And I could wish it upon them."

How shocked I was to hear him speak of the destruction in such approving tones! "Are you no longer a champion for law and order?"

I expected him to say that having seen the law perverted entirely for the purposes of greed, that law and order could no longer prevail. But he was still too much a lawyer not to sidestep my question. "We were forced to a choice. Not *whether* we'd pay this tax, but only in what circumstances we'd pay. So it's a matter of indifference whether it was drunk or drowned. It may take them ten years to get us to pay, in which time we'll save interest on the money. Whereas if we drank it, we'd have to pay immediately. And we'd also have been drinking to the final ruin of American liberties."

"Well, I think it's *sublime*," I said, for something in my nature always responded to principled defiance. No one had been harmed, and I could feel no pity for those tea leaves floating in the harbor—though I daresay I was thirsty enough for tea that I was tempted to taste it.

Even steeped in harbor water, it had to be better than coffee.

Fortunately, even without my beverage of choice, I could start this day with an elixir of pride. I knew John felt it, too, for he said, "There *is* a dignity, a majesty, in this effort of the patriots that I greatly admire. The people should never rise without doing something to be remembered—something notable and striking. And this destruction of the tea is so bold, so daring, so firm, that it must have important consequence."

WE HOPED THE important consequence of our civil resistance would be that Parliament would reconsider their intolerable acts.

Instead, the consequence was retaliation.

On a cold and damp afternoon in March, I was on the docks shopping for fish when redcoats with fixed bayonets flooded the harbor. One of the soldiers pushed my shoulder, barking, "Go home, woman. There'll be no business today."

In outrage at this rudeness, I snapped my cape and wheeled away, though it meant leaving without our evening's supper. And on the walk home, I saw the king's soldiers nailing up posts saying the harbor was now closed and would not be re-opened until we paid for the dumped tea.

All trade in the city came to a standstill.

In the days and weeks that followed, shops shuttered, boarding up their windows. Soon we couldn't buy bread from a bakery, nor flour to bake our own, even if we could've secured firewood. And over a cold meal of pickled cabbage and salt pork, I said, "So they mean to cripple Boston."

"All Massachusetts Bay Colony," John returned. "We'll no longer be allowed a fair trial by a jury of peers. And town meetings are forbidden without the express consent of the royal governor."

This last made my mouth drop open because town meetings were a way of life in Massachusetts, often taking place directly after our Sabbath services, with the citizenry still seated in the pews. So this felt like an assault upon the spiritual and social glue that held us together. "How will they keep us apart?"

"By stationing soldiers in every tavern and vacant building," my husband replied.

It was infuriating. Yet, panic did not set in until the royal governor mounted cannons on Beacon Hill.

"They want us to know they can fire upon us with impunity," Dr. Warren said when he stopped to check on Charlie and Tommy, who both suffered earaches.

Knowing that Dr. Warren was recently betrothed to a young patriot poetess of Boston, I wanted to both congratulate him and praise his choice in bride. But Warren's attention was riveted upon my husband. "Mr. Adams, they intend to quarter soldiers *in our homes*. To force us to obedience. To spy upon our doings and make us hold our tongues at our own dinner tables."

My husband rubbed his temples. "I must again move my family back to Braintree."

Dr. Warren leaned forward, forcing my husband to look at him. "Now is no time to shrink from hazardous duty, sir. I fear your country may soon call upon you."

This embarrassed my husband, who didn't wish to be thought a coward. "My country may call upon me as easily in Braintree as in Boston. But in the meantime, I don't think my wife will suffer a redcoat in the house. Not with four children under the age of ten. The first time a soldier woke Tommy from his nap, Abigail would be so wroth that I'd find myself clasped in leg irons to answer for her saucy tongue."

I smirked, because he was not far wrong.

But Dr. Warren was not amused. "They're going to dissolve our legislature. They're going to stop you from doing the work you were elected to do. And if we submit to these abuses, we'll become as exploited and downtrodden as India from whence our tea comes."

My husband sighed. "We cannot resist *alone*. If our sister colonies were to come to our aid, it could make a difference. If New York and Virginia and Pennsylvania would stand shoulder to shoulder with us, then we'd stand a chance."

"We hoped you'd say that," Dr. Warren replied. "A congress of colonial representatives has been called. From Massachusetts we want to send you as one of the delegates."

WE DIDN'T SLEEP that night, tossing and turning in silence. I knew that if John attended this colonial congress, he'd draw attention to himself. The kind of attention that was dangerous when royal officials were murmuring words like *treason.*

It wasn't until the next morning, as I readied a cold porridge slurry for the children's breakfast, that I found the courage to ask, "Are you going to accept?"

John took my hands with a wry but weary smile. "I *am* going to accept and become a delegate to this congress, thereby consenting to my own ruin, to your ruin, and the ruin of our children. I give you this warning so you may prepare your mind for your fate."

He said this in half jest, but I'm ashamed to say that I drew back with a burst of fearful tears.

"Oh, Abigail," he said, trying to offer comfort.

But I turned away. I'd already experienced the painful consequences of living in the public eye. John's political office hadn't enriched us—quite the contrary—and by abandoning his law practice, he'd be cutting his income from half of nothing, to nothing at all. Our financial situation would strain to the limits.

How was I to prepare for that?

But I remembered the words of Mercy Otis Warren.

He won't get far without your support, my dear . . .

So, I dried my eyes for my husband's sake. Then I grew very still as I took in the picture. Two confused children, wondering what this serious talk might mean. My hands gripping my porridge-stained apron. My husband bareheaded, neckcloth askew, his face wan from lack of sleep, his eyes beseeching me for understanding.

But his gaze was also determined and clear.

I felt clarity then, too. My husband must do his duty and serve. And I must do my duty, too.

Hadn't I said the act of dumping the tea was *sublime*? I would hate myself for a coward if I now cringed with fear. I had children who must grow up in this world; if I was to call myself a good mother, then I must take as a *blessing* any role I might ever be offered in shaping it for them.

As I stood there, my stays felt too tight; it was difficult to take a breath. For when I did, I knew I would speak something momentous into my little world. I would not merely prepare my mind but make a choice. "Well, then. I'm willing in this cause to run all risks with you and to be ruined with you if you are ruined."

At hearing this, my husband actually startled. Then, quite suddenly, he flew up from his chair to kiss me in a way that felt like communion. He kissed me and kissed me, unmindful of our children watching. And I knew we were in this together now, whatever may come.

Only later did I confess my fears. "It will be too dangerous to stay in Boston without you. I will have to take the children back to the farm in Braintree. But how will we get word to each other when you're in Philadelphia? Surely, we cannot trust the post."

"My law clerks have agreed to carry correspondence to you," John said. "If that route is compromised, rely upon Mr. Revere. He is courier now for our soon-to-be outlawed legislature."

I nodded, hoping to make closer acquaintance with the hard-riding silversmith. "I only worry, John, that I will be unequal to the trust you place in me for the farm."

"Truthfully, I fear myself unequal to the times that have put our little family at such a crossroads. I don't know if I really can do anything to help in congress. I am merely a country lawyer . . ."

"No, John. You're not *merely* anything. These *are* extraordinary times, but I've always known that I married an extraordinary man."

"Did you?" he asked, his eyes searching mine.

"I really did," I whispered, the certainty rising from the depths of my soul. In reassuring him, I renewed confidence in myself, too. Since these *were* extraordinary times I'd simply have to become an extraordinary wife and mother; there wasn't any other choice.

I could be frugal. I could be clever. I could stretch every coin to keep my children fed.

I'd find a way.

Chapter Six

BRAINTREE
Massachusetts Bay Colony
October 1774

I N THE TWO months my husband was away, my days were tedious and the nights unpleasant.

I did my best to oversee the farmhands and collect rents from our tenants. Of course, tenants like the truculent Mr. Hayden delayed. But I tried to be understanding because times were hard. Our widowed neighbor, Mrs. Copeland, was in such dire straits that she begged me to take in her eldest daughter, Patty, now a girl of fourteen.

I agreed, thinking it a good arrangement to have help with domestic tasks, but Patty was also another child to feed. And when I looked upon our drought-riddled, dusty field, I despaired of a harvest. Too little water made canning fruit and brining meat for the winter troublesome. We even struggled to keep the cows watered. Poor, thirsty creatures.

Still, there was nothing for it but to try. Nabby, Patty, and even little Johnny helped the field hands drag buckets of water until our hands blistered. Then after washing up, Patty and Nabby took turns churning butter while I dried pumpkin in the waning sun under muslin. I kept the fire lit in the hearth, boiling down jams, apple butters, and marmalades. I pickled eggs from our coop and cabbages from the field. I dried peppermint and lavender from my garden. I let nothing—not even potato peels—go to waste.

When the housework was done, and darkness finally fell, I scrubbed dirt from my body and from beneath my fingernails. And on the night of my tenth wedding anniversary, separated from my beloved, I spent lonely hours reading from ancient history, looking for clues for what might be our fate.

Neighboring families were dividing against each other into Patriot and Tory camps. A danger illustrated to me most personally when Nabby and I were invited to dine with my uncle Colonel Josiah Quincy at his grand spacious home with its tall windows and Chinese fretwork balustrade.

Though it was not our first visit, my daughter looked with new appreciation at the gleaming woodwork that had been polished with lemon oil. The gilded mirrors and porcelain dinner service made her gawp, too, as if she were only now coming into awareness of how much more humbly we lived.

I'd reminded her to be on her best behavior, but the adults at the table—who teasingly called me *Mrs. Delegate*—were decidedly misbehaved.

"These so-called delegates have no authority," complained the colonel's son Samuel, who, unlike the rest of our family, was an avowed Loyalist.

"They have *moral* authority," returned the good and patriotic Colonel Quincy, who often watched for British ships with his spyglass. "The most distinguished gentlemen are in Philadelphia, including our own John Adams."

The meal went on in silence for an awkward moment as Nabby and I tried not to gorge ourselves on roast duck with mashed turnips and ruby-red cranberry tarts waiting tantalizingly on the sideboard—better fare than we had eaten in ages.

But Samuel Quincy stared in the direction of the salt marshes until he suddenly set down his fork onto his plate with a clatter. "Do you know what our old royal governor says about this nonsense? He asked who the rebels were. He said he knew John Hancock, but where the devil *this brace of Adamses* came from he did not know."

It was an aggressively obnoxious thing to say in my presence. And something about the way he said it reminded me so much of John's cousin Samuel that I nearly wondered aloud if every family had an irritating cousin named Samuel. Fortunately, I bit that back but I wasn't willing to allow the insult to go unanswered altogether. "Mine came from Braintree, as you well know."

Samuel's wife met my eyes with sympathetic support. To her husband she said, "You do our guests a discourtesy! What's more, I think it's high time you supported the patriots."

At hearing that, Samuel Quincy threw his napkin down. "I'd rather sail to England and leave you behind!"

He tried to storm away, but his wife followed him, and oh, it was a terrible row.

Later, in the carriage ride home, Nabby was pensive. "When I stayed with Mrs. Warren last summer, she told me it's improper for a woman to quarrel with her husband over politics."

"Did she?" I was genuinely surprised to hear it, because I couldn't imagine Mercy Otis Warren holding her tongue if she disagreed with *anyone*. Mercy and I had opened a circle of correspondence in which we discussed books and the patriot cause. To a mother of four with a husband away, these letters sometimes felt as if they saved my sanity. So, I didn't contradict the venerable Mrs. Warren. I simply said, "I just thank the Lord that on important matters, your father and I see eye to eye."

Indeed, I was on my knees in prayer that very night when I heard a commotion outside on the road passing directly in front of our house. I rose, pulled my shawl round my shoulders, opened the window, and held the candle aloft to see men on horseback.

At the head of this mounted gathering, I recognized one of my patriot neighbors. He recognized me, too, with a touch of his hat. "Mrs. Adams," he said, glancing over his shoulder at a cart they were dragging, which looked to be filled with barrels. "We took this from the Powder House. We're going to hide it from our Tory neighbors lest they use it against us."

"Is there some reason you fear it?" I asked, for it was a bitter thing to distrust one's neighbors.

"You haven't heard, madam? The royal governor has dissolved our provincial assembly."

We'd been warned it might happen, but the blow still landed heavily. "So now we not only have no representation in Parliament, we have none on our own soil . . ."

"Oh, we have it, Mrs. Adams. The assembly has simply fled to meet elsewhere, even as the royal governor issued calls for their arrest."

Their arrest. My heart jumped to my throat. For I knew that if my husband had not left the assembly and gone to meet with representatives of other states, he, too, might be on that arrest list.

"Do you want any powder, Mrs. Adams?"

What need did I have of stolen powder? None, I hoped! Dazed, I replied, "Not since it is already in such good hands."

"At least take your children to your father's house or somewhere else with menfolk to defend you. And don't trust any slave along the way."

I blinked. "Why not?"

"Rumor has it the royal governor intends to free enslaved men of Massachusetts if they'll rise up against us."

We'd have only ourselves to blame if they did, I thought.

The day I first learned my nurse Phoebe could be sold on a block, I'd confronted my father about slavery's cruelty. He'd protested that he'd never sell Phoebe, that she was family. But family ought not hold one another in bondage, so his words had not appeased me then. And they embittered me now.

As the men rode off, I hoped it wouldn't come to violence. But if it did and it came at the hands of the enslaved, some part of me would wonder if we deserved it.

JOHN RETURNED AFTER three months' absence in Philadelphia, weary, dusty, and hungry. While I settled the children at the table, Patty helped me put dinner on and I was pleased to show my husband everything—from cheese to preserves—I'd eked out of our farm whilst he was away.

Smiling approvingly, John dug into his meal with relish. "Twelve of the colonies were represented in the congress. We've decided upon an embargo. None of us will import British goods; we propose also to end the slave trade."

That both surprised and pleased me. "I wish there was not a slave in the province. It's an iniquitous scheme to fight for our own liberty while daily robbing it from those who have just as good a right to freedom."

My husband nodded in full agreement, for he had always refused to traffic in slavery. "Had I to snap my fingers and make things right, I would. But America is a great, unwieldy body. Its progress must be slow. In the meantime, we wrote a petition to the king so he might redress our grievances."

While two-year-old Tommy flung peas at his sister, Johnny asked, "Is it over then, Papa?"

"Not yet." John paused, his fork held aloft. "But it soon will be if the king and his Parliament see reason."

"And if they don't?" I asked, disarming our youngest of his legumes.

John looked very much as if he didn't wish to answer me, but finally he muttered, "If Parliament doesn't see reason, well, we've voted for a Second Continental Congress."

At that, I groaned. To be without my husband these past three months had been the hardest work of my life. Whether I'd even put up enough supplies for winter and made sufficient plans for the next sowing remained to be seen. As a good patriot, I had agreed to run all risks with John, and share all his burdens, too, but that did not mean I could banish all my fears. Later with tremulous heart, I whispered against the pillow, "They are calling for arrests. Will the king think you a traitor?"

John laughed, pulling me against him. "Don't be absurd. None would dare call me that. I merely met with representatives from other colonies in Philadelphia and sent a petition as any free British citizen has a right to do."

He believed that, and I wanted to.

The petition sent to the king, signed by my husband, was decent and respectful. It addressed King George with a plea for clemency from his loyal subjects. It affirmed royal authority and restated our loyalty. But His Majesty's answer to our plight and our plea was a despicable silence.

Chapter Seven

BRAINTREE
Massachusetts Bay Colony
March 1775

WHILE THE KING remained silent, Parliament moved to punish all New England for our resistance.

And as the British prepared to make war against us, our own patriot leaders called upon militia to form a defense, hoard weapons, and store military supplies.

My husband played no part in that, but given the response of the king to our continental congress, it seemed as if John might indeed be considered a traitorous rebel.

Yet, fear didn't silence him. His legal cases went abandoned as he penned essays for the gazettes about the latest outrages.

We had never supposed our king to be a tyrant before, but now it was openly spoken of.

To mark the anniversary of that terrible night our neighbors called the Boston Massacre, the patriot schoolteacher James Lovell gave a stirring oration at the Old South Church in which he said the killings wouldn't have happened were it not for a standing army amongst us.

We all crowded close to hear, nodding our heads.

Why not constables or watchmen to keep order? The notion of using *soldiers* to enforce unpopular laws was tyrannical. "You see the danger of it," Lovell said, reminding us of that winter's night when anxious soldiers shot boys and left them bleeding scarlet in the snow. "When did our assembly pass an act to hazard our property, liberty, and lives? What check have we upon a British Army? Can we disband it? Can we stop its pay?"

We all knew the answer. And I, too, felt the indignation rise in my breast.

"Athens once was free," Lovell continued, proving himself a fine speaker. "Until a citizen—a favorite of the people—destroyed the commonwealth and made himself tyrant. In Rome, Caesar got the affections of his army, overthrew the state, and made himself dictator. By the same instruments, many lesser republics have fallen prey to the devouring jaws of tyrants."

Many who had doubted the king was a despot left Mr. Lovell's speech with their minds changed. I left it as fearful as I was defiant, for I thought it only a matter of time before the jaws of tyranny snapped down upon us, too.

The fangs sank in come April, on the day John banged into the house, his straw farmer's hat askew, so agitated that he still had a shovel in his hand. "Abigail!"

I rushed from the kitchen. "What's happened?"

John panted, sweat dripping from his brow. "Fighting in Concord. A rider just told me the British opened fire on militiamen there. Then a bloodbath in Lexington when they tried to retreat. Maybe two hundred, three hundred dead."

I couldn't credit it. Concord was more than fifty miles north, so I'd never been there, though my brother had a house up that way. "Any word of Bill?"

John nodded. "Your brother was one of the militiamen who returned fire, his whereabouts now unknown."

My brother had always been a wayward soul, and I had hard feelings about his drinking and gambling, but the thought Bill might be shot dead erased any feeling other than worry. "Dear God. What of his wife and children?"

"All I know is that your sister-in-law is trying to nurse one of the dying British regulars."

Dying . . .

Had it really come to this?

John's grave expression told me that it had. "The British were in Concord in an attempt to seize my cousin Sam and others, but they were warned just in time by Mr. Revere."

Learning this, my heart clenched such that I felt the need to lean back against the wall for steadiness. My first worry was that if the authorities were looking for Samuel Adams, they might confuse one Adams for another, as would happen again many times in our lives.

My second worry was that my husband might also now be a wanted man in his own right.

The same thought occurred to our son Johnny, who peered from the doorway where he eavesdropped. "Will you hide, Papa?"

I, too, desperately wanted to know John's answer. And I held my breath, waiting while my husband leaned the shovel against the door and took off his gloves. "No," John finally said. "I won't hide. Swim or sink, live or die, survive or perish, I am with my country. You may depend upon it."

My clenching heart swelled with pride and fear in equal measure. I couldn't have loved a coward, but I'd married a lawyer, not a soldier. I'd chosen my husband precisely because he was the sort to quarrel with a *pen*, not a musket.

Still, I was grateful that he had a musket. And when he pulled it down and sent Johnny to saddle his horse, I asked, "Where do you go?"

"To Lexington to see for myself what's happened," John replied. "I'll look for your brother. I'll send word. If danger approaches, take the children to the woods."

I nodded, trying not to clutch his arm and beg him to stay. If my husband were captured, the British might hang him. And even if he were somehow overlooked in this scene of war, all our worldly comforts were now at risk.

I felt weak in every limb. Only a terrible rage finally stiffened my spine. The king had chosen to *kill* us rather than let the East India Company lose money. Britain was now stained with the blood of its own children, and I'd never look upon her as a mother country again. So, as John readied to go, I pulled myself upright, kissed his cheek, and whispered, "What does this mean for us?"

"It means war," John said. "The die is cast. The Rubicon crossed. And if we don't defend ourselves, they will kill us."

THE BRITISH RETREATED to Boston. Now *fifteen thousand* militiamen from all over New England laid siege to hold them there. The fighting was no longer distant. It was ten miles away. And because our house was on the main road, militiamen and refugees from Boston passed hourly, so we heard bits of their conversation from our windows.

"Starve 'em out if they mean to attack us—"

"—stop them from launching raids—"

"They'll have no supplies or reinforcement over land!"

Some of the refugees included my own sister Mary and her husband, who had obtained a special visa to be allowed to leave Boston. Other passersby begged for help, including a minuteman who staggered to my house carrying a wounded comrade. "He's been shot. Thought we had it patched up last night, but now it's bleeding again."

We put the injured man on my kitchen floor, where I knelt to see if there was anything I might do. I'd asked Patty and Nabby to wind bandages and now they came to good use. Thankfully, the wound did not look mortal. Then again, how would I know? I was no doctor!

Once the wounded man was rebandaged and resting, I emptied my larder to feed bedraggled families who had fled Boston and walked through the night. For myself, I was determined to stay in Braintree doing what I could to help. To make room for refugees in need of lodgings, I said, "Patty, Nabby, you sleep with me, and the boys will, too, leaving room for the injured in the house. Surely, our tenant farmers will make room for the rest."

In this, unfortunately, I was firmly opposed by the surly and impudent Mr. Hayden, who was renting some rooms in our dairy. Though he had himself two sons in the Patriot militia, he refused to move his belongings to make space for those fleeing the fight.

"It'll only be for a few days," I argued with Mr. Hayden.

"Not even one day," he said, spitting tobacco juice altogether too near my boot. "It may be your milk house, but as a paying tenant I have the right of it, and it's not your place to demand I surrender an inch of it."

I tried a softer appeal. "I know you to be a great patriot, sir, and if you could—"

"Don't work your wiles on me, Mrs. Adams," he snapped. "You're a handsome little woman, but I'll not be stirred. And if you put my belongings out of place, I shall have the law on you."

The law. As if there were any such thing in this chaos! He'd never speak to my husband this way, but I had no recourse, because Mr. Hayden believed John wouldn't support my "womanly weakness" in taking in refugees. Worse, I didn't know if he was wrong.

I'd heard too little from John since he rode off with his musket. Only that my brother was alive and in the fight while my husband was on his way to Philadelphia to rejoin congress there.

Those shots at Lexington and Concord were, as they now say, *heard round the world.* And I believed the British would sorely regret it. Other colonies were rising up, too. New York seized royal arms and munitions. Men of Pennsylvania, Connecticut, and Rhode Island joined the militia in the thousands. Marylanders were already marching north to fight for us.

It was, indeed, to be war.

ON AN EVENING in mid-June, the thunder of guns startled me from my bed, the noise so loud it rattled the house and awakened my children. It was still the wee hours of the morning; two-year-old Tommy was crying, and after lighting a candle, I reached for him while Johnny and Charlie clambered to the window in their nightclothes, eager to see.

Charlie said, "Doesn't sound like muskets."

And his older brother, Johnny, told him, "It isn't. It's a cannonade from the British ships in the harbor. Mama, will you take me up Penn's Hill to see?"

What a brave and inquisitive boy Johnny was. But as I gentled his baby brother, I said, "We can't leave the little ones."

Hugging herself against the noise of the bombardment, Nabby said, "I'll stay with them."

She could be trusted, and there was Patty, too, who had tumbled from her bed with the rest of us as the cannons continued to rumble.

Now I felt as if I must put on a brave face for the children. So, as dawn lit upon us, I dressed and took our eldest son to climb to a perch where we could see. Johnny and I knelt together in the grass. And having had the foresight to grab his father's spyglass before we left the house, my eldest boy used it to peer in the direction of the rising pillars of smoke that blackened the dawn.

Breed's Hill blazed in red and yellow while British warships blasted away, illuminating the sky with explosions. It was far off, but not far enough, for already the air became tinged with the scent of sulfur and pulsed around us with malevolent force.

We kept low, holding hands.

"When will it stop?" Johnny asked.

Maybe not 'til they've laid us to ashes, I thought, but dared not say. With the light of dawn, I could see that neighbors were gathering at my gate to share news passed by riders.

"Farmer Whittemore has been shot in the face and bayoneted—"

"—but that man is nearly eighty years old!—"

"Old enough to fire a musket."

Upon hearing of the incident, Dr. Tufts had rushed to the scene to help the old farmer, though he despaired of his life. Meanwhile, patriots like Mrs. Warren's husband and brother were both fighting at Breed's or Bunker Hill. Everything was rumor and confusion. And every farmwife bustled out to the road with bandages and brews for the exhausted or injured.

One of the youngest—more boy than man—collapsed before me in tears. "Are you hurt?" I asked, reaching for his hands to offer comfort.

"It's Dr. Joseph Warren!" he cried. "He's dead."

I shook my head, refusing to believe it. But the militiaman told a grisly story. "Musket ball to the brain. But that wasn't enough for the villains. The British tried to sever his head for a trophy. Don't know where they buried him or if they left him for the vultures."

At this, a shriek of distress sounded from behind me, and I turned to see that Nabby had heard it all.

The good doctor had become a cherished friend. He'd tried to save my daughter Susanna. He'd been kind to John when he suffered that frightening attack of pain in his chest. And he was always tending my little ones of every sniffle.

Despite my children's eyes upon me, I burst into tears. Nabby and Johnny did the same, the three of us huddled together in grief as I reassured them that Dr. Warren would be remembered as a great patriot, and that he was in God's gentle hands, now.

I couldn't be so easily reassured, for I'd later hear that the British threw Joseph Warren into a common grave. Was that to be my husband's fate?

John wasn't a soldier, but he'd written that we must all become soldiers now. And as if reading my thoughts, a neighbor said, "We're only farmers. We don't have a chance against the finest fighting force in the world."

But as John had said, the die was cast. We would fight anyway. We would have to.

John and I might be separated by distance, but we were tightly united in this desperate struggle. And so were our children. Victory could be our only salvation. So that night I collected my pewter spoons and began melting them to make musket balls for the fight.

Chapter Eight

BRAINTREE
Massachusetts Bay Colony
July 1775

MY HUSBAND NOMINATED George Washington to be commander in chief of our patriot militias. We needed a seasoned soldier, and Washington was an experienced officer of the French and Indian War. It was also a good political choice, for a Virginian defending Massachusetts Bay Colony would remind the British that they couldn't simply crush us to force other colonies to submit.

Of course, appointing a military commander was a monumental, irreversible step. We had been *called* rebels before, but now we would rebel in truth. We would not meekly submit and let them kill us. The British had chosen the sword, but they were not the only ones who could wield one. More battles would follow. Now wives would lose husbands. Children would lose fathers. Mothers would lose sons. Women and children would fall victim, too. It was ever thus, in war.

And though my husband had done nothing in word or deed to encourage bloodshed at Lexington and Concord, in the congress, he'd given voice and form to our determination to defend ourselves. It was for that reason that on George Washington's way to camp in Cambridge, the celebrated soldier stopped to call upon me.

At the sound of light horse on the dusty summer road, I'd hurried from the garden, my basket filled with herbs—lavender, feverfew, and chamomile. The general had caught me out in plain brown homespun, dirt from the garden upon my sleeve. So, I'm afraid I was quite flummoxed in the presence of so *tall* and poised a soldier wearing a polished uniform of buff and blue.

I was apt to like him, but still I was struck by Washington's dignity and by the elegance of his person when I invited him inside and he stooped to enter our humble dwelling, his riding boots heavy on our creaky floorboards.

Washington smelled faintly of leather and tobacco when he stooped to kiss my hand in greeting. "Madam, it is my honor to present my respects to the wife of that fierce patriot leader Mr. Adams. The man everyone listens to in congress."

Delighted to hear my husband praised in this way, I bobbed a brief curtsey. "The honor is mine, sir, for *you* are the man everyone trusts to lead us to victory in this war."

Our new commander in chief towered over every other man in his entourage. With broad shoulders, steely eyes, and a lean military bearing, he projected a manly aura that inspired confidence. So I added, "I believe we cannot be in better hands. And I wish you well in this fight."

Washington smiled, modestly, then took in my spinning wheel with approving eyes. "We cannot win this fight without the patriotism of our ladies. We rely on your sacrifices, frugality, and industry with homemade wares."

It charmed me that he understood that. "Speaking for the ladies, we are happy to do our part."

Washington bowed in appreciation. "Until my wife arrives to lend her feminine graces to camp, I hope you'll come often to inspirit the officers, Mrs. Adams."

"I hope to try and so look forward to meeting your wife."

But in the meantime, I had many worries . . .

We were short of every sort of commodity at home. The war was creating financial havoc, and we'd need something to trade beside coin. Something valuable. Something we could easily carry if we needed to flee . . .

I was struck by inspiration on an afternoon in which Nabby, Patty, and I were sewing together. We were working our needles by the window, dust motes in the air. Now that Charlie was nearly in breeches, I was trying to cut down one of his old doublets for Tommy. That's when I dropped a pin to the floor between the boards. Nabby scrambled down to help pry it out, and I said, "Don't lose it. These days pins are more valuable than gold."

"Then we're doubly rich," Nabby replied, having found not one pin between the floorboards, but two!

I paused, a thoughtful finger upon my chin. The neighboring ladies all complained that pins had become scarce. If I could get hold of some, perhaps I could sell them like a hawker.

It might not be dignified—I feared what might be whispered about me at meeting during Reverend Wibird's sermons—but it'd give me more than the crops and eggs to keep us fed.

The only trouble was, where to find pins when Boston was occupied?

Well, Boston wasn't the only port in the colonies. So, by way of Paul Revere when next his rides took him by my house, I sent a note to John in Philadelphia, begging him to send pins.

He didn't send them with his next missive, but he *did* side with me against Mr. Hayden.

First, he commended me for my charity to refugees. Then he told the man who refused to make room for them to pack his bags and vacate our milk house altogether. John was finished with him as a tenant, and wrote, "I will not endure the least disrespectful expression to my wife."

I found this terribly gratifying . . . but where were the pins? In light of the weighty war that took up my husband's time, pins must've seemed such a trivial matter. But I had a larder to replenish if I were to keep his children alive and feed refugees besides. My spices were gone, the cornmeal much diminished, and I couldn't remember the last bite of salt pork we'd had for our stew.

So I felt no compunction about nagging for pins, insisting that he send them with *any* passing courier or friend until John sent more than a thousand in all.

Nabby and I counted.

But John had requested a favor in return: "I want to be informed from hour to hour of anything that happens in Boston—how the Tories subsist, whether the troops are healthy or sickly, and everything which passes in our army."

To gather that information I'd have to leave the farm. It meant donning boots, hauling saddle, and taking the horse myself to visit neighbors, the market, and relatives. It meant conversing with every passing rider on the road. Gauging loyalties. Testing the logic of the rumors before passing them on. And most of all, it meant writing letters—even embarrassed by my spelling as I often was.

It would be delicate and time-consuming work added to all my other responsibilities; nevertheless, I threw myself into it. I had, after all, promised George Washington that we ladies were happy to do our part.

JOHN LOCKED THE door of our rented room in Watertown and I flew into his arms like a girl half my age. He swung me up into those strong arms and carried me to a lumpy straw bed that groaned under our weight, but I didn't care because we'd been four months apart.

John rained down kisses upon me with the ardor of youth. T'was a sweet reunion, made sweeter by the anxieties we suffered, for our legislators had fled here to escape arrest. So we were, in a sense, in hiding. It was exciting. Intoxicating. And we came together trembling with emotions ranging from love to despair.

Later, our fingers twined in the candlelight, John teased, "*Mrs. Delegate*, they call you. A title you deserve for becoming my eyes and ears. People have little notion how important you are to me or to the cause."

"Perhaps they *should* know," I said, weary of the caution with which we now were forced to write to one another. I'd even taken to signing my letters under a pseudonym—*Portia*—in case any of our letters were intercepted.

It felt almost like spycraft, but if it was, I refused to feel shame for it. Nestling closer to my husband, I said, "I think the wives of all the delegates should assume your titles. After all, we give you up our names in marriage and hazard all with you."

It was not entirely a jest, for if our husbands were arrested, none of us would be spared of consequence. But John pointed out I was especially deserving, as unlike any of the other wives of the delegates, I'd gone to meet the officers of our ragtag army and made recommendations of who ought to be elevated over the others.

Fearing that he was teasing me, I said, "Military command may not be my sphere, but with so many clamoring for your favor, you need disinterested advice and information."

"Indeed. How did you come by so much information, Mrs. Adorable? Your letters were more useful than reports from scouts in the field."

"I made it my business," I said. "I suffered through so many cups of liberty tea with lady friends that I'm practically pickled in it. Ladies know more than you realize. Also, gentlemen like to talk to me and often forget what they're saying in the presence of a woman, so I paid attention."

One thing I'd learned this way was that the British General Gage was attempting to repair the lighthouse on Great Brewster Island to help his forces arrive. To prevent any such repair, our people went to recapture it or burn it to the ground if necessary. Fighting with more than thirty marines, our side had won the skirmish, but several were killed.

"I attended the funerals," I told John, gravely. "It seemed right that I should. And in so doing, I met with wounded British soldiers we'd taken prisoner."

John's sleepy eyes came more awake. "And what did they have to say for themselves?"

"I confess that I was still grieving the death of Dr. Warren and approached the prisoners with an altogether too haughty bearing." I was angry at what these soldiers were subjecting me to—fear for my children, my husband, our future, and our very lives. "I was unmindful of their injuries, though some were still bleeding through their bandaged arms. Arms that my own uncle, Dr. Tufts, had helped tend."

"But you spoke to them?"

I nodded. "I said, 'It is very unhappy, gentlemen, that you should be obliged to fight your best friends here in America under the banner of the Crown.' To my surprise, they said they were sorry."

"Not sorry enough to go home," John grumbled.

"One said he came with no thoughts of fighting but was obliged to obey orders. And that they wished with all their souls that those who sent them here would do the fighting instead."

That sentiment my husband could understand, but he turned slightly to the wall as he contemplated it.

"John, they were told if they were taken alive, we'd kill them."

"There is hope, then, that British soldiers will see how they're lied to."

In my experience, people were not easily disabused of lies they had swallowed, but I confessed, "I was affected by their contrition. It smothered my desire to rain down curses on their heads, and filled me with a hope that decent men might end the fighting."

But, of course, we could not wait upon it.

So, when the rooster crowed, I rolled out of that lumpy, too-narrow rented bed even as John tried to stop me. "Pray tell, where do you think you're going, wife?"

"We must both be about our business early today. While you speak to the legislators, I'll speak to their wives and sell pins. We need pins for our sewing—especially now that we have an army to clothe. I'm selling ten per packet. Nabby has tied them neatly with twine."

John grimaced and sighed as if he was indulging me in some lunatic idea. He couldn't afford to turn his nose up at a good honest trade. But neither could my husband's vanity be comfortable with his wife as a merchant.

Well, that vanity is going to cost him, I decided. "For every grimace or sigh about my pins, I will deduct some small portion of the profits for myself."

"By law, everything you own belongs to me," he teased. "And a small percentage of nothing is *nothing*."

That remark was going to cost him, too.

As it happened, I did such a brisk business selling pins for three, four, and even five times what we paid for them—that he didn't even begrudge me *my pin money*, as he called it. And I tucked those coins into the linen pocket tied round my waist, feeling fully entitled to them.

I liked the weight of money. Especially as it felt like the only secure thing I could cling to when John left again for Philadelphia. For this time, neither of us knew how long he'd be gone.

Chapter Nine

BRAINTREE
Massachusetts Bay Colony
September 1775

M Y HUSBAND OFT said that calamities come together. Fire, sword, and famine keep company and visit a country in a flock. Thus did pestilence steal into Braintree.

First, a farmhand collapsed in the barn. The illness spread to our tenants and boarders, then to our servant girl Patty, and then all three of my young sons. The disease leaped from person to person until our entire household sickened, and no visitor dared step over our threshold except Dr. Tufts.

I'd scrubbed everything down with vinegar to get rid of the stench. Yet, it still lingered. And with a kerchief over his nose and mouth, Dr. Tufts said, "It's dysentery." When he saw my confusion he added, "It's commonly called the bloody flux."

I wilted, finally apprehending the true danger. "What can be done?"

"Barley water calms the intestines," he advised, despairing that his physician's training didn't avail him of better remedies. "Molasses revives the spirits. Willow bark for the pain."

But I had none of these things, and he didn't either.

I would just have to make do.

With the servants all sick, and my sons writhing in their beds, only my daughter and I seemed immune to the plague that laid everyone else low. I was so grateful to Nabby for helping me keep a cauldron boiling in the yard for the bed linens, which were soiled anew every day. She was acquiring a maturity much beyond her years, and I didn't know whether to be glad of it or despair.

It was still hot that season—too hot to be standing out under the sun stirring boiling water with a paddle. I took off my straw bonnet to wipe the sweat away. And that is the last I remembered before I collapsed to the ground.

When next I awakened, cool water on my face and hair, I blinked up at my daughter standing over me, panic in her little eyes. "Mama!"

She'd dumped a rain bucket over me. But not before trying to rouse our near relations and neighbors. She'd run from house to house to get help, but everyone was sick. Even Reverend Wibird was so ill there were no meetings on the Sabbath. Now she was breathless, tears streaking her cheeks as she relayed the news that her uncle Elihu Adams and her baby cousin had died.

The rest of John's family were terribly sick, too.

Poor John, I thought in near delirium. He'd be pained to learn of his brother's passing. I could only pray that he wouldn't return to find the rest of us dead, too.

"Just help me inside," I whispered to Nabby, for I wasn't even strong enough to crawl unassisted. "We dare not ask anyone else to come. It's too contagious."

Nabby all but dragged me up the stairs, where I collapsed again, landing half atop the bed and half still hanging over the edge. I was so thirsty, so dizzy, so drenched in fever sweat . . .

"Where is John?" I murmured as I drifted in and out of consciousness. I murmured it again upon waking to tremendous pain in my abdomen, clutching my belly. I murmured it again hearing my toddler cry in his crib.

Little Tommy was dehydrated and suffering. I tried to reach for him, but I could scarcely lift my head.

Where is John?

Better he stay away, lest he die with us. Better that everyone stay away.

Below stairs, poor Patty shrieked in nightmare. Strange visions passed before my eyes, too, so I could scarcely believe that I wasn't hallucinating when I felt a cool cloth pressed to my cheek, and the rim of a glass of lemonade held to my lips.

I heard my mother's voice, serene but distant. "You did well to fetch me, Nabby. You took good care of your mama, your brothers, and all the others. But you're still a little girl, and you must let Grandmama take command here."

You shouldn't be here, Mother, I tried to say, shaking my head. *It isn't safe*. But as I spasmed in agony, I could only whisper, "No."

"Hush now, Abigail," my mother said. "So sickly and mortal a time the oldest man cannot remember. Dr. Tufts tells me there are eighteen dead amongst your neighbors alone."

Eighteen. I could scarcely believe it possible.

She told me that Patty's mother, poor Mrs. Copeland, was dead, Mrs. Randle lost her daughter, Mrs. Bracket hers, Mr. Thomas Thayer his wife. More dead in Weymouth besides. Then she asked, "Did you think I'd tend your father's parishioners while leaving my own daughter in want?"

Trying to ward her away with one hand, I rasped, "Take Nabby and leave here at once."

Nabby wasn't sick yet, so if my mother took her, at least one of my children might survive. These were the disordered thoughts that filled my mind.

My mother would not hear of it. "You need me now, Abigail. I remember when you were young—how my worrying after your health always vexed you. You ran from me whenever you had the chance. Well, now you are too sick to run."

In spite of all, it brought a smile to my chapped lips to remember the headstrong girl I'd been. Now my mother's solicitousness filled me with relief for my sake and anxiety for hers. She could see it in my eyes as I surrendered and took another sip of the lemonade. "Abigail, you must let me help you. Otherwise, I fear you'll be carried off and then who will mother my grandchildren?"

I didn't have the strength to make her go. I let her nurse me and the children that day. I let her return the next, and the day after that. I truly couldn't have survived without her.

When I was finally able to sit up in bed, I said, "Surely there's a letter from John."

Even in Philadelphia, he would've heard by now about the deaths in our town. He would've known his family was distressed.

Even a few scribbled lines would've been a healing balm. But having no letter at all made me agitated.

"Calm yourself," my mother said, lifting a bowl to my lips. "Letters often go astray. Now take some of this broth."

She was right, and I nodded obediently, deciding to save my strength for baby Tommy, who was unwilling that anybody but his own mama should do for him. Once a hearty and hale corn-fed boy, he'd become so lean and wan that his father would not know him. But thankfully his fever had abated. Charlie and Johnny also seemed to be coming through it. Would that I could say the same of poor Patty, who seemed to be putrefying where she lay abed in misery and suffering.

It wasn't until the latter half of the month that I finally regained the ability to wash and dress myself without assistance. Taking up a pen, I wrote a frantic letter to John asking him to find willow bark, rhubarb, nutmeg, cloves, and cinnamon for medicines.

Whether this note reached him, I didn't know, for woe followed upon woe, one affliction treading upon the heels of another as my dear mother fell ill.

Now, our roles were reversed.

In her bed at the parsonage in Weymouth, my mother groaned as I held the cold cloths to her head, lifted the glass of lemonade to her lips, and tried to coax her to take broth.

"It's special medicine," I told her, for Phoebe had allowed Dr. Tufts to transform the kitchen into an apothecary, every herb possible now hanging over the hearth where she had a fragrant brew boiling.

Meanwhile, my sister Elizabeth scrubbed the parsonage with vinegar. And when I tried to help her with the bucket she said, "Mama won't let me send for our brother because he's fighting. But she won't let me send for Mary either. I know it's a long journey and our older sister will expose herself to pestilence if she comes. But there comes a time—"

"Mama will recover," I insisted.

And I believed it even when, the next morning, I wiped my mother's fevered brow and she whispered, "It is all right, child. I'll be with God soon."

That could not be true. I didn't know how I'd bear the loss of her, much less the knowledge that she'd met this fate because she nursed me and my children. The guilt would surely kill me.

"*No*," I said, my voice quavering as I tried not to burst into tears over her bed. "You'll be well, Mother. I'll see to it. Because you cannot have given your life to spare mine."

Through her agony, she fixed me with a stare. "Abigail, wouldn't you give your life to spare your children?"

At her question, the vision of my little ones flashed before me. Johnny and his inquisitive eyes. Nabby's rosebud smile. Charlie's cherubic beauty. Tommy's pudgy little arms, always reaching for reassurance. I loved each and every one; I'd put my body between them and danger without a second thought. "But they're still *little* children."

"They're *your* children no matter how old they get," my mother replied. "And you are mine. God calls us all in the end. That I should be called instead of you gives me satisfaction."

This I could not accept.

I was back and forth from my house to the parsonage, from sickbed to sickbed, trying every cure I could think of, from sweet mulled cider to bitter coffee, from feeding to purging, from cold air to warm air, from cold water to warm water, from exertion to rest.

If I'd had leeches, I'd have tried that, too.

And as I worked to save my mother and all the others who ailed on my farm, I longed for my husband's strong hand at the small of my back to steady me in these grim times.

Try as I might, those in my care were slipping away. Our servant girl Patty died at the chime of midnight, and I sobbed silently at the cruelty of it. She'd lived under my care alongside my daughter, and now I washed her corpse and tenderly wrapped it in cloth, as if afraid to disturb her sleep. She'd be buried beside her mother—a woman who had done all she could to preserve her children and still failed.

Then, already shattered in grief, I returned to the parsonage where my own dying mother asked for tea. *Tea* of all accursedly precious things. With the soldiers still visiting punishment upon Boston, it was hard to find bread, much less tea.

But somehow Phoebe scared up a packet of leaves from amongst her fellow enslaved people. She pressed it into my hands with a grave expression. "You should be the one to give it to her, Honey."

I was unutterably grateful to Phoebe for giving my mother one last taste of pleasure on her deathbed and allowing me to deliver it to her. I resolved again to confront my father about giving this good woman her freedom. But first, I held my mother's sweat-soaked head up from her pillow so she could drink.

My mother swallowed a few sips, gasped, and fell back upon her pillow, then opened her eyes with a look that pierced my heart. For it was the eagerness of a *last* look.

She closed her eyes but lingered until five o'clock that evening with my father praying at her bedside. It had been his day to perform communions, but he'd led the congregation to pray for his beloved dying wife, and every eye had streamed, his own heart almost bursting.

Alas, I finally knew that prayers would not spare her. Nothing would.

My mother was leaving us for a world infinitely better than this one. She'd be gladder there in receipt of her happy reward. And yet, when she finally breathed her last, I nearly fainted with the distress of such a blow, for my grief mingled with such heavy guilt that I could not bear up under it.

I knew that till now my portion of the bitter cup was small in comparison with others. But now I drank a large draught of grief. And I couldn't overcome my too-selfish sorrow. I longed for my mother's smiling countenance, her kind advice, her tender care, her prudent example, and her thousand amiable virtues.

Virtues I knew I would never find again in this life.

It didn't matter that it was the natural way of things to bury a parent if we live long enough. Nor did it matter that our duty as Christians commanded us to uplift others instead of sinking into the abyss. I simply didn't know if I had the fortitude of a Christian or a philosopher to bear this grief.

Chapter Ten

I REFUSED COLONEL QUINCY'S invitation to dine. At least until my sister prevailed upon me. "But you *must* go," Elizabeth said, quite fretful. "You cannot grieve so hard and so long as you have done and survive to tell the tale, Abigail. You are *sinking*, and Mama would never want that."

Of course, neither would our mother have wanted for Elizabeth to fall prey to the commonest fate of unmarried daughters—to spend all her days looking after my father, supervising the servants, and trying to preside over a household that was not her own.

It was a heavy responsibility that Elizabeth now bore—one she would likely have no escape from. But that didn't mean she'd lost all interest in the world. "Besides, you say *Dr. Franklin* has come to see the situation here, so you must go with me to meet him!"

We'd first heard of Benjamin Franklin when our father taught us to fly kites. Papa told us about Dr. Franklin's experiments with electricity, which put us in awe. Then, when we were older, Colonel Quincy gifted us with copies of Dr. Franklin's almanac, taking great amusement from the man's wit.

The two had business dealings in chocolate, candles, and glass. And our maternal relation taught us to admire Franklin for his inventions and accomplishments in statecraft.

But we admired Franklin most for having introduced America to the idea of a lending library. Now I had the opportunity to dine with the man and tell him so. Nevertheless, I shook my head. "I can scarcely get through a dinner with my own children without dissolving into tears. How can I dine in society?"

"Because you aren't only a daughter grieving for her mother," my sister said. "You're *Mrs. John Adams*. You're a delegate's wife and it's your duty to meet with his colleagues and go where he cannot whilst he's away."

Elizabeth was right. Though I'd yet to receive a comforting word from my husband, he still needed me to be his eyes and ears. So, I dried my tears, tried to pinch some life into my cheeks, and dressed for my duty.

When I arrived at the familiar and beautiful mansion, I encountered Franklin by accident in the hall, and without introduction. I recognized him straightaway from a printed likeness—though at nearly seventy years old, the venerable old Franklin was now stout, balding, and bejowled. And I hadn't anticipated the flirtatious twinkle in his eye.

"I am Mrs. Adams," I said with a small curtsey.

Franklin tilted his head. "Sam, or—"

"John. Mrs. John Adams."

"Lucky John Adams," he murmured, gallantly offering to help with my cloak.

Fortunately, its removal revealed my black dress, which reminded him that I was in mourning. And he sobered instantly. "Madam, I offer my deepest sympathies in your time of sorrow."

Having come from the Second Continental Congress, where he now served with my husband, he continued, "When your Mr. Adams heard the dreadful news about your mother, he quite nearly mounted his horse to fly to you. I was the one who prevailed upon him not to abandon his country. And I sincerely hope that my safe delivery of his letters will offer solace, and an excuse for you to forgive me."

Thereupon he presented me a bundle of letters that I clutched like precious talismans to be opened in private. For the time being, I thanked Dr. Franklin, saying, "There is nothing to forgive, sir, for I, too, would have counseled him to stay. For our own sake, and for all our friends in distant colonies."

"Very good, madam. For as I always say, we must all hang together or, most assuredly, we shall all hang separately."

He laughed, but I could not. The possibility of my husband being hanged was far too real for me to laugh.

I joined Dr. Franklin at Colonel Quincy's table, where I was reunited with my sister and other prominent patriot wives and neighbors, including the wife of Sam Adams, with whom I was so often confused. The fare was considerably humbler than before the war. Cornbread with some scant butter. A watery soup of potatoes seasoned with salt pork and pickled cabbage on the side. All to be washed down with small beer.

Warmer fare, still, than our soldiers had to eat, not far distant from here, lacking firewood for cooking. And when I thought of the privations of those trapped in Boston . . . well, it seemed a feast fit for kings.

In conversation, I found Dr. Franklin to be social but not talkative. When he did speak, something useful or entertaining always dropped from his tongue. He was grave as the circumstances demanded, yet pleasant, and extremely affable. In truth, I thought I could read in his countenance the virtues of his heart, among which patriotism shined in its full luster.

The meal was finished with pears stewed in wine. And when the course was served, Dr. Franklin turned to ask all the intelligence I knew. "Congress sent me to take stock and I am interested to know everything a housewife in Braintree may have heard from friends, relations, and even the enslaved population of the area."

I liked being asked. And digging a spoon into my pear, I told him all I knew, from the supply of flour to the story of a cannonball shattering the sign in front of an inn.

"A thorough report," Franklin said, tipping his glass to me in compliment. "Perhaps I'll recommend you as a scout to General Washington if you'd like to enlist."

I laughed. "No. But if our soldiers should fail, the redcoats will find a race of Amazons in America wielding muskets against them. For the sufferings they've unleashed here are unendurable. Though I do worry about the southern ladies, given the example of their husbands."

"Why so, madam?" Franklin asked.

I leaned forward, wary to confess, "I have sometimes thought the passion for liberty cannot be equally strong in the breasts of those who have been accustomed to deprive their fellow creatures of theirs."

Franklin knew I spoke of slavery, which was not diplomatic to mention whilst a slaveholding Virginian led our army. And yet, I could see he heartily approved of my sentiments. "I've been told, Mrs. Adams, that you speak frankly. To my delight, I now know this is true. You'd make a lovely addition to our society in Philadelphia. Mrs. Hancock shall be joining us for the winter. I hope you shall, too, for your husband's sake, and for mine."

How tempting an offer! Winter fast approached and I'd been like a nun in a cloister, with no desire for company, my evenings lonesome and melancholy, still occasionally breaking down into a flood of tears over my dearly departed mother. So my desire to travel was engaged for more than one reason.

Elizabeth's eyes now encouraged me to accept, for she knew that to be reunited with my husband would be good medicine, even if I had to travel to the distant country of Pennsylvania.

But how would four small children fare on such a journey, and what would become of our farm? My husband hadn't the means of Mr. Hancock, so I thanked Dr. Franklin for the invitation and said I'd spend the winter wherever Mr. Adams thought best.

That night, closeted with John's long-awaited letters, I finally felt consoled and comforted. Among the many precious words John had written, I found, "I bewail more than I can express, the loss of your excellent mother. If I could write as well as you do, my sorrows would be as eloquent as yours, but upon my word I cannot."

And finally, "It's very painful to be four hundred miles from my family and friends knowing they're in affliction. But when I shall come home I know not. We have so much to do, and it is difficult to do it right."

Did any of us know anymore what was *right*?

Sunday, sitting in meeting, listening to our worthy Reverend Wibird, I found that I could no longer join his prayer that Britain reunite with her colonies in peace and brotherhood.

My mind was too agitated by the news that British regulars had attempted to seize the cattle that would sustain us during the winter. A skirmish erupted and they killed one of our sentinels. A young man dead simply for watching over cows. No, I would not join prayers for reconciliation with these savages.

Instead, I'd spend the rest of my Sabbath day thumbing through Thomas Paine's new pamphlet *Common Sense*.

Paine argued that we should declare our independence and sever all ties with the king to form our own nation—a sentiment we found appealing. But my husband ultimately called the pamphlet an "ignorant, malicious, short-sighted, crapulous mass."

Despite the seriousness of the topic, that critique had inspired a hearty laugh from me. I knew that John thought Mr. Paine's work dangerously populist in nature. In response, my husband wrote his own pamphlet, *Thoughts on Government*, carefully laying out a plan for a balanced government with co-equal branches to prevent the tyranny of one from overrunning the other, and the people besides.

But that was all too speculative for me. *I* thought the important part of Paine's pamphlet was how well it argued for a new nation. We did not feel British anymore, if ever we did. And we could not have suffered all this only to go groveling back to the king.

Britain was no loving mother, no benevolent parent giving guidance and discipline with our good in mind. In truth, she was a tyrant. Her people were unworthy to be our brethren. So, we'd have to govern ourselves or grovel all our lives.

Which was why I felt no hesitation in urging John to action. "Renounce them," I wrote him. "Let us declare independency and beseech the almighty to bring about their ruin."

Chapter Eleven

BRAINTREE
Massachusetts Bay Colony
March 1776

THE BRITISH WERE fleeing Boston!

Thanks to a daring plan to haul cannons over ice all the way from Fort Ticonderoga—a plan executed by Boston's own Henry Knox, the former bookseller—the British had awakened one morning to the shock of seeing our guns on Dorchester Heights pointing back at them.

Realizing that they weren't the only ones with cannons anymore, they turned tail and ran.

"Cowards," little Charlie said. "They stood it only one year, but we'd have stood it three."

I laughed, exhilarated. "Right you are, my little man." And that night I wrote to my husband, demanding to know where the British might go. Was the fight over?

Congress was soon to make my husband president of the Board of War, and I was keen to know the progress of it. Only a month before, I'd not known whether we could plant or sow with safety, whether we could rest in our own cottages or should flee to the woods. But now I felt as if we might sit under our own vine and eat the good of the land.

Was it unpardonable hubris to think we might actually *win* this fight?

With spring's arrival on the horizon, the long grief over my mother's passing lifted. The sun looked brighter, the birds sang more melodiously, and I felt bold and optimistic about the world's infinite possibilities.

Perhaps that's why I took up my pen to write my husband, "And by the way, in the new code of laws which I suppose will be necessary, I desire you would remember the ladies. Be more generous and favorable to them than your ancestors. Do not put such unlimited power into the hands of the husbands."

These words felt impertinent. Demanding. Audacious. Even a husband as indulgent as John Adams might take them amiss. I ought to scratch them out or feed the letter to the fire and start again. But as I looked to see Nabby studying alongside my sons, I could think of no good reason why we should fight for the freedom of her brothers whilst leaving her to the whims of whatever man she might one day marry.

All patriots now said they'd rather die than live without freedom. So, with this thought, I added, "If particular care is not paid to the ladies, we are determined to foment a rebellion, and will not hold ourselves bound by any laws in which we have no voice or representation."

I sent this letter with the highest hopes in my heart.

I received a reply that made it ache.

"I cannot but laugh at what you say about the ladies," John wrote. "We know better than to repeal our masculine systems, which would completely subject us to the despotism of the petticoat."

He plainly believed I'd written a bit of saucy jousting. But I'd meant it earnestly and now felt stung by his dismissal. Resentful, too.

My husband had wounded me in this exchange; he had, in fact, for the first time in our lives, truly *disappointed* me. Thus, I did not mind quite so much when he told me that he wouldn't be home in May.

And when I turned my mind to the finances that sustained our family, it was with a much more independent turn of mind. John—who had laughed at my plea for some small semblance of legal protection for women—had nevertheless asked me to begin making saltpeter for the soldiers' muskets. As if it was not all I could do to maintain his farm.

His financial fate rested on my merits. But the corn looked poor, I didn't have the strength to work the land by myself, and I couldn't make it rain. I'd have to lean harder on my own resources. So, when

Dr. Tufts stopped by on his way to Boston, I asked, "When you make house calls, do you ever encounter ladies who need pins?"

"Every housewife in Massachusetts needs pins," he replied. "Why? What scheme is brewing in your head?"

"I've been selling pins to friends," I explained. "I'm already trading with Mrs. Warren for soap, wool, and cloth from Plymouth. Now I want to expand my enterprise, but a respectably married woman cannot go from town to town hawking pins like a tinker."

"Why not?" he asked.

For a moment, I startled. His question wasn't just a flippant quip. The world as we knew it was coming apart, so, truly, why not? But unlike Mrs. Warren, I had to care about conventions and pleasantries. "Because it isn't done. Certainly not by a delegate's wife." We couldn't afford for our fellow citizens to wonder whether my husband was using his role in the public trust to corrupt advantage. Still, we needed to survive. "But your son is in trade. Might you and he consider, for some percentage of the profits, selling for me?"

My good Uncle Tufts grinned as if we were hatching a plot, and I supposed we were. "I don't see why not."

He hadn't hesitated, so neither did I, launching into a discussion of plans and possibilities. "I think even more money could be made in Boston."

"If only it were safe to go there," he warned. "The British have left smallpox in their wake."

In the aftermath of the siege, General Washington insisted upon inoculating the entire Continental Army against the disease, which was sometimes called distemper. I knew my husband wished for an inoculating hospital to be opened in every town in New England. Meanwhile, Uncle Tufts told me the city of Boston would embark upon the experiment of inoculating its populace all at once.

I decided then and there to be part of that experiment. I would not simply wait, complacently, for another contagion to carry off me and mine. For I was in a revolutionary spirit and would take fate into my own hands.

Chapter Twelve

BOSTON
Massachusetts Bay Colony
Summer 1776

MY DECISION COULD not be reconsidered; once we entered Boston we wouldn't be able to leave without a physician's certificate. But I did not have second thoughts. With my children, I patiently submitted to being smoked along with all our money and papers, as this was said to help prevent contagion.

Then we passed into Boston, a scene of such destruction as I never could have imagined. Eleven months Boston had been under siege, and now we passed a burned-out church, piles of rubble where houses used to be, and a stump was all that remained of Boston's Liberty Tree. Castle William was half blown to bits, and the Old South Meeting House was covered in manure, for the British had used it as a stable.

The British had left everything filthy, falling down, or forsaken—including our old house on Queen Street. One of our rooms had been used for poultry, another for coal, and a third for salt. The floors were mildewed, the ceiling collapsing, and the paper falling from the walls. I'd hire a girl to clean it and do my best to rent or sell it, but I feared it must be condemned.

I fisted my hands, thankful at least that not *all* the houses were destroyed. One of my uncles's town houses was in good, but spare, condition. There we were reunited with my sisters and their children, for we had all agreed to my plan to convalesce together. It was the most ideal situation I could conceive of to take the smallpox by way of controlled dose.

"Two percent don't survive the treatment," fretted my older sister, Mary.

To which my younger sister, Elizabeth, argued, "But a person is *much* more certain to die of smallpox if contracted the natural way."

Nodding in agreement, I said, "Twenty to thirty percent die if they haven't been inoculated. Simply hoping never to catch it the natural way cannot be chanced."

Still it was a frightful risk to take with my children's lives. I'd write to John about it only after the deed was done. He was sweltering in Philadelphia, debating a proposed declaration of independence. Nothing good could come of terrifying him for his family's lives.

I'd be frightened enough for the both of us.

I took the inoculation first—allowing the doctor to make a small incision in my forearm into which he placed an infected, pus-laden thread. Then I lined up the children, from oldest to youngest.

"Will it hurt?" Nabby asked, biting her lower lip and tugging at her lace cuff.

"A little," I said of the cut. "But whatever comes, I will be right here with you."

I am giving my child smallpox, some part of my mind screamed. If I should lose her, I would never recover. But the threat would come one way or the other. So, I would be with her through it all; that was my solemn vow.

I felt an echoing pain as the knife pierced her tender flesh and bright red blood flowed down to her elbow. But Nabby only winced at the cut, for which I was desperately grateful.

She provided a good example for her brothers, each of whom stood the operation stoically, like good little soldiers!

Nine-year-old Johnny watched the doctor work with obvious fascination. Six-year-old Charlie cheekily offered the doctor his toy horse if he wouldn't make it hurt too much. Finally, nearly four-year-old Tommy turned his mop of unruly hair into my shoulder with a whimper, but not a cry. And I promised them, "Once recovered, none of us need ever worry about smallpox again."

Even so, it was an anxious affair.

Mary and her little ones showed so few symptoms that we feared it had not taken—but in a house nearby, Mrs. Warren lay so dangerously ill her life was despaired of. I sent up a prayer for her, for I could not imagine the world without my courageous friend and mentor. For my part, my eyes were aflame, but only one eruption appeared on my arm. Johnny had it exactly as one would wish—enough to be sick but not troubled. Unfortunately, Nabby and the younger boys showed no symptoms and had to go through it all a second time to make sure the treatment took.

As per the doctor's instructions, we lay upon the carpet or straw beds or anything hard, abstaining from spirits, salt, and fats. Fruit we ate, and those who liked vegetables unseasoned could eat them, but that was not me. My easier trial allowed me to take constant care of my babes, for which I was grateful. Because I would do everything to return them to health, making me empathize with what I'd always felt was my mother's oversolicitousness. Somewhere in heaven, she was giving me a knowing smile.

And there were some compensations as we convalesced. For one thing, I had the finest room in my uncle's house. The window overlooked the flower garden, which was in full bloom. I'd always wanted a closet with a window I could claim all for myself in which to read and write my letters. It was there that I read John's most recent missive.

Someone told him I was in Boston.

The secret was out.

And now my husband wrote, "I feel like a savage to be here while my whole family will be sick in Boston. It is not possible for me to describe my feelings upon this occasion. Nothing but the critical state of our affairs should prevent me from flying to Boston to your assistance. Spare for nothing; I will repay with gratitude and interest any sum you borrow."

Poor John. There was little he could do for us, so I merely asked him to send me more pins and some real tea from Philadelphia. The *true* stuff was the only medicine I knew that might soothe our headaches and sore throats.

In the meantime, from our windows, we noticed patriot troops flooding into the streets under arms. I went outside and heard the buzz drifting about Boston.

"A proclamation from congress—"

"—what? Independency?—"

"Come to King Street and hear it read."

At last! I knew my husband was on the committee charged with drafting a proclamation of independence. He'd been working for weeks with Dr. Franklin and a Virginian named Thomas Jefferson, and then Congress itself had debated and rewritten it until they could finally get every colony to agree to its wording. That unanimity achieved, I now hungered to hear it. Gathering my skirts, I joined the multitudes in front of the redbrick State House.

From the little balcony overlooking the square, the words of the Declaration of Independence were read aloud, and I nearly swooned at their boldness.

We hold these truths to be self-evident, that all men are
created equal, that they are endowed by their creator
with certain unalienable rights, that among these are life,
liberty and the pursuit of happiness. That to secure these
rights, governments are instituted among men, deriving
their just powers from the consent of the governed . . .

I recognized John's sentiments in it, but the words did not ring with his style. Instead, they seemed a perfect distillation of the collective voice of the people. Almost like the sacred words of God . . .

I'd later learn that the wielder of so eloquent a pen wasn't my husband but the young Mr. Jefferson. At the time, all I knew was that these words stirred my very soul.

A fishwife come late to the reading leaned in to ask me, "What does it say?"

"It's enumerating the king's abuses," I replied quickly. "Explaining why he is a tyrant, and why we will throw him off or die trying."

The catalog of despotism went on in more detail, in better order and with lovelier language than I was able to memorize in one hearing. But I understood, and felt deeply, the truth of each accusation.

That the king had excited insurrections against us. Imposed tariffs without consent. Deprived the legislature of their rightful power. Undermined and corrupted the courts. Harassed and threatened public officials. Obstructed immigration. Sent soldiers against us in peacetime. Put military authority above civil authority. Quartered armed troops among us. Deprived us of due process and trial by jury. Sent prisoners to foreign lands to be tried for pretended offenses. Plundered our seas. Ravaged our coasts. Burned our towns. And destroyed the lives of our people.

To hear it listed for all the world lifted my soul more than any Sabbath meeting of my life. I no longer felt the aches of lingering smallpox, nor the grime of dust upon my skin, nor the sun's heat on my bonnet. What I felt was bathed and baptized in the refreshing *truths*.

And while I basked in it, the crowd went wild.

"Huzzah!"

"God Save our American states!"

"Heaven protect our Union!"

People swarmed the State House, pulling down the gilded lion and unicorn of the king's arms and tearing from the facade every vestige of royalty to be burnt in a bonfire.

We would have no more king. We would be colonies no more. We would be our own new nation. We would be free and we *must* be free.

John had made this possible. He was, I thought, a hero for the ages. And this made me wish to be a heroine. It'd been nearly six months since I asked him to remember the ladies. Now I felt obligated to try again.

"My dearest friend," I wrote, still in raptures. "If we mean to have heroes, statesmen and philosophers in this new nation, we should have learned women. The world perhaps would laugh at me, but you have a mind too enlarged and liberal to disregard the sentiment." Then, to twit him, lest he get too much vanity as a hero, I added, "Don't forget my tea, for your own sake as well as mine."

Chapter Thirteen

BRAINTREE
Massachusetts
November 1776

P apa!" Nabby threw her arms around John's neck with such enthusiasm that she knocked off his tricorn. Then the boys, laughing with happiness at their father's return, launched themselves at his knees, threatening to pull him down.

But my good man was a sturdy oak and could not be felled. He ruffled Johnny's hair, kissed Nabby's nose, then pried Charlie and Tommy off his legs and into his arms. "My little patriots!"

I hadn't expected him home and stood in mute shock. Thus, he scolded, "I suppose Your Ladyship has been in the twitters because you've not received a letter by every post. But come give me a kiss of forgiveness, because I've come to make my apology in person. Methinks the Continental Congress can do without me for a month or two."

A month or two. Then he'd be home well into the new year. It meant going to meetings together on Sabbath days followed by cozy candlelit suppers. It meant a happy Christmastide and help mending fences and creaky floorboards. And it meant that if the cannons boomed again, I could cling to him for safety . . .

Now John presented me with a tin. "I remembered your tea."

I gasped, clutching it to my bosom, then I playfully turned up my nose. "I wanted it for the smallpox, so it comes late. But I'll take it and be grateful."

"It's the second tin I purchased for you," he replied. "I sent the first to Boston when you asked, but the messenger delivered it to Mrs. Samuel Adams instead."

I spluttered with laughter. "Oh! Do you know I think I drank some? She invited me for tea in Boston, and I thought her husband far more considerate than mine. Especially since it was very fine tea."

"Only the best for my very fine wife," John said, puffing warm breaths into his still-cold hands.

I put the kettle on the fire and warmed some dinner for him, knowing it was his habit to ride hard without stopping for rest or sustenance. And as he tore into warm biscuits spread thick with butter, he asked, "Well? What think you of the declaration?"

"It was *marvelous*," I said. "Truly, John."

"No corrections or complaints?" He arched a teasing eyebrow.

"*Well*. I did think slavery would be denounced."

"It was," John replied, his shoulders falling. "But we removed the denunciation to appease the southern states or they wouldn't sign."

My nostrils flared. "And which states prevented you from re-membering the ladies? The declaration says all *men* are created equal. Whilst you are proclaiming peace and goodwill to men, and wishing to emancipate all nations, why must you insist upon retaining an absolute power over wives?"

John licked butter from his fingertips. "Does not the term *men* include all *mankind*?"

"So, then you *did* mean to include ladies?"

John smirked. "You'll have to ask Jefferson what he meant when he wrote it."

"I'm keener to know what *you* think. Because remember, hus-band, arbitrary power is like most other things which are very hard—very liable to be broken."

Now John held up his hand in a plea of mercy. "I thought I left Congress. I am scarcely in the door, and yet another constituency is heard from."

"I'll let you eat your biscuit in peace, Mr. Delegate," I said, kiss-ing his balding pate. "But we shall revisit the topic."

"Of that I have no doubt."

THAT NIGHT, AFTER I had readied the bed with a copper warming pan, our eyes met. The long-suppressed emotion of so many long months apart and countless tribulations now welled up inside me such that I began to tremble. I had pushed down every wish, and silenced every murmur, acquiescing in a painful separation. But now, as John moved to embrace me, my fingers tightened into fists, not knowing whether I wished more to thrash him for being so long away, or caress him in gratitude for his return.

"Abigail," he said, holding my trembling body tight. "I regret all that has conspired to keep us apart, but now I am yours."

I was tempted to tell him certain attitudes had also come between us, but never once had the flame of love dimmed, and now at the rumble of his baritone by my ear, love flared anew. "I have missed you, husband. Friend of my heart."

He kissed me, and I returned that kiss. Yet I knew he wanted more. I could feel it as his body pressed to mine, and an answering call warmed my blood. But as John's fingers began the nimble work of unfastening my clothes, I was seized with fear.

And as I pulled away, he mistook the cause. "Come now, my Abigail, don't be cross. You'd pity me if you knew what a lonely, forlorn creature I've been without you."

"I am not cross," I said, palms pressed to where I could feel the beating of his heart. "I think no man but you could've led Congress so nobly in these times. Who else could have persuaded the other colonies to band together for independence?"

He frowned down at my splayed fingers on his chest. "Then why do you fend me off?"

I flushed, finding it unusually difficult to explain. "I long to fold you to my fluttering heart, but our youngest isn't nursing anymore, and I fear the danger of another child."

John's frown transformed into a mischievous grin. "With all the other dangers we've hazarded, this is what you fear? I'd welcome another child. Each of our little ones is a delight, and you've oft mourned that they grow so fast . . ."

"I have," I admitted as his persuasions began to work upon me.

"We shall try for another little girl this time," he murmured against my hair, pressing upon what he surely knew was my weakest spot.

We still mourned our lost little Susanna. And he knew I still ached to give Nabby a sister. The thought of an infant girl mewling against my breast tugged at my maternal yearnings.

Yet, my mind raised a thousand objections. The farm, the finances, and the struggle to feed the children. Never mind *the war*. All of it weighed upon me. "Is it right to bring another child into a world of chaos?"

"We live in trying times, but my guardian angel whispers that we shall see happier days."

Suspicious of his optimism, I asked, "Is that guardian angel General Washington, perchance, with some hopeful military intelligence?"

But John would not be distracted with questions about the war and pressed a kiss to my neck. "Come to bed with me, my dear, and let's add another to our little flock. Think how nice it will be to walk in the garden with Charlie in one hand and Tommy in the other, Nabby on your right hand and Johnny upon my left, to view the cornfields, the orchards, and so on. And you the picture of fertility, another babe in your womb."

Certainly, I was tempted. But I felt so much *older* and less fit to carry a child as when last I was pregnant. Which is why I felt compelled to confess, "John . . . they told me you were dead."

The rumor had ripped through the colonies that John Adams had gone to inspect the troops in New York and been poisoned. A British spy had done it. Or a rival in Congress was the culprit. Or a Loyalist innkeeper had slipped the toxin into my husband's stew.

"Even after you wrote to reassure me you were still alive," I continued, "the story continued to reach me so brutally, so frequently, and with a nearly perverse glee by those I might have counted friends that I began to fear it was prophecy."

"No," he said, kissing my fingertips in tender reassurance. "That is superstition. Mummery and nonsense. Here I am, alive and well. And I mean to stay that way."

"But it's all I can do to manage without you even without a child at the breast."

At last he sobered a little at that, nodding thoughtfully. "I know how much I have put upon your slender shoulders, but you should not fear being alone. I promise that if God should bless us with another child, I will be home with you for the birth and difficult early months."

Now *here* was a temptation stronger than his honeyed words or silky caresses—stronger even than the thought of a milky-scented babe in my arms. To have John home again!

If a new child would ensure my husband's return, perhaps by adding to my family, I might unify it again. It was the one temptation I could not resist.

So it was upon his solemn promise that I surrendered to my good man. And when caught up in the throes of passion, he whispered, over and over again, "*I am yours, yours, yours.*"

Chapter Fourteen

WEYMOUTH
Massachusetts
January 1777

WE MADE OUR New Year's visits to friends and family, delivering gifts of fruitcakes. The parsonage offered a warm respite when we stopped to visit Phoebe and my widowed father, who was in much need of good cheer. There, we were also reunited with my sister Mary and her husband, Richard Cranch, with whom we shared mulled wine.

We also had at the table a very pleasant guest—the bespectacled James Lovell, who would this term go to Philadelphia with my husband to serve in the Continental Congress.

I remembered the man well from the marvelous oration he'd given to mark the anniversary of the Boston Massacre. But I wouldn't have recognized him because Mr. Lovell was still recovering from his arrest and yearlong ordeal on a British prison ship.

He was so thin that Mary plied him with slice after slice of my fruitcake, which he readily complimented. "Mrs. Adams, your servant deserves an increase in wages for this delicious concoction."

I tried not to preen. "It is my own baking entirely."

His eyebrows rose. "And here your Mr. Adams has described you to all and sundry as his stalwart *Portia*, such that I thought you more apt to wield a dagger than a baking spoon."

I laughed, glancing to my husband, who folded his hands before him as if in prayer. "Lord preserve me if Abigail should ever take up a dagger—her intellect alone is sharp enough to cut my vanity to ribbons."

I laughed again, resisting the urge to poke him in the ribs.

Then he smiled and said, "But she *is* my Portia. Even with baking spoon, she sacrifices for my sake and the sake of her country as courageously as any Roman matron."

I loved John then as much as I'd ever loved him and maybe more. For his good humor, self-knowledge, and the way he made me feel appreciated. For the warm affection in his eyes. For the man he was becoming. Not simply a foot soldier of good order, but the father of a new nation.

That night we spent long hours by the fire whilst Mr. Lovell shared harrowing details of his captivity. The tight, dark cell. The rats and the bite of irons at his wrists. The cold and maggot-infested meals. What kind of people held their fellow man in such conditions?

My heart truly went out to him. Mr. Lovell had been a Latin master—he'd never encouraged or been part of any mob. But the British needed to arrest *someone*, and he'd been easier to capture than Sam Adams. Owing his freedom to a prisoner exchange, Mr. Lovell now said, "Such injustices will *never* take place in the new nation we build."

I could see the doubt in my husband's less idealistic eyes as he considered human nature. But John kept his counsel, and I squeezed his hand in gratitude for that, and so very many other things.

WITH THE BLIZZARDS of January, my dearest friend was gone to Congress, but within weeks, I knew he'd left me with the stirrings of life within my womb.

It made me happier than I'd been in some time, despite the trials of winter. I stretched salt pork into stews seasoned with withered onions from the root cellar. I rationed pickled vegetables. I never *dared* crack open a jar of fruit preserves unless we had visitors—which we seldom did during cold weather. Occasionally Uncle Tufts sought respite after helping a patient, and I always saw to it that he was fed and warmed by my fire.

But few others stopped. Thus, I was shocked one wintry evening to find my father at my door, having come by horseback. Urging him in from the cold, I scolded, "Surely you didn't ride from Weymouth by yourself in the snow."

My father merely stamped his boots. "The Lord has seen fit to force me to do more in life on my own."

As a godly man, he'd always been forbidding, so I hesitated to reach for his hand to comfort him. Instead, I tried to convey with my voice that I understood—at least in some small part. "It's difficult to be without one's dearest friend."

If he appreciated my sympathy, he couldn't show it. "In any case, riding horseback is a trifle for someone so young as I am."

In truth, he was nearly seventy years old, but I dared not point it out, because if his grief over my mother was easing, I didn't wish to discourage his renewed vigor. "Nabby, help your grandpapa with his boots and set them by the fire to dry."

Nabby did as I bid while Johnny scrambled to pull an extra chair to our sparse dinner table. And while I tried to make little Tommy sit still and not spill his soup, I distractedly shared what news I had. "Dr. Tufts was here sharing tales of a woman who died in childbirth." Letting my hand drift to my pregnant belly, I said, "Would that he had kept *that* story to himself."

"Rejoice, for the woman is with her maker now," my father said. "She resides in paradise."

I did not feel much like rejoicing about a woman dying in pain and blood, leaving an orphaned infant behind. So, I remained silent until my father said, "I don't suppose you've heard the family news that your sister Elizabeth is to marry John Shaw this autumn."

John Shaw? I nearly choked.

Of all the men for my younger sister to wed! Shaw was a clergyman, like my father, but a dour Calvinist—the sort who saw sin everywhere and in everything. Incredulous, my hands gripped the back of the chair. "Don't say you gave your blessing!"

The same father who thwarted my own match for years now shrugged helplessly. "She loves the man."

This was news to me. "He'll take her away from us, all the way to Haverhill in New Hampshire!"

"Abigail, I know you've read the book of Ruth. A wife must go with her husband and his family. Besides, Shaw will let your sister read books and write those poems she dreams of publishing."

No, he will stifle her, I thought. There were few more conse-quential things for the quality of a woman's life than whom she married, and I could scarcely imagine a man less suited for her. My high-spirited little sister, Elizabeth, forced to adhere to every severe restriction, and held up for the community as an example as the Calvinist minister's wife!

I sat stewing about it during our meager supper, wondering at Elizabeth's strength of character if she could give herself over to the control of a man like that. "What does Phoebe say?"

"She won't speak against a love match," my father replied. "Es-pecially since Phoebe has her mind set to make the leap with a certain gentleman if he ever asks."

I knew Phoebe's *certain gentleman* was Mr. Abdee, a Black merchant of Boston. A far better choice in husband than Rever-end Shaw, in my opinion. "Does this mean you finally intend to free Phoebe? She's a deserving woman who has given us nothing but kindness in return for the cruelty of servitude."

"Abigail—"

"You are a parson meant to lead by moral example."

My father gave me the weary look of an exasperated elder. "Slavery is mentioned in the *Bible*."

"How many slaves did Jesus own?"

My father did not answer but plainly thought me a simpleton. "If Mr. Abdee asks for Phoebe's hand, perhaps I'll manumit her as a wedding present. Otherwise, I can't just set loose a woman alone in the world with no way of taking care of herself."

My lips pursed because my father was far less capable of tak-ing care of himself than any woman I knew. And here *I* was tak-ing care of myself alone, and my children, too.

I was still vexed the next day while taking inventory of the larder. I sent my little sister a letter in an attempt to dissuade her but now wondered if it would be better to ride to Weymouth and shake some sense into her.

In the end, I decided there was no accounting for what a woman would do when nearly thirty and still unmarried. My sister was leaping at what might be her last chance to be a mistress of her own household. It would be cruelly unfair of me to begrudge her.

But John Shaw!

Perhaps I was so cross because of my pregnancy; having spit up twice that morning already, I was out of sorts. I wanted a bite of fresh bread to soothe my stomach, but there was no flour to be had. There was not a bushel of rye within sixty miles of this town. We were also out of sugar, rum, coffee, and chocolate.

Peering over my shoulder, Nabby said, "We have just enough molasses to make Indian pudding."

We did at that! How fortunate I was to have a daughter who was both a companion and an assistant, possessing a prudence and steadiness beyond her years. In truth, Nabby's help sustained me through that hard winter, into the first buds of spring. And though Johnny wasn't nearly so helpful, he was at least now big enough to ride to the post and back.

Their father often sent a few lines to the children—who, shivering over a fire, would compare each letter's length to see which one was longest, bickering over whom their father loved best.

"Not me," Tommy whined. "Papa never writes me."

"Only because you can't read," Nabby consoled him.

As for me, as my time of birth neared, I looked round with a melancholy sigh for my absent partner, wondering what would happen if, like Dr. Tuft's patient, I should perish in the ordeal of childbirth.

Most widowers would take another wife to be a mother over his children; but I couldn't imagine John courting anew. It would all fall upon Nabby to tend to her father's household and raise up her brothers. A fate from which I wished to spare her, as much as I wished God to spare me and the child in my womb.

A DROUGHT-CURSED SUMMER baked our fields, leaving me to wonder if I was forever to be standing in the dust, praying for rain. The farm work went hard because our gray horse was lame with age. The wise thing to do would be to sell her for stew meat, but my husband had a soft spot for animals, and I was relieved that he wrote from Congress that I should let the mare enjoy the rest of her life in our pasture as a reward for long service.

Certainly, the horse served us longer than my head farm worker—

a formerly enslaved man who came to us with Phoebe's highest recommendation.

"He can't just *leave* us, can he?" Johnny asked. "Not in the middle of haying."

"He's a free man in what we hope to make a free country," I said, realizing that I had no cause to blame the man for having been tempted away with an offer of one hundred dollars. Congress had issued continental currency to finance the army, resulting in dizzying inflation. Money was already worth only a third of what it used to be, and soon our currency would be worth less than blank paper.

When I explained this to Johnny, he asked, "What's inflation?"

"It means the money we hold today will buy less tomorrow."

My boy looked thoughtful. "Then shouldn't we buy as much as possible today?"

"If it's something that keeps or can easily sell . . ."

Congress was promising to pay 6 percent interest on war bonds. It was, as far as I knew, the only way of defending our savings against depreciation. So that night I sent money to the loan office. Of course, I couldn't keep this secret like my pin money. And I feared my husband's judgment because John held so-called stockjobbers and "paper men" in low regard. But thankfully, he was far too absorbed in his work in Philadelphia to lecture me; instead, he expressed gratitude for a friend who looked after his interests so well.

Meanwhile, I eagerly awaited his promised return to be with me for the impending birth of our child. If the birth should go hard, at least I'd be comforted by John's presence. When I closed my eyes, I could still remember him whispering, "*I am yours, yours, yours . . .*"

Then I received brutal evidence to the contrary.

John's latest letter sent me retreating behind a bolted door to the darkest corner of the bedroom where I sobbed secretly into my hands. He said he couldn't return for the birth of our child. Nor could he be with me for the delicate months after. For Washington's victories at Trenton and Princeton weren't enough.

We were losing the war.

John was needed in Congress, where he presided over the Board of War, so he would not, *could not*, keep his promise to come home.

I had done well, so far, without him. But how could I manage our home and our farmhands from childbed? I had little choice but to go to my husband's only surviving brother for help—a brother who testily reminded me that he had hay of his own to bring in.

In the end, it was left to me and my children and our few hired hands. We did our best. Nabby carried water for the men. Johnny drove the hay cart and used a rake to turn the field. Charlie rescued critters who put themselves in the way of the scythes, thereby befriending a singing sparrow that he made his pet.

Even little Tommy tried to help when he saw some hens robbing the pea vines. He went into the garden to shoo them, but someone had carelessly set a scythe, and he ran against it, badly cutting his leg.

We had to send for my good Uncle Tufts to come sew it up.

"Your little ones are too young for dangerous work, Abigail," Uncle Tufts scolded, rolling his sleeves up to help with some farm chores that were much beneath his dignity and training. "As much as your Johnny wishes he was ready to be the man of the house, he cannot yet carry the burden."

I thanked him profusely, shaking my head, not knowing what would become of us were it not for Cotton Tufts. "What my boys need is a preparation for manhood that only a father can provide."

"Their father is still in a better position to help them than some," he said, reminding me that my brother, Bill, serving as captain of the marines on a privateer ship, had been captured by the British. He, too, was a father of little children and now I had to worry he might starve on one of those prison ships.

Not long after, I carried that worry with all the others into my own personal battle upon the midwife's chair, pulling hard on the cloth straps as I strained to bring forth another child.

Tragically, it was a battle lost before it had even begun.

For nine months I had pleased myself with the idea of presenting to my husband a fine babe, born into a free country. But those dreams were now buried in a little grave, transitory as the morning cloud, short-lived as the dewdrops.

Another ill-fated daughter.

She had been a *very* fine babe, with hair as dark as mine. When she was born, it looked as though her eyes were only closed for sleep. But she'd died in my womb in the small hours of the morning when I awakened to convulsions.

I'd known even as I heaved and screamed upon that birthing chair that I would deliver a dead babe. As the drying blood chilled my thighs and no cry came, I realized I would have to bury another child—a daughter without even a name. Tiny lips tinged with blue, tiny fists with rigid fingers that never once opened to reach for me in this world. A daughter with no father at home to press a farewell kiss to her little brow before putting her in the ground.

I was convinced that if I hadn't been so distressed, the babe would have lived. Blame stole into my painful grief as I sobbed over the little body. I blamed the British. I blamed the king. And I tried desperately not to blame my husband.

I *understood* why he hadn't come home. I knew his time was not his own, nor mine.

Nevertheless, John had made a vow to me—not only respecting this pregnancy in particular, but also in marriage itself, to forsake all others. A vow he'd made before God.

Yet, in a choice between ensuring the safety and happiness of his wife and child, or that of the country being birthed, John had chosen the country. And I was only beginning to understand that he always would.

Chapter Fifteen

THE SUMMER HAD made us tremble. The fall of Fort Ticonderoga. The scalping of Jane McCrea. The Battle of Oriskany, where Mohawk, Seneca, Cayuga, Onondaga, and Mississauga warriors helped slaughter patriot forces.

It wasn't until autumn that we had good news. The best possible news. We'd won the Battle at Saratoga, capturing British General Burgoyne and more than six thousand of his men. *His whole army.*

Hopefully this meant the tide was turning. Either way, my husband was now coming home for a visit. Waiting for him, I stood in the yard, pulling my coat tight around me against an unseasonably cold wind with hopeful eyes on the muddy road.

From our earliest days of marriage, John had ridden circuit for the courts, returning home dusty and smelling of horse, with toys for the children. But since the start of the war, the distance between our partings and reunions had grown such that I could no longer bear for partings and reunions to be the whole pattern of our marriage.

We've sacrificed enough to the cause was my guilty, sullen thought. Whatever I had said or consented to before, from this day hence, I wanted John home with me. Here on this farm in all its frosted bleakness. Here in our simple saltbox house that the stinging wind had washed of its color. Here where all that remained of our hopes and dreams resided.

At last, through the cold fog of the morning, I glimpsed my husband's red roan emerge, John astride a cheery saffron saddlecloth. And at the sight of him, no sense of decorum could hold me back.

Lifting my skirt to fly into his arms, I quite outran all semblances of dignified reserve, chased by our geese who followed the trail of grains and garden trimmings I dropped in my wake.

Oh, the flapping, hissing, and honking fuss they made at the return of a master they'd quite forgotten. I behaved little better—nearly dragging my poor husband off his mount into my embrace.

John laughed as we rained down profligate kisses upon each other's cheeks, lips, noses, and brows. What a spectacle we made—the delegate and his lady.

Or, I hoped, *the former delegate* and his lady.

With the familiar scrape of John's unshaven cheek against mine, my fingers tangling in his snow-dusted cloak, my laughter suddenly dissolved into sobs.

"Now Mrs. Adams, what is this?" John asked, wiping my tears with his gloved thumbs. "I expected well-deserved remonstrations. A welcoming embrace if I was lucky. But not tears. Why do you weep?"

"For love. Do you know I dreamed that you'd finally returned home but met me coldly—as if you cared little or nothing about me? To feel your rejection was so distressing that my heart ached half an hour after I waked, even as I tried to reassure myself it was only a dream."

With a shake of his head my husband drew me against his warm chest. "Your dream will never come to pass. You can never be coolly received by me. Not while my heart beats and my senses remain."

I could feel for myself that his heart was still beating under his coat. Steady and strong. I paused a while longer to hear it before I was willing to go inside where I must share him with the family.

I thought Nabby would come bolting from the house, her braid flying behind. That the boys would crash into his knees as they'd done before. But nearly a year's absence is a long time for children—letters are a poor substitute—and I think it broke John's heart to see our little ones regarding him with cautious eyes.

"Such a reserved girl our Miss Nabby has become," John said, greeting our daughter with a hug and a parcel. "But I doubt she'll remain shy when she sees what I've brought."

Nabby tore off the paper and held the book inside close to her heart, though she knew not what it contained. "A book of French?"

"Every day I see the French language will become a necessary accomplishment of American ladies and gentlemen," John said. "Thankfully, your mother can read it and understand it."

More gifts followed. Toys for the boys and a loaf of sugar for me, along with pins and tea. It made our cozy winter evening very agreeable. I held a teacup near my nose, savoring the precious drink almost as much as I savored the feel of my husband's warm fingers in my other hand.

That night, in the quiet of our canopied bed, we grieved together over the loss of the baby we conceived during our last brief reunion. And we came together in love and relief that the war was finally turning our way.

For two weeks we basked in the glow of family harmony and the blessings that remained to us. During the day, John bundled up the boys against the cold and took them to look after livestock, sharpen blades, repair the barn, and chop firewood.

It pleased me to see how John Quincy blossomed under his father's direction. The two would get to talking philosophy as they worked, each insisting that any trees planted in the spring would shelter and provide for the new nation in the future. But when it came to the younger boys—especially our sweet Charlie—their father could be a touch too stern. When our cherub suggested a snowball fight, his father snapped, "How can you boys even *think* of play fighting when young men—now soldiers—are making war in earnest in this country?"

What weighed upon John, of course, was that he'd helped send young men to fight in this war. Those soldiers were suffering, even now, in their winter encampment at Valley Forge. But I hated to see our boys shrink from their father in shame. Boys who were not so unmindful of the suffering of others as their father supposed, for they'd seen soldiers bleeding on our floor.

They ought not be robbed of *all* semblances of childhood. But before I could find the words to say so, Nabby stepped forward to wrap her arms around her brothers. "Instead of a snowball fight, might you take us to build a snowman instead, Papa?"

Building something appealed to her father's nature. But still my husband hesitated. "With all that must be done around this farm? Why, your mother will think me a wastrel for abandoning her near a year only to return for tomfoolery in the snow."

"Oh *balderdash*!" I cried. "After all our struggles we deserve a little frivolity. Come, children. I believe I can even spare a carrot from the root cellar for a snowman's nose."

In the end, it was six carrots.

For as we frolicked in the yard, the children insisted upon making a snow family. A stout snowman father with a lawyer's tie wig. A mother with stone eyes both front and back—for I'd told the boys all mothers have secret eyes behind their heads and that's how I always knew what mischief they were up to. Then we built three boys, with twiggy arms. Johnny's had pinecone buttons. Charlie and Tommy had turkey feathers because they liked to pretend they were Sons of Liberty dressed as Mohawks dumping tea in the harbor. Lastly, we built a snow girl and used berries to give Nabby's likeness her enigmatic smile.

When we finally went back inside, our noses stinging from the cold and our faces sore from smiling, I couldn't remember when last we'd had such a wonderful day.

At dinner, John was in much better spirits. "Abigail, I'm grateful for how well you've maintained the farmstead. And how frugal you've been with our dwindling savings. Fortunately, I mean to refill our coffers with my next case at the bar."

"You're taking a case?" I asked, hoping with all my heart and soul that it was true. "You're not returning to Congress?"

He shook his head. "I have done my part. I am wearied with the life I've been leading, and if I spend any more time away, I shall scarcely know my own children. I think Elbridge Gerry will take my place. In any case, it's someone else's turn to serve."

I smiled, savoring these words, until he added that his wandering ways were not *quite* over. "There's an important shipping case that ought to pay quite well, though it will involve a little ride to the courts in New Hampshire." Feeling me tense beside him, he added, "New Hampshire is not so far. I shall visit your sister Elizabeth and Reverend Shaw and return home before you notice I'm gone."

Brooding, I whispered, "Oh, I shall notice. After the bruising my heart has taken this year, it shall notice every absence the rest of our lives."

John smiled indulgently, pressing a kiss to my hand. "Can you make yourself amenable to it anyway?"

I knew I was being unreasonable. My good man had to earn his living. And it was only a short trip. So, returning a kiss at the corner of his lips, I teased, "I suppose I can resign myself to it for the sake of small matters like keeping food on the table."

"Small matters indeed," John said, pulling me into his arms. "Small matters indeed to hearts bruised by my wandering."

WHILE JOHN WAS away in New Hampshire, an official packet from Congress arrived adorned with elaborate wax seals. I let it sit on the table because we were finished with that business. Someone else would take John's place in Philadelphia. Someone else's poor wife would be left home alone. And someone else's children would wonder when their papa might return.

But in the end, I thought it might be too important to ignore, and so I tore open the seal, revealing the terrible news. Congress had appointed my husband to go to France and negotiate a treaty of alliance.

This hit me with the shock of a thunderclap from a clear blue sky. My heart dropped to the pits of despair. This couldn't have been a surprise to John, and yet, he'd sat at our dinner table pretending that he'd leave off public service for the sake of our family.

The nerve of him.

The moment I heard John's horse approach upon his return from New Hampshire, I hurried to the barn, my bonnet askew and my breath puffing steam on the air. Instead of greeting him with an embrace, I asked, "When did you know?"

Without meeting my eyes, he said, "Word reached me on the road."

He didn't say he had refused the position, which was all I wanted to hear. Instead, all I heard was the jingle of the bridle, buckle, and other horse accoutrement. And every moment of silence that stretched between us only made me more wroth. I'd had my husband back only a few weeks. A few happy weeks. Now he forced me to ask, "Have you accepted?"

John finally looked me in the eye. "No."

My voice took on the most pleading tone of my life. "Then tell me you won't. Tell me you won't allow Congress to rob me of my newfound happiness. Tell them no. Tell them other men are making fortunes for themselves while your children are growing up in something very much like real want."

John sucked in a long breath. "I've already told them I'm ill qualified to be sent to France, but they do not agree . . ."

So they'd appealed to his vanity, which I knew was a strong appeal indeed. As panic rose, I needed for him to see reason. "Don't you know what will happen if you're captured on the high seas? They'll throw you in the Tower and hang you for treason. That is, if you even survive the trip. With good reason do few reputable ship's captains *ever* cross a winter's sea."

John couldn't argue that. Instead, he said, "Abigail, an alliance with France will win the war."

"Isn't that why Dr. Franklin is in Paris? Surely, he's more than capable."

"Dr. Franklin is aged and ill. He needs assistance."

I could see in the squareness of my husband's shoulders and the firm line of his mouth that he'd made up his mind. And though my heart flailed at the very prospect, I screwed up my courage. "Then we'll go to France together. We must hazard it all for our country as a family. If disaster strikes, then it strikes us one and all."

With a look akin to pity, John reached to stroke my cheek with his gloved hand. "Let us go inside, where we can get warm and speak sensibly."

"John, we cannot withstand another year apart." Tears flooded my eyes and I tried to brush them away because they made me feel childish. I willed myself to be calm and forced a cheerfulness I did not feel. "I've always wanted to see more of the world than the twenty miles around this farm. Think of the opportunity for your boys to learn diplomacy at their father's knee. And think of the opportunity for our daughter to learn French and meet well-off suitors."

John frowned. "Our daughter is yet a child. And you've already pointed out the dangers of this venture. What sort of man would I be to risk my wife and children's lives over a winter's sea with British warships lying in wait?"

Mercilessly, I reminded him, "You risked all our lives the moment you accepted a role in politics. This venture is merely an extension of a gamble already undertaken. A gamble I undertook with you. All I wanted then, and all I want now, is to share in it. To be your companion. To meet God or glory together, come what may."

My husband drew me to him, pressing his cold nose into my hair as he tried to soothe me. And I might've let him if he hadn't said, "I'm fortunate to have so courageous a wife, but if we go to France together, who will look after the finances and the farm?"

The finances and the farm . . .

I'd pleaded with him as a wife, lover, and patriot. Yet, he'd replied with cold practicality. And though I was a practical woman, this was too much to bear.

"Who indeed," I muttered frostily.

I pulled away from him, turning to go, and he called after me, "Abigail!"

"I'm going inside," I said over my shoulder. "For I am suddenly feeling quite *cold*."

"Wife!" he snapped, following me. "It's one thing to risk my life, quite another to doom my family to poverty."

I spun back around to face him. "Then don't *go*, John."

No sleep was had that night as I argued with him. He said he couldn't duck his duty to end this war if possible. Yet he forbade me to go with him. He wished to shield me, and he also wished to guard a future for our family because if we went together, everything would fall to ruin.

"You'll have the help of neighbors," he promised. Of our family members. Even of his colleagues and members of Congress. "You'll be able to call upon Mr. Lovell at any time. He's promised to stand in my stead and send you word and wages."

John's reasons were sound, and by the wee hours, I couldn't argue any longer. He was too good of a lawyer. Yet, I felt as if my primary worth as a partner had been laid bare as a manager of his affairs. And, perhaps more crucially, as an enabler of his rise.

BY MORNING, I sat by the window, my shoulders slumped in defeat. I pressed my cheek to the glass lest anyone catch a glimpse of my distress. Perhaps I ought not to have worried, for my face felt too leaden with shock to lift into any sort of expression at all.

I knew now that it had been foolish for either of us to think—for even a moment—that John could retreat and leave the revolution to others. It was a fantasy born of exhaustion and grief. The truth was that our whole fate still depended on the outcome of this war.

If it was lost, the king wasn't going to pardon my husband simply because he'd returned to his law practice in the midst of the fight. So, our discussion, which had gone long into the night, had only managed to persuade John that he must go and take our eldest two sons with him.

He feared his own sons wouldn't know him if he went away. And we both feared that I couldn't provide for four children on my own. If each of us only had two to feed, it would be easier.

Besides, ten-year-old Johnny's mind was exceptionally agile and avaricious for knowledge. He'd surpassed the learning he could find at his mother's knees. Visiting France would give him a depth of experience as well as learning; any career he wished for would benefit greatly. Then there was my little Charlie Cherub, who hadn't even yet turned eight. He was already suffering for the want of manly example. To prosper, he'd need more of his father's attention.

I told myself that for the boys, this might be a grand adventure—the making of great men. If I wanted what was best for them, I had to let them go. And yet, my mother's heart cried out with indignation at risking my sons on a sea that I could not cross myself.

Even my faith could not soothe me. When we read scripture together on Christmas Day, John urged me to surrender all to God's hands. But I couldn't. And neither could five-year-old Tommy, who, when being tucked in for the night, wailed, "Papa, why can't I go, too? Don't you love me as much as my brothers?"

My husband climbed into bed with our little boy and cuddled him close. "If you dry your tears, I'll tell you a secret, Tommy."

Tommy fisted both his eyes, trying not to blubber.

Then John whispered, "You are Papa's favorite. Which is why I'm leaving you to enjoy the company of your mama and your sister, whereas we will be bereft without them."

I couldn't bring myself to go to the docks on the wintry February day of their departure. We said our farewells at the house. My fingertips stroked Johnny's cheek, trying to memorize the shape of his face—round like his father's, with dark brows and eyes like mine.

My precious oldest son hugged me tight round the waist before making a solemn promise. "Mother, I will remember everything you have taught me."

My heart squeezed, knowing that he was still the same brave boy who took me up Penn's Hill to see the fighting. I could no more hold him back now than I could then. "It's a difficult task for a tender parent to part with a child. Nor could I consent if I didn't know your father will care for you well. But I want you to remember, John Quincy Adams, that young as you are, the cruel war into which we've been compelled may stamp upon your mind this certain truth: the welfare of all countries, communities, and individuals depends upon their morals. And you must guard yours."

There would be many snares and temptations in Europe. Some of the worst of which my sons were likely to escape because they were young. Yet there were many that might stain their morals even at this early period of life. Even so, to exclude my sons from temptation would be to exclude them from the world in which they were to live—to fix a padlock upon the mind.

A thing I would never do.

Johnny promised he'd guard his morals, then said, "You have been so kind and tender a mama that I believe I shall never be able to repay you."

"*Repay* me?" I said, laughing a little through tears. "You shall repay me by being a dutiful son and by watching over your younger brother."

With this, I turned to Charles, who was fearful and didn't want to go. If I could only offer him a reprieve! Sniffing back emotions that he feared were unmanly, Charlie asked, "You'll take care of my songbird?"

"I'll take the very best care of your little songster," I promised. What advice I gave him in parting was no doubt pinched and distant, for if I said anything warmer, I'd grasp him to my bosom and refuse to let him go. My husband would have to tear him from my arms!

"All will be well, Abigail," John promised. "And I have something for you."

With that John pressed something cold and delicate into my palm, grasping my fingers, and enclosing them with his own over my heart.

When I opened my hand again, I found within it a gold-rimmed pendant. "Oh, John," I said, staring at the portrayal of an ancient heroine staring out at the sea, shaded by a sturdy tree. "It's beautiful, but the expense!"

"More than you know, for if you look carefully, you'll see the leaves of the tree are made from our hair. Yours and mine."

It was a romantic gesture, the most romantic he'd ever made. For he was not prone to lavish gifts or baubles. But this one had a practical purpose. In the portrait, a shield supported the matron's arm, and emblazoned upon it were the words *I yield—whatever is—is right.*

"You are my Portia," John reminded me, encouraging me to face this separation stoically.

In truth, this locket did put iron in my spine.

My husband—once a simple country lawyer—was now to prove himself upon a world stage in an effort to found a new nation. And despite being left behind, I meant to help him do it. So, I sent my husband and sons off with kisses, watching them go under an arrow of wild geese winging their way south. My own geese made plaintive cries as if they yearned to follow, and I felt their sorrow in my soul, for my wings, too, had been clipped.

Chapter Sixteen

BRAINTREE
Massachusetts
June 1778

O N MY KNEES with brush and bucket, I thought, *I should have heard from them in April*. I was scrubbing the floor because I needed to keep my hands and brain occupied with mundane tasks, lest I go quite mad.

We'd heard reports that Dr. Franklin had been murdered in Paris—which left me to worry that even if my husband and dearest little boys safely reached France, they might be targets for assassination.

The only person who could provide me with good intelligence was Mr. Lovell, who had promised to stand in my husband's stead while he was gone. So, I wrote to him of my alarm and distress.

Thankfully, Mr. Lovell assured me that reports of Dr. Franklin's death were not true. But then he added the strangest postscript. "Call me not a savage when I say that your alarms and distress have afforded me delight. If you expect your griefs to draw only pity from me, you must not send them in such elegant language or I shall be far more apt to admire than feel compassion."

Was that a flirtation? If so, strangely made.

Because I did not know what to think, I made the grave mistake of telling Mrs. Warren about it on a visit to Plymouth.

"The impertinence!" she sputtered, fanning herself with the suspect page. "Oh, my dear. What will you do?"

"About the letter?" I asked, taken aback by her dramatic reaction. "I suppose I shall thank Mr. Lovell for putting my mind at ease about Franklin."

Her lips pinched. "He did more than that. And what about the *other* letter?"

I had, to my profound regret, also told her about a letter in which Mr. Lovell had professed *affectionate esteem* for me. While there was nothing unusual in a married gentleman conveying his esteem to a lady, *affectionate* esteem was altogether something else.

Now Mercy said, "Some husbands might call a man out for professing such a thing."

"Oh, for goodness' sake, let us not make too much of it." After all, my husband considered Lovell to be both a patriot and a friend. Special consideration must be made. Besides, it *was* rather flattering to have an admirer. "Thankfully, my husband is not a man for senseless duels of honor and what Mr. Lovell wrote is harmless."

Mercy did not agree. "What if a letter like this was to fall into British hands and be printed for all the world to see? You think it would cause no scandal?"

Nauseated at the thought, I had to admit she had a point. Now I wanted to throw these letters in the fire, and I said as much. "But what else can I do but ignore these flirtations? I depend on Mr. Lovell."

"Nevertheless, my dear, you must discourage this man in no uncertain terms."

I pinched the bridge of my nose. "You're right. I know you are right. I simply cannot think straight because I am so distressed to be parted from my husband in these trying times."

"You've been parted from him before," Mercy reminded me.

"Never by an *ocean*. He may be gone as long as a *year* with my boys."

"But then he'll be back and all will be well," she said, a little impatiently. "Abigail, you are young and have many years left to spend in peace with your dearest friend after he's finished his work. And think of the advantages that will come from this honorable appointment. Advantages to yourself and your children."

"Advantages?" I wondered if she knew how little my husband was paid. "I cannot imagine any that would recompense me for my worries."

Mercy sighed like a patient schoolmistress. "If I were in your situation, my dear, I'd strive for less worry and more heroism."

I startled with a flash of anger. The truth was that Mercy was not in my situation because she'd complained so bitterly about *her* husband's absences that he resigned his post as major general of the Massachusetts militia. So, it was a bit galling to hear this from her . . .

Nevertheless, I stifled my irritation because I admired her so very much. Mercy was, to me, a heroic figure. She had, after all, published her own play to be scrutinized by the public. Something that took more courage than anything I'd ever done.

Besides, we were now doing brisk trade together in Plymouth, and that wasn't a business relationship I could afford to endanger. So, I decided that if Mercy were precisely in my situation—younger and healthier—she would indeed exert the heroism she called upon me to exert.

Heroism. Heroism. Heroism.

This I repeated to myself when, upon returning home to Braintree, I found both my sisters and Phoebe waiting. All three together, hands clasped fretfully, which could only portend bad news. "What is it?" I asked, frightened that Elizabeth had come all the way from New Hampshire. "What's happened?"

Mary ushered me inside with motherly solicitude. "Come sit and let us make you something to drink."

It was Elizabeth who reluctantly showed me the newspaper clipping that reported: JOHN ADAMS CAPTURED BY THE BRITISH.

It was good that I was sitting, for my knees would've buckled otherwise. And as I tried to catch my breath, my younger sister hastened to say, "But you mustn't believe everything in the newspapers. They make mistakes."

I nodded, though my mind was already racing to the worst possible outcome. My husband captured, starving in a rat-infested prison ship . . . and what of my boys?

"We need to corroborate this story," said Mary, ever sensible. "I've already sent messages to friends, family, and neighbors who might have cause to know the printer and learn where he gets his information."

Phoebe added, "Folks I know say it might be a trick by the British to put the war into more confusion."

I was grateful for their solicitude and support. And I said so.

"It's what family should do," Mary replied. "Since Mama is gone, we need to do more for each other. Hence, Mr. Cranch has heard my pleas to move to Braintree to be near you."

This welcome news was soured only by the knowledge that she wouldn't have pleaded with him on this score unless she believed John *was* captured. That he'd be tried and executed. And that I'd need my sisters nearby to survive as a traitor's widow.

They feared I was to be an object of charity.

It was all so upsetting that I needed to lie down. I let my sisters take charge of the household and the children so I could wail fearful tears into my pillow. I was tired, so tired. But whenever I closed my eyes, my dreams echoed with my husband's footsteps on a ladder to the gallows. John would hope, being stout, that the fall from the trapdoor would break his neck; but my husband had such a *strong* neck that he might strangle to death . . .

Would my boys have to witness it? Even if the king spared my sons that monstrous cruelty, how would I ever get them safely home again? Those were the terrors I endured night after night until at last, one morning I was awakened by the sound of feet pounding up the stairs.

The women in my family burst into the room as one. Nabby jumping onto the foot of my bed. Elizabeth waving a packet of letters. Mary helping Phoebe into the doorway. "Abigail!" Elizabeth enthused. "Letters from France."

From *France*. Not England, but France.

I sat up abruptly, breaking the seal to read of the safe landing of my husband and sons. And I made a sound—almost a shriek—of relief. I read the letters aloud, though the words had little meaning. All that mattered was that my husband hadn't been captured.

The newspaper told it false!

Mary finally took the letters from my exhausted hands and read them to me. "Your dearest friend says that the treaty of alliance he'd been sent to negotiate had already been signed before he even set foot on French soil."

"An alliance?" Elizabeth chirped. "So, the French are going to help us win the war!"

It was marvelous news. French warships would be our salvation, but my husband and sons had never needed to expose themselves to danger to secure that salvation. Which made the news bittersweet.

My daughter worked it out for herself. "It means Papa didn't even have to go to France. Now that he's not needed, will he take the next ship home?"

"I don't know," I said. Though on second thought, I doubted it. Having undertaken the expense of sending John Adams to Europe, Congress was likely going to find a way of getting their money's worth.

For the time being, I must continue embodying the heroine of the pendant I wore round my neck. Which was easier to do now that I knew my husband and sons were safe. Or at least as safe as anyone could be in this world.

DABBING SWEAT FROM my forehead with a kerchief as I melted from the early summer heat, I told my newest farmhand, "Sir, I cannot pay what you're asking."

He jutted his chin. "I've been offered more by others."

I wasn't too proud to plead with him, but I could scarcely afford to pay what I'd already promised. "With the high tax levy from Congress—"

"In which your husband served," he interrupted with a snort. "And to think we rebelled against the *king* for high taxes."

I laughed at what I took for a jest. "Taxes were only part of the reason."

"Be that as it may, your husband was one of those who saw fit to start the war, so you cannot complain of the taxes to fund it now. It's only fair Mr. Adams pay his share."

Mr. Adams is paying more than his fair share, I thought.

"The *king* started the war by sending an army to strip us of our liberties. Not Mr. Adams," I said, arguing with the man even though I knew I shouldn't.

"Aye, we wanted our liberty," the farmhand said. "Now you certainly have *yours*, Mrs. Adams."

That struck me as a bold and insolent thing to say; unfortunately, I must suffer this insolence because without farmhands, I couldn't sow or harvest or bring any crop to market. I'd have to somehow charm and cajole this man into staying. I simply needed to put on a cheerful smile, govern my tongue, and convince him to accept the wage I offered.

It's what I needed to do.

But out of my mouth flew the words "And *you* shall have *your* liberty, sir. I cannot begrudge you taking a higher wage elsewhere. Not during trying times such as these. I release you from any obligation."

The man startled, so offended that he spat. "You won't find anybody else willing to take orders from a woman at a lower price. Any man with pride would rather work his own land if he could get a parcel."

"I'm sure you're right," I said, now convinced of my decision to send him packing even if all I'd have to eat in the coming year was pride. But I was not going to be insulted on our own family land. A man wouldn't stand for it, so why should I? "Indeed, I may have to let every single worker on this farm go. You're merely the first. I wish you good luck, sir, and a fine day."

With that, I turned back for the house, raining curses down upon myself with every step. What would I do now? How was my family to live?

As was my habit when vexed, I strode directly to the larder to count my bottles of cider and jars of pickled eggs and vegetables. I still had sacks of cornmeal and wheels of cheese in the milk house, so these could be stretched for some time. And the small investments of my pin money were proving fruitful.

That might sustain us. But wouldn't pay the tax bill.

Ruefully, I remembered the words of the farmhand. *Any man with pride would rather work his own land if he could get a parcel.*

The farm was our most important asset, but I couldn't sell John's land. For one thing, even if I could arrange the legal niceties, it was a moral precept of the Adamses that they never sold land.

Still, I thought, with sudden inspiration, *there are plenty of men without land*. And they could rent ours. Farmhands might not wish to follow my orders, but tenants worked for themselves. The idea spun in the web of my mind until I was entirely caught up in it. And now I knew what to do.

Since moving to Braintree, Mary and her daughter Betsy often made the trip by horse and buggy to visit me and share family gossip. Now she said, "Uncle Tufts says you've let go of all your hired help. But I wouldn't have believed it until now to see you boiling your own brew."

Stirring a pot of peppermint, chamomile, and rose hips, I said, "I hope it is drinkable. But I haven't let go *all* my help. I still have two domestics. One is at market, and the other is out back with laundry."

Mary looked out the window. "And who are those men working your fields?"

"Tenant farmers. Uncle Tufts helped me find two brothers just starting out. They're going to pay me half of anything they make."

Mary, who took on boarders to make ends meet, looked suitably impressed. "Without having to manage a farm, I suppose it leaves your mind free for other pursuits?"

I decided to confide my latest scheme, even if she might think me a fool. "I'm going into trade with European goods. Linen. Glassware. Spice, sugar, and paper. If John could send these goods to me from France—"

"You'll be a shopkeeper?" Mary interrupted, eyes wide, for this would be considered quite unseemly.

"Not precisely," I replied. "I shall use some goods for barter, as goods are likely to hold value better than paper currency. But Uncle Tufts will see that the rest is sold to shopkeepers. That is, if the goods I order can make it past a British blockade."

Mary winced. "What if they do not? Oh, Abigail, you risk losing your whole investment sunk to the bottom of the sea!"

I swallowed, knowing it wasn't the kind of gamble either of my sisters would've been able to stomach. But I believed it had to be tried. Trying to project an air of confidence, I said, "Well, Uncle Tufts likes the idea. And now with France on our side of the war, we're sure to break the British blockade."

"What does Mr. Adams say?"

"Precious little from France," I replied, taking the pot off the fire. "Mostly he writes to reassure me of the welfare of the boys."

"How did my nephews enjoy their adventures at sea? They will have tales to tell . . ."

"Oh yes. They nearly wrecked in a storm—the mast was split. Then there was a skirmish with a British ship, one so serious that my husband grabbed a musket and took up his place with the marines. All to say nothing of a cannon exploding and killing an officer on board."

My staid sister blinked in obvious horror. "Oh, how glad you must be to have remained on land."

"To the contrary! When I think of my helpless little boys tossed on the ocean with cannons exploding around them, I wish a thousand times I'd gone with them."

"Well, as your older sister, I do not wish it."

"In any case, they are safe now," I said, pouring the oddly colored brew into a teapot. With that, I called, "Nabby! Fetch cups and cornbread."

When my daughter did not reply, I looked up to realize she was nowhere to be found. "Now where have those girls gone?"

Mary laughed, again peeking out the window past my lace curtain. "Who can guess? Our daughters are thick as thieves these days."

We both took pleasure in the closeness of these two cousins; I'd always wanted it, even before I knew Nabby would never have a sister of her own. And now Mary leaned forward to confide, "I have it on some authority that our daughters have staked out a tree on a hill between our homes where they climb into the foliage to share their secrets."

"*Secrets*?" I asked, somewhat shocked by the notion that my daughter might be old enough to *have* secrets, much less keep them from me.

Mary gave a knowing smile. "She's almost thirteen, Abigail. Surely you remember how we were at that age."

I did remember. Mary had been motherly and obedient. Elizabeth had been bright and precocious. And I had been tart and defiant. "Thankfully, Nabby takes more after you than me."

Placing cups on the table, Mary smiled and said, "You know, our girls are about to start upon the serious business of courting . . ."

"Nabby is too young."

"You were only fifteen when you met Mr. Adams," Mary reminded me. "Our girls should begin training in the necessary arts of attracting a *worthy* beau."

I'd been teaching my daughter needlework and how to write elegant correspondence. What's more, Nabby was already an excellent housekeeper. But I knew my daughter would need to be more accomplished to attract the right kind of suitor.

Mrs. Warren had provided her lessons in the refined arts of poetry and literature, but she'd also need to know how to sing or to play a musical instrument. Her social graces ought to be enhanced with lessons in elocution. She ought to dress fashionably with a bit of the fripperies that other girls her age prized.

Thinking on it, I said, "I suppose as a birthday gift, I shall have to scrape together a few coins and send her to Boston for dance lessons."

Mary nodded approvingly. "A wise investment. Betsy wants to learn to play the piano, but we can't afford it. Especially now that our brother has vanished and it shall fall to us to help support his family."

I sighed in commiseration.

Released from captivity, our brother had returned only long enough to drink and gamble away what savings he had, abandoning his family altogether. Last week, one of his creditors had come banging on my door looking for him, and I'd had to fend the man off with my broom. "Do you think Bill is gone for good?"

"I do. Our father has sent letters to reason with him, offering forgiveness to a prodigal son, yet there comes no reply."

It was an altogether too common happenstance for a husband to abandon wife and children, but never did I think to see it in my own family. "The imprisonment must have done something terrible to our brother's mind."

"Oh, he was always the proverbial black sheep. You remember the furor when he forfeited his opportunity to go to Harvard."

"I remember it well, for I wished aloud that I could go in his place, and he mocked me."

Mary smiled wryly at that old family story. "You'd have done better at Harvard than he would have. You know our brother and his weaknesses."

I did. But must we now pick up the pieces of the life he'd shattered? I tried in vain to summon the hard-heartedness I had found within my breast when dismissing my workmen. But all I felt now was a melting sympathy for my brother's children, who were left abandoned through no fault of their own.

If there were still jars of vegetables and bottles of cider in my larder, I could never turn them away. I would support them. I would, if necessary, take them in. And without word from John, I made this decision like I made all the others recently: *on my own*.

Chapter Seventeen

BOSTON
Massachusetts
Autumn 1778

I N THE AFTERMATH of a dreadful storm, the battered French
fleet lay in the harbor with torn sails flapping helplessly in
the wind, broken yards yawning upon scarred decks, and
snapped ropes dangling from the rails. Nevertheless, the sight of
the gilded fleur-de-lis flying over fancifully carved prows inspirited
every patriot in our poor beleaguered Boston.

We weren't alone anymore in this war.

We hoped our new allies would make the difference.

The French Admiral d'Estaing had put into our harbor for repairs, then sent sailors in blue coat, white lace, and red breeches
to my door to apologize that he could not call upon the wife of
Monsieur le Commissaire Adams personally.

His officers had, instead, handed over a formal dinner invitation,
written upon paper so rich and creamy I was tempted to press it
to my cheek. Now my daughter and I were to dine with the French
aboard the *Languedoc*, said to be the finest warship in the world.

The admiral's dinner party promised to be the only highlight
in Boston's social season, but for some reason, Nabby balked at
the occasion. She didn't like the feathers in her hair or the brooch
I gave her to wear upon a ribbon at her throat. And unwilling to
admire herself in the mirror, she said, "I dread it, Mama. I cannot
speak French well enough to converse."

I could myself read and write French well enough but my
tongue was another matter. With a hopeful breath, I said, "I'm
sure some will speak English."

"I'll be the youngest person there!"

"I'm certain other young people will be aboard for the music and dancing," I said, lightly dusting her cheeks with powder. "You'll have a chance to practice your new accomplishments."

And to meet eligible young bachelors, I thought.

I certainly didn't wish for my daughter to attract the attention of a Frenchman, but prominent Bostonian gentlemen would also be there. Still, Nabby protested, "I won't have anything to say!"

"Then just *smile,*" I advised. "You're a young lady now, and as the daughter of John Adams, you'll be expected to charm our allies."

Nabby didn't argue further; she was merely sullen. Unfortunately, I was sullen, too. My gown wasn't even fit for a Quaker, for I hadn't had a new dress in years, and had not received the silk I asked John to buy me in France.

In fact, three shipments of goods had been lost. *Three!* I wanted to wail at my bad luck, fearing when my husband learned of our misfortune, he'd refuse to invest more, saying we had no use for textiles, handkerchiefs, and gloves that were sunk in the sea. No doubt, he'd tell me to count it an expensive lesson and cease wasting money on baubles.

Then again, John rarely told me anything at all. What few letters I received from France were clipped. Brief. Parsimonious. And cold.

It was as if he had changed hearts with some frozen Laplander.

By way of excuse, he'd scribbled, "It's not safe to write anything that one is not willing should go into all the newspapers of the world. Notwithstanding this, I've written you nearly fifty letters but they've all been sunk or taken."

Fie on the newspapers of the world. A loving wife could not survive on guarded missives alone. These were my gloomy ruminations as the admiral's barge ferried us across a murky autumn's sea to the large warship, its French flag snapping in the wind.

As it happened, I could not remain sullen or gloomy under that festooned mast. Especially not when greeted so politely by both Admiral d'Estaing and his French officers. Another Frenchman was present, too—this one wearing an American uniform of buff and blue. In greeting, he bowed with a flourish. "I am Gilbert du Motier, the Marquis de Lafayette."

I knew his name, of course. The French hero had come long before his naval compatriots and had been wounded at the Battle of Brandywine. He was not *quite* so good-looking as I'd been led to believe by the breathless accounts of ladies who admired him throughout the colonies. But he had an aristocratic visage, and the overall effect of his person was extremely agreeable. "I'm happy to meet you, sir."

"I am happier," he said, in heavily accented English. "Because I am highly sensible of the honor that I have to present the wife of John Adams with a tribute of my gratitude and respect. For I know this man by reputation to be a *colossus* of liberty."

I flushed with pride. "Well, you also have a reputation here, sir, as you are quite young for the rank of major general."

Lafayette grinned. "This campaign is a good school for a young soldier like me. God grant that the public does not pay for my lessons."

At that point our conversation was cut short by the boom of celebratory guns, a dinner fit for a princess, and glasses raised in toast after toast.

The French toasted America. We toasted the King of France. They toasted Congress. We toasted the French fleet. They toasted General Washington. We toasted the French-American alliance. They toasted Dr. Franklin and my husband; we toasted Admiral d'Estaing and the Marquis de Lafayette. They toasted Commerce, Art, and Architecture. We toasted Liberty and Friendship.

This went on until we had toasted seemingly everyone and everything of importance in the world.

Later, warmed by the liquor of so many toasts, Lafayette said, "I feel as if your husband and I have traded places, Mrs. Adams. Here *I* am in America, having left behind a daughter and a worthy wife devoted to enlightened ideals. And there *he* is, in France, having left behind a daughter and a patriotic wife who I am told is no less devoted to the cause of worldwide humanity."

It was too generous a compliment, for I had committed myself only to the freedom of my own country. I'd given little thought to the idea that our revolution might elevate mankind. "Do you really think the ideals we are fighting for will change the lot of the average person?"

"I wouldn't have come to America if I believed otherwise. Given my title and holdings, I am more free than anyone to bestow my services where I please. And in offering my services to this intriguing republic, I bring only my frankness and goodwill; no ambition, no self-interest; I work only for the glory of human happiness."

I actually believed him. He was, after all, only twenty-one. An age when men allowed themselves to be shaped by ideals, before life's cruelties hardened them. Fortunately, my own husband—so tough and crusty on the outside—still harbored a softness in his breast for high-minded purpose. It was the true source of my love for John, so I hoped for the sake of Lafayette's wife that he did not lose this idealism. "I assure you, Marquis, you secured your own personal glory, too, by shedding blood in our cause."

He shrugged, color coming to his cheeks. "It was a trifling wound. The sort one should wish for if wanting to take a bullet only for curiosity."

With that, he extended his long, stockinged leg, so we could see that he had quite recovered. Which made me laugh. For of all the things I might have expected from a French nobleman, humility wasn't one of them. "Hearing that you've now been cured of such morbid curiosity about bullet wounds must be a comfort to your wife."

Now Lafayette cringed. "The post is so unreliable over the sea that my lady wife believed me dead until a letter from my own hands reached her. You can imagine the mischiefs made by rumor in this war."

"I don't have to imagine. I have lived it. And if your wife loves and esteems you as much as I do Mr. Adams, she must miss you very much."

Lafayette gazed into his glass without taking a sip. "I did not have the opportunity for a proper farewell to my wife and child before I sailed. And I know my beloved Adrienne has suffered cruelly for my absence."

I did not doubt it. I'd heard that the Frenchman's wife was pregnant when they parted company, and that their daughter had since died. I didn't know if it was their first or second child; I only knew that I, too, had suffered the loss of a daughter in my husband's absence during this war. So I felt deep sympathy for his beloved Adrienne.

Lafayette sighed. "If providence sees fit to allow me to return, I shall beg her pardon. Given your own husband's long absence, I think you are one of the only women in the world who can tell me whether she will forgive me."

"She will," I replied, unexpectedly moved by his vulnerability. "*Of course* she will forgive you. For she must know that you are about an extraordinary task."

Lafayette smiled. "As is your husband."

He made me feel better. He soothed the heart that had been bruised by my husband's cold letters. He made me feel optimistic, patriotic, and brave. Truly, the young Frenchman had a gift for it. For though he only sipped at champagne, Lafayette effervesced in conversation, arguing for human equality. And he repeatedly pulled the ladies into respectful discussion of matters in which we were normally seen as trespassers.

He asked our opinions. He even tried to engage my terribly shy daughter. "What must you have thought, Miss Adams, the day independence was declared? How proud and pleased you must have been."

Uncomfortable to be the subject of attention, Nabby stared down at her lap. "I—I was too young to know what to think about it, sir."

Lafayette smiled, indulgently. "And now?"

It should've been an easy question to answer. All Nabby had to say was that she was proud of her father. I nudged her because my daughter seemed tongue-tied. But when she finally spoke, I wish her tongue had stayed tied.

"I don't think much about politics," she said, fingering her napkin nervously. "Perhaps it's better that way, so I can have friends upon either side of the war with whom to take tea."

She tittered, as if she thought this a very fine, feminine answer. Doubtless, in many circles, it was. Yet around *this* table, shoulders slumped, fingers fidgeted, gazes fixed upon the distant horizon, and French officers about to do battle for our liberty deflated, all undone by the notion that even John Adams's daughter thought they risked their lives for a disagreement that didn't merit disrupting her seating arrangements at a tea party.

Later, in the carriage, Nabby cried, "I told you I wouldn't know what to say!"

"I'm sure it is all forgotten," I said, hoping the Lord would forgive my little fib. "The Marquis de Lafayette smoothed matters, and with luck, by morning it will be lost in a drunken haze."

Nabby tore the ornamental feathers from her hair. "I *never* know what to say in company. Much less in the presence of important people."

Why should she? She spent her days sequestered with me on a farm. There were no provisions made for women, much less girls, to study the art of international diplomacy—not even in this era, when it was so plainly necessary.

"I don't always know what to say either," I admitted. "But we'll both have to learn. We have little choice but to become lady diplomats. We haven't the luxury of being indifferent to politics. No one in our country does."

"But they say ladies must not trespass in politics."

I raised a brow. "Those who say it are the very same who conspire to deprive us of the education we need to inform us on such matters. So, we must educate ourselves."

Which is why I decided to send Nabby to Mrs. Warren over Christmastide, for more politics took place in Mercy's salon than in the legislature. It would leave me even lonelier in the bleakness of that winter, and I'd dearly miss Nabby's company, but it was far more important that my sons *and my daughter* learn to be good, productive, and informed citizens in the free country we were struggling to bring about.

Chapter Eighteen

BRAINTREE
Massachusetts
January 1779

WHEN I HEARD a new merchant vessel from France had slipped past the British ships and now lay at anchor in our harbor, I hastened to Boston to receive long-awaited mail from my husband. Eagerly, I bundled against the cold in a new red scarf that my sister Mary had knitted for me.

I did not mind the nip in the air. It was a bright winter's day, the sunlight shone on the snow like a scatter of diamonds, and I intended to make the most of my trip.

I'd taken a few bottles of cider to give as gifts while making visits. My supplies of everything else had dwindled, but that would soon be remedied. For whatever goods John had sent me, I'd either keep for myself or easily find buyers.

Everyone was much in need.

I knew Congress wanted John to stay in France and convince the French to send more ships, money, and guns. Still, I hoped John's letters would say he was coming home. My husband and sons had been living a whole new life in Paris these past months, one that I had no part of. And the distance, both physical and emotional, was growing painful.

Clasping the pendant I still wore every day around my neck, I resolved yet again for *heroism*. Heroism and hope. Thus, I jostled with the others at port for deliveries until a sailor said, "Nothing for you, Mrs. Adams."

"I'm sure there's been some mistake," I said. "This ship came with cargo from Paris, no? Surely it carries packets from our representatives there."

The hapless sailor nervously glanced at his superior, a whiskered older man who held the manifest. "I am sorry for it, Mrs. Adams, but we aren't carrying anything for you."

My chest tightened even as denial sprang to my lips. "Perhaps it was arranged under a pseudonym. Or, instead of letters, some packages? Linens. Gloves. Handkerchiefs."

The weathered old sailor must have recognized my crushing disappointment, because he suggested, "Mayhaps Mr. Adams sent his packets by way of Philadelphia. Safer that way."

It wasn't inconceivable that John might've sent packages to that city. But the delay put yet another obstacle in my way of paying the tax bills and feeding Nabby and Tommy. They deserved more than potato peel pie and whatever other scraps I found in the larder.

I *relied* upon John to send goods for our survival. All this to say nothing of the fact that I relied upon him for news of himself and my sons!

How long did he think a mother's heart could stand not knowing about the health, happiness, or schooling of her beloved boys?

Nearly a year they'd been gone with nary a word.

Now I fought off the urge to sink to my knees, for seldom in my life had I ever felt as low-spirited. Not wishing to make a spectacle of myself, I took a few steadying breaths of nippy air. "I'm sure you're right. Mr. Adams must've sent his packets by way of Philadelphia. I'll write Mr. Lovell and I'm sure it will all be straightened out swiftly."

That night I took up my pen and wrote to the only person in Philadelphia who could tell me with some authority whether I had cause to despair. Mr. Lovell's reply came swiftly, but it was not what I wished.

You may be assured, dear lady, that not a line for you has arrived, or anything material under your husband's hand. Personally, I have not had a single line of answer, though I have written sixteen times or more to him.

Should I be comforted or horrified by this report of my husband's silence? I could think of no reason that did not trouble me.

Another thing that troubled me was the way in which Mr. Lovell continued to dance over the line of impropriety. For this latest letter also contained an impertinence far beyond anything attempted before.

In the first place, he'd addressed me as *Lovely Portia*. Then he went on to say he was relieved that my husband's "rigid patriotism" hadn't left me pregnant before he left.

The cheek of this! It was nearly obscene. I flushed hotly at the thought any man but my husband might tease me about the sex act. It mortified me to imagine how Mrs. Lovell might feel if she were to see this letter.

And it somehow made me feel as if *I* ought to be ashamed. What was my recourse? I'd tried to discourage him the way Mercy had advised, telling him his flirtations were dangerous and unwelcome. But there was little else I could do. My husband had left me to this man's mercy, so I dared not offend him.

WHEN I VISITED Plymouth to fetch my daughter home, Mercy was gossipy as a Boston fishwife. "Well, *this* is a scandal."

Fearing she'd somehow got wind of Mr. Lovell's increasingly improper letters, I trod carefully. "What scandal do you mean?"

From her sickbed, she leaned close to confide. "They say Dr. Franklin leads a debauched life at Versailles. Our patriotic sage may be a widower, but to embrace the French custom that every man of importance must have a mistress? Outrageous."

I blinked at her. "That cannot be the custom."

"My dear, it is so much the custom that even the king—*the king*—endures mockery for his fidelity to his wife."

I was shocked into silence, and she mistook its cause.

"Oh, my dear, you have nothing to fear when it comes to the fidelity of your good man."

Instantly, I bristled. "Madam, I never doubted his fidelity."

That was the plain truth of it. I'd felt increasingly abandoned, taken for granted, and even condescended to. But the idea that John might disgrace our marriage bed . . . never.

Mercy reached to pat my hand. "Good. I think your Mr. Adams to be the most honest man I've ever met. If by living among European courtiers his integrity should be undermined, I shall never trust another man again."

Stoutheartedly, I said, "I am quite sure that you will never have cause to mistrust men on my husband's account, and neither will I."

"Of course," Mercy said, smiling conciliatorily. "But Mr. Adams would have to forgive you if ever you doubted him. You've been snowed in all winter, without a line from him, alone with your thoughts, and without even the comfort of your good little girl, our dear Nabby, whom I really love, and love more the longer she resides with me."

Happy for a change of subject, I said, "A sacrifice I was glad to make for her education."

"Nabby is such an amiable girl. Obedient and polite with an assemblage of other virtues that do you great honor. She's certainly blessed with the intelligence one might expect of such parentage—an intelligence that would render her opinions on political matters interesting should she care to form any."

I couldn't hide a scowl of disappointment to learn that, apparently, no intellectual passion in my daughter's breast had been stirred by the unique opportunity to spend an entire winter here. Surely if *I* had been offered such an opportunity when I was Nabby's age, I'd have devoured every book in the household and peppered the talented playwright with so many questions she'd have been eager to send me away . . .

My disappointment must've been evident, for Mercy reassured me, "It won't dim her future prospects a jot. It's her lack of interest in a different direction that might cause her difficulty, though."

"A different direction?"

Mercy gave a helpless laugh. "Most girls her age fall in love with a different fellow every week. Nabby, however, is quite indifferent to romantic prospects."

"Well, she is not grown into a woman yet . . ."

"She is woman enough to have attracted the attention of some young men," Mercy replied. "Yet, she confessed to me that she's never been pierced by the arrow of love and finds boys to be tiresome."

I sputtered an unexpected laugh at that.

Mercy chuckled, too. "In any case, it's only right that the daughter of John Adams set a high standard for herself. But she takes after her father in plumpness, so she cannot afford to haughtily shun every boy who offers a tender heart."

I sucked in a little offended breath, wanting to defend my daughter's beauty against this unnecessarily brutal appraisal. It felt *so* unnecessary, in fact, that I began to wonder if any of the boys for whom my daughter confessed indifference were, in fact, Mercy's own sons.

To soothe hurt feelings if any existed, I said, "Oh, I doubt my daughter harbors a haughty indifference toward anyone, much less a boy offering a tender heart. She's more likely sad and homesick."

Of course, this put Mercy on the back foot. "If our Nabby has been unhappy, she conceals it from me; she says living in Plymouth is just as pleasant as Boston or Braintree."

Apparently, living arrangements were yet another matter about which my daughter was *indifferent* . . .

Mercy smiled, sipping at the teacup a servant brought on a tray to her bedside. "Don't be vexed. You're blessed to have a daughter whose only fault is that she's aloof!"

Aloof. Haughty. Indifferent. Were these really faults that could exist in a girl with good disposition? No matter what she claimed, Mercy wouldn't have reported them if she didn't believe I *should* be vexed. And I *was* vexed. So vexed that I wished to quarrel. "I believe you've misjudged her."

Whatever else I was going to say died on my lips at the sight of Nabby in the doorway, just returned from a sledding expedition with Mercy's rowdy sons.

"Mama!" she cried, throwing her arms around my neck in a way that was decidedly not aloof, haughty, or indifferent.

"Oh, I've missed you," I said, looking down upon her beloved round face, which did not seem too plump to me in the slightest.

In that face I saw not only my daughter, but also the husband I pined for. Not to mention the shining hope I still clung to of a better world that might yet be built for her and all my country's children.

Heroism, heroism, heroism, I exhorted myself on the carriage ride home to a near-empty larder. For surely, one day soon, John would return triumphant and relieve me of my cares.

But still a dark question now bedeviled my brain.

What if he doesn't?

Chapter Nineteen

BRAINTREE
Massachusetts
Spring 1779

FEARFUL OF MORE disappointments, I didn't allow myself to believe it when I was told that a long-awaited packet of letters from John had finally arrived with parcels and gifts. Only when the trunks were stacked in my entryway and the letters placed in my trembling hands did I feel my heart soar at the sight of my husband's familiar handwriting.

Nabby and I opened the packages first. Inside, we found a jar of marbles for six-year-old Tommy, who gleefully poured them onto the floor. We also found tea, precious tea! Giddy with excitement, we started unboxing things faster, unpacking gloves, pins, house brushes, china bowls, ribbons, and fabric, too.

But when Nabby unrolled a furl of muddy orange silk over her knees, she winced. "What a *ghastly* shade."

"Oh dear," I said, reaching to finger the cloth. "The quality is good, but this color is not at all to my mind."

We'd asked for gray or lavender—suitable for serious occasions. Now I wondered what use I could make of *orange*.

"I'd look sickly wearing this," Nabby said, holding it up against her rosy-cheeked complexion, which favored bright blues and pinks. "People would run from me fearing I had some plague. To send this for my dresses, my dear father must approve of my notion to be a spinster all my days . . ."

I laughed that she was contemplating spinsterhood rather than indulge in romantic play. "Why would you wish to be a spinster?"

"Because boys are so *tiresome*," she replied.

Tiresome had become her favorite word as of late and I tried not to encourage her by taking notice of it. "Perhaps your cousin Betsy will want this fabric," I said, rolling the fabric up again. "If not, we'll try to sell it, though it will not fetch much."

Nabby laughed. "*What* could Papa have been thinking?"

"Given his important work in France, we must be grateful he thought to send fabric at all—as I suppose ladies' fripperies are quite beneath his notice."

Besides, the silk really *was* of very nice quality, and amongst the other articles he sent, we soon found linens and handkerchiefs—both of which always made me a tidy profit.

I chastised myself for all the months I feared he'd forgotten us. He'd now sent more than enough to keep us afloat and a few treats besides. That was to say nothing of the letters, which I lovingly cradled to my bosom until Nabby asked, "Aren't you going to open them?"

"Not until the kettle is ready." I intended to indulge myself. I took a tea tray upstairs, my heart as light as a feather and my spirits dancing. In anticipation of many pleasures so long denied me, I rocked my head slightly to one side, then the other, to loosen the aches in shoulder and neck. When I stirred the tea, I enjoyed the tinkle of the little metal spoon against the porcelain cup before setting it down ever so gently in the saucer. I finally brought the cup up warm between my hands, watching the steam rise from the amber whirlwind. How *wonderful* it smelled. And the taste!

Though I had no sugar to sweeten it, the leaves imparted a sweetness of their own, floral notes melting to something earthier on the back of my tongue, and I moaned with the pleasure of it.

The tea was *excellent*. The best I ever had, and according to John's manifest, not even high priced, which made it all the sweeter.

I knew there was much to do around the farm before sundown, yet I found myself removing my shoes and taking down my hair. I even scented my wrists with a little lemon verbena on a whim before sprawling abed like a wanton with my letters . . .

John said he feared to write love letters lest they fall into enemy hands. So, I told myself to be content if all I received was a packet of terse little notes that told me next to nothing. As long as they reassured me of the good health and happiness of my boys,

I promised myself to read between every line the unspoken sentiments of my husband's heart. I would simply trace each letter, each word, until I could feel his hand as mine.

With trembling, joyful fingers, I broke the wax seal and unfolded the pages, pressing my nose close, imagining I could scent some lingering essence of my dearest friend.

The first letter—from November—was all business except to reassure me that our boys were "very well" and that "Europe is the dullest place in the world."

I smiled at the charm of this dubious sentiment, but that smile faded upon reading the next letter, in which he wrote, "This moment I had, what shall I say? The pleasure or the pain of your most recent missive from late October. The complaints in it gave me more pain than I can express."

I stopped short, trying to recall what complaints I made six months ago. Surely only that he didn't write often enough or with the warmth I was accustomed to. But I could remember nothing that justified what he wrote next. "This is the third letter I've received from you filled with complaints. I wrote several answers but could not send. One was angry, another full of grief, and the third too melancholy, so I burnt them all."

Then came something from my husband I could never have conceived: a threat.

"If you write to me in this style I shall stop writing back entirely. Can professions of esteem be wanting from me? Can protestation of affection be necessary? Can tokens of remembrance be desired? The very idea of this sickens me."

Heavy distress spread through my limbs, making my arms weak as he continued to rage at me. "How shall I convince you that my heart is warm? Shall I declare it? Shall I swear to it? Is it possible you should doubt it? I know it is not possible for if I could believe you truly doubted me, I cannot answer for the consequences. And you will be very sorry for them."

I lay there upon our empty marriage bed, stunned, letting my tea go cold, my mind reeling to remember what could possibly have occasioned such a rant.

This letter, with its anger so blunt . . .

I should've stopped reading. I had, after all, meant to savor this packet of letters. Unfortunately, now I needed to know that this fit of temper was only that. My good man always regretted his outbursts. Perhaps I'd learn in the next letter that he apologized for his harshness. Perhaps he'd write to me gently, remembering that I was his partner in this life, left quite vulnerable and alone.

But the next letter was all Paris and politics. "Last night I saw the illumination for the birth of the Princess. Splendid indeed. The military school, the hospital of invalids and the Palace of Bourbon were sublime."

I smoothed out this letter on the quilt next to the one in which he assured me that Europe was the dullest place in the world. Then I stared, counting back.

So it had been Christmastide when he strolled the Parisian streets enjoying these sublime sights. And if he thought of me, it was apparently with anger for having dared to ask for reassurance of his love.

The idea of it had *sickened* him.

Just as I now felt sickened to remember what *I* was doing during that same Christmastide. I'd been cold, hungry, and lonely, pouring my heart out to him in letters—my tears flowing faster than the ink—and suffering a dreary winter without my daughter, without flour to make bread, shivering in threadbare clothes without hope of paying our bills . . .

Now teary, I beseeched myself to lay these letters aside. All for naught. I couldn't stop flipping page after page, the rest of John's cruel letters passing before my eyes in a blur.

A New Year's wish urging me to find a way to embrace poverty.

A Valentine mocking me as "Her Ladyship" for having had the temerity to ask him for news, which he somehow believed I wanted for gossip to impress my friends. This followed by an assertion that he was surrounded by spies and an accusation that perhaps someone was whispering malicious rumors about his doings into my ear.

Nearly every letter was suffused by his disgust that I should wish to know any detail, political or personal, about his daily life. Every letter impressing upon me his importance, and my unimportance.

Finally he wrote, "Leave me alone. You know that I shall not injure you and you ought to believe that I have good reasons for what I do."

Oh, but he had injured me. Never before had I felt so unjustly treated. Certainly, he'd given me cause for frustration and disappointment. But that was to be expected in any marriage, and I'm sure I'd given him cause for the same. But *this* . . . this was different.

If he had slapped me, it would not have felt more like abuse. All at once, the pendant I'd worn felt as if it were strangling me, and I tore it from my neck. Still, the breathless sensation spread until I felt a tightening in my chest and my breath began to stutter.

I couldn't get enough air. I stumbled from the bed to the window, dragging in ragged gasps. Was this what John experienced during the Boston Massacre trial? Then, I'd been at his side, coaxing him to breathe, soothing him until the pain subsided. But I endured this frightening pain alone until I sank down to the floor for fear I might lose consciousness.

I lay there, gripping the edge of the dusty, old Turkey carpet until my heart stopped thudding in my chest and swallowing became easier. The sharp stabs of panic transformed into a dull but deeper heartbreak.

I did not leave my room that day. I couldn't eat a bite. Nor did I take more than a nibble in the days that followed. When I finally roused myself, I floated through the farm like a fog—quiet, insubstantial, and scarcely there.

Perhaps this was the terrible consequence that John warned of if I should doubt his love.

Because doubt his love, I now did.

From whom could I seek comfort?

It would be too dangerous to confess to any friend or neighbor. Too cruel to confide in my children. Too shameful to tell my sister Elizabeth, whose marriage to Reverend Shaw I had judged so harshly. Nearly as shameful to tell my sister Mary, who must have always suspected my smug belief that my husband was a better match than hers. And it would be too humiliating to tell my father, who had never approved of John in the first place.

Pride goeth before the fall. Yes, I'd been proud of my marriage, and now worried for the depths to which it could yet fall.

Bottling up this fear made for sleepless nights. My mind had suffered a distress that could not be described and a wound much deeper than it seemed. But apparently my daughter noticed my distress and whispered to our relations, for I eventually received a visit from Phoebe, carrying jars of medicinal broths.

Looking me up and down, she said, "Word is that you're ailing, Honey. Dr. Tufts wants you to take these."

"I'm in perfectly good health," I protested, ushering her inside. "Just tired. Nevertheless, I welcome your visit! How is my father?"

"Same as always," Phoebe said, commandeering the hearth. "But don't think I can be put off the subject. If you're not ailing, then why are your cheeks so pale and your hair a bird's nest?"

Self-consciously, I tucked tangled curls under my bonnet. I was pale from lack of rest and my hair unkempt because I couldn't muster the dignity to brush it. Of course, none of this could I tell anyone.

But Phoebe . . .

I realized that she might, indeed, be the only person in whom I could confide, which made me burst into sudden tears. Without a word, Phoebe came and wrapped her arms around me, as if I were a young girl again at the parsonage, weeping over some childhood trouble. And I melted against her, wetting her neck with my tears.

Phoebe rubbed my back, saying, "There, there, Miss Abby. What sort of trouble have you got yourself into?"

"It's Mr. Adams," I hiccuped. "I fear he does not love me any longer."

There. I said the dreaded words aloud. Now they floated dangerously between us until Phoebe batted them away. "Well, if it's true, it's not the end of the world. Love's not good for much anyway. But dry your eyes and tell me why you think his heart's gone cold."

It took me some time to pull myself together. I had to resort to drying my tears with my fichu and wrapping myself in a shawl for comfort.

Then, over a hot bowl of broth, I showed Phoebe the letters. The cold ones, the angry ones, the spiteful ones.

We had taught her to read—my sisters and I—and now I watched Phoebe's wizened old eyes linger on the nastiest parts. "Well, your Mister is in a mood . . ."

Exposing my wounds like this—even to an intimate—made my despair turn to fury. "Never did I know Mr. Adams capable of being so *mean-spirited*! Whatever I've done to displease him, it cannot be so great an offense to justify this. I begin to believe . . ."

I could scarcely articulate what I'd begun to believe.

In revisiting these letters, I'd noticed that while John found nothing to praise in me, he had only praise for France. "The delights are innumerable. The politeness, the elegance, the softness, the delicacy, is extreme." How delicious the cookery. How charming the manners. How elegant the entertainments. How educated the women. How pleasant the climate there being, he said, "not a softer air, a warmer sun, or a more delicious appearance of things about Boston."

It was a suspiciously romantic turn of phrase for the likes of John Adams. Had he, perhaps, made the acquaintance of a softer, warmer, more delicious woman? I had tried to shake the thought away, but now miserably whispered to Phoebe, "Mrs. Warren told me it is the custom of every important man in France to take a mistress."

I could've cursed Mercy for telling me that, but it wasn't *Mercy* who had made me wonder. It was John, and I resented him all the more for it. "If he loved me, he would never!"

Drily, Phoebe said, "Oh, people can hurt you plenty even if they love you. But I don't think you have to worry about Mr. Adams taking a mistress."

Eager for any scrap of hope, I asked, "Why not?"

"Well, by my reckoning, Honey, a husband like Mr. Adams—a churchgoing husband who prides himself on personal honor—

well, he'd feel guilty. Knowing he's sinned, he'd scrawl sweet nothings to his wronged wife and press flowers between the pages to ease his conscience."

Well, I had not thought of that. The few times in our marriage that John knew himself to be wrong, he'd been very contrite. Remembering this flooded me with relief. "That is an astute observation about husbands; how did you come by it as an unmarried woman?"

Phoebe snorted. "Enslaved people don't survive to be my age without studying human nature."

That ought to have prompted some soul-searching on my part about Phoebe's situation, but I was too absorbed in my own troubles. "Well, what am I to do? Even if Mr. Adams hasn't strayed from our marital bed, he's made a mockery of it. I didn't think him capable of mistreating me. And I won't tolerate it."

Phoebe snorted again. "Oh, yes you will." This brought me up short, but she continued on without a care for my bruised pride. "You don't have a choice. When you were a'courting, you did your best to find a groom who would treat you well. That's the last freedom you had. Now you're married, and in marriage, you belong to him."

That set my teeth on edge, for as a religious woman I had never believed it. "Men who wish to be happy willingly give up the harsh title of Master for the more tender and endearing one of friend." Then, remembering to whom I was speaking, I added, "The ownership of *any* person is unjust and immoral."

Phoebe stared at me hard, for she would always understand the injustice and immorality of owning human beings in a way that I would *never* be capable of understanding. "You don't say?"

Now I felt shamed. "I did not mean to imply that marriage is slavery—"

"No," Phoebe said. "It sure isn't. But there's plenty in common. My people say you might get a kind, loving master. You might get a cruel one. Either way, you've got a master."

I swallowed, not daring to meet her eyes, for no matter how often I'd challenged my father, he refused to give up the right to her, even though he knew it was a sin. Yes, my beloved father. A pastor and man of God. A kind master, but still a master . . .

"There shouldn't *be* any masters," I said in mounting determination. "A thing I intend to say to my father again when next I see him."

"You'll do no such thing," Phoebe said, wagging a finger in my face. "It won't help me. And it won't help you to argue with your husband across the sea either. Perhaps he has some reason to make the British think he's a stern and unfeeling patriarch—a facade meant for his protection and yours. But it doesn't matter if he has a good reason or a bad one. Do you think vicious little letters are the worst thing Mr. Adams can do to you? He's fallen in love with France, you say. Well, what if he stays there? You wouldn't be the first wife in this family to be deserted."

My mouth ran dry, because she was right. My drunken brother had abandoned his wife, leaving her bereft of hope, housing, and sustenance. And though I helped to support his children, I did not dare ask what humiliations my sister-in-law endured to survive.

What recourse did she have? None. She could attempt to divorce him, but the process was not only rare, costly, and uncertain, but would impart a stigma she'd carry all her days. The truth was that women had little protection. It would be better if my sister-in-law were widowed, for whilst my brother lived, his wife and children were tied to him, his absence an anchor that dragged them down into poverty and shame.

A fate my children and I might share, Phoebe insisted, if I didn't follow her advice. "You write back sweetly to your husband. Apologize for even the slightest shadow of a complaint. Be solicitous of his health and flatter his vanity. And if he *has* taken a mistress, do not imagine you'll ever benefit by taking the slightest notice of it."

That was too outrageous a suggestion to be borne. "I cannot apologize and mean it. It would be dishonest, and he'd know it."

Phoebe eyed me for a fool. "Then you best take the pieces of your broken heart and glue them back together in such a way that you can make your apology ring true."

I knew she was right. And rarely in my life did knowledge of the truth cut so deeply. All my marriage, I imagined myself to be in love. Now I believed that what passed between John and me must be something less than love—that it had *always* been something less than love. Because true love can only exist between equals. And we had never been that.

John had always indulged me. He'd made me feel as if my opinions mattered. He'd flattered me with his trust. He'd refrained from using the powers the law granted him to oppress me. And in so doing, he'd given me the illusion that we were a union of hearts and souls.

Now that illusion was shattered, revealing the cruel reality that a union of hearts and souls was not possible so long as his sex tyrannized mine. And if I wanted any measure of freedom or dignity, I couldn't write to him in anger, asking for reassurance or explanation or justification. I couldn't even plead with him to treat my heart more gently and help me mend it. I'd have to mend my own heart with the glue of self-regard and a determination to be independent from this day forth.

Henceforth I'd remember the painful truth that John Adams was merely the father of my children and the man to whom I was pledged by a marriage contract. No matter how much it hurt, from that legalistic point of view, his regard and affection for me was entirely unchanged, leaving me in the wrong for expecting more.

So I took up my pen and wrote to John, "You chide me for my complaints, when I had so little occasion for them. I entreat you, my dear sir, to forgive it as an anxious solicitude to hear of your welfare. Bury in oblivion every expression of complaint—erase them from the letters as I have erased from my mind any idea contrary to the regard and affection you've always manifested towards me."

There. That was apologetic. Now for gratitude.

"Accept my thanks for so kindly providing for me. The articles you sent will be a great assistance."

I encouraged him to send more—for even if two out of every three shipments sank to the bottom of the sea, I could still profit. And I aimed to profit. I aimed to study every possible method of economy in my power, all with an intention to add to my pin money.

About which I had told John nothing.

I doubted I ever would. Why should he feel entitled to the details of my life if he was unwilling to share the details of his?

I finished the letter with a customary closing that now held a much darker, cold, and legalistic meaning.

I am wholly yours.

Then I folded that letter so carefully that the edges were sharp enough to cut. I melted the wax, pouring a perfect bloodred puddle on the page, before pressing a seal and watching it harden along with my heart.

Part Two

Chapter Twenty

BRAINTREE
Massachusetts
Summer 1781

I LEARNED TO LIVE without John.

And as the war dragged on, my marriage also felt like a battlefield. My husband now objected when I drew a bill against his salary. He claimed he needed the money in Europe whereas I should be able to support myself exclusively by way of selling the goods he sent.

In light of this, I could no longer afford to merely *dabble* in mercantilism. I must now wholly embrace it, turning my trade into a more efficient operation. To that end, I made over the bedroom where my eldest boys used to sleep into a place to store and catalog my wares. I wrote up pleasing little descriptions to entice customers who were increasingly desperate because of wartime shortages. And the more attention I paid to this business the better I profited, collecting enough to pay the exorbitant taxes, feed my children and my brother's children, and buy a small carriage besides.

From afar, John balked at the price of that chaise—three times more than before the war. But I paid for two-thirds of it with the sale of lace handkerchiefs alone, so he could scarcely complain. Or if he did complain, I'd take no notice, since owning my own chaise—and driving it myself—was a *necessity* to transport goods.

I could not always presume upon Uncle Tufts, who was a doctor before he was a merchant.

So, in buying that chaise, I remembered the example of Boudica, the ancient warrioress who drove her own chariot into battle. I likely made an equally curious sight on the roads of staid

Braintree. Nevertheless, I harnessed our horse to the conveyance, took the reins in my own hands, and set off.

My first stop was at the new house of James and Mercy Warren in nearby Milton, bringing a little gift of cider and preserves to make them feel welcome. Mercy had a gift for me, too: a copy of her latest essay for the newspapers, for which I'd written an anonymous introduction.

My first published work!

I wasn't yet so brave as to publish under my own name, but oh, those were my words for the world to see. It pleased me more than I ever thought it could. What my husband would think, I didn't know. Or perhaps I didn't care because I was too happy in my knowledge that people had read my thoughts. And seeing them in print was a very precious gift indeed.

With gratitude, I told Mercy, "I couldn't be gladder that you've moved closer to us."

"We needed a change of scenery," she replied. "My boys need a more rural setting to keep out of trouble. We also wanted to live in a place where we'd hear less from that buffoon who is now our first governor of Massachusetts."

She meant John Hancock—against whom we both would've voted had we been able. Hancock had been patriotic enough at the start of the war, but he was using his money to get elected, which we thought unseemly and corrupt.

Since we couldn't vote against him, we'd had to content ourselves in counting votes and trying to dissuade our neighbors from voting for him. But Hancock had won easily, and it taught me a powerful lesson about the nature of raw power. Money mattered. And I needed more of it. Which was why I told Mercy, "I'm thinking of investing in land in Vermont."

She looked surprised, for we both knew a woman couldn't buy land. "How shall you do it?"

"I don't know yet. My husband would respond too slowly from France for me to take advantage of a good deal."

If, that is, John could be moved to respond at all.

He seemed altogether too enraptured with France to take an

interest in my struggles. In fact, my husband now permitted me to place my orders directly to traders in Europe so that he wouldn't be bothered playing intermediary.

"He must allow an agent to act on his behalf here in Braintree," Mercy advised. "Perhaps some man of your family. Though Mr. Adams has your two sons with him in France, he ought to make it easier for you to provide for Nabby and Tommy here at home."

I dared not tell Mercy that my husband had even begun to grouse of the inconvenience of caring for our sons, writing, "Although my boys behave very well, my affections I fear got the better of my judgment in bringing them."

I was furious to read that, for though I'd learned to live without John, I'd never learned to live without my boys, or to harden my heart against them. John should be grateful to have the boys with him! Especially since I was left with merely the fond hope of seeing the return of my dear sons in some future day, improved in person and mind.

Now I sighed, confessing to Mercy, "I miss them terribly. I console myself to think that Johnny and Charlie now reside in a place that gave birth to many great men. Surely, they must learn something in Europe that would benefit them."

"Of course they will. Did you not say that John Quincy sometimes writes to you in French?"

I nodded with pride. "And both boys are now also learning Dutch—a thing I dutifully reported to Charlie's little songbird. Against all odds, I have managed to keep the sparrow alive and singing sweetly. A poor substitute for my cherub, but still a comfort . . ."

"I cannot but smile to think of your Charlie," she said. "That cheeky little creature! Whenever I saw him, I wanted to stuff him with candies."

"I suppose it's good that he went with his father, then. For he would've been spoiled by the fondness and caresses of all his acquaintances."

"Indeed. In your next letter, please tell Charlie that Mrs. Warren sends her love. Though perhaps it is wiser not to commit any thought to paper these days."

Mercy leaned forward in the way she did when she had gossip to share. "Have you seen the intercepted letter from Mr. Lovell that was published?"

My throat tightened, nervous it may have been one of his flirtatious letters to me. "Do I wish to see it? I pray it was not intended for my hands."

"Thankfully not! It was a letter to his congressional colleague Mr. Gerry. But there are things said in it that will make his wife miserable."

"What things?"

Mercy's expression tightened with disapproval. "He wrote that he had no desire to go home and see Mrs. Lovell, even after leaving her three or four years altogether. I believe he cares very little for his wife."

Given that my own husband was now three years absent, I cringed. "Pray do not measure a gentleman's regard for his wife by how long he is absent. You'd wound me if you think thus of my own dear partner."

In truth, I was already wounded by my husband's disregard. But this was nothing I wanted Mercy to know.

Now she fanned herself. "The case is different with Mr. Lovell. He's only in Philadelphia. It's in his power to visit his wife without much hazard."

"Perhaps he has reasons to stay away from his wife that he does not wish to share with the world," I said, not wanting to reveal that Mr. Lovell had already told me he couldn't afford to return home because he relied entirely upon his wages in Congress. And he also feared that his wife might get with another child he could not support.

But Mercy insisted, "I think it more that this gentleman looks upon our whole sex as common prey and plunder."

"Oh, I cannot think he has so bad a heart!"

Mercy eyed me with suspicion. "Why do you defend him, even after the way he has written to you? I know this man has been a line cast to you in a turbulent sea. But I believe he's formed an attachment to you, Abigail. To indulge it may be your ruin."

I didn't want to believe this—perhaps because Mr. Lovell *had* been a line cast to me in a turbulent sea. He forwarded news, packages, letters, and even procured for us supplies when we were in need. But if Mercy suspected an improper attachment, then there might be gossip I must fend off.

To that end, I issued an invitation to the lonely Mrs. Lovell to come to Braintree and stay as my guest.

To my consternation, she refused the invitation.

But then a letter arrived that erased this snub from my mind. Though it was addressed to *Mrs. Adams*, I soon realized it wasn't intended for me. I was about to seal it up again and take it to Mrs. *Samuel* Adams when I noticed my husband's name mentioned on the page. Scanning the news reported by a woman friend in Philadelphia, I discovered that the French—and Benjamin Franklin, too—were unhappy with my husband's independence as a diplomat.

There was a plot afoot to recall John or *order* him to defer to France's wishes in negotiating a peace with Great Britain. Well, this would never do. We couldn't trade the bullying of an English king for the bullying of a French king!

However hard I'd made my heart against John, I couldn't simply ignore this letter, which threatened not only his career but also our country. So, I sprang into action, writing a blizzard of letters to Mr. Lovell, Mr. Gerry, and every other person of importance I knew, asking them to exert their influence in Congress on my husband's behalf.

Fortunately, my swift action had good effect. Friends took up John's cause, defending his honor, patriotism, and good service until no one in Congress would dare recall him.

Of course, I'd soon have cause to regret this good deed. For by autumn there was talk of naming my husband to be the American minister to the Netherlands to secure a loan from the Dutch in support of our war effort, and to convince them to recognize American independence.

It was a prestigious post and a worthy mission, but would mean at least another year apart.

A younger, less-disillusioned version of myself might have put up a protest, but I wrote indifferently to John. "You will do what you esteem to be your duty, I doubt not, fearless of consequences."

He accepted the post as I expected. But never did I think he would then send my sons away—news that came to me like a bolt out of the blue. And as I tried to explain the whereabouts of her brothers to Nabby, she wanted to know, "Where is Saint Petersburg?"

"In Russia." I shivered at what little I knew of this place—a forbidding, savage empire of ice and snow. This is where my husband had sent our Johnny, now fourteen years of age, to serve as the private secretary to Mr. Francis Dana, our minister in the court of Catherine the Great.

Due to my son's fluency in French, the language of diplomacy, Johnny was thought to be a fit apprentice. I ought to have been proud. I *was* proud. Still, how was a mother to reconcile herself to the idea of her young son being sent off without family into a country as far away as the moon?

Then there was Charlie—a boy of only eleven, sent in the other direction toward home, braving British warships, to say nothing of storms, by himself.

Uncharitably, I wondered if my sons, who had been all but torn from my arms and dragged across the sea, were now such an inconvenience to my husband—in all his importance and pomposity—that he'd simply put them on ships and scattered them to the winds!

And when I wrote to my husband, it was a struggle to keep the venom from my pen. "Charlie's desire to return home must have been great indeed to induce the poor fellow to cross the Atlantic without father or brother. I cannot say how much the anxious heart of a mother feels upon this occasion. I would have felt easier if you had at least written to me about it before doing it."

What was done was done. I promised myself that if I clasped my middle son again in my arms, I'd make up for every moment we spent apart. His ship, the *South Carolina*, departed Amsterdam on the twelfth of August. If the seas were fair, I could expect my boy home in September, so I tried not to fret.

But September came and went.

Then most of October, too.

No one had any news of the *South Carolina*.

In the eyes of everyone I met, I could see pity. Ships often foundered at sea and were swallowed up whole. And now I was left to hope that my boy had merely been captured by one of the British warships prowling our shores.

Finally, lest I go mad, I took the carriage on snowy roads into Boston myself to interrogate sailors on the docks of Boston Harbor. "Have you any word of the *South Carolina*?" I asked officers, common sailors, and even dockhands alike. "My son is on board. A boy of eleven. Charles Adams. Have you heard anything?"

"*Nothing*," was the usual reply, given with a sorrowful shake of the head.

But one day in mid-November, I received a different answer. "The *South Carolina*?" asked a sailor just come from Bilbao, his breath puffing steam into the cold air. "She's in Spain. Or at least she was."

My knees threatening to buckle in relief, I asked, "You're certain, sir?"

"Aye, madam. I was on that frigate. I went ashore one day, and they sailed without me. But before that I saw your boy. Memorable little fellow. Golden curls, dimpled smile, always singing a tune or feeding the seagulls at the rail."

"Yes," I said, brightening. "That is Charles! But I don't understand. Why is he in Spain?"

"The captain of the *South Carolina* turned privateer midjourney," the man explained. "More profit to go after prizes while the war is still on."

I felt the blood drain from my face. A privateer was simply a licensed *pirate*. Dear God, my husband had put my eleven-year-old son aboard a pirate ship that, according to the sailor, had indeed attacked, boarded, and seized the cargo of enemy ships.

Seeing that I was on the verge of swooning with fear, the sailor hastened to reassure me, "With the rumor that the war might soon end, the captain is surely making his way from Spain to Philadelphia."

I'd not sleep a full night until Charles was safely home in my arms again, but I clasped this kind man's hands in thanks for giving me news of my boy. Then I thanked God for preserving Charles thus far.

Though what I might do to my husband, John, if his neck was near enough to throttle, I could not say . . .

In the meantime, I'd do what I could to provide the best home-coming a boy could want—enough Indian pudding to make Charlie burst. For that I'd need coin, but my trade goods weren't selling so easily now.

"Your prices are too high," Mercy warned. For she had herself been unable to sell the goods she took on consignment, going into my debt.

I didn't press her for repayment, nor did I point out that though she might be a very fine playwright, her salesmanship was decidedly lacking. For example, she refused to believe ladies wanted white handkerchiefs, not black, which she deemed more practical. So, she wouldn't take my advice to discount the black ones and sell the white for much more.

Rather than let her go further into debt, I advised that she surrender her unsold goods back to me. I was sure Dr. Tufts and I could find buyers at my price. Admittedly, it was harder than before. And it didn't help that the Massachusetts legislature was about to devalue paper currency, of which I had too much on hand.

For that mistake, my husband found the time to scold me. "I am heartily sorry to hear you have a sum of paper. How could you be so imprudent?"

Imprudent?

Firstly, I was tempted to point out that no other housewife in the colonies would be expected to know so much about currency that she might be called *imprudent* for not anticipating this financial turn. And in the second place, I was tempted to point out that nearly everything *he* knew about wartime economy he'd learned from me. Finally, I was even tempted to tell him that because of my pin money, I had a much greater sum of paper than he supposed.

But I said none of these things, because in scolding me, John had given me just what I had needed to buy that land in Vermont.

Now all I needed to do was take my carriage to Weymouth and visit Uncle Tufts.

"Mr. Adams wishes for me to invest," I said.

Tufts lifted a snowy eyebrow. "Does he?"

Because it was not a lie, I brazened it out. "He does. He thinks it *imprudent* not to." When I suggested the purchase of land with our paper currency, my husband hadn't forbidden it. He hadn't answered at all, so I'd do as I liked. "But a woman cannot buy land, and certainly not in her own name. So, we'd need you to make the purchase in trust."

Eyebrow still aloft, Dr. Tufts said, "For Mr. Adams, of course."

I saw that we understood each other. "Yes, for Mr. Adams. Of course. It's too difficult to manage his affairs from his new house in Amsterdam. Will you do it?"

"Yes," Dr. Tufts said. "I rather enjoy helping you get around these obstacles. I approach it as some manner of surgery. A corner cut here. A little stitch there, and all will be sewn up in your favor."

"For a small commission, of course," I said. To get around the law, women had need of friends like these, but I wouldn't take advantage of him.

He smiled indulgently. "We'll find a way to put your money to good use." I liked that he said it was *my* money—for he knew who earned it. And when I wilted in relief, he added, "Don't fret, Abigail. You have enough other worries. How fares your boy in Russia?"

"Johnny arrived safely, praise God."

"No doubt already doing credit to the family. But no word yet from Charles the Charmer?"

"Not since learning he's in Spain. I've written Mr. Lovell but have nothing back yet."

He made a sound at the back of his throat. One of discomfort. "Well, your friend Mr. Lovell has other troubles at present. Given the rumors."

"Oh, Cousin Cotton," I scolded, crossly. "Surely people aren't still harping on that business about his intercepted letter saying he didn't wish to return home to his wife."

"Oh, he'll be *forced* to return to her now. Too many are calling for his resignation now that it's said he's having an illicit affair with his landlady!"

I went rigid with both shock and humiliation. If it was true that Mr. Lovell was a rake, neglecting his wife and seducing his landlady, all while sending flirtatious letters to me, then I'd blot the man from my memory with shame that I'd ever been flattered by his attentions.

And even if it wasn't true . . . well, there was a pattern in the man's conduct that made this easier to believe. It didn't reflect well on my own character that I'd ignored his flirtations and continued a correspondence. That would end now. Whatever my husband might be up to in Europe, I'd give him no cause to doubt *my* fidelity.

I had learned to live without John. Now I'd have to learn to live without Lovell's help.

I'd simply rely upon myself more than ever before.

Chapter Twenty-One

THE NEW YEAR finally brought my darling boy back home. At nearly twelve, he was no longer small enough to leap into my arms and be spun round. But he ran to me, crying, "Mama!"

After being smothered in hugs and kisses from his mother, his sister, and his little brother, Charlie told harrowing tales of his journey. Of storms and learning to gamble for additional biscuits for his dinner. He told me how he'd clung to the soldier into whose hands his father had entrusted him, begging him not to abandon him in Spain.

Yet, despite five months at sea with rough, hard-drinking sailors— my son's heart was still soft. And I delighted in his joyful reunion with the little songbird he loved so well.

"I heard you were homesick," I told him, running my fingers through his curls.

"It was no fun in Holland without Johnny. Then I was sick, and Papa got much sicker. So sick the servants said he'd die."

I startled. "This is the first I'm hearing of it."

Thereupon Charlie described to us a terrible scene. "Papa fell from his chair, sweating and panting. I couldn't wake him. Six weeks he lay abed, and on the days he was awake, he couldn't even hold a book."

John Adams abed for six weeks? I couldn't imagine it. "What ailment could possibly render him so?"

"The doctor said malaria," Charles replied, continuing on with one breathless story after another until the fire burned down and he finally fell asleep in his father's chair. While I cherished the return of such spirited conversation with my son after so long a separation, my thoughts kept returning to John's illness.

Malaria. A disease so often fatal. Debilitating to those who survived it. Regret for my most uncharitable thoughts swamped me. For I realized now that when my husband sent our sons away, he was completely unable to care for them—so bedeviled by malaria that he wasn't in his right mind.

When I was ill with dysentery, struggling to care for the children, begging my mother to take Nabby with her, my illness had not been six weeks. To think of my husband so monstrously sick and suffering amongst strangers . . . well, my heart was not so hard that I couldn't feel a pang of pity.

Certainly, the news seemed to weigh on Nabby.

Our daughter was going on seventeen now, with a lovely oval-shaped face framed by soft auburn curls. All about her was refinement, from her almond-shaped eyes to her rosy lips. Majestic as a princess, she cared nothing for the increasing interest of young men in town. In fact, she'd refused numerous invitations to join them at Harvard commencement—the highlight of every year's social calendar.

Pensive since the news of her father's illness, she finally said, "Papa could've died in Europe and the last we would've seen of him is *years* past now."

With that, she lapsed into one of her chronic silences that lasted all the next day. When the silence continued through bedtime, I was finally exasperated. "Why are you so quiet?"

"In *this* family, I should not get a word in edgewise even if I tried."

"Impertinent child." Hers was a saucy reply, but I much preferred a show of spirit to her brooding silence. "It's true your family are talkers. But that's because the world is too interesting not to talk about. And we now occupy a prominent place in it."

"I wish we didn't," she said wearily. "My friends tell me I ought to be happy about Papa's exalted station. And I endeavor to appear so, because it would be wrong to wear a sorrowful countenance during the war. But a girl with a heart of *adamant* couldn't be truly happy when never having her family together."

I eyed her with growing concern. "I didn't know you were so unhappy."

"I don't talk upon the subject, because I don't wish to add to your woes, Mama. But I seldom reflect upon our situation without tears." Tears did well in her eyes as she asked, "Why not send me to Europe? Papa complains that he has a house in Amsterdam but no housekeeper. *I* could keep house for him, tend to him if he's still ill, and otherwise see this interesting world you speak of."

It would be absurd to send my young, unmarried daughter alone across the sea. Nevertheless, I could see the child really believed herself to be quite serious. After all, it'd been just as absurd to send my sons, who were both younger. Now Charles, speaking three languages, had returned with tales of adventure. And Johnny was well into an apprenticeship in the dazzling court at Saint Petersburg.

Nabby said, "I've scarcely visited as many *towns* as John Quincy has *kingdoms*."

It was natural that Nabby might envy her brothers. I almost envied them, too. And I remembered well my own wanderlust at her age, so I didn't have the heart to tell her she couldn't go. I'd let her father disabuse her of these notions as he'd disabused me of so many of mine.

JOHN LET HER down gently. He told our daughter there was no point in her coming to Europe, because though Congress had not yet seen fit to release him from his duties, he might be sailing home at any moment.

Of course, he wouldn't commit to that. And fists clenching with frustration, Nabby said, "If I am ever married, I could never imitate my parents. I simply could not endure this uncertain way of living."

I looked up from my knitting. "Life will soon instruct you how much more you can endure than you think you can. But is there some reason to believe you won't marry?"

She became quite focused on *her* knitting. "Because romantic sentiments—like patriotism and love—are very dangerous."

My eyebrows inched up. "Why do you say so?"

She waved a hand, as if to encompass our drafty, distressed home and the empty beds upstairs. "The life you lead has instructed me, Mama."

Amused, I asked, "Are you certain your mind hasn't turned to the subject of patriotism, love, and marriage because of the attentions of a certain young lawyer who has hung up his shingle in town?"

"Of course not." Her knitting needles clicked together with more force.

I hadn't wished to broach the topic for fear of upsetting her burgeoning friendship with Mr. Royall Tyler, a handsome young lawyer who had dazzled the town with his learning and talents. He was boarding with my sister Mary, and we first met him there where we ended up talking late into the evening about books.

Since then, he'd made himself a regular visitor at my fireside where my children were variously occupied—Charlie reading, Nabby sewing, Tommy studying grammar.

But I knew Mr. Tyler's attentions weren't for me and my literary conversation. His growing attachment to Nabby was too obvious not to notice. Now I teased, "I think you aren't as indifferent to Mr. Tyler as you pretend."

Nabby threw her head back. "You were never more extravagantly mistaken, Mama."

"Is that so?"

"Your Nabby is the same cold indifferent girl she ever was. But I long to be in love, if only because it must be a strange feeling and it would let me know whether I have a heart or not."

"Of course you have a heart." I put down my knitting. "Not even one so hard as adamant."

"One made of ice then. That's what I tell everyone."

I knew she was indifferent to the sons of Mrs. Warren—which was for the best in my opinion, as those young men seemed like rogues. But in town, Nabby was acquiring a reputation for fickleness when it came to the attentions of the male persuasion. One day, Mr. Storers was at least agreeable. The next day, she was not fond of him. To say nothing of Mr. Guild, who she now said *was quite out of her books*.

She'd have to be more charitable to find a partner in life. "I think you have a warm heart, Nabby. I know you love your siblings, cousins, parents, and family. I've seen you cry over the loss of people dear to us."

"Those were the days of my weakness," Nabby said.

I suppressed a laugh at her world-weariness, for in that moment, my daughter reminded me very much of myself when I was close to her age, piercing the pretensions of everyone who sought to tame me with a determination never to fall prey to the passions that led other girls astray.

Though I believed she could be won by Royall Tyler, I didn't believe she'd be won *easily*, for in truth, my daughter had loathed him upon first meeting—warning her cousins that he was too charming to be sincere. "Our sex cannot be too careful when it comes to the acquaintances we form," she had said.

Which was, of course, very true. But from what I could surmise about the young lawyer, he was perfectly respectable, if love-addled. For the colder she was to him, the more it seemed to ignite his pursuit.

In fact, the very next afternoon the young barrister appeared at our doorstep ostensibly to look at one of my husband's law books, but in reality to present Nabby with a heart that he'd carved from ice, accompanied by a little poem in her honor.

"I shall never be won with trinkets," she insisted to hush her younger brothers, who both taunted her gleefully. Thereupon she abandoned the ice sculpture to melt by the hearth. But I noticed she tucked the little poem into her sleeve for safekeeping . . .

NOT LONG AFTER, Mr. Tyler declared his intentions. "Madam, I wish to court your daughter, but with her father absent, I'm at a loss as to how to proceed."

I had, of course, already made every secret inquiry after this young man. I'd learned of his good education, the steadiness of his learning habits, and the estate he stood to inherit, which was not inconsiderable.

"If you wish to court my daughter, sir, you must know that one aspect of your history brought to my attention troubles me. It seems you spent several years after your father's death squandering a third of your inheritance."

Mr. Tyler had the grace to flush before admitting it. "Even then, madam, I always applied myself to my studies with a mind to business. Thankfully, I have reformed and put those days behind me."

I had no reason to disbelieve it—especially since he was never found but with books under his arm. Nevertheless, I felt compelled to inform him, "Even if my daughter were willing to be wooed, my husband and I must speak in one voice, and he's across the sea. Besides, now is the time to build your practice. You're not yet established enough to form a connection with any young lady."

Though clearly heartsick, Mr. Tyler professed to accept this. He said he could be patient. "Whether I'm blessed in my wishes or not, I'll endeavor to be worthy of consideration for your daughter."

I was impressed and wrote John about this, never suspecting the effect it might have upon him. At first, my husband flew to his pen to deny that our daughter was old enough for a suitor—never mind that she was older than I was when he met me. In the next letter, which came swiftly upon the first, he was wroth at the notion that I might've encouraged Mr. Tyler, who he imagined to be a wastrel, a scoundrel, and a prodigal son. "My child is not to be the prize of any rake, even a reformed one."

He forbade any attachment between them, demanding an end to the entire affair. Then, his letters—a veritable avalanche of them—became sweet and tender, gently advising his daughter. "I am so uneasy about this subject that I'd come instantly home if I could with decency."

It seemed that after nearly four years away, the realization had finally struck him with a forceful blow that everyone he'd left behind did not simply stand still whilst he was gone. We all went on with the business of living, and if he wished to have any place in his family's affections—or to have any part in guiding his daughter's heart—he must be more attentive.

So now he wrote and wrote and wrote. Unfortunately, his letters came too late. For with the coming of springtime, Nabby was in love.

"YOU ARE IMPERTINENT, sir," Nabby said to Mr. Tyler.

"To the contrary. When a young gentleman is alone with a

young lady he *must* say soft things to her fair cheek—indeed, the lady will expect it."

"Only if you mean these soft things. Otherwise, how cruel to win the affections of an amiable girl and, though you leave her virtue unspotted, discourage men of decency who suppose her heart engaged!"

Mr. Tyler inclined his head. "May I ask the names of these rivals you fear might be discouraged?"

"You may not," Nabby said, with a laugh.

He laughed, too. "Ah, Miss Adams, from the moment I first saw you, you struck me as the lady whom I have long loved in imagination and never dared hoped to see."

As the young couple conversed, they'd forgotten the open windows, unmindful of an audience. Now they paid the price, as Charlie and Tommy made a pantomime show inside.

With a mop on his head and a fist full of flowers he stole from my table, Charlie pretended to be his sister. And fluttering his long pale eyelashes, he broke into high falsetto. "Oh, Mr. Tyler, how dare you romance me!"

Tommy—less talented at such plays—took the part of the suitor and dropped to one knee. "But it's your fault, Miss Adams, for you have bewitched me."

"Boys," I said mildly.

From outside, their sister gathered her skirts and flung open the door, giving chase. "Oh, you little brats!"

She'd forgive Charlie, no doubt, for he was too sweet to hold any grudge against. But Tommy was such a rogue, the grudge might last a bit longer.

For my part, I was highly amused. Both by the antics of my sons and by the unexpected fervor with which my daughter befriended Mr. Tyler, eventually defending him even against the mild criticisms I'd heard. "Mama, those days when he is said to have squandered part of his fortune were spent serving with the militia in defense of our country."

She was both heartbroken and indignant when she read her father's admonishment. "The man to whom you give your heart must be a thinking being, and one who feels another's woe. One may dance or sing, play or ride, without being good for much."

Having been silent for days upon the receipt of these letters, my daughter finally ventured to say, "It wasn't dancing, singing, and playing that led me to like Mr. Tyler. I didn't know him when those were his amusements."

"I understand," I said, well aware of how deeply her father's disapproval could cut. Especially when delivered from leagues away, without the softening comfort of voice or touch.

Her cheeks pinkened. "And when my father says that he's not looking for a poet for a son-in-law, does he not know my friend was his class valedictorian at Harvard and is now a prospering country lawyer, just like Papa used to be?"

"Your papa is just venting his spleen," I said to reassure her. "He can be stern and acerbic, but he has only your best interests at heart, my dearest."

She paced before the fireplace. "Well, I have so few memories of my father and such meager evidence of his affection that I shall have to take your word for it!"

"That is unfair and untrue," I said, though I wished I could've said it with more conviction.

Chastened, Nabby apologized. "But is it right for Papa to form a bad opinion about Mr. Tyler without knowing him?"

"That is the trouble," I said, taking her hands in mine. "Your father cannot be happy without knowing the man to whom he gives his daughter. And you cannot be happy without your father's approval."

She was too dutiful to gainsay me. "Then what's to be done?"

"Don't give up hope of a future connection with Mr. Tyler. But until your papa returns home and sees for himself that you have a worthy suitor, you must put a pause on this romance and be patient."

Of course, patience was not a family trait.

The pendant John gave me was meant to inspire patient endurance and acceptance. But it had sat unworn in my jewel box for nearly three years now as I took my life into my own hands. So, I felt quite the hypocrite for telling my daughter she must sit idly by and let others determine her fate.

Chapter Twenty-Two

BOSTON
Massachusetts
December 1783

T HE WAR WAS over.

It hadn't ended all at once, of course.

It began with a battle won at faraway Yorktown two years earlier, followed by treaties and endlessly slow negotiations. Then, at the end of November, British soldiers had evacuated New York City. Before the enemy had even vacated the harbor, George Washington's troops raised our new flag to mark the momentous occasion.

We won.

We were *free*.

I wanted to fall to my knees and give thanks to God that we had prevailed. And what was once the whisper of a new nation was about to be a reality.

"Huzzah! Huzzah! Huzzah!" As news of the British evacuation spread, crowds thronged Griffin's Wharf, the site of the Boston Tea Party ten years before.

"It started here," I told my children, though the road to revolution had been more than dumping tea into a harbor. Even those who lived through it were likely to forget all the outrages that led to rebellion.

But we wanted to remember this *one* act of proud defiance as the spark that lit the torch. And though my family hadn't suffered as much as others—those who gave their lives and limbs, those who lost fathers, sons, and brothers to the violence—I still felt entitled to some measure of pride.

Gratifyingly, Boston recognized this by offering me a viewing box from which to watch the parade. Now, at my side, my boys watched soldiers muster, and I watched Nabby who was, in turn, not very surreptitiously watching Mr. Tyler cheer for the procession.

She'd broken things off at her father's insistence. In truth, the two lovebirds had been so convincing in ending things—flitting from heartbreak to quarrel to disdain—that I'd been utterly persuaded it was over.

But from the way she gazed longingly at him through the passing crowds, I deduced that the fire still burned. As if to confirm it, Nabby asked, "Shouldn't we invite Mr. Tyler to sit by us?"

"Nabby," I said, with warning.

"I don't see why he cannot visit with us with the freedom of a friend, though not with the intimacy of a nearer connection," she argued. "I will never act contrary to the advice of my father. I've surrendered all notions of love. But why should I treat a friend who has done nothing to forfeit my esteem with neglect or contempt?"

This might've been more words than I'd ever heard my taciturn daughter string together at once. And let no one doubt she was, indeed, the daughter of John Adams, because she made a very good case.

Besides, I knew that my husband's stance was softening. The longer John wrestled with the realization that he'd have to come home to exert his paternal authority, the less exertion he made. For he had not yet been released from his duties abroad, Congress believing that the infant nation needed senior diplomats in Europe possibly more now than ever before. Thus, he wrote, "Nabby's felicity is very near my heart but I must resign her to your prudence and the advice of your friends."

Since the decision was now apparently mine, I took a cautious approach. "Very well. Invite Mr. Tyler to join us with the freedom of an acquaintance."

Thereupon I turned and noticed my thirteen-year-old Charlie, recently recovered of measles, squinting in the winter sun, trying to get a better look at the parade. And now I, too, strained to look, because I thought I glimpsed my brother.

I hadn't seen Bill since before he abandoned his family, fully embracing his wastrel ways. Still, if, indeed, my brother was marching in this parade amongst other soldiers—some of them freedmen—I thought he deserved to cling to the one proud moment of his life: his service to our country.

For I could begrudge *no one* their celebration.

Certainly not Sam Adams, who had thrown off his austere demeanor to express real pleasure after so long and hard-fought a struggle. Nor could I begrudge Governor Hancock, who paraded about in a peacock-embroidered coat. Many other Sons of Liberty were missing, however. I mourned their absence. Mercy's brother, James Otis Jr., who had led the rallying cry of "no taxation without representation," had died in May, having been struck by lightning. An absence dearer to my heart was Dr. Joseph Warren, who'd so long ago been martyred to the cause. I took some solace in the fact that he'd finally been given a proper burial after Paul Revere identified his body by some silver dental work he'd made for him. So now I joined in the cheers for all the men who fought against the British, like Henry Knox, the Boston bookseller who'd turned general of the artillery, and Farmer Whittemore, who was now, thanks to Dr. Tufts, somehow *still* alive at the age of eighty-six to tell the tale of how he'd taken thirteen bayonet wounds and a bullet to the face. Merchants, tradesmen, and common working men of Boston looked forward to freedom with pride.

I was also gratified by the expressions of joy and satisfaction displayed by the women, who waved kerchiefs, cried open tears, and pinned ribbons to their bonnets. I searched in vain for Mrs. Warren in the crowd but knew that she would also feel joy on this day. Naturally, an end to the war ought to mean easier days for us at hearth and home. We wives and mothers had a right to anticipate that with pleasure. Still, it was more than hope and gratitude that women felt when I spoke to them. We counted ourselves patriots and participants in this cause.

And I was pleased when Mr. Tyler acknowledged this with a tip of his tricorn. "I hope you will bask in this moment of triumph, madam. No doubt, Mr. Adams would attribute part of it to you for keeping the home fires burning."

I'd done that and *more*. So had my countrywomen. We'd sewn shirts to clothe and inspirit the soldiers. We'd prepared bandages, tended the wounded, run messages, provided military intelligence, and even taken up pitchforks to guard strategic locations.

We, too, were patriots. Which, considering our situation, I considered heroic. After all, excluded from honors and offices, we would never be rewarded for it. Our property was still subject to the control of our husbands. Deprived of a voice in legislation, obliged to submit to laws imposed upon us without our consent, we ought to have been indifferent to the public welfare.

Yet all history and every age exhibited instances of patriotic virtue in women.

Therefore, I'd praise myself for having sacrificed so large a portion of my peace and happiness to promote the welfare of my country, even if that country would never thank the hand that rocked its cradle.

In truth, I *swelled* with pride. And when I thought about my husband, I could trace his conduct through this war and find an undaunted character. He'd faced the dangers of the ocean though he risked captivity and the noose. He'd contended with wickedness in high places. He'd hazarded his life against the revenge and malice of a now-defeated king.

In so doing, he had contributed to the happiness of *millions*.

These were facts. Solid truths no one could dispute. My anxieties and distresses at every period bore witness to them. Whatever shortcomings John had as a husband, I could never fault him as a patriot. And now, as the enormity of what he'd accomplished sank in, these recollections were more sweet than painful.

Perhaps this showed upon my expression, for Mr. Tyler asked, "If you knew Mr. Adams would've remained so long abroad, would you have consented that he should have gone in the first place?"

I collected myself with a deep breath while looking overhead at the evening's illuminations. "If I had known, sir, that Mr. Adams could've achieved what he has in creating this country, I'd not only have submitted to the painful absence I've already endured, but I'd have not opposed even more years apart. For I consider the happiness of myself and family the smallest dust in the balance."

"PRAY TELL ME you did not mean it," Nabby said, whirling upon me later that night. "You'd consent to Papa being away longer still?"

"I was answering a hypothetical question," I said.

"It is not hypothetical when Papa remains abroad even though the war is done!"

She already knew the myriad reasons her father was still in Europe as Congress dithered over whether they yet needed him there. But Nabby cared nothing for these reasons, and how could I blame her? In a fit of high-minded patriotism, I'd called our happiness *but a speck of dust in the balance*, but for a girl Nabby's age, it was everything.

Her life's prospects depended on a successful courtship before she reached a spinster's age. It was one thing for me to sacrifice my own happiness for the country. But I also had a duty to my children.

The war was done. We had *won*. We'd sown the seeds of independence, then struggled and suffered mightily to harvest that crop. Now it was time to enjoy the plentiful bounty in peace.

It was time for John to come home. It was time to stitch our family back together. Time for my husband to meet our daughter's suitor. Time for John to be the guiding influence our boys so badly needed.

His children needed him. The farm needed him. And with the war over, I'd have fewer freedoms to operate independently without a husband.

So, perhaps, to my chagrin, I'd need him again, too.

As I fiddled with my quill over the balance books that night, I knew my mercantile business was done. Now was the time to invest in something less volatile. Something that would help pay for the education of my sons.

I'd reluctantly consented to send Charlie and Tommy to learn under Reverend Shaw in New Hampshire because my sister Elizabeth housed, fed, and cared for them as if they were her own. It was affordable, but was it the best situation for them? And must I always worry about money?

Yet, it wasn't the boys' schooling or money that kept me awake at night. It was the question of why I had said I'd consent to

John staying away longer. Was it because I feared we might never again be to one another what we were before the war?

I disliked the cold, distant, scolding man he had become in Europe. I still grieved the husband I once knew. The husband I still somehow longed for . . .

Whatever I might think of the inequalities of marriage, life was meant to be done with someone else, wasn't it? Despite all, I wanted companionship.

However hard I'd made my heart against John these past years, it had only encased the remains of our love and preserved it like a flower in amber. I'd never know if it could blossom again unless I persuaded John to come home.

I wrote to him frankly, begging him not to accept another appointment from Congress. In case my pleading was not enough, I resorted to bribery, hinting at my pin money. "If you come home and take the farm into your own hands, I can assist you in getting our living this way instead of running away to foreign courts and leaving me half my life to mourn in widowhood. I have a hundred pounds sterling I could command upon such an occasion."

In letter after letter, I beseeched him to come home.

I could have never imagined his reply.

For now, in letter after letter, John beseeched me to join him in Europe.

AT WEYMOUTH, WHERE I joined my older sister in caring for our ailing father, Mary asked, "Abigail, why do you sound as if this comes as an unwelcome shock?"

"Because it *is* an unwelcome shock!" Years ago, John insisted it was too dangerous to join him, financially impossible, and that there was nothing so disagreeable as a woman at sea.

Now his feelings had changed, but so had mine.

I'd once *begged* my husband to take me with him, but in the five years he'd been gone I'd built my own life here. "The notion that I must drop everything, including the happy company of my sister and the care of our father, does not appeal."

Mary sighed. "I'm flattered to think my company might rival

the glories of Europe, but I fear our father will not much longer be a tie that binds you here."

She wasn't wrong, though my eyes stubbornly refused to see until the last possible moment when we sent for Elizabeth to say her farewells. Before he died, my father blessed us and whispered, "God gave me for children three comforts and one affliction."

Our brother, the Affliction, did not attend the funeral. No doubt Bill thought himself justified in staying away to avoid his creditors—especially since my father broke custom and left his property in trust for my brother's wife and children. That was surely a humiliation for him.

But the parson was deliberate with his arrangements, including for my sisters and me, and those for Phoebe.

Because Mary was the oldest, we let her explain it to our old nurse. "Papa's will gives you the choice, Phoebe. You may have your freedom, or you may belong to me or Mrs. Adams or Mrs. Shaw as you please. It would be ownership in name only, of course. To provide you security. None of us would demand services of you."

Slavery in name only was still slavery, and I tried mightily not to remind everyone that Phoebe was *already* entitled to her freedom according to recent court cases in Massachusetts. She was free due to the state constitution my own husband had drafted. But I knew that both my sisters feared for Phoebe's safety to live as a freedwoman, so I only added, "Whatever you choose, there's also a behest to support you in old age."

Phoebe didn't hesitate. Eyes shining with deliverance, she said, "I will have my freedom."

"*Yes*," I said, scarcely restraining myself from leaping up to embrace her.

"You're certain?" Mary asked.

Phoebe stood taller, her eyes gazing heavenward. "Miss Mary, I'm more certain than I've ever been in my life. Should a bitter cup come to me from the choice, I'll still savor it for having been my choice."

We were all struck by these words. By her willingness to leap out into the unknown with faith in the future. She was, I thought, a remarkable woman, and we each owed much of ourselves to her example.

Would that I could be as firm in a decision whether to join my husband in Europe. Later, after we'd toasted Phoebe's freedom and reminisced of loved ones passed, conversation turned to my dilemma, and my sisters fretted over the dangers of a sea crossing.

"I cannot go in any case," I said. "What would I do with the farm?"

Mary suggested, "Put it in the care of your tenants and Uncle Tufts."

Elizabeth groaned. "Mary, why do you encourage her? I scarcely see Abigail as it is. She'll be even farther from me in Europe than now."

"You're a reverend's wife," Mary said, her tone scolding. "Surely you know that if Abigail's husband calls, she must go. It cuts me to the quick to part with her, but we ought to make it easier for her to obey."

Well, I might not obey, I thought.

John hadn't commanded me to come. And even if he had, it'd never been my way to meekly submit. For that matter, it'd never been the way of my once-spirited little sister, Elizabeth, either. Yet at the mention of her stern husband, the Reverend Shaw, she shrank into herself in a way that pained me.

Apologetically, Elizabeth suggested, "I'd care for your boys while you're away, Abigail. You needn't worry for them."

We all knew that Charlie and Tommy were destined for Harvard. John didn't wish to interrupt their schooling with travel, and neither did I. But how could I abandon them? "It's impossible. Who would take on our account books and collect from our debtors?"

Biting her lower lip, Elizabeth said, "Prevail upon young Mr. Tyler. I'm told he's a fine young lawyer."

With a sharp brow raised, I glanced to the parlor, where my daughter was engaged in close conversation with her cousin Betsy Cranch. "I wonder where you hear that from . . ."

"Your boys," Elizabeth explained. "They say Mr. Tyler is Nabby's very special friend."

Well then, there was no use denying it. While the behavior of the two was without fault, my daughter and Mr. Tyler were so terribly in love that anyone could see it. And, in truth, Mr. Tyler was a convenient man to have around. He made himself useful chopping firewood. He helped collect rents. He ran errands for me. All welcome behavior from a potential son-in-law.

I was also impressed by the large and stately house he'd just purchased in the north precinct of Braintree. It was a *very* fine house in which Nabby might go into housekeeping and bring forth children. Certainly, it was finer than the saltbox in which I'd raised her. No doubt every time Nabby passed Mr. Tyler's new abode, with its elegant front door, she imagined herself its future mistress.

As if following my train of thought, Mary said, "Take Nabby with you to Europe."

I winced. "And separate her from her special friend?"

"It will do her good," Mary advised. "If their love is true, it will survive the separation. Yours has."

I wasn't certain that was true. There had been hours, days, and weeks when I wandered from room to room, feeling myself deserted by John, despairing of lost love. Moreover, I was comfortable without him now. Did I not deserve to enjoy the comfort of the community I'd helped sustain through all the long years of the war?

The truth was, I did not want to go to Europe.

I did not need to go.

So, I did not go.

Instead, I delayed. I answered my husband's letters only sporadically. Perhaps realizing that he had no means by which to force me, John invoked my sense of marital duty. "I am in ill health and cannot live much longer without my wife and daughter. I want two nurses at least."

When that failed, he appealed to my sense of adventure. "Come to Europe with Nabby as soon as possible, satisfy your curiosity, and improve your taste by viewing these magnificent scenes. Go to the play—see the paintings and buildings—I am in earnest."

When that, too, failed, he finally—unexpectedly—appealed to my heart. "Abigail, I cannot be happy, nor even tolerable without you. Pray embark as soon as you can. The moment I hear of your arrival, I'll race with post horses to receive you. And if the balloon should be carried to such perfection as to give mankind safe navigation of the air, I will fly to you."

The warmth of this last letter gave me hope that we might rekindle a love that had nearly been snuffed out. I found myself at my jewel box, thumbing the pendant. The one of the woman and her shield, staring longingly after a ship at sea.

That woman yielded. That woman waited. That woman did not make her own fate.

But I would.

I wouldn't risk everything for marital duty. Nor for adventure. But always in my life I'd risked everything for the call of love. And despite all the pains of recent years, it was still a call I could not deny.

Chapter Twenty-Three

BRAINTREE
Massachusetts
January 1784

N
ABBY WAS CRESTFALLEN. "I presume you don't ask whether
I consent to your leaving this country without me with
any intention of being influenced by my reply."

"I wouldn't have asked otherwise," I said.

"I wish you hadn't," Nabby said, turning away. "I wish I had no
choice in the matter at all."

"I don't understand you, Nabby."

Hugging herself, she said, "I'd rather go from necessity than
choice—the latter would never carry me, the former must."

Nabby felt it was her duty to go with me. She'd been the constant in my life, and I'd been the constant in hers. She feared for
my life and didn't wish me to face the sea alone. "For you, Mama,
I'd willingly sacrifice my happiness, my peace, pleasure, and every
agreeable idea, if only it didn't cause Mr. Tyler such pain."

Oh, hearing this shattered my resolve! "Then forget this madness. I'll appeal again to your father to come home."

Nabby shook her head so vehemently that one errant auburn
lock escaped its pins. "It's my opinion that by going to him, my
father will return much sooner than otherwise."

"Why do you think so?"

"Because he can ignore our letters, but not our tears."

I thought my daughter might be altogether too optimistic about
the powers of our persuasions in the flesh, but then she met my
eyes. "Mama, I've known your sacrifices. I've shared them with you

and dread their continuance. So, I will go with you. What I have said is all I shall ever say on the subject."

With that, she made ready to face the ocean.

She broke the news to her Mr. Tyler, who took it hard, though eventually he conceded. "It's your duty to obey your parents—mine to obey my honor. Let us, therefore, both follow the path of rectitude; and if we're not happy, we shall, at least, deserve to be so."

A few days later, he was in better spirits, proposing marriage. My poor girl nearly swooned, both overcome by the romantic suggestion and fearful of its consequence. "But—my father—my papa—"

This made Mr. Tyler laugh. "I've written to ask his blessing. If he agrees, will you?"

No heart of ice had she! My daughter went pink with pleasure, nodding before she looked to me to know whether I'd countenanced it. In truth, this development took me quite unawares. It also gave me a great deal of relief, for I thought it proper that the young man should finally address her father directly.

But what would John say?

THE HAPPY BRIDE had no father on hand to give her away, and I didn't know what traditions must be observed in this unusual circumstance, but given my love for her, I'd done my best to ensure that marital bliss should be celebrated to everyone's satisfaction.

As the fiddlers took up their instruments and the scent of Indian pudding spiced with cinnamon, ginger, and nutmeg wafted from my kitchen, the groom paced nervously by the pine-garland-festooned fireplace.

Then all eyes turned to Phoebe as she entered wearing her best dress—an English-style pale cotton robe embroidered with sprigs that matched her brown eyes.

We all liked Phoebe's choice in groom well enough, for Mr. Abdee was a respectable gentleman. Certainly, I couldn't fault Phoebe for seeking love and companionship. But I remembered that she'd once said marriage had much in common with the enslavement from which she'd *just* been freed.

When I reminded her of this, she had said, "It's my heart that's the trouble. Since the defeat of the British, it's gone soft with hope. By my reckoning, it's a new world. If the Commonwealth of Massachusetts has seen fit to grant human rights to enslaved people, they'll someday have to give women equality, too."

I hoped she was right, however far off that day might be. But then Phoebe said, "In any case, Honey, you're the very last person who should be questioning what a woman might do for love."

I laughed, helpless to deny it. No one in the family truly wanted me to cross an ocean for John Adams. I still wasn't sure *I* wanted to, either. Nevertheless, I'd spent recent weeks putting my affairs in order, including this one.

I wanted to host Phoebe's nuptials as a token of my love and a farewell to family and loved ones. So, the vows were made, toasts were raised, bread was broken, and jigs were danced across my floor.

Nabby, however, did not dance. She was sad in anticipation of our forthcoming trip and held back from the celebration, no doubt wishing this was her own wedding feast.

"Be of good cheer, my dear girl," I whispered. "When you demonstrate that your love for Mr. Tyler can survive a trip to Europe, you shall have your father's consent and your heart's desire. The sooner we go, the sooner you'll meet marital bliss."

Nabby nodded, trying to reassure herself. "Yes. I have given Mr. Tyler—as a token of affection—my portrait in miniature, and he swears he'll keep it close to his heart and write every day."

"Good. Now join the celebration, because you don't wish for Phoebe to think you begrudge her, do you?"

Nabby flushed. "Of course not. Though it seems some people do . . ."

Her eyes shifted to neighbors who were apparently reluctant to celebrate due to the unusual social mix gathered round my hearth. A sizable portion of the local population of enslaved and freedmen had come to see Phoebe pledge her troth. And, of course, people had biases and bigotries.

Lord knew I still had my own.

But it was a new year, and I hoped it really could be a new world. So, I simply behaved as if it were the most natural thing in the world for different races and religions to celebrate a wedding together and hoped to lead by example.

I started by being downright pleasant to my dour brother-in-law Reverend Shaw, who opposed any dancing at weddings. To distract him from discomfiture, I said, "Thank you for the marvelous job you're doing in educating my boys."

The reverend gave a barely perceptible nod, which was as close to a smile as the man was capable. "I think well of your lads. Charles wishes to be ready for college at fifteen, and Master Tommy is determined that he shall not be outstripped, requesting that he take the same lessons as his brother."

"It's wonderful to hear," I said. "My mind is put at ease knowing that their morals and manners will be strictly attended to while we're abroad."

"Yes, *strictly*," he said.

I hoped he'd not be *so* strict that he sucked all the joy out of my boys. But having settled nearly all my affairs, now all that remained was to reassure those who relied on my generosity—my nieces and nephews, and other pensioners.

They were frightened to see me off. Not only for me, but also for themselves to be left in want. I made presents to my poorer neighbors, reassuring them they'd have a friend and a welcoming presence here in my house while I was gone.

To that end, I spoke to the bride before she was whisked away. "Phoebe, would you and your new husband be willing to live here as caretakers while Mr. Adams and I are abroad?" Not much surprised my old nurse, but this did. And she covered her mouth, which made me regret my presumption. "You mustn't feel obligated," I hastened to say.

"Oh, I'm happy to do it, and I know Mr. Abdee will agree. I'm simply sensible of the honor. You could've asked one of the tenant farmers."

"Oh, I'd never trust a man to look after my teacups or keep the damp out of my furniture. They're always throwing the windows open at night without a single care!"

Phoebe laughed. "Better to ask a kinswoman."

"You *are* my kin," I told her, though I knew it was facile to say. Nevertheless, it felt true. Papa was gone, and she was free without any formal tie or obligation to our family anymore. But I felt a family obligation to *her* and I wanted her to know it.

Phoebe squeezed my hand as her voice dropped to a whisper. "There's something I didn't think was my place to tell, but if we're kin . . ." Her eyes flicked to where Nabby sat by Mr. Tyler. "Miss Nabby can do better."

I was uncertain how to respond. "You must say more. Do you know something about Mr. Tyler that makes him unworthy?"

Phoebe sucked her teeth. "It's the way he rides."

"The way he *rides*? He's a skilled horseman."

"Skilled," Phoebe agreed. "But he applies that whip mighty regular. And you can tell *everything* about a man by the way he treats living creatures in his power."

I couldn't argue that. "You've mentioned this to Nabby?"

Phoebe shook her head. "Might not matter to a girl so much in love, but her mother ought to know. Fortunately, your journey will give you a chance to think."

"Our *journey*," I said, with a rueful headshake. "I will only admit this to you, Phoebe, but I'm terribly frightened."

"Of the ocean or of the man you might find on the other side of it?"

"Both," I confessed. "Decidedly, both."

I WON'T RECOUNT in much detail the pain of taking leave of my boys and other loved ones. Fourteen-year-old Charlie sent us off with a few token locks of his still-golden hair. Eleven-year-old Tommy broke down blubbering that he'd never been so far from his mama and wanting to know why he was the only Adams who was never to see foreign shores.

"We'll be gone only twelve months," I said, kissing away his tears. "Eighteen at most."

Alas, that was an eternity to a child.

Suffice it to say that mine was truly a house of mourning, neighbors, honest yeomanry, and their wives and daughters almost like a funeral procession, all come to wish us well and to pray for a speedy return.

Good Heaven, what were my sensations on this occasion? I'd fortified my mind, determined to possess myself with calmness, but this was too much, so I shook them by the hand, mingling my tears with theirs, and left them.

The next morning in Boston, Nabby said farewell to friends in town while I occupied myself with several important personages who called upon me, including the honorable Thomas Jefferson, esquire, former governor of Virginia.

The primary drafter of the Declaration of Independence had, even then, a developing reputation as a mathematician and philosopher. My husband had always spoken highly of Mr. Jefferson's role in Congress during the grim years of the revolution, but somehow John had never mentioned that the Virginian was so very agreeable to the eye.

With the ginger hair and freckled complexion of a Scotsman, he towered over me at such a height as I'd never seen in any man but George Washington. Which left me to wonder: With what elixir did Virginia water her sons to grow so tall?

Mr. Jefferson bowed to me with a gentlemanly flourish. "Mrs. Adams, I beg your pardon that I carry no letters of introduction," drawled the man who needed none. "They were forgotten in my rush to reach Boston."

"Why, Mr. Jefferson, you're as well known to me as if we met eight years ago. My ears still ring with the immortal words you penned in our Declaration of Independence."

"You are too kind," he said, though I think he was pleased by the praise.

"What brings you to Boston?" I asked.

Jefferson inclined his head, genteelly. "I'm sent to Paris to join forces with your husband on a commission to negotiate treaties of commerce with France. When I learned that you and your daughter were to sail there also, without the protection of father, husband, brother, or son, I hastened hither in hopes of having the pleasure of accompanying you to Paris and of lessening some of the difficulties to which you may be exposed."

"How gallant, sir," I said, genuinely touched.

"I also took the liberty of making arrangements on the French packet, which will sail early next month aboard which I've ensured your choice of accommodations." Then, to reassure me of the propriety of the offer, he added, "I shall have with me my daughter Patsy, who along with her younger sisters has had the misfortune of losing a mother."

I knew little about the circumstances of his loss—only rumors that his wife had died in childbed two years ago in consequence of having to flee the British invasion of Richmond. Now I couldn't help but think back to the last time I was in childbed—alone and frightened, birthing a dead child.

It was only providence that spared my husband from the same widowhood as his Virginian friend. And in the realization of it, a certain tenderness stole over me for Mr. Jefferson. "Sir, you do me a great favor in making this invitation to travel with you. But alas, I'm thirty-six hours away from setting sail for Paris by way of Deal, then London. I've already booked passage and don't think these arrangements can be changed at such a late date."

The gentleman's surprise at my having made all my own arrangements was evident from his intake in breath, but he recovered himself well enough. "Then perhaps I can change my plans and see if there's room for my daughter and me on your vessel. Is it a good ship?"

"It is," I promised. "But you cannot possibly re-order your affairs to accommodate mine. I'm certain you must have many preparations to make, given that you didn't intend to leave for another two weeks."

"I did hope to visit the cities of New England before I go. If I'm to negotiate a commercial treaty on their behalf, it seems advantageous to understand their manufactures."

"Not only advantageous, sir, but necessary for the good of your country. You must keep your plans, even though it deprives me of your amiable company."

Either truly disappointed or a very good actor, he said, "I surrender to the necessity of my country, but might I at least be of service to you in some way before you sail? Is there, perhaps, something you need for the journey that I can procure?"

"I believe I have everything," I said, before remembering, "except something good to read."

"Ah," he said, countenance brightening. "I'm also in need of good reading. Might you accompany me to a bookshop? Which do you recommend?"

"I've not found one I like since Henry Knox closed his store. But he's gone on to grander things."

Jefferson smiled a little tightly, for I gathered he was as concerned as my husband about the new fraternal organization of revolutionary war soldiers styling themselves the Society of the Cincinnati, in which Knox was intimately involved.

I was careful not to criticize Knox, but I did tell Jefferson my worries that this society might usher in the sort of hereditary noble titles we'd just fought a war to extinguish.

"I share your worry, madam," Jefferson said, holding the door for me, as somehow, without realizing it, I'd already assented to join him on a shopping trip. "We shouldn't risk an American aristocracy."

"Still, my heart bleeds to deprive these soldiers of ribbons and decorations they earned. Especially when they're otherwise so poorly rewarded for their service."

Our conversation continued down the street and into a bookstore where, between the rows of pamphlets, we found our tastes and opinions in nearly perfect accord. I caught Jefferson wistfully eyeing a copy of *Tristram Shandy*. "A favorite of mine," he admitted.

"Mine, too. I enjoy its affectionate humor and its indulgence of human foibles."

With a hand over his heart, Jefferson feigned surprise. "Truly, madam. You astonish."

"How so?"

"Because my friend Mr. Adams, while courageous and honest, has led me to believe all New England must be filled with *misanthropes*. Yet here we find in his wife the picture of true benevolence."

I couldn't even take offense on my husband's behalf. Someone who had served so intimately with John—surely experiencing daily his irritability—had the right to poke gentle fun. And together we chuckled at John's expense.

Later, laden down with books and pamphlets, Mr. Jefferson saw me back to my lodgings. "*Bon voyage*, madam. I hope to enjoy your company again soon in Paris. *Au revoir.*"

I smiled and laughed in parting. It was the first time in a very long while that I'd smiled and laughed so easily. And I was grateful to Mr. Jefferson for easing my anxieties for the journey ahead.

To those who'd never been at sea it's impossible to imagine the nausea arising from the smell of the ship. The continual rolling, tossing, and tumbling. I could not count the times Nabby and I retched into a bucket or over the side. It was days before our sickness abated, allowing us to go on deck, where we beheld the vast and boundless ocean before us with astonishment and wonder.

Naturally I had less awe about the filthy ship. To fill the time, I demanded a mop, bucket, and brushes with which Nabby and I could scrub the ship from stem to stern. I believe the captain was grateful for our service, but the cook didn't appreciate my advice about how to spice the food or store his utensils.

"*Mother*," Nabby said, thinking me particularly meddlesome.

"I only offer friendly advice," I protested. "*Everyone* can stand a little improvement."

"Even you?" she asked

"Especially me," I said, newly apprehensive. "I'll have to better myself. For one thing, I shall have to learn how to engage in a parade of debauchery and nonsense at a royal court, where I'm likely to make an awkward figure if my manners remain those of a mere colonist's wife still dressed in homespun."

Nabby looked genuinely surprised. "I didn't know you worried about such things. You're otherwise a person of such certainty."

If only she knew. "It's true I'm not apt to be intimidated, but now we enter upon the world's stage . . ."

In truth, I looked forward to seeing such places as I'd always dreamed of—yet also wondered how I might be received on our stopover in England, for that country had called my husband a traitor not long ago.

After a passage of thirty days from Boston, my daughter and I rejoiced to set our feet again upon land.

Standing there on the British shore, I was overtaken by the enormity of our undertaking. Never in my life had I thought I might travel so far. Most American women lived and died in their own towns. Visiting a city like Boston would be the grandest adventure one might ever attempt. I remembered when even riding to Plymouth had seemed an exotic delight. Now here I was in *England*, a place that used to be my mother country, then my enemy—and now what was it?

She felt like an estranged mother. One with whom relations were still frosty. but from whom I'd learned much—good and bad.

So, what were our impressions after leaving behind forbidding white cliffs battered by the sea? Along the way to London we saw cathedrals of Gothic construction—so gloomy I mistook them as jails for prisoners. Then we came to London, quite unprepared for the crush of people, but I was better pleased with London than I expected. It was a large, magnificent, and beautiful city, with wide streets built straight, the houses uniform, and many fine open squares where the nobility and public buildings resided.

The stalls of Covent Garden featured such a wide array of fruit, vegetables, and flowers that Nabby said it must rival the Garden of Eden. We took a meal of hot pies from a passing vendor before settling into our hotel, where ladies swanned past with decorative fans, lace sleeves, and summer gowns in every pastel shade from carnation to mint, apricot to periwinkle.

While Nabby gawped at the gowns, I gawped at the hotel bill! "These expenses frighten me. The sooner your papa comes to fetch us, the better."

Of course, it wasn't only the expenses that made me anxious for his arrival. It was also the state of agony and doubt in which I'd dwelt for so very long. If I was to find, in reuniting with John, that our hearts had been irretrievably severed, then I should like this blow to strike me swiftly rather than leave me trembling any longer under the hammer.

Chapter Twenty-Four

LONDON
England
August 1784

W E SOON FOUND better lodgings with a friend of my husband's in London. And one afternoon, shortly after being ensconced in our new dwellings, a manservant poked his head into the parlor. "Are you at home, Mrs. Adams?"

I blinked in confusion. "I am right here, sir."

"Quite, madam. Shall I *say* you are at home?"

I stared at him.

He stared back at me.

I was the first to blink. "To whom would you say otherwise, when you can see I am here?"

The manservant gave a long-suffering sigh. "If someone comes to call upon you, and I say that you are *not* at home, a card will be left. If I say that you *are* at home, you would receive visitors."

"You cannot be serious . . ." It would take time to understand the rules and customs of the strange place in which I now found myself. Customs that apparently included routine dishonesty about one's whereabouts. "And what am I to do with these cards?"

"You return the visit at your leisure. If the card was left by someone you don't wish to see, then you return the visit at a time they are similarly unlikely to be at home."

"That will end the matter? Or will the person I do not wish to see then return my visit?"

"They may, indeed, return the visit, madam."

Bewildered, I asked, "Wouldn't that create an endless loop of fruitless visits between people who don't wish to see each other?"

"Precisely, madam. Unless, of course, you wish to offer a deliberate snub."

Blinking, I nearly declared this all to be a ridiculous waste of time, but as my mouth opened to utter the words, I remembered I was a diplomat's wife. It wouldn't do to disparage the rules of British society if my husband was now to promote good relations between nations.

Besides, I didn't expect that I'd receive many visitors.

In that, I turned out to be quite wrong.

To my astonishment, former American colonists who had fled to London during the war now left an avalanche of little cards. And perusing the names on these cards, Nabby asked, "Do you think these Tories have come to admit they were wrong?"

My ill-mannered cousin Samuel Quincy, who had once threatened to sail to England and leave his wife behind, had done just that during the war. I hoped to see his name on one of the cards, but my hope was in vain. "People don't like admitting a mistake. More likely those who have called upon us believe I might help them return home or better their circumstances here."

"Then you should return the visits," Nabby said, surprising me. "Because I think you'll take great satisfaction in offering Loyalists forgiveness while drinking their tea."

I laughed. "Do you think me so petty?"

With a quirk of her lips, she replied, "I know my mother to be a godly woman for whom observing Christian charity—no matter the incidental vindication—offers the sweetest reward."

Thus, absolving myself of my smugness toward those who once cursed us but now curried favor, I returned these visits eagerly and with good cheer.

This and the marvels of London occupied my time.

I was fascinated by the shocking grandeur of Westminster Abbey, so large that footsteps echoed as we explored the monuments to dead kings and queens. I was amused by colorfully dressed jugglers in the Hay Market while hawkers tried to sell us roasted chestnuts. And I was refreshed by the verdant splendor of Kew Gardens with its great, red-painted pagoda ornamented with gilded dragons.

All this offered distraction as we waited for John to come from The Hague.

But still, what took so long? If I'd come across an ocean only to be deserted again, I would not account for my actions!

One afternoon while I attended my correspondence in the main parlor, the butler burst in with a surprising lack of decorum. "Mr. Adams is come! The young Mr. Adams that is."

Johnny? Overcome with excitement at the unexpected arrival of my eldest boy, I leaped to my feet. "Where is he? Downstairs in the parlor?"

"In the guesthouse, madam. He stopped to get his hair dressed."

"His hair?" I laughed, perplexed, for no son of mine had heretofore so much as straightened his waistcoat to make himself presentable for his mother. It had been hard enough to make my boys wash their faces, comb their hair, and wear clean stockings! The idea that my eldest son now felt the need for a *barber* before greeting his mama confounded me entirely.

When Johnny finally crossed the threshold, I drew back, not really believing my eyes. Good God. John Quincy Adams was no longer one of my boys. He'd grown into a man. His jaw and shoulders squared. His cheeks freshly shaved, but a whisper of hair upon the backs of his hands. Truly, if it weren't for his penetrating dark eyes, I wouldn't have known him as my own dear son.

Much taller than me now, Johnny had to stoop to take me into his embrace. "Oh, Mama! And my dear sister, now a lady!"

His *voice* was changed, too. When I last set eyes on him, it had been high and boyish. Now at the age of seventeen, his voice had a depth to match his stature. And I couldn't find words to express the feelings that overcame me. *Pride*, perhaps, to see the boy that I birthed grown into a self-sufficient man of the world.

Grief, too, to have missed so many years of his growing.

"My boy," I kept saying, grasping his hands. I supposed I ought to call him Master Jack now. He dressed like a young nobleman, and his hair was powdered like one, too. I could scarcely believe that he belonged to me.

In the days that followed, he entertained us with tales from the Empress Catherine's court at Saint Petersburg. "I wish I could tell you how very cold it is in Russia, but it's also a very criminal place and someone stole my thermometer almost upon arrival." He made us laugh and he piqued our curiosity. In speaking of Russian religious traditions, Johnny said, "Easter is a great holiday. They present each other with colored eggs."

"*Eggs?*" Nabby asked, puzzled.

He explained the holy symbolism to her, then followed it with a story truly unfit for his sister's ears. "At court it was rumored that Catherine the Great has a special room with exotic furniture where she takes her lovers. Of course, I cannot confirm it, as, I regret to say, she never invited me there."

"*John Quincy,*" I scolded, though he only laughed. And as Nabby tried not to do the same, I knew I would forgive him anything. I couldn't stop looking at him, touching him, and marveling at the miracle of this reunion.

But another reunion was yet to come . . .

I was now so anxious to see my husband that my hands daily shook. Even if our love still burned, would the resentments and disappointments finally gutter out the torch? I couldn't know until I laid eyes upon him. After all these years, would he be a stranger to me?

I might, indeed, be a stranger to *him*.

I'd carefully hidden my wounds. I'd pretended that his desires were law to me, all while becoming my own mistress. It'd be far more difficult to keep up a ruse of self-abnegation when my husband could look into my eyes. Would he still love the woman he found behind their surface? For that matter, would he still love the surface?

Standing before a mirror, I smoothed my dressing gown over my belly, frustrated by the fleshiness of my hips. I'd eaten very little during our voyage at sea. What I had eaten, I'd thrown back up. Yet, I hadn't wasted away even a little. Indeed, I'd survived a decade of scarcity and hunger without becoming thin, which made me believe that nothing less than death would ever carry away my flesh.

Certainly, I'd never again have the tiny waist of my youth. I'd given up on that idea after the birth of my children. But what I saw now was a matronly and unfashionable woman. Well, that settled it. Both Nabby and I needed new clothes, and my husband had written that we should spend whatever was necessary to make ourselves presentable in the public eye.

So, my daughter and I set about getting ourselves *pretty*. We visited the stay maker, the mantua maker, the hoop maker, the shoemaker, the milliner, and the hairdresser—all necessary to transform me into a fashionable lady of London.

And how bold these English ladies were, wearing their hats at a jaunty angle like gentlemen! Of course, this appealed to Nabby, who insisted upon a riding habit. "Mama, riding habits are perfectly acceptable attire for women here in all manner of situations I wouldn't have expected!"

I worried she might appear to be an Amazon, given that she'd inherited a taller frame than the rest of the family. But I indulged her if only because, having been dragged to Europe against the inclinations of her heart, she had a right to any small enjoyment fashion could afford.

Moreover, I was pleased by her sudden curiosity. Nabby wanted to see everything, and with her brother, she strolled the British Museum marveling over ancient artifacts. They saw Shakespeare's plays performed at Drury Lane. They enjoyed late-night fireworks at Vauxhall Gardens and were out again at sunrise the next morning with the energy of two young people on holiday.

Try as I might, I simply couldn't keep up with them.

One Saturday morning before the rooster crowed, a soft knock came at my door. I ignored it, pulling the lavender-scented bed linens higher round my shoulder and burrowing down into the feather pillow for more slumber.

The knock came again.

Assuming it was my children come to wake me, I peeked out from behind the damask curtains of the four-postered bed to murmur, "I'm too weary to join you this morning. I'm going to sleep in late."

The door opened with a squeak of hinges to reveal my husband in the low flickering light of a lamp. I gasped. I hoped this vision of John was a mere byproduct of my sleepy haze, because I hadn't wished for our reunion to be this way.

I'd picked a new gown, a wig, and jewelry in which to greet him, but now I was in disarray with sand in my eyes and curls having escaped my sleeping bonnet. My hands flew to my hair to straighten it, but John crossed the carpeted room with hurried steps and dropped at my bedside, bareheaded, dusty from his travels.

Our eyes both went teary as we beheld one another for the first time in so very many years. My first words were both a sob and a sputter of relieved laughter. "*Oh, John.*"

"Yes, it is I," he said, huskily. "But are you Abigail? Because I've never heard my wife express a wish *to sleep in late.* Are you sure that you are she?"

No, I wanted to say. *No, I am very much changed.*

So was he—at least in appearance. John was still stout and solid. But as my trembling hands caressed the thinning of what hair he still had, I couldn't help but feel renewed worry for his health. His eyelids sagged, his pallor was alarmingly ashen, and his hands were swollen in mine.

I whispered. "*Husband, husband, husband*," as if to convince myself he was the same man.

Pressing a kiss into my palm, he murmured, "*My beloved wife, my dearest friend . . .*"

I didn't wish to break the spell, but my worries overcame loftier emotions, and I couldn't hold them in. "How tired you look."

"Only because I've been traveling all night, my dear. Rest assured, I'm twenty years younger than I was yesterday. By coming to me, you've made me the happiest man upon earth."

Despite everything, I smiled to hear it. In fact, I let out another unexpected laugh, a sputter of joy and relief merely to be *touched.* My skin wanted to soak it in like a thirsty desert as he folded me into the conjugal tenderness of an embrace. So many years I'd gone without a caress that my tears now flowed in a torrent. They wet his face and mine.

Though I turned away, pressing the base of my palms to my cheeks to hold them back, they poured silently down my wrists in rivulets to my elbows.

If he'd asked why I was crying, I couldn't have explained. Even if I understood all the reasons, I wouldn't have dared. Because the years of yearning, disappointment, anger, and hurt—they might've all come pouring out with my tears. So, I was silent.

At length, John stroked my shoulder and said, "How terribly I have abused your love." I shook my head to deny it, but he knew me too well. "Abigail, let us not add dishonesty to the distance I've put between us. I know I've wronged you. I've cursed myself a scoundrel even *as* I wronged you. And yet, still I wronged you. Probably in more ways than even I know."

I could only stammer. "I have felt—I have *been*—so alone."

Somberly, he nodded, lowering his head.

"That first year, John, when you didn't write with any tenderness—"

"I *could* not, Abigail," he started to argue. "I was surrounded by spies and didn't wish for the British to use my tenderest vulnerabilities against me." He trailed off, then let out a sigh as his shoulders slumped. "The truth is I thought I had good reasons, but I was too wrought up in my own vanity. I knew you were in distress, and I could've done better by you. I should have."

At the sob that escaped me, I saw a new flash of pain in his expression. It wasn't easy for John Adams to admit when he was wrong. But he admitted it now. "If I made you doubt my love, it's the greatest regret of my life. I am sorry, Abigail."

I took a moment to becalm myself. Then I thought it best to bring levity. "You are very thorough in your pleadings, sir."

With a quaver in his voice, he whispered, "A good lawyer knows when to throw himself upon the mercy of the court. I've been a faithful husband, but not a good one. I mean to remedy that now. If you'll still have me and if you're still mine. I know it will take time to forgive, but I will do everything I can to win back your love."

"You never lost it," I said, wiping the tears from his face and then my own. "Not even when I willed it so. I've told myself many lies to survive, but in the end, I'm still most affectionately, most tenderly yours and only yours and wholly yours."

It was not then and there all resolved between us, of course. How could it be after so many years of pain? Yet, I knew this to be a new start between us.

When we were young, we used to jest we were akin to steel and the magnet—always pulled together. I'd always assumed my husband to be the steel, but now I thought him the magnet. Because even with so much still unsettled, I was drawn to kiss him.

Poets and painters wisely draw a veil over those scenes that surpass the pen of the one and the pencil of the other. And so as for what happened next, I, too, shall draw a veil.

Later, propped on pillows, we spoke of our children.

"And how do you like our son?" my husband asked, his fingers tangled with mine.

I grinned. "How grown Johnny is! A real man of action. He's rented a coach for our travel—made all the arrangements needing no advice from me whatsoever."

"Did I not speak truly when I said he was the greatest traveler of his age and without partiality as promising and manly a youth as anywhere in the world?"

"You were truthful, indeed. Now, believe *me* when I say what a fine young lady our daughter has become."

My husband sighed happily. "My princess. My jewel. I cannot wait to see her. Shall we wake her?"

Given the sunlight blazing in the window, I said, "She's no doubt already gone out without realizing you're here. She's enjoying the city with her brother—and deserves the enjoyment. She's been a great comfort to me, you know, all these years."

"As has her brother been a great comfort to me. Johnny is everything you could wish him. Miss Nabby's *special friend* must rise in the legal profession quickly or he'll be overtaken by her worthy brother."

I hadn't expected John to raise the specter of Mr. Tyler quite so soon. Now I readied myself to explain the perplexing matter. "Speaking of Miss Nabby's special friend . . ."

"Is she terribly glum without him?" John asked. "I'm surprised you didn't marry her off and have them look after the house."

My eyes popped open. "Marry her off? After you made such objections? Though I've become a bold woman, I'm not *that* bold."

John tilted his head. "But I gave my assent back at the start of the year when I began to think the delay in your coming to me might be because of this entanglement. I realized how bullheaded I'd been. How little cause I had to judge a situation from across the sea. How my trust in you should be commensurate with the responsibility placed in your hands. I sent a letter saying Nabby should listen to you, in whose wisdom I have the greatest confidence."

Oh, how time and distance and a disruption of the mail could change everything! "We never received that letter. It must have miscarried."

I imagined the precious missive dumped into the sea. Fluttering in the dirt on the roadside. Or perhaps it had been sent to Mrs. Samuel Adams by mistake. It gave me a twitch at the temples to think of all the ways in which such an important letter might go astray.

That twitch became a genuine ache in the head when John said, "Well, no matter. The young man in question wrote asking my consent to a union with our daughter, and I gave it."

Now my breath caught in distress. "I knew he'd written for consent to wed, but you gave it?"

"Yes, and quite graciously, too. I told him to make free use of my law library. I said I prayed God would bless the pair." My husband looked well-pleased with himself, and a small bit confused by my reaction. "Isn't that what you wished?"

"Well." I squinted in the morning light as it fell over my pillow. "It *was* what I wished, but then . . ."

Given the turn of events, did I dare confide in him the doubts Phoebe had planted? They were, perhaps, trivial complaints. And I didn't wish to poison my husband against the man who would become our son-in-law.

Having received my husband's blessing, the betrothal could be considered akin to a signed contract. So Nabby's options had abruptly, and considerably, narrowed. Thus, I didn't speak to John of misgivings. I only said, "I hoped to see whether distance would weaken the bonds of affection. I suppose it should be enough to reassure us that having been kept from a union this long, their affection remains unflagging."

John, in a jovial and decidedly nostalgic mood, said, "It still vexes me to think how long your parents kept us from marrying. It was, of course, a seemingly prudent course of action from loving parents. But now, greedily, I wish to have back every moment they kept us apart."

Kissing the corner of his mouth, I said, "Well, then, husband, before we leave for France, let us make up for lost time."

Chapter Twenty-Five

I FELT MYSELF A young woman again. It was my joy in my husband, in my children, and in the world itself that made me so. Never had any family had so agreeable a journey—feasting on picnic lunches, reading aloud to one another, and laughing over jests until our sides hurt.

John and I were raucous with merriment and our children both teased us for our volubility. In return, we wondered aloud how two garrulous parents might have produced such constrained progeny. For where his father's sense of humor was lively and playful, Johnny's was quiet and dry as a bone, and his sister always apprehended it first, snickering behind her fan.

As for France, it was a marvel to us. Everywhere we looked, something novel and interesting came into view. But the countryside was poorer than England's. The sight of downtrodden peasants working the fields certainly sobered us. And John warned, "You'll smell Paris before you see it."

It was true; Paris was dirtier than London—shockingly so— and from the carriage window, I stared openmouthed at noblewomen in ridiculously tall wigs walking not far from where notorious whores openly plied their wares.

"It takes getting accustomed to," John said. "But this is a delicious country. Everything that can soothe, charm, and bewitch is here."

"*Indeed?*" I asked archly, as a scantily clad woman passed while both husband and son pretended not to notice.

At length, under my scrutiny, John laughed. "Fine. I admire the ladies here. Don't be jealous. They're handsome and their accomplishments are brilliant. Their knowledge of letters and arts exceeds that of the English ladies, I believe. Then again, I think women better than men in general."

"Since when?" I snapped my fan. "I think you say it with hopes of earning my pardon."

John grinned. "Is it having the desired effect? No matter. All will be forgiven when you see the house I secured for you."

To save on costs, our house would be in Auteuil, four miles outside the city. And as our carriage rolled down the lane, I stared at the white stone, the carved archways, the tall glass doors. "This cannot be our house."

Stepping down from the carriage, John offered me his hand. "It is for our time here."

I remained in shock, for our little saltbox in Braintree was but a hovel by comparison. "But this is much larger than we need. How many rooms?"

"I'm told forty beds may be made in it," John said.

"Forty!" I froze. Would I play hostess to so many? And who would keep so many fires lit? "It must be cold in winter."

John led me inside. Dining room to the right, with faded blue silk draperies. Elegant salon to the left with pools of light on the floor. Beyond the glass doors: a garden spilling with roses, orange trees, and china vases of flowers. My hands flew to my mouth at the sight.

"Why, Mrs. Adams," John teased. "I do believe you're in raptures."

I couldn't even reply, stumbling out into the garden to discover green, gold, and crimson bursts of growing things in geometric plots. A wall of grapevines. A fountain.

Oh, the hours I could pass in this paradise . . .

While I stooped to smell a fragrant white flower, Nabby called excitedly from the house. "Mother! Did you see these clever floors?"

John steered me back inside, where my reverie was brought to earth by the state of the place—it was quite dirty. It would take twenty maids to scour it clean. Still, beneath sheets we found fine furniture and mirrored rooms, paintings and carved fireplaces, to say nothing of an elegant bathing convenience set in a room of mirrors.

As for the floors that fascinated Nabby, they were made of strips of wood resembling black walnut that were fashioned into squares.

"It's a parquet floor," Johnny explained. "It must be brushed and waxed instead of washed."

Sighing, I said, "As always, it seems beauty comes with inconvenience."

Nabby waved her fan. "You insisted we scrub the decks of a ship, Mama. You wouldn't know what to do with yourself if you weren't keeping busy."

John arched a quizzical brow, and I shrugged. "Those decks were filthy."

"No doubt," John said with mirth. "You won't be doing the brushing and waxing here, my dear. We'll have servants."

"Did she really swab the decks of your ship?" Johnny whispered to his sister.

Nabby laughed, murmuring in reply, "More than once."

With an exaggerated sigh, I feigned a stern look. "Whatever have I done to have such saucy children?"

Johnny kissed my cheek. "We were merely lauding your industriousness."

"Spoken like a budding diplomat," I said, grinning as my impertinent offspring made off to explore. In truth, the playfulness between them absolutely delighted me.

The family apartments upstairs allowed us each our own chambers. Mine connected to my husband's. Johnny and Nabby would share a sitting room, where I already knew she'd spend every day writing to Mr. Tyler.

"It's a wonderful house," I said, clasping John's hand. "At least it *will* be wonderful once I set up housekeeping here."

I'd need bed linen, table linen, spoons and forks, tea furniture, china for the table, and all this to say nothing of the servants we must procure. I soon learned France had a policy about servants. A coachman would do nothing but carriages and horses. A hairdresser would not sweep the room—that was for the chambermaid. And no one but the frotteur de parquet would polish the floors and empty the chamber pots—which I was appalled to learn everyone used for dirty business rather than go outside.

Living here would be costly beyond my imagination, but John promised it would be less expensive than setting up a household in Paris.

Our first guest was Dr. Franklin, who poured himself an overfull glass of wine. And when my husband stared a little too pointedly, knowing his colleague suffered from gout, Franklin defiantly drank it down in one long gulp. "Mr. Adams," he said, wiping his mouth, "don't you know that wine is constant proof that God loves us and loves to see us happy?"

I laughed, but John did not.

In the Continental Congress, Franklin had worked harmoniously with my husband. Unfortunately, tensions between them had erupted in Europe, where my husband had concluded Franklin was a talented patriot but an irredeemable libertine. In turn, Franklin had written that John "means well for his country, is always an honest man, often a wise one, but sometimes and in some things absolutely out of his senses."

Privately, I thought both men to be substantially correct.

Thankfully the responsibility of moderating between them fell to their new colleague on the commission, the dangerously amiable Mr. Jefferson, who finally arrived in Paris with his daughter Patsy—a lovely young girl of eleven or twelve.

Patsy was all her father with ginger hair and freckled nose, but she'd come in such a state as only a motherless daughter might, without proper clothes or shoes for a girl her age. I set out at once to help remedy that. Meanwhile, Nabby took the lonely girl under her wing in friendship despite their age difference.

"Thank you for trying to put Miss Jefferson at ease," I told Nabby one afternoon, thinking it was good for my daughter to have someone to think about besides her betrothed.

"She's a sweet girl and her manners are lovely," Nabby replied over tea. "I only worry that she can scarcely tear her eyes away from her father. Mr. Jefferson is her sun and her moon."

"She's no doubt frightened to take her eyes off him. She lost her mother and now finds herself here in France, a place with odd customs and a language difficult to master."

I, too, struggled to speak French, though I could read and write it tolerably well. Thus I counted myself lucky to have a close circle of English-speaking friends for society, including the delicate and charming Mrs. Angelica Schuyler Church and her British husband, a dealer in armaments for our side who'd therefore had to go by an alias during the war. In addition to the venerable old Dr. Franklin, there was his friend Dr. Bancroft, a renowned scientist and secretary to the American diplomatic mission. Another handsome Virginian, twenty-four-year-old Mr. William Short, served as Thomas Jefferson's personal secretary. And, of course, there was Mr. Jefferson himself, who was unfailingly kind to both my children, inviting them to outings in Paris and making them both feel quite sophisticated.

Mr. Jefferson was gallant with Nabby at musical occasions, and a fine mentor for Johnny, taking him on scientific expeditions. And my husband—who had a complaint about every man he ever met—simply *adored* Jefferson. Truly, I'd never seen him take to anyone like that before.

"He's an excellent hand," John gushed as he told me of their work negotiating protection for American ships against the Barbary pirates. "Congress couldn't have sent better. Since Jefferson's arrival, our affairs have gone on with the utmost harmony."

"You sound smitten," I teased.

John swatted this sauciness away. "He's an old friend with whom I worked through many knotty problems. Age has only seasoned his steadiness and abilities. I don't trust easily, but I trust in Thomas Jefferson."

Personally, I found the Virginian to be a wonderful conversationalist. Over tea in our window-filled conservatory, I found that everything interested him, from politics to architecture, and from animal bones to even the plant I brought with me on the trip, sitting now on a marble-topped console table, gilded with finely carved vine leaves and grapes.

"It vegetates in air?" Jefferson asked, eyes wide with wonder.

"You must wet it once a week," I explained. "That is all. It requires no soil. You simply set it upon a table near a window and it thrives."

"Wherever did you come upon such a plant?"

"It was a gift from a friend who visited Connecticut," I said, warming to the subject. I brought it as an American marvel to impress the Europeans, and it was the only bit of my gardening I could trust to a sea voyage. "I don't know if the plant is native to that place. Dr. Franklin believes it may be called Tillandsia. Or he says it is perhaps an orchid or fungus of some kind."

"A wondrous thing no matter its name," Jefferson said, peering closer. "Does it flower?"

"I didn't think so, but since bringing it to Europe, I was surprised to see it bloom."

Jefferson gave a grin that tilted toward rakish. "Much like you, my dear Mrs. Adams?"

This was gallantly understated flirtation, which made me flush with pleasure. "I forgive your impertinence because you make an apt comparison. During the war, I went so long without the companionship of my dearest friend that I sometimes felt as if I, too, must subsist only on the nourishment I could grasp from the air."

The widowed Jefferson suddenly sobered. "Yes. Sometimes we must learn to thrive without our beloved companions. For the sake of our children, if for no other reason."

Realizing I'd stumbled into a tender place, I gave him a moment to collect himself. My eyes drifted across the garden to where our girls sat—Patsy weaving together a necklace of flowers for Nabby. "It is a delight to see them together."

"It is." His blue eyes warmed as he watched the girls. "A friend from America is a comfort for Patsy. Is your daughter as homesick as mine?"

I tapped my chin. "Difficult to say. Nabby is separated just now from her betrothed, and it dampens her mood."

Jefferson shook his head and offered some reason for optimism. "Oh, young Miss Adams may be down in the dumps now, but the education she shall receive here will be worth it."

"Ah, the education of young ladies! You've hit upon one of my favorite topics . . ."

I thought he might laugh, but instead he laced his hands behind his back in thoughtful contemplation. "It is a subject very much on my mind. I'd like Patsy to learn the best poets and even the graver sciences. She may one day head a little family whose education will probably rest on her alone because the chance she will draw a blockhead in marriage I calculate at about fourteen to one."

My laughter tinkled like a French fountain. "A grim calculation, sir."

Jefferson laughed a little, too. "I envy you sons, whose futures are in their own hands. To be the parent of daughters seems a more fraught exercise."

"But uniquely rewarding."

That elicited an unexpectedly tender smile. "So true. In the hour of my greatest loss it was my daughters who were my solace, comfort, and tie that bound me to earth. Especially Patsy."

It'd been two years since the loss of his wife; yet, still, I heard his raw pain in speaking of it. Like me, he seemed to harbor too much sensibility. Like me, he'd been forced to leave his two youngest children with relatives in America. Like me, in his loneliness, he'd forged a tight bond with his eldest daughter. We had more in common than I might've ever supposed, and I wanted very much to make him a friend. Especially since I had so few others in this new country.

To remedy this isolation, I wished to become acquainted with France's educated ladies. For years, my husband had written to me of their excellence and sophistication. Mr. Jefferson also alluded to Frenchwomen's prominent role in political matters. None so prominent, they said, as the wealthy widow Madame Helvétius, whose salons were frequented by luminaries like Diderot, Condorcet, and Turgot.

They said she was the model Frenchwoman, and that sculptors, politicians, jurists, and playwrights all attended her while her eighteen ribbon-adorned Angora cats mingled amongst the guests.

But I could scarcely believe this when we encountered her at a visit to Dr. Franklin's house, where she came with not cats but a little lapdog she carried into the parlor.

She threw herself upon a settee in such a way as to expose leg and thigh and my daughter blinked in shock, which caused her brother Johnny to whisper something, and both made faces behind her fan.

But the wealthy widow wasn't even slightly abashed. She sprawled, crooning to her little dog, who piddled by my foot.

Jumping away, I said, "Oh, he's made a mess. Let me call for a towel."

Madame Helvétius pressed a finger to her lips. "Please do not. Dr. Franklin accuses me of loving this little dog more than I love him. So, we must keep this our secret."

With that, she used the hem of her gown to wipe up the puddle. Then she disappeared into the crowd of guests who went outside.

Am I dreaming what I just saw?

"It would seem the lady's rank sets her above the little formalities of modesty and cleanliness," said Mr. Jefferson, who had, until this moment, situated himself in the corner by a potted plant, quiet and mysterious as a sphinx.

Abashed, I cried, "So it seems!"

"Would that we might all be excused from formalities," Jefferson continued, offering me a small pastry from the sideboard. "The expense of appropriate garments for court at Versailles has me afraid to examine the receipts."

Nibbling the proffered pastry, I commiserated with him. "I feel the same every time I review our books. It seems quite unconscionable what Congress thinks diplomats should be able to survive on."

Jefferson's head tilted in what seemed to be genuine surprise. "Mr. Adams permits you to review accounting books?"

I'd become a manager of finances by necessity during the war, but I supposed a gentleman of Virginia would consider it unladylike to continue the practice. So, I was careful with my words. "Oh, yes. Mr. Adams is so accustomed to the role of statesman that he prefers to leave matters of smaller importance in my less-capable hands."

My hands were more than capable, and I'd saved us quite a bit of money over the past ten years by countermanding my husband's instructions when they made no financial sense. So, John now really preferred not to be troubled by money. But I didn't wish to diminish my husband in the eyes of a colleague, so I diminished myself instead. "With prices what they are here in France, I fear Mr. Adams's trust in me may be misplaced. My meager talent at economy will not prevent us from being losers by the year's end."

"I feel the same pain," Jefferson said, and I didn't doubt it, because he'd taken a house in Paris proper and was sending his daughter to take her education in an exclusive convent school.

I gently expressed my worries about young Patsy being exposed to papist thought there, but Mr. Jefferson reassured me religion would be no part of her education. And to lessen my prejudice, he sent tickets for us to witness a ceremony of nuns about to take the veil.

Between this and John taking me to visit the hospital for abandoned infants, I learned nuns provided love and tenderness to these little orphans. But what could account for the number of abandoned children here in France?

As a mother, I couldn't understand it. It hardened me against the French. I didn't care for their morals, their manners, or their mode of living. And though we were on a diplomatic mission, I worried that judgment would show upon my face to every person here. For my heart and soul felt more American than ever. But like that hardy plant from Connecticut, I'd have to find a way to thrive here without my native soil.

Chapter Twenty-Six

I T WON'T HURT as much as you think it will," John Quincy said, helping me into the carriage. In this, my son was echoing his father, who insisted I must summon the courage to leave our safe little circle of American friends and go calling.

I had special cards for the occasion, with my name printed on one side in a decorative frame of laurel. The back was blank for any message I might wish to write.

I'd provided the driver with the addresses of ladies upon whom I meant to call—and the driver took some umbrage, as if I thought him incapable of knowing his way around Paris.

Thankfully my eldest son, with his well-trained courtly manners, soothed tempers and now assured me of a painless affair. "You'll simply have your servant knock, ask for the lady, and wait to be told whether she's at home."

Well, of course, none of these French ladies were *at home* when I called. And why should they be? I was merely a stranger sprinkling my card all over Paris like seed corn.

Knock. Ask for the lady. Leave the card.

From my carriage, I watched my servant repeat this for several hours until we finally reached one of the grandest homes in all Paris—the Hôtel de Noailles—and the last name on my list.

The Marquise de Lafayette.

The formidable doorman in livery of red with gold lace said the lady was not at home. The card was left, the gates closed, and my servant returned to my carriage grateful to be done with this business for the day.

However, no sooner had our carriage wheels started to turn than did appear that same doorman, banging on the side of the coach to make us stop. Breathless, he said, "*Excusez-moi, madame, je suis désolé.*"

As it happened, the lady was indeed at home, and she was now waiting in the majestic doorway, my card in hand. "Mrs. Adams, I am happy to be seeing you by your visiting. So happy!"

Thereupon Lafayette's young wife threw her arms around my neck like an old friend and pressed kisses to my cheeks with such warmth that it melted my New England reserve. Breathlessly, and in tolerably good English, she said, "I pray you forgive the mistake. Today I am in a family way with mother and sisters—who you must meet."

She took me to her ornate chambers where the women of her family were indeed knitting together in familiarity—and I was sensible of the honor to be admitted into such intimate company, so I tried not to gawp at the gilded mirrors, silvered sconces, and ornate moldings. Everything elegant, expensive, and refined as far as the eye could see.

I was introduced to the lady's mother and sisters, who were all most kind to me. Then the marquise said, "I foresee we will make good friends, Mrs. Adams, for the sake of our husbands. As mine teaches me to love Americans."

I happily recounted for her the few meetings I had with her heroic young husband during the war, and she expressed regret he couldn't greet me himself, as he'd recently returned to America for a visit with George Washington at Mount Vernon. "But you must be meeting the children," she enthused, sending nursemaids to fetch the heir, four-year-old Georges; his older sister, Anastasie; and his younger sister, Virginie, who was just learning to talk.

I saw how fond and attentive she was to them—which was very much *not* the custom for women of her class. But the Marquise de Lafayette was a different sort of lady than I'd come to expect. She was pious and possessed the gentlest ease in her manners that can possibly be conceived of. Almost studied as an art and rendered as nature. Best of all, she was thoughtful—so much so that she gifted me with a little songbird.

"To remind you of your dear boys left in America. When you told me how much you missed them, you mentioned your Charles loved songbirds, so I hope this puts you in remembering him. Unfortunately, I do not know how to remember your Thomas for you."

"This little bird will make me remember both boys," I said, touched by the noblewoman's gesture. In truth, I also came to love that little French bird in its cage. In the weeks that followed, it chirped to cheer me every day, making me think even more fondly of Adrienne Lafayette.

The marquise eventually came to dine at our home dressed neatly, but without rouge, diamonds, or elaborate coiffure. And to my surprise, I heard the American women at my table whisper with sneering disdain. "No lady of *our* country would go to dinner so unadorned."

Irritated, I remembered what Jefferson had said about Madame Helvétius and repeated it this time with sincerity. "The lady's rank sets her above the little formalities of dress. For her husband is a hero of our revolution, and she presents herself with the simplicity of a good republican."

In truth, Adrienne was so wonderful a creature that I felt ashamed of myself for forming too hastily a bad opinion of France and the French. And though Lafayette's wife was closer in age to my daughter Nabby than she was to me, we did indeed become good friends.

When I complimented her wisdom for a young woman of only twenty-four years, Adrienne said, "It is because I was forcing to put away childish things too soon. The custom in our country for families like mine is to marrying young. I was myself betrothed at only thirteen."

I hoped I'd misunderstood. "Ten years and three?"

She nodded. "It is why the husbands and wives in France do not love. We are just children when matching." Her doe eyes went soft and wistful. "I was married before capable of love. But my friends made so wise a choice for me that I learned to love *mon Gilbert* with all my heart."

Hearing this, Nabby blushed a little, which led me to tell the Frenchwoman about my daughter's betrothed. Nabby, of course, had nothing to say—seemingly mortified by the discussion. And as she stared out the window, I gave an exasperated laugh. "She has been a quiet girl most of her life. Silent and sad."

"What does it mean, *sad*?" Adrienne asked.

"*Triste*," Nabby replied. "Mama believes me to be *triste* by nature."

"Oh, no, I do not think so," Adrienne said at once. "If I am a physiognomist, I say Miss Adams is not *triste*. She is grave. A serious girl thinking serious thoughts in a serious world."

This characterization absolutely delighted Nabby, who repeated it several times to forestall my criticisms. And while I couldn't entirely discredit what Adrienne said, I knew my daughter well enough to know her silences—and the one she fell into by winter was *triste* indeed.

"Mr. Tyler does not write me," Nabby finally admitted.

"Be patient," I told her. "I've written Mrs. Warren numerous letters and have yet to receive a reply. Those letters must make a long journey over the ocean. They're often lost."

Nabby crossed her arms. "Less so, one would think, now that there is no war."

I was sorry to see the way a lack of letters soured her mood; she was, in this way, too much like her mother. For weeks she'd thrown herself into our travels, eager to improve her French, practicing with me every day. But now, with no letters from her betrothed, she withdrew into a silence so long and so provoking that it annoyed even the hairdresser.

Working Nabby's locks into a high coiffure, she asked whether the pins were too tight. "*Les épingles à cheveux vous font-elles mal, mademoiselle?*"

Nabby did not answer.

Only when I poked my daughter did she murmur, "I'm sorry. I do not speak French."

And the hairdresser snapped, "Mademoiselle does not speak English, either!"

I laughed at that, but then and there I decided that Nabby needed cheering.

Diversion was to be the order of the day. So, while my husband attended court in Versailles, we shared mid-day meals with American ladies. We supped with French ladies in the evening. And because Paris was so much less dangerous than London—perfectly safe for ladies to traverse without fear of pickpockets—we did our share of sightseeing at ease. We took chocolate in a shop outside the Tuileries Garden and looked for bargains in boutiques. We saw *Figaro* at the Comédie-Française, though Nabby airily dismissed it as a production of *low wit*.

We dined with Mr. Jefferson and his daughter most nights. On one evening when we were entertaining foreign diplomats, the ambassador of Sweden made eyes at my daughter and leaned over to tell Johnny, "Your sister is of such perfect porcelain complexion that she looks ten years younger than anyone else her age in France."

My poor son was torn between what he felt was his diplomatic duty and his duty as a brother to warn the man off. He nearly tore his cloth napkin to shreds in his fisted palm, which *did* make his sister laugh.

In the new year we toured the courts of justice with its grand architecture. We browsed glassware in the shopping arcades, running our fingertips over the smooth and intricately designed decanters and perfume bottles. Jostling for good deals, I found gifts to send home: sweets for Charlie and Tommy, ribbons for my sisters, and lace kerchiefs for Phoebe.

We went to see the hot-air balloon land in Paris, followed by a tour of Notre-Dame, in all its awe-striking grandeur. Truly, the gigantic gray structure with its fascinating gargoyles made me feel humbled as a human being!

Then came a celebration in early January when the servants followed the chicken course with an especially large pie. My husband eyed it suspiciously. "What is this?"

"Tomorrow is to be celebrated La Fête des Rois," our servant replied, as if we should know what this celebration portended. But it was quite impossible to keep track of these celebrations because the religion of this country required an abundance of feasting and fasting, and each person had his particular saint, as well as each calling and occupation.

"It's to celebrate the three magi," Johnny said, always informed. "The tradition is to serve a galette with a bean hidden inside. Whoever is served the slice with the bean is dubbed king or queen for the day."

My husband's expression darkened as he gnawed at his chicken bone. But Nabby was already taking the first slice. Alas! Poor girl, no bean, and no queen.

Licking her fork, she declared, "At least the almond cream is delicious."

Johnny took a larger cut, bisecting his paste with mathematical circumspection until he finally conceded. "*Bah*. No crown for me."

"For what purpose would you need a crown?" I asked.

"*Height*," my boy replied. "I'm determined never to marry a girl as tall as Nabby lest her height give her a sense of superiority over me."

"Oh, are you thinking of marrying?" I asked, knowing that it would make Johnny go crimson, for it seemed he formed a new crush on a new lady every week.

Cheeks aglow, Johnny mumbled, "It was a *jest*, Mama."

Grinning at the mischief I'd made, I was ready for my dessert. "Though I have no cravings for royalty, the puff pastry is wondrously aromatic." When I finished every delicious crumb, I declared myself in no way dissatisfied that my slice had no bean.

My husband, who was all this time picking his chicken bone, had watched us divert ourselves without saying anything. Now, to the servants' horror, he seized the entire remaining half of the pie and began stabbing and slashing it with his knife and fork until he found the bean.

"Behold!" John said, keen to prove a point. "*This* is how kingdoms are attained."

We all laughed except for the enraged servant, who could not countenance the havoc wreaked upon the cook's finest pie. "No, sir. You are no legitimate ruler for you seized the bean by *force*, which is against the laws of God."

A slow smile spread over John's face. "Very good. Now I have you speaking like an American."

OUR WHIRLWIND OF merriment came to an end with a terrible piece of news from America—Mr. Jefferson's youngest daughter, Lucy, had died at just two years old.

A man of great sensibility and parental affection, our Virginian friend took it hard. Afflicted with a migraine that left him prostrate with grief, Jefferson could not work. Neither could Dr. Franklin, as he was too ill.

Thus, the work of the commission in negotiating treaties of commerce with France fell almost entirely to my husband—though he did not complain of it. Instead, he leaned upon his family. To help him, Nabby and Johnny did their best to manage the correspondence and translate ciphers while I made our house an embassy for foreign diplomats.

At a dinner with a representative from the West Indies, my husband was asked if American women spoke much on politics. He replied that we did. "Indeed, the liberties of a country depend on her ladies."

How gratified I was to hear it. I was pleased, too, by the rhythm of our days. We rose in the morning, not quite so early as I used to when feeding the turkeys and geese on the farm, but as soon as my fire was made and my room cleaned, I woke Nabby, then knocked at Johnny's door, who always opened it with his book in hand.

After breakfast, my husband sat down to either writing or reading while I directed the chambermaids in their work and took up mine, for I still darned stockings. Meanwhile, Johnny retired to his chamber to translations of Horace and Tacitus, Nabby to her writing table to pen letters home. At noon, John found his hat and cane for a four-mile walk while Nabby and I retired to our toilette to be dressed.

At two we all met together to dine. And after tea, the table was covered with mathematical instruments and books, and nothing was to be heard until evening but of theorems, as my husband taught Johnny about the bisecting and dissecting of tangents.

Occasionally, Nabby and I would be called upon to relieve their brains with a game of whist—a game I always won.

"How is a parson's daughter so adept at cards?" Johnny wondered.

"Because your uncle Bill is a gambler," I said. "He taught me what the parson said I ought not learn."

Johnny grinned. "Then you shall not mind anything I teach Nabby . . ."

Nabby sniffed from behind the fan of her cards. "Why should she? I'm incorruptible."

We enjoyed each other's company until ten, when it was time to rest. And if you had asked me what the business of life was here, I would have answered *pleasure*. Indeed, but for the absence of our friends and loved ones in America, I couldn't imagine living a more pleasing existence.

One afternoon in spring, John was scribbling at his desk and said, "I fear Jefferson's grief befuddles his mind. He's sent for his remaining daughter. He says he must have little Polly here. Must be able to see her, touch her, and ensure her safety."

It was a sentiment I could understand, though I feared for such a young child to cross the sea without a parent—look what had happened to Charles!

"In his place, I'd resign and go home."

"Have you had your fill of France already, then?"

I shook my head ruefully. "In spite of all my better judgment, I've fallen in love."

"Truly?"

"Truly." I smiled, hoping he understood that the love into which I had fallen was not only with France. But I said, "Paris. The countryside. The people. The churches. The artwork. I've even come to love the obscenity of the ballet, not to mention Madam Helvétius and her incontinent little dog."

"Then I'm sorry to tell you of some news that has come lately from Congress . . ." My husband was now grinning like a Cheshire cat. "I've been appointed to England to serve as the United States's first ambassador there."

My hands went to the backs of our red velvet chairs for balance. "Oh, John . . ."

His grin fell away. "No, don't say it. You're right. I shall have to refuse it. I'm ill-suited to the role. I'm not elegantly made, not sparkling in conversation, not agile in ballroom dance, nor quick with flattery—"

"You cannot refuse! It's the greatest honor. My husband, the *minister*. It's your *destiny*, John."

He rose, wrapping his arms around me, pleased by my reaction. "Do you mean it?"

"I do," I said, cupping his cheeks in my hands.

"Don't think it will be a bed of roses. They'll have no love for me at the Court of Saint James."

That did give me pause. "Will it be safe for you there?"

"We have a treaty, now. It will be perfectly safe."

"Then I'm only sorry to be leaving France. It's felt like a magical hour in my life, and I'll always love every person who played any role in it."

John smirked. "You mean Jefferson. I'll miss him, too, but letters will swiftly cross to London, and there's little reason we cannot visit."

"He's staying in France?"

John nodded. "As minister. He'll replace Franklin."

There was a delightful symmetry. John Adams and Thomas Jefferson had toiled together like brothers to declare our independency and now served as ambassadors to secure that independence, separated only by a narrow channel.

I felt the hand of providence in it.

But now we'd have to tell the children.

Nabby, who came to Europe to persuade her father to return to America, would no doubt want to go home and marry Mr. Tyler at the soonest opportunity. I supposed Johnny would not wish to accompany her because, speaking five languages fluently, he'd have the best opportunity to further his career as his father's personal secretary.

But in the end my predictions were wrong in every particular. "It's time to finish my education at Harvard," Johnny said. When

I pointed out to him the many fine institutions of learning in England, he wouldn't hear of it. "The son of John Adams ought to be educated in his own country and—well, that's enough reason."

I'd caught the hesitation. "Is there another reason?"

"I should be at home for my brothers. I know Charlie and how sad he can get."

I scoffed, for my middle son was the most cheerful boy I knew. But Johnny pointed out, "He was so homesick when I went to Russia that he was willing to undertake a sea voyage."

"Well, he's home now," I argued. "Or at least, in his own country with his own relations."

Johnny's lips thinned. "I should also like to meet Mr. Tyler."

"Oh dear. Do not make trouble for your sister."

"To the contrary, my sister wishes it."

"What can you mean?" I sensed a secret. Unfortunately, my eldest son was, in his way, even more stubborn than his father, and there was no prying it out of him.

Guessing the reason, I confronted my daughter. "I suppose you want John Quincy to escort you home and down the aisle to marry your sweetheart."

Then Nabby flummoxed me by saying, "No. I hope to stay longer with you and Papa in Europe."

I was selfishly pleased, if surprised. "What will Mr. Tyler say?"

Nabby turned to stare out the window. "I cannot guess. And in any event, I'm certain to be the last person to hear of it."

This pained me with curiosity. "What is it that you and your brother know?"

She shrugged. "I simply believe Mr. Tyler and I could both stand to mature before we wed."

And that was all she would say.

"I don't know what I'll do without Johnny," my husband complained.

"Congress is sending you a personal secretary," I reminded him. But my husband's sorrow in sending Johnny home had less to do with the young man's helpfulness as scribe, and more to do with how close father and son had become.

For my part, I grieved to let Johnny go after so little time together again. Nabby often teased that John Quincy was *the golden child*, for in our eyes he could do no wrong.

Now my husband mused, "Once he graduates from Harvard and I return to my life as a simple country lawyer, we can hang our shingles together. A law practice of father and son."

I couldn't imagine how my husband—after living a life as an important statesman, and now a minister—might return to a modest law office and a ramshackle house on a little farm. "I think when we return to Braintree that we should buy a new house. Johnny can scout property for us."

Naturally, my frugal husband despised the idea. "Corrupted by European opulence already, my dear? No, my money already flows through our fingers here, and we shall end up very much in debt."

He would not end up in debt, but I let him think so. My pin money continued to grow under the watchful eye of Cotton Tufts, to whom I wrote a private letter about how I thought it best to invest the money.

In the meantime, we made ready to leave France.

One night, the weather being very soft and pleasant, I asked John to take me on a walk through the garden so I might impress it all upon my memory.

Ah, I would miss it.

We made fond farewells to Franklin and other members of the delegation, Mr. Short, who had become a favorite of mine, and our French friends, including the Condorcets and, of course, the Lafayettes.

Then, at last, the Jeffersons.

That John didn't wish to part with Thomas Jefferson—the only person outside our family with whom he felt he could communicate with perfect freedom—was most evident by how brusquely he said farewell.

A thump on the back, then a grunt of "*My good man.*" Then an abrupt disappearance into the house.

I worried Jefferson might take offense, but I think he knew my husband well enough to be sensible of the honor. After I'd embraced and blessed his daughter, I sighed with deep regret.

"Thomas. It's only the knowledge that we'll likely have your company on a visit to England that keeps us dry-eyed."

Jefferson took my hand, upon which he planted a kiss. "Madam, you are one of the most estimable characters on earth."

They say nobody ever leaves Paris but with a degree of tristesse, and that was certainly true of me. As we set off in the carriage, my beloved little songbird thrashed in its cage so much that I feared it would dash itself to death.

"You are a little French bird," I said, stopping the carriage to surrender the beloved creature to my former chambermaid. "It's right that your first attachment must be to your own country above all others."

And thus we quit France with a wistful sigh.

Chapter Twenty-Seven

T
UT TUT, MINISTER Adams," I teased. "Such *stiff* republican knees."

We were practicing what he'd say and how he'd bow to King George in their first meeting. And now John grouched, "It's no use. I called the man a tyrant and led a revolution against him. I can hardly now expect to be received in warmth. Or to give it."

"That is the art of diplomacy, John," I said from the chair upon which I'd taken my role in the king's place, using my husband's cane as a scepter.

John tugged at his lace cuffs, then started again. Three bows, one upon entrance, one halfway across the hall, and one when he was close enough to address me. "Sire," he began, voice strained, then colored when he realized his mistake. "I mean, *sir*!"

I waved his cane impatiently. "Yes?"

John cleared his throat. Then cleared it again. "The United States of America have appointed me their minister plenipotentiary. And it is in obedience to their commands that I have the honor to assure you of their desire for friendship and their wishes for the health and happiness of your royal family."

"Oh, that is a fine opening, John. You've removed the personal animus altogether. It's very good."

"It *ought* to be, considering how many versions I've thrown into the fire."

The rest of his speech continued this way, cleverly distancing John from his past utterances and transforming him into the mere instrument of the country he served.

Despite my praise, John rubbed his throbbing temples. "The awkwardness of this encounter. It's likely to be the most mortifying of my life!"

"Don't you think it'll be worse for the king? Ultimately, you're the victor and he's the vanquished. He lost his war and thirteen colonies. Surely you can find it in your heart to be a little merciful to the man."

I said it not because I cared for the feelings of the king, but to put my husband at ease. It would give him confidence to enter the king's presence on that footing.

On the fateful day, Nabby and I awaited John's return at our handsome new house in Grosvenor Square, which was to be the first American embassy in Britain. For company we had Colonel William Smith of New York—a former aide-de-camp to George Washington who'd been sent by Congress to serve as John's new personal secretary.

Smith was a tall, upright military man thirty years old by my estimation, with square shoulders and a dashing confidence. I had no doubt that standing next to my portly, bookish husband, Colonel Smith might be mistaken for the ambassador rather than the assistant. Which may be why it was thought prudent for him to stay behind.

In any case, the colonel made himself useful in diverting us with tales of the war. We already knew of his heroics at the Battle of Harlem Heights in New York, where he was wounded, though he didn't mention it. And I thought him a modest, worthy man, if I could judge from so short an acquaintance.

The only thing I might hold against him was his membership in the Society of the Cincinnati, but he wore no badge of that hereditary order and claimed no intention of ever doing so.

What he did speak of was his service under Washington and then foreigners like Lafayette. "Mine is a military family, so I thought the proudest service a man could give was to offer his life in service of his country. But how much greater is the glory of men who fight for the freedom of others an ocean away."

"Well said," I murmured, distracted by the jingle of a carriage at the gate.

Soon my husband burst in, throwing his wig on the chair in triumph. "Success!"

Flying to him, I asked how he was received. And John positively puffed up with pride. "I cannot recall every word King George said precisely. But some of it is emblazoned on my brain."

Caught up in the excitement, Nabby said, "Do tell, Papa!"

"The king said: 'Sir, the circumstances of this audience are so extraordinary, the language you have adopted so very proper, and the feelings you have expressed so just to the occasion, I not only accept and return the offer of friendship from the United States of America, but also I'm very glad that the choice has fallen upon you as their minister.'"

I gasped, for it was a better reply than we had any right to expect. I hoped it meant our diplomacy here in London would be fruitful.

Unfortunately, the newspapers the next day were less generous than the king. It was thought that by sending an *Adams* to court, the United States had been impudent. Then again, many in Britain thought the very existence of the United States to be impudent. We couldn't allow it to dispirit us. And in any case, we had too much to do.

As the ambassador's lady, I needed to purchase new furniture, for it had been too expensive to transport what we bought in France. And even before I set up housekeeping, we were beset by every manner of unfortunate American in England. I found myself in the unexpected position of receiving refugees and petitions.

It was my duty as well as my honor to help these unfortunates in whatever way I could. Sometimes that meant I convinced John to give them money from our own purse without knowing whether Congress might ever reimburse us.

Not all the supplicants were deserving; some pretended to be soldiers from the war—and we were grateful to Colonel Smith for sorting out the legitimate cases from the frauds.

Then came the flood of cards from ladies, which obliged me to return the visits with a shower of my own cards all over London.

It was in this way that the Countess of Effingham and I went several rounds before I finally gave in and decided to be *at home*.

I also needed new dresses, because at court a lady couldn't wear the same gown more than once. Worse, the shoes in London were so inferior that I had to beg of Mr. Jefferson to send me some from France.

For our first audience with the queen, Nabby and I both wore white. Mine was a white crepe festooned with purple ribbon, ruffled cuffs, and lace kerchief. I wore it with a pearl necklace, pearl earrings, pearl pins in my hair, and two white feather plumes.

"Do not laugh at me," I warned John, feeling entirely above myself for wearing such pearls and riches. "Here I am, the daughter of a parson and the wife of a farmer wearing white crepe."

John assured me, "You, my dear, are, in all seriousness, a heavenly *vision*."

But it was Nabby who stole our breaths, trailing down the stairs in white lace and decorative petticoats, her auburn hair adorned in a wreath of white flowers. John, much affected, shook his head in wonder. "When did my little girl become such a beauty?"

Nabby flushed at her father's attention, taking his arm as we went out to the carriage. I was escorted by Colonel Smith—which was how I noticed the strong pulse of his heartbeat, and eyes artfully averted from the sight that occasioned it.

Oh, it was not only Nabby's father who realized she was a beauty!

At two o'clock we went to the queen's drawing room, passing through several apartments lined with spectators. I spoke with the Dutch minister, Count Sarsfield, Lord Carmathan, and Sir Dormer and several other gentlemen with whom I was slightly acquainted. But not a single lady did I know until the Countess of Effingham pulled me into the circle round the drawing room, which was very full.

The royal family was obliged to go round to every person and find small talk enough to speak to all of them. The king, with red face and white brows, went round to the right. Meanwhile, the diamond-adorned queen and princesses to the left.

When the king came to me, his royal majesty kissed my cheek. "Have you taken a walk today, Mrs. Adams?"

A bit stupefied to be kissed by the man whose name I cursed whilst revolutionary soldiers bled on my kitchen floor, I replied, "No, sire—sir."

Seemingly perplexed, he asked, "Don't you love walking?"

"I'm rather indolent in that respect," I replied.

At which point he bowed politely and passed on. And that was that.

It was a preposterous, almost hallucinatory experience. The King of England had seemed almost . . . *daft*.

But an even stranger experience was still to come, for Queen Charlotte made certain that my daughter and I were left waiting another two hours before she approached in radiant purple and silver, her expression as hard as the diamonds in her hair. "Mrs. Adams."

"Your Majesty," I replied, with a curtsey.

She stared at me frostily, as if *willing* me to drop my gaze, but I did not. And her mouth twisted in contempt. "Have you got into your house?"

"Yes, at Grosvenor—"

The queen interrupted me with a feigned yawn. "Pray how do you like the situation of it?"

She made no effort to hide her hostility, which was quite all right with me, because I had disagreeable feelings, too. These people were, after all, the cause of a war that had consumed nearly a decade of my life. "It is a fine house, though naturally I prefer those in *my own country*."

I thought I heard a little snort of offense from one of the princesses. Then, abruptly, the queen moved on with great hauteur—much beyond that which her personal charms might justify.

I remembered long ago jesting with John that someone like Queen Charlotte would never welcome me as a guest at Buckingham House. In truth, she had not. She was rude, ill shaped, and her hair was of a ridiculous height. And I thought it a very foolish thing to waste time and ceremony just to pass a few insipid words with royalty if she were any example of the species.

But that was not something a diplomat's wife could utter. It was my duty to ignore these slights. And in any case, I was left too exhausted by the ordeal—standing more than four hours in total without respite—to utter anything at all.

Naturally, the newspapers were outraged that we were given even an ostensibly polite reception. One said that if they were in the king's place, they'd hang my husband as a proscribed rebel, peace treaty be damned.

"Cheer up," I told John. "The newspaperman calling for you to be hanged thinks you are *Samuel* Adams."

That did not cheer him.

If anything it made him gloomier, so I wrapped my arms protectively around his beloved neck. "Well, let our presence bite them like a serpent and sting them like an adder. We will do our duty no matter what the newspapers say."

And no matter how they misrepresented us to their countrymen. For I was asked by many strangers, "How can you live without laws, Mrs. Adams? Everyone knows the former colonies are in anarchy."

Then there were the merchants who insisted my husband would have nothing to do as ambassador even to regularize trade. "What do we need from America anyway?"

Still others insisted there was little point in our embassy. "Mr. Adams may have authority now, but this union between colonies will all dissolve in civil war and his acts here will be meaningless. Mark my words."

This was the attitude we must counter at all costs. It was our mission if we wished for the United States to remain a free nation. So, I saw as many visitors as I could, imparting to them the *truth* about our country, keeping too busy even to write my own letters.

"Write to John Quincy in America for me," I told my daughter. "Tell Charlie and Tommy that we love them and that we're sending sweets."

"I will," Nabby said, diligent with her pen.

"Oh, and be sure to mention the sweets in a letter to Reverend Shaw so he doesn't forbid it. That man would eat sawdust imagining it might please the Lord."

On my way downstairs, I heard a commotion in the parlor. Men's voices raised, and I heard Colonel Smith bark, "I assure you sir, I owe no debt."

His visitor sneered. "You are Mr. William Smith, are you not? Here in the household of Mr. Adams, as one might expect you to be. I have here the proof of your indebtedness by way of gambling from Weymouth, Massachusetts. I've come all this way to collect it."

"I assure you I have never stepped foot in any place called Weymouth," said the colonel.

All at once, I realized the source of the confusion but was too mortified to intervene. Fortunately, the colonel didn't need my assistance. "You are misinformed, sir. You may take up the matter in court or let it come to fisticuffs, if you prefer, because I certainly do."

At this threat, the creditor sized up John's secretary and decided against an altercation. Out the man went with a shout. "This won't be the end of it!"

"Oh, I rather suspect it will be," said the colonel, who then turned and paled to see that I had witnessed it all. "Dear God! Madam, I assure you I am no debtor. On my honor, I know *not* what that was about."

"I do," I admitted, shamefacedly. "I beg your pardon. You see, my brother . . ." How was I to explain? "He shares your name. William Smith. How sorry I am that your reputation might ever be touched by his."

The colonel was very gracious—promising to keep this to himself so as not to bring scandal upon my family. "My dear lady, do not worry for a moment. In the future, I'll be sure to emphasize that I am Colonel William *Stephens* Smith."

I liked William Stephens Smith. And I wasn't the only one. One afternoon Nabby stared after her father's secretary with a wistful sigh. "It is little wonder that the Marquis de Lafayette sent such a warm letter of recommendation for Colonel Smith. Do you think him a man of honor?"

"I do indeed. And I wish I could say that of all your acquaintances."

She stared at me, her lower lip wobbling. So long she had been holding a secret that I felt she might finally burst. "Nabby, I know Mr. Tyler has broken his promises in writing you scarcely at all these past fourteen months. But I sense there's more."

She shook her head, as if unwilling to betray him. "Can a breach of honor in one party justify the want of it in another?"

"Oh, Nabby," I said, grasping her hands. "If you're conscious of any want of honor on the part of Mr. Tyler, I—along with every friend in the world you have—would rejoice if you liberated yourself."

Thereupon my daughter dissolved into sobs, fled to her chamber, and locked the door.

An hour I paced, wondering if I should knock and demand entrance or wait until morning. Just as I had decided to knock, there was a tear-streaked Nabby in the doorway holding two letters from America. The first letter was from many months ago when we were in Paris from her cousin Betsy Cranch, alleging much conduct unbecoming on the part of Mr. Tyler.

Betsy said he burned letters from friends that he had promised to forward to Nabby. That he flirted with other young ladies. She shared the rumor, even, that he had impregnated two servant girls and dumped them on Phoebe's doorstep to care for.

Now, I knew Betsy Cranch could be an imaginative and emotional girl. Her gossip couldn't be given too much weight.

But the second letter was from John Quincy, who had let no grass grow under his feet. Upon his arrival in America, he set about immediately to interview Mr. Tyler, and he now believed him to be both neglectful in business and deeply dishonest in love.

Swiping at her eyes, Nabby said, "I couldn't act based on Betsy's rambling account. Having been promised to Mr. Tyler, I've lived in dread that Papa should think me a dishonorable girl if I entertained the idea of breaking the engagement. So, I was determined to go through with it, whatever the truth."

I felt horror to think that a girl could ruin her life for the sake of manners and empty form. "Nabby, you mustn't just *go through with it* when it comes to a husband. Your choice will form the whole shape of your life. The man you marry will have legal *power* over you."

Far better to be thought a bad woman than to marry a bad man, I thought. But I knew it was not that simple. As I rubbed my poor Nabby's shoulder and offered her my kerchief to sniffle into, she explained, "I wanted Papa to give his assent and once he did, how could I then say I was trapped? I thought I could just bear up under it. Then the pain of it became more terrible when I met Colonel Smith, a gentleman I could *truly* love. A gentleman I've been obliged to tell that I'm already promised to another. But now, with John Quincy's letter, I don't know what to do. Do you think Papa—"

"I'll speak to him at once," I interrupted.

Thereupon, I awakened John from his slumber and told him everything.

As my husband blearily blinked away sleep, I took responsibility for this disaster. For I had encouraged Mr. Tyler's courtship without the stern scrutiny that a father would've given it.

John listened to everything, trying to keep his nightcap from falling into his eyes. Finally, he sat up in bed and crossed his arms. "Summon Nabby."

"What will you say?"

"You will hear it when I say it," John snapped.

Our poor girl crept inside the room, timid as a mouse. John motioned her to his side. "Nabby, this is a serious matter, and I hope it's upon mature deliberation that you've come to a conclusion about your feelings. The truth is, Mr. Tyler is a perfect stranger to me, and I gave my consent to wed only because I conceived your affections to be engaged."

"They were," she admitted. "But I didn't know him capable of these things I'm now told he's done. I would wish to break this connection, but I'm so afraid of what people will say."

"Fie on that!" John cried. "I tell you, my dear girl, if you have reason to question the honor of this gentleman or suppose him capable of lying to you or your brother, well, then I'd rather go to my *grave* than see you married to him."

"Oh, Papa!" Nabby flung herself into his arms. He soothed her, kissing the top of her head, patting her back, and assuring her that all would be well.

And I never before loved John Adams more than I did that night.

Chapter Twenty-Eight

LONDON
England
March 1786

M R. JEFFERSON STAYED with us on his visit to London, which was very much to our liking. He'd come to help negotiate a treaty with Portugal and to meet with the minister from Tripoli. If one could call him a minister. In truth, the turban-clad, bearded fellow represented the Barbary pirates, who were demanding protection money from the United States.

My husband and Mr. Jefferson both believed we ought to pay this ransom, but I protested, "It's extortion!"

"Indeed, Mrs. Adams," Jefferson said, crossing his stockinged legs at the knee. "Of the basest sort."

John chuckled ruefully. "My dear, we can either purchase a peace or have a war that will cost us three times as much—if we had a navy fit for the purpose, which we do not. We mustn't be afraid of two hundred thousand pounds to procure treaties with the Barbary powers which will save us millions."

Jefferson added, "Alas, it falls to Mr. Adams and me to divine where we'll get the money."

"Money for bribery or tribute," I groused. "Oh, I like it not! And I can well imagine what will be printed about it in the British press."

With that, I handed a few of the day's sheets over to both men. Mr. Jefferson perused them and made a sound of disgust. "I tell you, John. You're a rock to withstand these slanders. I wouldn't trade places with you for all the world in this matter."

Jefferson's expression then turned wry as he bounced his foot in its buckled shoe. "Or that other, more *personal* matter."

I smiled my own wry smile, knowing he was needling my husband about Colonel Smith's recent request for our daughter's hand in marriage.

It'd been eight months since Nabby broke things off with Royall Tyler, during which time he proved himself every bit the scoundrel. At first Tyler wouldn't accept the end of the relationship, threatening to come to London and drag Nabby back with him. He then refused to return Nabby's miniature, questioning her honor and fidelity.

Nor would he pay his rents to my sister Mary, who had been his kind and indulgent landlady, but was also the aunt of the woman who spurned him and therefore must pay the price.

I was embarrassed that I'd ever taken his part.

Thankfully, a better suitor was on the scene.

Before pursuing my daughter, Colonel Smith had taken a four-month tour of the Continent. But since his return, he'd wooed ardently and won Nabby's heart.

I cautioned patience, but Smith wished for a speedy union.

"From the frying pan into the fire," John said, but saw no reason to object. He liked Colonel Smith—a war hero from a prominent New York family with a rising future. He simply did not like the speed of it.

I had sought to ease his worries by saying, "A soldier is always more expeditious in his courtships than other men, and they know better how to capture the citadel."

But now my husband asked Jefferson, "Is he good enough for my daughter?"

"Not *remotely*," Jefferson replied. "Miss Adams is a rare gem. As a father I concur with your own unspoken judgment that no man could ever deserve her."

John laughed. "Yet . . ."

"Yet, they are of age," Jefferson said. "And I think Colonel Smith to be of worthy character."

And that settles it, I thought. For there were few men whose judgments my husband trusted as much as Jefferson's.

Truly, it was a blessing to have the Virginian's diplomatic help and family advice. He'd procured for me more shoes from France, and for him I'd purchased some table linens he'd needed from London. He was charming with Nabby, who served ad hoc as her father's secretary whilst Colonel Smith was away, and she was delighted Jefferson wrote her under cipher as if she were a regular member of the delegation.

For my part, I was happy to accompany Jefferson to the theater and on his tour of English gardens, during which he expressed his frustration that though he'd sent for his youngest daughter, Polly, her relations in Virginia had been dragging their feet in sending her.

"It's painful to be away from them even for a worthy mission," I said, confessing my own longing for my boys. "The servile ceremonies of court certainly don't compensate."

"How do you otherwise enjoy the duties of Madam Ambassador?"

"Never the same two days in a row. I never know if I'll need to rearrange the seating at a dinner to account for a gentlemen's feud or if I'll receive as a diplomatic gift from the West Indies a hundred and fourteen pounds of turtle meat."

Jefferson laughed. "And for amusements?"

"I observe the absurdities of Britain. I've noticed the people here think even more of their titles than in France. Oh, the airs they put on."

Jefferson nodded. "You must not repeat this, but I would not be averse to sinking the whole island." When I laughed, he asked, "By the way, what did you do with the turtle meat?"

"Ate it, of course. It was a fortunate thing we had a banquet coming up. The rest we gave to charity." For just as in France, I never set my foot out without encountering many starving persons in tattered clothing or riddled with disease. "I do not see how the British consider themselves a superior nation when there are so many poor. There must be some essential defect in the government and morals of a people who tolerate this."

At home, our communities attempted to make small basic provisions for the unfortunate. Even in Boston, we didn't walk amongst the poor as if their woes were not our care. But I dared not question Jefferson on how it stood in Virginia, lest we trod upon the subject of slavery—a subject upon which he professed to agree with us, but which he could not discuss without awkwardness.

Back at Grosvenor Square we discussed another matter on which we did not *quite* see eye to eye. John and I despaired that a brewing insurrection against tax collectors in Massachusetts fed into British stereotypes of American anarchy. "We mustn't let liberty become licentiousness," I said.

But Jefferson was less troubled. "We've had thirteen states independent for eleven years with only a little protest. What country can preserve its liberties if their rulers are not warned that their people preserve the spirit of resistance? The tree of liberty must be refreshed from time to time with the blood of patriots and tyrants. It is a natural manure."

It was not a shocking statement to hear, given that we'd all so recently lived through scenes of violence. We now had the luxury of thinking in abstractions. And having received from American friends copies of the proposed new Constitution, John asked, "How do you like the plan for our new government?"

Jefferson grimaced. "I confess there are things in it which stagger me. Their proposal for a president seems a bad edition of a Polish king—he may be reelected from four years to four years for life. Once in office, possessing the military force of the union, he would not be easily dethroned, even if the people could be induced to withdraw their votes from him. It would be better if the president were to serve one term and be banned forever from seeking a second."

John nodded thoughtfully. "It is a fearsome responsibility that trusts men of honor to quit it." We all knew what little stock my husband put in *trust* when it came to mankind. "Yet we shall need a strong executive. And in any case, I like the checks and balances of this government. It is not a pure democracy, but mixed, which will preserve it longer. Remember, there never was a democracy yet that did not commit suicide."

The two gentlemen continued their debate well into the night, long after exhaustion sent me to bed. By morning, I found that they were now discussing Jefferson's forthcoming unpublished book, from which he read a quote about the evils of slavery. "'I tremble for my country when I reflect that God is just and that his justice cannot sleep forever.'"

I thought it a remarkable statement from a man who had inherited many enslaved persons from his late wife's estate. "Some at Monticello are relations, in truth," he now confided, punchy from the late night before. "My wife's father took to him a half-African woman named Elizabeth Hemings, and now her children serve mine."

That his father-in-law had done this disgusted me. It also opened my eyes. For we had, when in France, met Jefferson's cook—the light-skinned James Hemings, who I now realized must be near kin. I'd seen for myself that Jefferson gave that man wide latitude; certainly, James Hemings did not behave as if he believed himself to be enslaved. But the fact that Jefferson was master over his wife's relations was a shameful situation—one that probably pushed him to champion a failed move for abolition in Virginia, about which he said, "Doing so nearly ended my political and financial life."

How glad I was that my husband had never trafficked in persons! Gladder still that the constitution my husband had drafted for Massachusetts had been interpreted to abolish slavery altogether. Of course, I sympathized with Jefferson in the matter of inheriting a moral problem, for my own father's freedwoman was tending to our house whilst we were away. Phoebe was serving me, I assumed, in a similar family capacity as the Hemingses served Jefferson. But of course, Phoebe was free to go whenever she wished . . .

Before Jefferson took his leave of us, he sat for a portrait, and my husband insisted on purchasing a copy to grace our home. The visit with our Virginian friend had refreshed my husband as if he'd rested idle abed for a month. Truly, none of us wanted him to go. But thankfully, Jefferson reassured us all it was not the final farewell of *adieu*, but only *au revoir*.

A FEW MONTHS after Jefferson's visit, we gave our only daughter in marriage to Colonel Smith, a man who swore to make it his purpose in life to bring about my daughter's happiness. Yet the occasion was too momentous not to feel anxiety equal to what I experienced the night before I married.

"Well, marriage turned out all right for you, didn't it?" John asked, having ambled down the stairs, eyes bloodshot and weary, to find me awake at four in the morning.

"Indeed, it did," I said, brushing a kiss on his cheek. "So, then, what has bestirred *you*, at this hour?"

John was quiet. Then all at once, he burst out, "I want to see Nabby! Our innocent baby girl. Knowing what scene is likely passing between them this very night, I have half a mind to march over there and—"

"Oh, John, that is a scene of love you *do not* wish to interrupt."

John pulled at his chin. "What if he hurts her?"

"He's a gentleman!"

"Still, it could happen; she might feel she must suffer in silence. Does she even know . . ." He waved his hands in frustration. "Does she know the general *idea* of the coming together of husband and wife?"

I chuckled, trying to settle his mind. "She *knows*, John. She's a girl of more than twenty, having been raised on a farm and having lived two years now in the most sophisticated courts of Europe."

He scowled. "We are never going to see her again!"

I laughed and felt badly for it, because he was truly distressed. "Don't be absurd. They've only gone to live at nearby Wimpole Street. And I've made them promise to dine with us every day."

That eased his mind, which eased mine. Soon enough we were nestled again in bed, and I fell into a deep slumber that lasted until mid-morning, when I awakened to see my husband coming in with hat and cane.

"Well, I've been to see them," he said.

"*What?* Could you not wait until our midday meal?"

"No, I could not. I wanted to see Nabby before breakfast."

I covered my mouth. "Was Colonel Smith as vexed to find you at his door before breakfast as *you* may have been if *my* father had done the same?"

"He was relieved, actually." John's expression softened. "Our poor girl—happy as she is to be carried away in marital bliss—had cried to think of us lonely without her."

I sat up with concern. "She *cried*?"

"While we were worrying about her, she was worrying for us. So, I met her with such cheerful reassurance as to dispel the clouds over her head. She's well. We're well. All will be well."

Oh, letting go of children was a trying business. It would be easier, I hoped, with my boys. Their wives would likely feather our nest, whereas Nabby would be obliged to fly off with her husband.

For now, though, Nabby's husband and mine both had important diplomatic work here in London. And for that I was grateful.

BY SUMMER OF the next year, at the age of forty-two, I was made a grandmama for the first time. Nabby gave birth to as fine a boy as I ever saw, and as we beheld the infant in his cradle, I said, "He has your brow, John."

"Poor devil," my husband replied. "The rest of his shape is his father, at least."

I patted John's arm. "This will be no bad assemblage when years mature the one and time strengthens the other."

Our grandson was to be named William, and I sighed, wary of more confusions. "Yet another William Smith in the family? I do believe, counting my dearly departed father, that makes four."

"We'll call him our Willy Magpie," John declared, for the babe liked to reach for shiny baubles, like his mother's ear bobs.

Nabby, for her part, had come through the birth with ease, despite all my worries. "You aren't too sorry for a grandson, are you, Mama?"

I'd hoped, in vain, for a granddaughter, but now that it was a boy, I convinced myself to be happy about it. "It's just as well. For any granddaughter of mine must be an educated and accomplished young lady. And I have ever observed that it's a dangerous thing for a female to be distinguished for any qualification beyond the rest of her sex."

I had been bickering with John about this at breakfast, and I was not finished making my case, even though he pretended not to hear. "Whatever may be a woman's deportment, she's sure to draw upon herself the jealousy of men and the envy of women. Of course, I do not see any way to remedy this evil but by *increasing* the number of accomplished women."

Nabby laughed. "Mama, forget all that for today. I'm so happy. I didn't know I could ever *be* so happy."

My darling girl was radiant. And I rejoiced for her lucky escape from the charming but debased Mr. Tyler—who had, by all reports now, gone on to commit adultery with his new landlady, leaving a cuckoo for the woman's husband to raise. More scandalous still, the landlady was the mother of the young lady he now intended to marry!

His lascivious treachery was worse than Mr. Lovell's, but similar enough that I wondered at my own judgment for having ever been taken in by either man.

Then again, it seemed as if bad behavior in young men was a contagion. For news from my sisters at home told me that under the pressure of financial embarrassments, Mrs. Warren's sons were becoming rascals. I was sorry for the financial embarrassments, but I didn't like that her sons were being foisted as friends upon my own boys, who might well follow their bad example.

It made me nervous, too, to learn that my Charlie Cherub was apparently now so good-looking that the young ladies in town all gave him tokens or clippings of their hair.

"The Misses all think Charles an Adonis—a perfect beauty," mused my sister Elizabeth in a letter, explaining that she'd advised my son not to give in to the temptations that arose from such attention.

I'd always be grateful for my sisters taking on the role of substitute parents for my boys. In my place, Mary had hosted a gathering of more than three hundred people to celebrate Johnny's graduation from Harvard—a party at which Phoebe had been an enormous help, too. I knew the women in my family would extend love and guidance to our sons.

Still, I couldn't help but fret about them, especially when news reached us from Harvard that our youngest boys stood accused of having taken part in a Thanksgiving food riot at Harvard in which windows were smashed and furniture overturned.

"The shame of it!" John raged.

To calm him, I said, "We ought to reserve judgment until we've heard a defense against these accusations."

But John set his cup down with altogether too much force. "Charles has been fined as a suspected instigator and may well be expelled."

At the other end of the table, our son-in-law, Colonel Smith, who usually adopted *rectitude* as his motto in all things, smirked a little, as if imagining the rough-and-tumble fun of such a rowdy food fight at school. But Nabby—protective of the little brothers she'd helped me raise—argued, "John Quincy believes Charles to be innocent."

Whatever the truth, our minds couldn't be set at ease until we were in America to take a more active part in the upbringing of our children.

Alas, my husband's work as ambassador was crucial, for despite our treaty of peace, the British made practice of seizing American soldiers and pressing them into the British Navy. Whitehall insisted these were mistakes, but we knew it to be a lie, and as America's ambassador, John must stand firm.

I was acutely aware that I, too, was representing our nation upon the world's stage. And it was a role I liked better than expected. In addition to hosting dinners, I toured the countryside, attended lectures, and otherwise made of myself as public a figure as possible.

I was as active as Colonel Smith in managing my husband's correspondence. There was a feminine art, after all, to weaving a net of important political and social figures in Europe for the benefit of our country.

Here in London as the ambassador's lady, I had found some part of myself that I had not known existed. A desire, as well as a true *penchant*, for public service. And I was not ready to give it up.

Chapter Twenty-Nine

LONDON
England
Summer 1787

JEFFERSON WROTE THAT his youngest daughter would soon arrive and asked me to look after her until he could come from Paris to fetch her. It was a favor I was glad to do, at least until the little waif arrived at my door . . .

There I found the eight-year-old clinging to the leg of the ship's captain who delivered her. My frustrated butler had summoned me, unable to persuade the little girl to cross the threshold.

Now I wasn't having any more luck.

Whereas her older sister Patsy had the look of her father stamped on her freckled features, the younger Miss Jefferson must've favored her mother—delicate as a sparrow, with darker hair and eyes.

I assumed a girl of such delicate frame would have a soft temperament to match. But I realized how mistaken I was on that count when Polly refused to come inside. "You're just going to trick me like everyone else!"

The captain's cheeks colored at her outburst, explaining, "Miss Polly's relations enticed her onto the ship with a promise of picnic and play with her nursemaid here. We were told not to set sail until after the girl fell asleep for a nap."

With that, the captain's eyes flicked to the shadowed portion of my stoop, where I was startled to see another girl—this one a taller copy of the first, and not much older. She must be a relation, but I'd eat my bonnet if she was any older than fourteen.

Why, Mr. Jefferson had said his daughter would be traveling in the company of an *old* nurse. How could his relations entrust his precious daughter into the charge of another girl scarcely old enough to care for herself?

"This is Sally," the captain said, drawing the servant girl into the sunlight, at which point I realized that if she were kin to Polly Jefferson, it could never be acknowledged. For Sally was a mulatto, with amber eyes and a complexion of pale but unmistakable fawn.

Nevertheless, she had the temerity to correct the captain about her name. "Sally *Hemings*," she said, with a curtsey.

I recognized the name and smiled. "In Paris, Mr. Jefferson introduced me to James Hemings. Is there a relation?"

Sally gave a prideful tilt of her chin. "My brother."

"Well then, you see, we all know each other after a fashion. We shall get to know each other even better over some cakes and lemonade. Won't you like that, girls?"

It had been a while since I dealt with children so young, and I practically had to pry Polly's hand out of the captain's so she could take a seat at my table. There, with tears on her face, she gulped down lemonade. Then she shoved bites of cake into her mouth like a savage. She'd been five weeks at sea and, but for Sally, with men only, so that she was as rough as a little sailor.

She continued to express how very angry she was at all the deceptions; I was apprehensive that she'd be a troublesome child. But my heart went out to her when she began to sob all over again.

"Now, Polly," I said, gently. "Why must you sob? Soon your father will come fetch you to France, which is a marvel. You know, I met your sister after she crossed the ocean, and I didn't see her cry one tear."

"Patsy is *older*," Polly blubbered. "She ought to do better, and she had her papa with her besides."

"He's your papa, too, is he not?"

"I don't know him or you. You're a stranger!"

What was I to say to that? It was a tragedy that in having served his country so well, Mr. Jefferson's own daughter did not know him. And I was momentarily struck with a pang for my own boys. They were old enough to know us, but would they grow up feeling themselves to have been similarly abandoned?

Thankfully, just then, I heard Nabby in the entryway. "What in the world is all that wailing?"

I hustled out of my chair with very little decorum to greet her and my grandson. "Oh, Nabby, I'm *so* glad you happened by! It may help little Miss Jefferson to see another young person."

"I'm hardly a young person anymore," Nabby said, smiling down at her baby. "Unless you mean your grandson. But surely that's not Miss Jefferson crying in your parlor?"

"I'm afraid so. Come help me reconcile her to making new friends."

Nabby surrendered my grandson to a servant and joined me in the parlor, where the younger Miss Jefferson continued to wail. "More strangers!"

"No, no, Miss Polly," I insisted. "This is my daughter, and we're family friends. Your father was our guest here in this very house not long ago."

"We have a portrait to prove it," Nabby said, by way of sudden inspiration. "Your papa posed for it when last he visited."

We took her to see the portrait and I asked, "Would we have Mr. Jefferson's likeness in our home if we weren't the best of friends?"

Alas, the painting didn't comfort Polly, who stared forlornly. "I don't know who that is."

"I recognize him," Sally said, helpfully, but without any identifiable emotion.

I reached for Polly's hand. "Well, you girls may both rely on us to give you every attention and care."

"And *fun*," Nabby promised. "There are so many amusements to be had in London."

I took up the suggestion. "Yes! We'll take you to the theater at Sadler's Wells for puppet shows, treats, and all the fun you can imagine."

Polly blinked her tears away, so I thought we were making progress. But then she told me, with raw emotion, "I'd rather see Captain Ramsay again for just one more moment than have all the fun in the world."

"Oh, my heart aches for this honest little one," Nabby murmured.

Mine did, too.

Polly Jefferson was another child who had been sacrificed for her father's public service. Neither she nor any of my children had any say in it. Though none of them had less say, I supposed, than Sally Hemings.

Once the two Virginian girls were ensconced in their beds for a rest after their travels, my daughter said, "Mr. Jefferson had better bring Patsy when he comes. Or Polly may not be reconciled to going with him. And you must persuade him to send Sally back to Virginia."

I shook my head. "His kin should've sent an older woman to help manage things, but after Sally has come all this way, to subject her immediately again to the sea? That might be too cruel. Besides, Sally seems to be a good-natured girl and fond of Polly."

Nabby took a deep breath. "*Mama*, people in France already whisper about Mr. Jefferson's chef and how unseemly it is for the spokesman of liberty to carry with him a man in bondage."

"You've heard what Mr. Jefferson has written about slavery. He surely has a plan for the gradual emancipation of his people."

Nabby tilted her head. "Are you going to pretend you haven't noticed the *resemblance* between those girls?"

My cheeks burned. "You cannot think that Mr. Jefferson, of all people . . ." I trailed off, not daring to put into words the sin for which she apparently suspected him. "There's a family connection with the Hemingses through his wife's father."

Poor Sally was a living example of race-mixing, from which we'd been taught all our lives to recoil. I was still, in fact, smarting from my own visceral reaction to seeing the play *Othello*, in which the romance between the dark Moor and the fair Desdemona had disturbed me because of either the prejudices of my education or a real antipathy for which I ought to be ashamed.

But my words confirmed the true wickedness; masters abused their servants in the most depraved ways—even in families as fine as the Jeffersons. And this elicited a shudder of disgust from my daughter.

In the end, I reluctantly agreed that Sally should be sent back to Virginia. And I tried to encourage this in the letter I sent. But while we awaited Jefferson's reply, it was wonderful to have children in the house again.

After a trip to puppet shows with our grandson Willy Magpie, and a visit to purchase some new clothes for both Polly and Sally, the younger Miss Jefferson decided I wasn't such a frightening stranger after all.

Polly was promptly restored to the amiable and lovely child one might've expected her to be. In fact, she quickly became the favorite of every creature in the house. Even John, who exclaimed, "Do you know that impudent little filly sidled up to me in my library today, slipped into my lap without so much as a *by your leave*, pulled a book down from my desk, and began reading to me!"

Far from being annoyed, John was smitten. "I cannot understand why you so foolishly wrote to tell Jefferson that his child was here. We should've kept it our secret."

I laughed. "I was foolish indeed. Now I'm loath to part with her."

Truthfully, I'd have been happy to keep Sally with us indefinitely, too. She was a neat and modest girl who confided that she had a mother in Virginia who wished her to see the world and considered this a rare opportunity. "My mama volunteered me to go because she wants for me to set foot in France."

An odd phrasing, I thought.

But then I wondered if Sally's mother knew of the French Freedom Principle, which held, in theory, that any enslaved person was emancipated when setting foot on French soil.

There are no slaves in France, they said. This was, unfortunately, mostly a fiction. But were I Sally's mother, would I not have jumped at the chance to test the legal premise?

"Well, then, you must go to France," I told Sally.

For how many times had I vowed to do all in my power to protect my children? I would not be the one to thwart another mother's effort to do the same. So, I no longer tried to persuade Mr. Jefferson to send Sally home—even though I knew it would mean less embarrassment for our country and our diplomatic corps. Indeed, my indignation over the whole matter grew the more I got to know the sweet, demure Sally whose quiet reserve so reminded me of my own Nabby. Indeed, our good friend quite deserved to be embarrassed to still hold people in bondage—and I intended to press him on the matter when he came to London to fetch the girls.

As it happened, however, Jefferson did *not* come to fetch the girls. Instead, he sent a French servant, which set Polly again into a frantic state.

Men! Jefferson was as reckless as my husband had been sending Charles home from the Netherlands. And now I wondered if there'd been some well-meaning Dutch woman warning my husband the way I had warned Jefferson, only to be ignored.

For how was I to answer Jefferson's daughter when she angrily said, "As I left all my friends in Virginia to see my father, I did think he'd take the pains to come for me himself and not send a man I cannot understand. So, I will go, but pray don't ask me not to cry about it, Mrs. Adams."

"In your place, my dear, I might cry, too."

For however great my fondness for Thomas Jefferson—and it was very great indeed—I felt sorry to count him amongst the men who were better statesmen than they were fathers. My own husband included on that score.

Chapter Thirty

LONDON
England
Spring 1788

OUR THIRD LONDON season was upon us, a vibrant whirl of balls, court presentations, and rides through Hyde Park. Everything seemed to be blossoming, from the colorful blooms I cultivated in my small urban garden to my Willy Magpie, who was now less a baby and more an adventurous and cheerful little boy.

By contrast, his grandfather was increasingly sour as spoiled milk. "Prime Minister Pitt is not the friend to America we'd hoped he'd be."

Knowing how difficult it was for John to sway the British leader to pay attention to any of our concerns, I tried to encourage him. "I daresay he has been consumed with domestic affairs; we must commend him for ordering an investigation into the slave trade with an eye towards abolishing it."

"Yes, but that is all I'll say for him."

My husband was frustrated. He wanted to go home. And so did I.

Indeed, we had been so long abroad that in our absence an entirely new Constitution had been drafted, debated, and was soon to be ratified in the United States. And I'd finally had my fill of the foggy weather, the pretensions, and the ridiculous customs of court. Not to mention the London newsmen who continued to mock my husband for want of better sport.

When we first arrived, they'd condemned John as a colonial bumpkin. By the end of our term, John was accused of being too *much* a genius in having displayed an unseemly knowledge in the book he published entitled *A Defense of the Constitutions of Government of the United States of America.*

In three volumes my husband had spelled out all the reasons why a mixed government with different branches best protected liberty and prosperity. Now we gladdened at the prospect of returning to partake of both at home.

Eventually, John would be replaced as minister by the distinguished South Carolinian war veteran Thomas Pinckney. But we could not wait for that to come to pass. So we set sail, leaving the post as empty as the British deserved it to be.

"You won't miss Europe?" John asked in the privacy of our berth aboard ship. "All the finery and entertainments?"

"Oh, I've seen enough of the world," I declared. "Henceforth, I shall be content to learn from the pages of history. And you?"

"For a man who has been thirty years rolling like a stone," he said, "I welcome going home."

The only pangs I felt were in parting with Nabby, who was pregnant with her second child. She would be settling with her husband's family in New York. But in making our farewells, she'd reassured me that we'd see one another again soon. "Everyone is saying that Papa will be elected vice president in the new government."

"*Heaven forbid*," I had replied, because our private affairs desperately needed our attention. Besides, I doubted that, after so long away, our countrymen would even remember us.

But those doubts were put to rest by the hero's welcome that awaited us in Boston Harbor. Well-wishers mobbed the docks and cannons roared in salute to welcome my husband home with a thousand people who greeted us with shouts of "Huzzah! Huzzah! Huzzah!"

At the rail, I turned to John to exchange a private smile, and I do believe I glimpsed his lower lip actually wobble. Tears misted his eyes before he managed to compose himself, standing ramrod straight, shoulders squared manfully with pride.

Meanwhile, I gave what I hoped was a dignified wave, overwhelmed with emotions of my own that made me bubble with sudden happy laughter.

Boston, oh Boston, always in cacophony!

As we were ushered from the barge to the carriage, hands reached for us from every direction. They all wanted a better look at Minister Adams and his lady. Even our old friend Henry Knox—now round as a barrel—pushed forward to shake our hands and deliver letters reassuring us of Nabby's safe arrival. Francis Dana—Johnny's old mentor in Russia—had come, too. An aging Sam Adams and a humbled James Lovell congratulated us. Meanwhile, church bells tolled all over the city—one of the most joyous sounds I ever heard in my life.

I knew all this pomp and circumstance might fan my husband's vanity and make him insufferable, but in that moment, I simply couldn't find it within myself to mind if it did.

After being whisked to a gracious reception at the residence of the governor, from whom we received the most pointed civility and attention, we declined an escort to Braintree in his coach and four.

Not wishing to cause more of a stir, we quit Boston quietly to stay with the Cranches, where we met with delightful reunion upon reunion.

Oh, the gladness to be once again folded against the bosom of my older sister, Mary! And there was her daughter Betsy, a woman now, preparing the feast. Friends, neighbors, and relations arrived from everywhere. Phoebe and her husband came with cider from our orchard. Uncle Tufts, now a distinguished elder, welcomed us with good news about our private affairs. My younger sister, Elizabeth, came by carriage from Haverhill. And our sons rode out to us on horseback.

In my mind's eye, I could only imagine my boys as they were when we left them. But as they dismounted and approached us with affectionate but reserved regard, I could see they were both Harvard men now.

Eighteen-year-old Charlie presented me with a dimpled smile and a bouquet, and I almost gasped at his appearance. He cut *quite* the figure in tight buff breeches and matching embroidered waistcoat atop a high-collared white shirt over which his still-flaxen hair curled. Then, after kissing my cheek, Charlie clasped his father's hand, giving it a firm shake. "Welcome home, Father."

"*Charles*," my husband said, one hand on his son's shoulder as he scrutinized the boy he hadn't seen in seven years. "By God, you're so fair I'd wonder if you were a foundling did your mother not swear you were mine."

"John," I said, scandalized, giving his arm a swat.

John only grinned. "Then again, you don't take your looks from your mother's dark-haired tribe either!"

Next came fifteen-year-old Tommy, dressed in his Sunday best—with John's stocky build and my dark hair upon his head. A foundling, he was surely not.

"Mother," Tommy said, kissing both my cheeks.

I returned those kisses and drank him in. He flushed at the attention, as if time and distance had put a polite stiffness between us all, despite the love shining in our eyes. Then, at last, John Quincy arrived, pleading our forgiveness. "I couldn't get a horse!"

My husband's closer relationship with our eldest son was evident by the way he grabbed John Quincy round the neck and loudly professed his love. "Johnny, my boy, my boy . . ."

"Don't blame my brothers if they are shy," Johnny whispered when we embraced. "They're in awe of Papa. And fearful you'll scold them for what they've been up to at Harvard."

At that moment, I didn't give a fig for what either of them had got up to there. Let them instigate all the food fights they liked! "There's nothing sweeter than to be with our children again," I promised my sons. "Today it's the only thing that matters in the world. I'm only sorry your sister isn't here with us."

Of course, there were others missing from this reunion.

Strangely, Mrs. Warren and her husband hadn't come to greet us. And I asked my sister Mary, "Are they terribly ill or have we offended them in some way? Mercy's pen went dry when I was in Europe."

"Mrs. Warren has been unwell for a long time," Mary said over cider. "But she's also embarrassed because she owes you money. And jealous because she believes she was better destined than you to become a prominent lady of the republic."

I thought my sister was being uncharitable. Mercy could be prickly, but I didn't think her petty. And I hoped we might yet be reunited in friendly company. So, I saved my griefs for those with whom I would never again be reunited but in heaven. Colonel Quincy had passed. My Aunt Tufts was gone. My Aunt Smith, too. Perhaps most painful of all was the loss of my unhappy connection to my brother, who had died penniless, drunk, jaundiced, and alone, far from the children he'd abandoned.

I felt ashamed and angry by all the pain Bill had caused his family and himself. I'd spent countless hours thinking about how we'd been raised together but turned out so differently. Yet, mingled with that shame and anger was genuine grief for the brother I'd known in childhood, who'd taught me to play cards. And for the heroic soldier he'd been in our revolution.

Now I hoped his wandering soul was, at last, at peace. Just as I felt mine to finally be.

Home, we were home.

But we wouldn't return to the saltbox in which I'd raised our children in Braintree. Phoebe and her husband were eager to show me how well they'd kept the old place in our absence, but we were to have a new home upon eighty-three acres of the finest land in the area.

"Now you've got the best mansion in Braintree, Honey." Phoebe grinned widely, wearing her Sunday best, and the little tokens I'd sent her from France.

"Indeed, I do," I told her.

I took special pleasure in the purchase of a new house not only because it was the finest mansion in Braintree, but also because I got it for a steal—all owing to a most unlikely benefactor.

Royall Tyler.

In the wake of his romantic scandals, Nabby's former paramour had simply abandoned the place and his creditors like a no-account scoundrel. The jilted owner was so desperate to sell that he accepted two hundred pounds less than his set price. Thus, Tyler's villainy delivered into our hands the most wonderfully situated domicile, with fields to plow and fruit trees to pluck and a picturesque view of the bay besides.

Now Uncle Tufts, stately and seemingly in his prime at the age of fifty-four, was pleased to present John with the keys. "I pounced on it the moment you sent your approval, and now it's yours, sir."

"The idea to buy it was Abigail's," John said graciously. "She has a keen eye for a bargain."

"It is that," Tufts said. "But needs improvement. As you'll soon see for yourself."

I looked forward to hanging wallpaper in the parlor, painting my chambers French Gray, and furnishing each of the seven bedrooms to my liking.

Perhaps it was because I had spent so many hours making such plans that I was so disappointed with the place when I saw it again. The truth was that I'd been spoiled by the grand homes of London and Paris. So much so that this home, with its low ceilings, now seemed as cramped as a wren's house. I'd hoped for a home to give formal entertainments but now teased that a lady guest dared not wear a feathered headdress nor a gentleman heels if he wished to walk upright under our new roof!

Then there was the shocking state of disrepair in which Mr. Tyler had left the place—almost as if he'd somehow *known* we'd purchase it. Perhaps he did possess that warlock power, for it seemed only witchcraft could explain the damage. Every manner of tradesman from carpenter to mason must be hired for the inside.

Tyler had also let the garden run to complete wilderness. Which I supposed was just as well, since it was the only place in which we could put the cows until a new dairy could be built to replace the old one.

"Ah, well," John said, surveying the pile of rotted timbers. "Are not these the rural domestic cares to which we so desperately wished to retire?"

He *said* he wanted to retire, but I knew his mind. The new federal Constitution had been ratified by nine states just days after our return, which made it official. By the end of July, both New York and Virginia had ratified it, too, which meant the new government had a chance to survive. And we'd been informed that John had been elected in absentia to the first Congress.

But John Adams had no wish to be a congressman.

"It'll be the vice presidency," he said. "Or nothing."

Many of my friends, family, and countrymen had grave reservations about this new government. Our son John Quincy feared it wasn't democratic enough. I was told Mrs. Warren opposed it because it lacked a bill of rights. And we already knew of Mr. Jefferson's reservations. Some advised my husband to steer clear of it entirely. So, I should have discouraged John.

Instead, I said, "Any lesser position would surely be beneath your dignity."

Part Three

Chapter Thirty-One

BRAINTREE
Massachusetts
April 1789

M Y HUSBAND PACED before our open windows, spitting venom. "*Half* the votes George Washington got!"

"No one else came close," I reminded him, idly flipping through a pattern book of drapery samples from London.

"It's an insult," John said, utterly disinterested in my improvements at our new farm. "It shows how little my countrymen think of me."

Exasperated—for he'd been ranting and raving about it for hours—I was unable to indulge him for even another moment. "Oh, John. They think so little of you that they've *made you the first vice president of these United States.*"

He crossed his arms. "Only if I accept."

I laughed. I couldn't help it. "You will accept once you've nursed your wounded pride."

"Do you presume to know my mind, Madam?"

"I do indeed, sir. Better than you know your own."

My husband turned from the window, spun on his heel, then spun back again. "And you feel no shame for me in the way this has been offered?"

Again, I laughed. "I feel nothing but *awe* for the man you've become and satisfaction that the rest of the nation appreciates you, too."

His cheeks colored. "Well, then . . ."

As he trailed off, I abandoned my pattern book and rose to capture his cheek in my hand. "Listen, husband. A federal cavalry has been sent to escort you in the morning. A cavalry in Braintree for the new vice president! Never could we have imagined something so grand."

"You'll follow?" he asked, the edge of anxiety in his voice. "You'll join me in New York?"

"*If* I must," I replied, pretending weariness.

In truth, I did not relish the idea of packing up all the furniture from Europe just as I finally had it arranged to my liking. Even less did I relish the idea of leaving my family again. My sisters would be disconsolate. But John Quincy was a grown man, studying law like his father before him. And the younger two boys were both at Harvard, with Charles nearly graduated.

Soon our nest in Braintree would be empty—our flock of children all flown away. Whereas in New York, we could at least be close to Nabby, who now had another little baby at the breast, whom she'd named after her father.

Very seriously, my husband said, "I'll need you there, Abigail. Even if you must leave this place to the birds and the beasts."

I gave a quick look around, calculating the expense of the repairs and improvements we were making, and it didn't seem such a bad idea to let it go to wilderness. "Very well. Find a new house for us in New York and I'll make *that* a home. I know you want your own bed and pillows, your hot coffee. I know how many of these little matters make up a large portion of our happiness."

He stooped to kiss me. "*You* are my whole happiness, Abigail."

It certainly pleased me to hear it, even if I knew it wasn't entirely true. He couldn't be happy without pursuing his grand destiny. If I was jealous of America, that was my own fault. For if I'd wanted an ordinary marriage, I wouldn't have married John Adams.

MY HUSBAND WAS seen off by cheering crowds at the sides of the road. It was to be the beginning of an entirely new chapter of our lives, and we were writing the first page of the new nation under the Constitution besides.

But, of course, first, much had to be managed.

To begin with, our son Charles could not be left to his own devices. His latest escapade at Harvard involved running nude through the courtyard—which he swore he did only to cheer a companion who was down in the dumps. Whatever the motives of the softhearted fool, Charles was getting a reputation—not entirely undeserved—as a beautiful but bad young man.

He simply *must* have a fresh start. Which was why we obtained permission for Charles to forgo commencement in order to take up an offer my son-in-law had declined: to study law in New York City under the well-regarded Alexander Hamilton.

Like Nabby's husband, Hamilton had been Washington's aide-de-camp during the war. Though unlike my son-in-law, he never rose above the rank of lieutenant colonel.

Nevertheless, Hamilton was already a brilliant lawyer and one of the authors of *The Federalist Papers*, which had persuaded the states to ratify the Constitution. His views on mixed government and checks and balances had much in common with those my husband expounded in the volumes he published in London.

Now, Hamilton was a man very much on the rise. So, if our middle son was to learn the law, he couldn't have a better master.

Meanwhile, our youngest moped at hearing Charles would be coming with us to New York. "Tommy left behind yet again. All alone."

"All alone?" John Quincy asked, taking umbrage. "I'll be only a day away by horseback should you need me. Sometimes I think my own brothers forget I ever returned from Russia."

Tommy gave his big brother a nudge in the ribs. "Trust that we can never forget about *you* John Quincy. Our brother, the prodigy."

Charles confirmed it. "We never hear an end to the praise of your wisdom and good behavior, Johnny."

I could imagine how Nabby would add to the teasing. *John Quincy Adams, the golden child . . .*

But she wasn't here, and it seemed our destiny as Adamses never to be all together at the same time.

That night, pacing the room in his sleeping shirt, John pleaded, "Abigail, you *will* come after the inauguration, won't you?"

"I already said I would, Mr. Vice President."

"You're a saucy woman, Mrs. Vice President," he replied. "But I simply cannot do without you."

IT TOOK MONTHS before I could close up the new house and farm. My husband's brother had promised to take it on in our absence but now refused. In consequence, I found myself fertilizing the meadow. Ah, from the glories of Versailles and the Court of St. James to emptying buckets of manure in Braintree! But someone had to tend the fields.

Though immersed in his legal apprenticeship, Johnny helped me sell a troublesome horse that had smashed a wagon to bits. Meanwhile, Tommy volunteered to quit Harvard, help on the farm, and live with Phoebe at the old place so we could rent the new.

I knew Tommy was eager to be helpful, but also that he would be happy to escape his books. Of course, this his father would never countenance, so I resigned myself to doing what I could by myself and leaving the farm nearly in the state that I'd got it— with bare pastures but some asparagus beds made.

Fortunately, my bonny son Charles arrived the week before departure and cheerfully pitched in with the remaining tasks, all while fending off the flirtation of a neighbor's daughter who lingered to watch him working shirtless in the field on an unseasonably hot day.

When I scolded him, Charles swept those golden curls out of his blue eyes and grinned. "I cannot help that girls flock to me like songbirds."

"You can try keeping your clothes on!"

When Uncle Tufts stopped by to settle some of our mutual finances, he couldn't help but laugh at my predicament with shirtless Charles and his lady admirers. "It's good that you're taking him with you to New York, where he'll be under your watchful eye."

"Let us hope my eye is watchful enough to ward off mischief," I said.

As it turned out, Charles was a delightful traveling companion who kept out of trouble, eating and sleeping without the slightest inconvenience. "I know how to duck my head and adjust to my circumstances. You forget, Mama, how much time I spent roving the world."

"Oh, I will *never* forget it. And there were moments I feared I might never forgive your father for it, either." But those harrowing days were now tales of family adventure.

And now we were about to start a new one.

WHEN CHARLES AND I arrived in the port of New York, a forest of ships' masts and fluttering flags welcomed us, the music of Trinity Church's bell not far off.

And to every gentleman we came across in the harbor, my son chirped, "Well met, sir. I'm Charles Adams! Son of the vice president. I have the honor to be your obedient servant."

We were sorry to have missed the inauguration, for which the newspapers informed, "His Excellency John Adams, one of the ornaments of our age, has received an elegant suit of American broadcloth manufactured in Hartford in which to make his appearance as Vice President of the United States."

I was sorrier to have missed my husband's speech before the Senate. But I was recompensed in seeing our new home on Richmond Hill, where my daughter bounded out the door without any sense of decorum to embrace us.

Despite now being the mother of two clinging little boys, Nabby positively glowed with energy and good health. "Mother! I hope you approve of the place and what I've done to prepare it for you," Nabby said, showing me how delightfully situated this home was, with a beautiful view of the Hudson River. The verdant fields were ornamented with mighty pine and oak trees. The manse itself was grand, with stately columns and a hawthorn-hedged flower garden round back.

"It is perfect," I assured her. "More to my mind than any other place I have ever lived in."

"There are many species of birds here," came a voice from behind us.

It was Colonel Smith, at home and at leisure midday, as was his habit since returning to America. "Pigeons. Partridges. Woodcocks. They'll all sing to you, madam."

Colonel Smith was himself a great aficionado of poultry, and, like a country squire, was almost never to be found without hunting dogs at his heels.

"I shall delight in their song," I assured my son-in-law.

Charles was keen to make the acquaintance of his new brother, for though he'd heard much of Colonel Smith, they'd not yet met. "I'd like to see them, sir, if you will show me."

We let the two gents go off to make friends over their mutual love of birds. And inside, I saw that Nabby had everything so well arranged that only beds and a few additional articles seemed necessary for our comfort.

While I unpacked, Nabby attended the cradle in the corner, where my newest grandson—John Adams Smith, named for his grandfather—slept fitfully. And watching her rock her little Jack with pride, I said, "You've done so well that I begin to think my own furniture will stay packed. At least whilst your family remains with us here in New York, which I hope will be for some time."

I had more than a maternal reason to hope so. I had scarcely rested from my travels before the house was a scene of levee. The city's leading lights descended daily in ornate carriages. First to call upon me was a friend I made in Paris, the beautiful Angelica Church, who introduced me to her sweet younger sister, Mrs. Alexander Hamilton. Next came Mrs. Morris, dripping in jewels, followed by Mrs. Knox wearing hoop skirts so wide I feared for my end tables. Senators' wives, the ladies of foreign diplomats—somehow they'd all heard of my arrival and wished to pay call.

If I meant to do anything useful here, I'd need my daughter's help to fend off well-meaning callers and keep up appearances. Especially as the only person I wished to see was my very own husband.

How upright and distinguished the vice president looked when he finally strode in the door at one o'clock to clap Charles on the back and fold me into his embrace.

Yet, there was a certain hint of fear in my husband's eyes that I couldn't account for when he said, "Your first call must be to Lady Washington."

"*Lady* Washington? Is that what we are to call her?"

John scowled. "No one in this new government knows what to call anyone. We're living in bedlam."

How annoyed he was on that point! I could scarcely blame him. Had there been a republic of the sort we'd founded since the days of the old Romans? It felt as if we were creating everything anew.

"President Washington has been very ill," John finally said. "His life was despaired of."

"*No*," I said, quite horrified.

We'd heard some rumor along the journey that the new president was suffering a mild fever, but now John explained, "He had an infected tumor of the leg; he had to undergo surgery. It was feared that gangrene would take him."

My hands went to my mouth. "Is he—Washington—er, His Lordship—or is it His Majesty—recovered?"

John only said, "The immediate crisis has passed. The tumor was cut out and the fever has abated, so we believe he'll survive. But that is hardly a guarantee, is it?"

No man's life was guaranteed in this world, and my husband stood only one man's breath away from the presidency. The weight of responsibility descended upon me, making my limbs weak. Washington was chosen to be the president of our new government because he was the only man they believed could hold it together.

If he died, could my brilliant but irascible husband do the same?

I simply did not know. And everything felt in such a precarious state.

"Washington cannot even sit up," John said, all but wringing his hands. Had any provision been made in the Constitution about what might happen if a president was alive but too feeble to serve? "But he must survive because this nation is too young to survive such a calamity."

Nabby and I went the very next morning to pay respects to Mrs. Washington at the three-story redbrick presidential residence on Cherry Street, with its freshly painted white stoop and a uniformed sentry standing guard. The drive was roped and chained out of fear that carriages might wake the president while he recovered, so we were obliged to come down from our carriage and walk part of the way.

I was prepared to be told that the Washingtons couldn't receive us but we were taken to Mrs. Washington's drawing room to call upon the woman who not only held the first position of ladies in our nation, but who must also be living in fear she might lose her husband.

For the occasion, I'd worn one of my best gowns from the Court of St. James. But Martha Washington, as it happened, was plain as a Quaker. Every bit of her clothing was of the finest quality, but it was plain, nonetheless. And she greeted me with great ease and politeness, her soft Virginia accent at the fore. "Mrs. Adams, you do us the greatest honor."

"The honor is all mine," I said with a curtsey.

Nabby also bobbed a curtsey, glancing to me nervously for direction as to how she ought to behave. But truly, I didn't know how to behave, or what I expected of Washington's lady, for despite her visits to her husband's winter camp during the siege of Boston, we'd not met before. And I feared that I stared too long taking in her appearance.

The plump Martha Washington had white hair, and when she smiled, I saw she had beautiful teeth. Somehow, all the parts put together gave her an air of dignified femininity without even the tincture of hauteur.

"I'm grieved to hear of His Majesty's illness," I told her. "And I regret that I came at a time that I cannot present myself and my daughter to him."

"I assure you, he regrets it more," she said, offering tea and cakes.

The cakes were bright and tart with lemon, and the tea a rich and fragrant brew I hadn't tasted in America since long before the war. As we ate and drank, we traded social niceties about the weather and our new home on Richmond Hill but soon turned to our business as the wives of the nation's most public men.

"I never expected to find myself in this position," Mrs. Washington confided. "I had hopes, after so much toil and sacrifice during the war, to spend the evening of our lives in domestic peace. I think this a position better suited for a woman such as yourself—a woman with more gaiety and youth."

I was flattered that she could possibly think me youthful. "My dear lady, we are *both* grandmothers."

That pleased Martha to hear. "In any case, henceforth I'm determined to be cheerful about my situation because I firmly believe that the greater part of our happiness or misery depends on our dispositions. But I find this business of receiving and returning calls most tedious."

I sympathized. "In Britain, there's quite an elaborate system. I found it helped to return the calls in the early evening when ladies were exhausted from the day's business and less apt to say they were *at home*."

Martha smiled at my ingenuity but then offered her own. "I believe I've devised a means by which to dispense with it efficiently. I will hold public levees on Friday evenings. And I should hope you may often be in attendance."

"Of course," I said, only belatedly realizing this would be, for Mrs. Washington, like a queen holding court. Which meant that I'd be . . . *what*? Her lady-in-waiting? The etiquette was quite vexing.

She then informed me that as I was the lady second most in rank, the public would expect me to host entertainments of my own at a given time every week at which they'd be offered refreshments and the opportunity to chitchat by my warm fire.

Trying to be agreeable, I said, "I'll receive guests on Mondays, so as not to conflict with your levees."

Martha smiled approvingly. "*Do* be a dear and let the other ladies know. They've been waiting for your arrival to make firm plans."

Having quietly nibbled at her cake, Nabby now glanced up. "The other ladies?"

Though we didn't know it at the time, each of the important ladies in the new administration would hold receptions on a different night of the week. Henry Knox was now secretary of war and his wife, Lucy, would claim Wednesdays. Mr. John Jay would be serving as the chief justice, and his wife, Sarah, would claim Thursdays. And so on.

There wasn't a public budget for these entertainments. We'd have to pay for them ourselves. But before Mrs. Washington could tell me all this, a servant bent to say, "The president has awakened, and upon hearing of Mrs. Adams's visit, would like to receive her. Perhaps you'd be so kind as to visit his rooms?"

Nabby and I rose swiftly, duly sensitive to the honor, and a servant ushered us into the president's presence, where we found him lying upon a settee. Though his manner forbade overfamiliarity, he was still quite personable. Half raising himself up, he said, "I beg you to excuse me for receiving you and your daughter in this posture, Mrs. Adams."

I curtseyed with true reverence. "Given your illness, it is perfectly understandable, Your Majesty."

I'd been impressed by Washington all those years ago when he was the general in whom we put all our revolutionary hopes. Age had only made him more venerable. Like my husband, he'd come out of retirement to make these states into a nation, and in so doing, he seemed to have grown in stature. Now I felt his eyes sweep up and down my elaborate court gown. "I congratulate you and your husband on your good service overseas, Mrs. Adams. Though I do wonder if you can relish the simple manners of America after having been accustomed to those of Europe."

I couldn't help but tease, "Oh, I think Americans enjoy more of the same luxury and manners of Europe than they're willing to admit."

The president smiled at my unwillingness to pretend Americans were inherently humbler people than those found across the sea. "As I have discussed with your Mr. Adams, it will be a difficult balance to instill our new republic with power and majesty whilst refusing to festoon it with the trappings of monarchy."

"A continuing discussion I know he'd welcome, should you honor us with a visit to Richmond Hill when you are able. It is a beautiful spot. Peaceful. You must make it your resting place, as it'll restore your spirits."

I meant it but didn't anticipate that he'd come so soon. Not long after this visit, the president had a bed put into his carriage so he could ride to our home. The stairs into the house gave him quite a bit of trouble. Nevertheless, I counted it amongst the honors of my life that he *did* visit and somehow managed the obstacle of those stairs. Over dinner, he gifted some sugar plums to my two little grandsons. And in very short order, I decided that George Washington was a man of unassuming kindness, which left me much more deeply impressed than I ever felt before the monarch of Great Britain.

Chapter Thirty-Two

RICHMOND HILL
New York
Fall 1789

THE NEWS FROM France was almost too dramatic to be believed. The Bastille stormed. Uprisings in the provinces. Officials hanged, beheaded, and eviscerated by angry mobs . . .

We often read the latest dispatch aloud as we sat on the portico, enjoying the breeze from the Hudson. According to headlines, the French were in rebellion against their king, and despite the violence, my fellow Americans welcomed the idea that our revolution was now spreading across the world.

I was frightened for the safety of our French friends. My husband, even more so. "I hope this will end in liberty for the people, but the way this moves forward I foresee great calamities."

This was not, however, the great subject that concerned the United States under its new constitutional government. Instead, our Congress debated the matter of titles—a controversy in which my husband played a central role.

And now his indignant shouts frightened a squirrel in a nearby tree.

"*John*," I winced, wanting to cover my ears against his tirade. "I already said I agree with you."

But he was still arguing with the Senate in absentia. "We cannot simply address George Washington without a title as if he were any other citizen. It isn't monarchical to insist on some distinction such as *His Highness* or *His Majesty*."

"Yes, you're right," I said for the tenth time.

But on he went to the invisible jury. "Whenever mankind means to respect anything, we give some special ceremony to it. Why build monuments and erect gravestones? Why do children call us *Father* and *Mother* instead of our given names? I daresay we called George Washington *His Excellency* when he was our general—and that didn't make him king."

Thankfully, a servant announced tea, and I seized the excuse to escape into the warmth of our carpeted parlor, where Charles was already pouring a cup for his sister.

But John followed me, still on his rant.

Nabby had also been treated to her father's arguments since his arrival in New York, and now she whispered urgently, "You must make him give this up before people poke fun at him."

"Too late," muttered Charles into his cup. He was studying law under Alexander Hamilton—a man whose talents he much admired—and because of his proximity to Mr. Hamilton, he oft heard news before the rest of us. "I've heard they're calling my father *His Rotundity, the Duke of Braintree.*"

As my husband reddened, Charles added, "I fear I shall soon have to challenge someone to a duel."

"I sent you to study under Mr. Hamilton, not to ape his youthful foolishness," John snapped, for Hamilton had a reputation for involving himself in so-called affairs of honor. "I thought you had better sense."

Charles grinned. "Well, I have sense enough to know that Mr. Hamilton will not long be my master. He's spoken of as Washington's choice for secretary of state."

John blinked, genuinely surprised. "A fine soldier he might've been. A fine legal and economic mind, too. But secretary of state? What foreign experience does that man have other than having been born in the Caribbean? The president should have a seasoned diplomat for his minister of state."

In the end, my husband lost the fight about titles. It was resolved that our leader would be called simply *President Washington*. But in the matter of the cabinet, John's point of view prevailed.

Washington offered Hamilton the post of secretary of the *treasury* instead of state. Which was all right with me, because we were owed quite a bit of money from our time abroad, and Hamilton seemed just the man to set accounts right.

When I said so at some dinner party, Mr. Hamilton leaned over with blue eyes that gleamed almost wicked. "I shall take the *greatest* pleasure in fulfilling your wish, madam."

I merely smiled, having been flattered in foreign courts by men far more seasoned. But I understood why others found Hamilton charming in company. It was his evident genius and the passion with which he presented his clever views. Not to mention the intoxicating sense of power that he projected. Of course, it grated John's nerves the way Hamilton strode about the capital as if he were prime minister, and not merely secretary of the treasury.

But I thought indulgences must be made for men of genius.

Then one night, after one of Mrs. Washington's levees, my husband returned home in a rage, tearing off his cravat. "*Villainy!*"

John had finally discovered why he received fewer votes for vice president than he expected. "Hamilton wrote to electors instructing them to throw their votes elsewhere to avoid the procedural trouble of a tie, and embarrassment for Washington."

I hated this obsession of my husband with how many votes he received. But I knew from experience that if I disagreed, it would only prompt him to marshal his powers of argument. So I tried a different tactic.

Feigning shock, I said, "What corrupt intrigue. Why, John, they must have had real fears that you'd get the greatest number of votes, defeat Washington, and win the presidency!"

My husband's puffed chest deflated as reality struck his brain. "More votes than Washington? Surely not, my dear."

I blinked as innocently as a doe. "Why else would Hamilton engage in such an underhanded scheme? Personal animus?"

"None that I'm aware of," John grumbled. "No doubt, he did it out of simple loyalty to Washington, worrying about the mischief a tie would make."

I blinked again. "Do you think so?"

John threw up his hands. "Well, he could've been open and honest about it! But Hamilton has too much disposition to intrigue."

I coaxed, "What will you do?"

My husband was too caught up in himself to notice the unnatural fluttering of my lashes. His finger pointed in elocution, as if he were back in the courtroom. "I could make an official inquiry into my election!" Then the fury leeched out of him, and the finger wilted. "Yet, in truth, it's better forgotten."

This was the conclusion I hoped he'd draw. Now I asked the only question about which I was still of two minds. "Can Secretary Hamilton be trusted?"

"No. He's too *ambitious*." John sighed. "Still, I think he has good abilities and great industry. And I know not where a better secretary of the treasury could be found."

From all reports, Hamilton was a first-rate talent. A great deal more worldly and sophisticated than Congressman Madison, whose bad ideas stacked up in the legislature every day. Among them, Madison had proposed to force buyers of government securities to split the payouts with the original holders who had been forced to sell them during difficult times.

If that proposal passed, I stood to lose quite a bit of money. Thus, for the time being, I was for Hamilton. Charles was, too.

But my son-in-law, Colonel Smith, was less impressed, which had everything to do with his frustration. Having gone without employment for seventeen months whilst awaiting a federal appointment, Colonel Smith—bitterly disappointed—had been passed over for lucrative offices. As a genuine hero of the American Revolution, and a Washington loyalist to boot, he'd expected commensurate recognition from the new president. Instead, Washington named him to be a federal marshal—a position with vast responsibilities and personal risk but very meager pay.

I was distressed to think how Colonel Smith could possibly support his family on the wages proposed, but I couldn't let my distress add to my daughter's, so I tried to find the silver lining. "It's a vitally important job," I said to Nabby, for as one of the first federal marshals in the country, my son-in-law would need to protect judges, ensure the smooth operation of the courts, conduct a census, serve warrants, and make arrests. "President Washington couldn't appoint anyone whose patriotism he didn't trust completely."

"Well, he *should* trust my husband's patriotism," Nabby said, quietly. "For without it, he would've lost his army twice over during the war."

I knew this was true. Colonel Smith got Washington on a barge at the Battle of Long Island. Later in the war, Colonel Smith had destroyed a bridge to keep Howe from overrunning Washington's army. My son-in-law never spoke of this heroism. He probably felt as if he didn't need to. That the public would remember. But in recent years Colonel Smith had been serving the country overseas, where his accomplishments went unseen.

Years away had erased him from the public mind.

Nabby told me his pride was deeply wounded. "Both Hamilton and my husband were trusted aides-de-camp. Yet Hamilton is in the cabinet, whereas my husband is to be a glorified jailer."

On the one hand, it did seem unjust. Hamilton fought in fewer battles, was never injured in the cause, and once resigned in a fit of pique during the war. Yet he was widely considered George Washington's favorite son.

On the other hand, my son-in-law had ignored our advice to complete his legal education and boasted of no expertise in government. He hadn't done an honest day's work since returning from London, preferring to wait for a choice appointment while hunting partridges.

I gave my daughter an encouraging smile. "I'm sure it's only a start. If Colonel Smith does well as marshal, surely he'll rise."

Or at least I hoped he would.

My husband had written personally on Smith's behalf, which may have hurt his prospects more than helped. For as cordial as Washington was to us in society, appointing our son-in-law to a more prominent role in government might invite the criticism that he was bringing men into his administration by way of heredity rather than merit.

If I were in Washington's place, I might shy away from it, too. But none of this did I tell Nabby. "Well, we must simply do what we can to advance our husbands in a different arena. The *social* one."

In that arena, I was at least a little adept.

Every Friday evening all manner of people turned out for Mrs. Washington's levees dressed brilliantly to be entertained with lemonades and ice creams. And while other ladies tried to outdo one another in pearls, gloves, feather ornaments, and embroidered silk shoes. I had the honor to attend the president's lady on the dais. President Washington even did me the honor of gently removing any other lady who tried to take my place. And there, at Martha Washington's side, I carried myself with what I hoped was a dignified bearing—trying to convey the sense of authority and sureness that would've rivaled any lady-in-waiting at a royal court.

But, of course, this was a republican court.

Mrs. Washington's simpler levees—held in her neoclassical drawing room with its Wilton carpet and gilded paintings— were grand enough for me. For if I closed my eyes, I could easily remember myself on my knees scrubbing floors, feeding geese, milking cows, and scraping together meals for my children from old root vegetables in the cellar.

Fortunately, I'd come a long way from the days of the war. And what diplomacy I'd learned in Europe made me better able to manage being pressed on all sides by those who now sought to curry favor.

I found myself besieged by hangers-on who wished me to get an audience for them with my husband. I was approached by strangers who somehow thought they had some right to presume upon me. I was also pressed by friends of long-standing acquaintance, like Mrs. Warren, who—despite her indebtedness to me, her lack of letters, her new coolness to us, and her virulent opposition to the Constitution—now asked me to convince my husband to find some government position for her sons.

I couldn't do this in good conscience. To spare us both the embarrassment, I threw the letter into the fire and pretended never to have received it.

"OH, FOR AN English butler and housekeeper," I muttered while fixing the place settings, lighting the parlor, and fussing over my own hair, since we had no friseur.

Still, we were managing. I might complain about my weariness in making idle conversation with the wives of every government official, diplomat, or other stranger who happened to make the trip to Richmond Hill. But I was becoming *exceedingly* good at it.

I'd learned well in Paris and London. I knew that my quick, acerbic wit could be an asset in political circles, because society ladies feared me a little bit, and under the circumstances, that was no bad thing. It meant they were more apt to aim their darts at someone like the round and jolly Mrs. Knox.

I was well content. And why shouldn't I be? Surrounded by my children and grandchildren, I told Nabby that if only I could pluck my remaining loved ones from Braintree and transport them here, I should be the happiest woman alive.

Nabby's brow inched up. "That is all you want for?"

I glanced down at my expanding waistline. "Well, I should also like to develop an aversion to Mrs. Washington's lemon cakes before I grow ro—round."

I'd nearly said the word *rotund*, which called to mind the mockery of my husband as His Rotundity, the Duke of Braintree. And Nabby smirked at me. "Papa cannot pass them by either. It would seem to be a family trait."

"Now that you mention it, your brother Charles grows fat as a goose."

My daughter chuckled. "Because you domesticated him! He was once a wild slender songbird, fluttering about Harvard's courtyard in nothing but the clothing of nature. Now that he's caged, he has naught to do but gorge on the seed."

I eyed her for her poultry references. "It is good for wives to have different interests than their husbands, you know."

"*You* likened Charles to a goose!"

I laughed. "Truthfully, he eats quite sparingly. So, he mustn't take enough exercise. Or, perhaps he too often sacrifices to Bacchus with your husband at his social club."

Nabby understood this to be a veiled accusation. "It is more likely the sweets my unmarried sister-in-law plies him with. There isn't a girl who doesn't want to watch the dimpled Charles Adams eat her confections."

Scandalized, I flapped my fan against her arm. "He had best be careful, or those dimples of his will be his undoing."

"WELCOME TO NEW YORK, Mr. Jefferson!" I said, beckoning our old friend into my drawing room.

Having only recently returned from his stint as ambassador in Paris, Jefferson had been made secretary of state. And we couldn't be happier.

Now the Virginia gentleman lifted my hands to give a courtly kiss to the back of each one. "Mrs. Adams, you are a sight for sore eyes after a journey in such snow I could travel no more than three miles an hour. How pleased I am to find you looking well."

Jefferson was also looking well. Very well indeed. Still tall, freckled, and lean—but with a new gravitas and a more sophisticated wardrobe he acquired in Paris.

"Are your little girls with you?" I asked.

Jefferson smiled. "Not so little now. Patsy is seventeen and soon to be married."

"I had not heard!"

He nodded, hands behind his back. "A distant cousin. Not a blockhead. I'm delighted by the match."

"We will send a gift!" I said, then teased, "Though I hoped we might match your Patsy to one of my boys to strengthen the federal union."

Jefferson chuckled. "Well, I still have Polly. When I'm better settled, she'll join me."

My heart filled with warmth, remembering that little girl. "That would be wonderful! And how fares Sally?"

Oddly, Jefferson curled inward at the question, as if I had somehow stabbed at a vulnerable spot. "Well. She's well."

I was confused; perhaps Virginians didn't ask after each other's enslaved servants, but he had never flinched when I'd asked after James Hemings. In any case, the discomfort of the moment was fleeting, as Mr. Jefferson was charming as ever.

We fell swiftly into amiable conversation as he asked after Nabby and my grandchildren. Jefferson smiled broadly and his eyes settled upon the decorative table where little Willy's childish chalk crayon drawing lay, as the maids had yet to clear it away.

"I see your grandson is an artist in the making," Jefferson said with a wink. "You ought to frame it to ornament the walls of this lovely abode. And it is truly lovely. I'm envious, as I'm lodging at a boardinghouse just now, though I hope to take a house on Maiden Lane."

"A good location. Colonel Smith found a place on Nassau Street. You'll be neighbors."

I didn't mention it was a foolish expense for Nabby's husband to undertake, considering a third child was soon to be born. I kept my own counsel about my son-in-law's expenses, since no one is without their difficulties, whether in high or low life, and every person knows best where their own shoe pinches.

"What news from the House of Representatives?" Jefferson came around to asking as we waited for John to return from the ferry.

"I was in attendance myself to hear Secretary Hamilton's report on the public credit and his proposal to assume state debts; I looked on from the galleries with Mrs. Jay. It was a spectacle."

Time with the ladies of France seemed to have accustomed Jefferson to women in public affairs, for he no longer showed surprise at my involvement in politics or finance. "And what think you of the proposal to move the nation's capital?"

I made a face. "I'd rather not move again." I doubted there was a spot in the United States so beautiful as this upon which I lived now. But I knew southerners feared northern influence. Cheekily, I suggested, "Perhaps Philadelphia would be convenient."

"Or even Baltimore," he replied, ever the diplomat. "In any case, I'm curious to see what compromise may be had."

"*I* am curious about what is happening in France," I said, unable to resist interrogating him on the matter even a moment longer. "We've heard positively dreadful reports. Violence and mayhem."

"Some," he said, his tone measured. "So far it seems that their revolution has got along with a steady pace, with occasional difficulties and dangers. But we are not to expect to be transported from despotism to liberty in a feather bed."

"But I'm so fearful for the Lafayettes."

He grimaced. "Yes. I've never feared for the ultimate result, though I fear for Lafayette personally. France would work out her salvation, but were she to lose Lafayette, it would cost her oceans of blood, and years of confusion and anarchy."

He seemed disconcertingly philosophical about it. And I sensed, even then, that small political fissures were beginning to open between us. But we were all only too glad that Jefferson would be secretary of state—that, and knowing he would add so much to our social circle over the season.

And so he did, though I cannot say everyone was happy for his company.

Alexander Hamilton greeted the secretary of state's debut as if a rival for his lady love had swept into town.

At Mrs. Washington's glorious New Year's party, the chandeliers dripped candle wax onto clusters of lemon-verbena-scented ladies in feathered plumes, while gentlemen gulped down warm spiced wine.

Mr. Jefferson tried valiantly for light conversation with other guests, but Hamilton cornered him near the table of sugar-dusted honey cakes, and like an angry hornet, dove straight in for the sting. "A national debt, Secretary Jefferson—if it is not excessive—will be a blessing."

Jefferson frowned into his glass of punch, apparently fascinated by the orange slice bobbing in his drink. "I wish I could agree for the sake of agreeableness, sir. But I sincerely believe the principle of spending money to be paid by posterity is but swindling futurity on a large scale."

I stared into my own cup of syllabub, feigning distraction. But I was still listening attentively when Hamilton began to needle Jefferson about the progress of the French Revolution, disparaging all who took part in it.

I saw that Jefferson took great offense, though he was too much a gentleman to ruin the merriment of the evening by saying so. But his fury would later be vented behind Hamilton's back.

For the two cabinet secretaries apparently started the year as they meant to go on, and by spring, it was already known they were dedicated foes.

THE WEATHER REMAINED uncommonly wet and cold, as if the sky itself grieved the passing of Benjamin Franklin in Philadelphia at the ripe old age of eighty-four.

Here in New York, we had more snow in spring than through the whole winter. And everyone was now sick. Most especially President Washington.

"We are in great anxiety for the president," John confided. "Be prudent and say little upon the subject. We cannot have general alarm."

"I'm certainly in no state to gossip," I said, vexed by a frightful cough and the idea he could think me so foolish. "I thought he was recovering in the countryside?"

"He returned with a violent fever and such a rattling in his throat that Mrs. Washington left his room thinking him dying. The physicians warn me we may need to be prepared to step forward."

He meant that if Washington died, he'd become president, and I'd replace Martha Washington as the foremost lady in the land. I'd seen enough to know what that meant, and it was a position I had not the least ambition to attain.

That night, as freezing rain lashed the windows, I lay awake, haunted by a single thought: the government's survival depended on George Washington's life.

If he died, John would be called to replace him, and it would be an impossible task. The burden could crush him—our public finances in chaos, the government untested, the people unsure.

Leadership in such times was filled with peril. In France, the king and his family were prisoners of the mob. And John warned that this was the fate of leaders when government failed.

I feared that fate for him. I feared it for us all.

Even if Washington recovered—he had already been at death's door twice. And if he didn't last to the next election . . . where would we be?

Chapter Thirty-Three

NEW YORK CITY
New York
August 1790

WASHINGTON RECOVERED, AND that summer every important man in his administration hurried to cement necessary changes in government lest we again be thrown into such a panic.

Thanks to a compromise forged at a dinner between Secretary Hamilton, Secretary Jefferson, and Mr. Madison, we were to move the capital. First to Philadelphia, then later, to a stretch of swampy wilderness on the Potomac between Maryland and Virginia, where they aimed to build a city from scratch.

Hamilton would have his financial plan—the federal government assuming the war debts of the states and filling the pockets of those who had invested in those government notes long ago, myself among them. Hamilton's plan might make us wealthy, but I detested the idea of leaving New York.

Especially since our family was already experiencing so many private changes.

Having swept into Nabby's new house on Nassau Street, immediately setting everything better to my liking, moving furniture here and there, I said, "Your baby brother is through commencement now, though it was not the affair it might've been. Gone are the days I can ask your Aunt Cranch to make a plum cake for three hundred."

Nabby looked a little appalled. "Surely Tommy at least had a celebratory *dinner.*"

I sighed in reply, glancing around the parlor, trying to decide where better to relocate her tea cart so visitors would not bang into it every time they walked in the hall. "I shall have to make it up to him somehow. For now, I'm glad my boys have all passed through college, and have done so well, despite the almost constant absence of their parents."

It was my daughter who worried me now, soon due to birth another child—*much* too soon after the last—which made me hover. "This house is too small and hot and stuffy in the summer for you to give birth here. You must come to Richmond Hill to bring forth your child."

I think she took it for implied criticism of her husband, because she argued, "This house is in the midst of the hustle and bustle. It shall be easy for the doctor to be called, if need be. And in any case, I cannot leave my husband."

"Whyever not? There are at least servants at my home to watch after the children so you can lie in restfully and regain your strength."

"Colonel Smith is happy to look after our boys while I rest."

I gave her the most skeptical look of my life. "I scarcely even trusted your papa to look after you when you were the age my grandsons are now."

But I could no longer command her. Nabby would likely move her furniture back to the way she had it the moment I left the room. And in the end, she insisted upon giving birth where she was.

When our newest grandson was born, blue eyes glistening with wonder at the world, I couldn't help but laugh at his size.

"Such a big fellow," John said, pretending to grunt under the weight in his arms. "And ginger hair! What branch of the family do we owe that to?"

I laughed. "Not mine. What shall he be named?"

"*Thomas*," Nabby said. "In honor of my little brother who graduated from Harvard without fanfare."

"Poor Tommy," Charles broke in. "Always an afterthought."

Nabby poked his arm. "Well, now he has a namesake."

To which her brother crowed, "The next one ought to be named after me!"

"The next one?" I cried. "No man ought to talk about *the next one* so soon after a woman's labor unless he wants his ears boxed."

Towering over me, Charles said, "You cannot even reach my ears anymore, Mother."

My husband snorted with amusement. "Oh, do not dare her, my foolish son. Where the vice president's lady has a will, she finds a way."

OUR FAMILY WAS happy in New York that summer mixing in an entirely new social circle—one inhabited by no lesser figure than Alexander McGillivray, a chieftain of the Creek Indians who had come to New York to negotiate a treaty with President Washington.

"I should never have suspected him to be of that nation, as he's not very dark," I told Nabby. "Indeed, he dresses in our own fashion and speaks English perfectly well."

"Well, that is a dull report," Nabby said.

"Never fear, his fellow chieftains are much more exotic to our eyes. All of them very fine-looking men in deerskin breeches, silver armbands, and feathered turbans. The painter Mr. Trumbull has pronounced them perfect models."

The treaty signing was expected to draw more than fifteen hundred Creek Indians and eight hundred Cherokees. Rations were given for the celebratory bonfire, around which they danced like spirits, hooping, singing, and yelling.

At Washington's official function later, the gentlemen mingled to one side of the room, while ladies mingled on the other. And I noticed many of our ladies either felt distaste, or felt obligated to pretend distaste, for these tribal people.

All except for the young Eliza Hamilton, which surprised me. Of the cabinet officers' wives, she'd always seemed the most timid. "You didn't take alarm by the bonfire dancing, Mrs. Hamilton?"

"Oh, no," she said, sipping from a crystal goblet, then dabbing her cleft chin with a kerchief. "My father, Senator Schuyler, is a longtime Indian agent. I'm much accustomed to such things."

"I wish I could converse better with them," I said. "For they seem friendly, manly, generous, grateful, and honest. Not at all what people say of them. And they certainly know how to express their pleasure in true savage style."

"It's true," said Mrs. Hamilton, adorned for the occasion in a

plain powdered wig and black ribbon round her throat for deco-
ration. "But are they the savages or are we? I wonder."

It was an interesting comment. One that seemed quite out of
place coming from the wife of the suave Secretary Hamilton, who,
sporting a peacock silk tailcoat with gold lapels, never seemed to
harbor the slightest doubt about our enterprises.

Nevertheless, as the evening went on, and dinner was served,
I felt true delight when one of the chieftains bent his knee and
conferred upon me an Indian name. "*Mammea.*"

I was honored, though I had absolutely no idea what it meant,
and did not wish to offend by asking. I looked about the room to
see if anyone might offer a translation; but no one did.

The secretary of war was studiously cutting into his ham, and
his wife, Mrs. Knox, seemed rather flummoxed, for a change,
about the etiquette called for on this occasion. Yet, on the other
side of me, I noticed Secretary Jefferson smirk. And I leaned in to
whisper, "Do you know what the chieftain is saying?"

Still smirking, Jefferson replied under his breath. "I cannot
swear to it, but in their language, I do believe that he either proffered you the respect due a woman leader of the people . . . or else
he called you a *pluck-able round grape.*"

"*No!*" I gasped, covering my splutter with a napkin.

"Don't worry. I won't tell Mr. Adams."

With a strangled laugh, I said, "You must never tell *anyone.*"

Jefferson smiled into his Madeira wine. "It will be our secret,
on my honor as a Virginian."

And I do believe he kept that secret all his days.

The lovely evening went on, and I was happy to have Mr. Jefferson for a partner in conversation. We spoke of family and the
delights of New York, because we both knew our time here was
coming to a close.

Thanks to the bargain he'd brokered with Hamilton, we must
follow the government to Philadelphia. I did not wish to go, but
what else could a woman leader of the people do?

Chapter Thirty-Four

PHILADELPHIA
Pennsylvania
December 1790

I N THE COBBLESTONE streets and redbrick buildings of the City
of Brotherly Love, I heard more languages than in any other
place I'd been. German settlers still spoke their native language
in the marketplace, where one might also hear Dutch, Algonquin,
and Iroquois. The growing black population, both enslaved and
free, switched freely between English and a mixed tongue that
drew upon their native African languages. And *French* was heard
everywhere, as the city had become a haven for refugees fleeing
unrest. Many Americans greeted them with open arms, inspired by
the notion that France, too, might cast off a king.

Philadelphia was the most populous city in the United States.
And as winter descended, so did high society, leaving calling
cards every afternoon while our new rooms were still heaped
with boxes and trunks I had yet to unpack.

The president's house was on Market Street, just south of
Independence Hall. And Mrs. Washington's drawing room announced the season with garlands of pine and candles aplenty.
As guests thronged and a constellation of beauties each came to
curtsey before Mrs. Washington, I overheard conversations whispered behind the flutter of fans.

Some guests enthused over Hamilton's dynamism and exciting
financial plans. Others, wearing tricolor cockades of red, white,
and blue, praised Jefferson for championing the common man
against the overreach of a too-powerful federal government. And
some were still whispering that the volumes Vice President Ad-

ams wrote in London proved he distrusted democracy so much that he'd make us a monarchy in all but name.

Hearing absurd nonsense like that made me exceedingly sour. And attending the president's lady on the dais, I whispered in her ear, "I don't think Philadelphia beauties quite compare to New York's."

Mrs. Washington revealed only the hint of a smirk. "Certainly, the occasion is poorer for the absence of your lovely daughter, Mrs. Church, and Mrs. Van Rensselaer, but we are recompensed by the company of their sister, Mrs. Hamilton."

We both looked in the direction of Eliza Hamilton, who was, in that moment, modestly demurring an offer to dance from Senator James Monroe. The poor young lady was besieged night and day with those seeking favor and influence, for it was now openly and notoriously said that her husband was the most important man in government.

And that Washington was merely the figurehead.

Hamilton's tireless but aggressive efforts to establish American commerce were masterly, but his tendency to behave as if he controlled all the levers of government rubbed many the wrong way.

Including and especially Secretary Jefferson.

"I feel caught between them," John often grumbled. "That is, if either deigns to involve me in matters of state. Nevertheless, public affairs go on so smoothly that we scarcely know Congress is sitting. I fear I'm quite ornamental. The vice presidency of these United States is the most insignificant office ever the invention of man contrived or his imagination conceived."

I would laugh, asking, "If the vice president is ornamental, then what can be said of the vice president's wife?"

The truth was that I had little to do in Philadelphia but fan Martha Washington at public levees and spend our savings fixing up our rented house on so-called Bush Hill—which I disliked, not least because there wasn't a single bush upon the property.

For this insignificant office of the vice presidency, we'd been away from Braintree nearly two years!

Oh, how I longed to tend my *own* rosebushes and plant herbs in my own garden. And if I was to fling our money about like rain, I'd rather shower it on our friends and family.

I tried not to let it gall me that we were emptying our coffers to serve strangers tea, coffee, cranberry tarts, and gingerbread cake. But at least we had the comfort of our sons, as Charlie and Tommy had both joined us in Philadelphia to read the law.

When the boys weren't studying, they squired me about the city. We visited the State House Bell, its inscription proclaiming liberty to all the land. They also took me to the playhouse, and I enjoyed the performance—until someone nearby remarked that the author was Royall Tyler.

My head snapped up in shock. Charlie feigned innocence. Tommy laughed aloud.

"You rogues!" I cried. That Nabby's one-time suitor—father of an illegitimate child—had become a successful playwright was galling enough.

That I'd enjoyed his work? Nearly intolerable.

"He's now attorney for the state of Vermont," Charlie said when we returned home.

I cursed myself for thinking—just for a moment—that he was doing better for himself than Colonel Smith. "You boys had better outstrip him in accomplishment. You're the sons of John Adams, after all."

"We will," said Tommy, putting his feet on the table to vex me. "One day, Papa's three sons will all practice together with him."

"The law offices of Adams, Adams, Adams, and Adams?" Charlie grinned. "It sounds like a farce."

From behind his paper, John muttered, "Don't think I'll share my clients with you. As it happens, Johnny already lost his first case in Boston, so I may have to disown him."

The boys exchanged a glance.

I shot John a warning look.

"I *jest*," he said. "Am I not allowed levity in my own home—especially after I sit bored all day presiding over the Senate?"

Unless Congress was in session, there was nothing of import he could do. So when the Congress went into recess, we saw no reason to stay in Philadelphia. Indeed, I could scarcely contain my excitement to return to the house we'd left to the wilderness in Braintree, making our escape from the political whirl.

Unfortunately, politics followed us wherever we went. Upon our return home, John Quincy arrived for supper carrying a pamphlet by Thomas Paine: *The Rights of Man.*

John rolled his eyes. "I can guess what it says and it may go directly into the fire."

But our eldest son insisted upon reading it to us anyway. It was important, he said. People were reading it everywhere in the country—farmers praising it, merchants cursing it.

So, we sat down to listen.

We knew, of course, that Paine championed the violent overthrow of the French monarchy, but this pamphlet also attacked the very concept of a balanced government that had been adopted in the United States. The Constitution that my husband had so ably championed in his *A Defense of the Constitutions of Government of the United States of America.*

"Now comes the coup de grâce," John Quincy said. "*Jefferson* has endorsed Paine's pamphlet."

There it was, printed in plain black and white for all to see.

It was no secret that Jefferson considered our Constitution to be flawed and the French Revolution to be an extension of our own. But he was secretary of state now. For him to say it—nay, to print it!—gave it the stamp of American policy.

The president wouldn't like that.

Alas, my husband was more upset that Jefferson wrote he was glad "*something is publicly said against the political heresies which have sprung up among us.*"

At hearing that, John nearly choked on his cider. "Heresies?"

I tried to calm my husband. "Don't read too much into it." Though we'd sensed a growing difference of opinion with Jefferson, we remained extremely warm friends. "I'm sure he meant Hamilton, not *you.*"

John shot out of his chair. "It wasn't Hamilton who wrote *three volumes* defending the very separation of powers Paine mocks."

I blew out a slow calming breath. "Nevertheless, you ought not think Thomas Jefferson, of all people, would attack you personally."

"It gets worse," our son said, ignoring the plea in my eyes to leave it alone before his father burst a blood vessel. "'No doubt our citizens will rally a second time round the standard of common sense.'"

Now my husband looked stricken. "What can Jefferson mean, saying our citizens will rally a second time? Is he encouraging citizens to rebel against the very government in which he serves? And for what reason?"

John Quincy now put down the pamphlet. "Whatever he means by it, this endorsement is indiscreet and disloyal."

Our son was now a rising, but struggling, lawyer in Boston, deeply ashamed whenever he borrowed a few coins to keep afloat. We sensed a frustration in him. His brain—once employed in the intrigues of foreign courts—was dulling with legal matters no weightier than an overdue tavern bill or a family quarrel over the inheritance of a cow.

But Jefferson's folly set the rusting gears of my son's political mind into motion. "It doesn't matter if Jefferson named Papa as a so-called heretic. Everyone has inferred it. In Boston, they say my father is such a monarchist that he'd welcome King George back to our shores. And this will only confirm their worries."

"One will always hear slanders," I murmured.

Nevertheless, our son took umbrage against what seemed a betrayal by a family friend and government official. "Jefferson is abusing his position of high authority to frighten people with his paranoia about the powers of the presidency."

Looking pained, John grumbled, "Well, a free man has a right to believe what he likes."

"Does Jefferson think so?" John Quincy asked. "If he did, he wouldn't accuse those who disagree with him of *heresy*. Who elected Jefferson to be the Pope of Democracy?"

No one. No one, indeed.

Now John Quincy said, "Father, this must not be suffered with silence."

My husband shook his head. "Jefferson has misstepped here, and Washington will be wroth. I won't add to the president's burdens by carrying on a pointed quarrel in public with his secretary of state."

"Then I'll do it," said John Quincy.

My husband thought it a bad idea but did not forbid it. For my part, I felt as if a veiled accusation could not simply sit unanswered. And did my son not deserve to express his political beliefs? We'd fought a war for just that principle.

In the end, John Quincy published a series of letters in the paper under the pseudonym Publicola, which prompted a letter from Thomas Jefferson.

Jefferson wrote to my husband, "I have a dozen times taken up my pen to write to you and as often laid it down again, suspended between opposing considerations. I determine however to write from a conviction that truth, between candid minds, can never do harm."

Thereupon he explained that his endorsement had been published without permission. Someone had lent him the pamphlet, and to excuse the delay in returning it, he scribbled a line of colorful praise. Never did he think this little note would then be forwarded to the publisher and printed.

"I hoped it would not attract notice," Jefferson now claimed. "But a writer came forward under the signature of Publicola, attacking not only the author and principles of the pamphlet, but myself as its sponsor, by name."

Still, Jefferson closed his letter on a conciliatory note. "We have always differed as friends should do, respecting each other's motives, and confining our differences to private conversation. And I declare that nothing was further from my intention than to have had your name or mine brought before the public on this occasion."

John groaned. "He thinks that *I* am *Publicola!*"

My husband took up his pen to deny it. Then wrote, "The friendship which has subsisted for fifteen years between us, without the smallest interruption, and until this occasion without the slightest suspicion, ever has been and still is, very dear to my heart."

As it was to mine.

Unfortunately, whatever our personal feelings, the incident exposed an expanding chasm inside our own government. Differences between friends that might grow too wide to ever paper over.

Divided between Federalists and Anti-Federalists, factions were hardening. And if forced to choose, I feared Thomas Jefferson and John Adams would no longer be on the same side.

Across the ocean, another people yearning for freedom were awash in blood. Jefferson thought it a mirror of our own revolution. But was it a distorted picture of corrupted ideals, or a reflection of a fratricidal struggle here yet to come?

Chapter Thirty-Five

QUINCY
Massachusetts
March 1793

AFTER FOUR YEARS of the vice presidency, I could no longer afford to accompany my husband to Philadelphia. Though I couldn't regret our service to the country, neither was I willing for us to go into debt just so I could stand on the dais next to Mrs. Washington and let guests eat us out of house and home.

Besides, as the lady of only second rank in the capital, I was superfluous. I longed to be useful in preparing for our eventual retirement, so after Washington's re-election, I remained in Braintree—or at least our precinct of the same, which had been renamed *Quincy*.

Oh, the relief not to rise too early in the morning. To spend my days gardening, tending livestock, and increasing our investments. For my dream now was to have a home in which all our family might one day be reunited happily under one roof.

For the moment, however, our children were scattered to the winds. Thomas in Philadelphia. Charles in New York. And Nabby back in London of all places, where her husband had decided to pursue some mysterious financial opportunity.

They'd lost their infant son Thomas to an unknown childhood disease. We'd mourned that tragedy with them but could not solace Nabby's wounded mother's heart. So, while I hadn't liked the idea of Nabby going overseas, I hoped a change of scenery might help mend her heartbreak. London had, after all, been good for that once before.

Now only John Quincy, practicing law in Boston, was close enough to visit. One fine errand day, walking on his arm through a crush of shoppers in Faneuil Hall's marketplace, we looked for bargains on writing paper and sealing wax.

In the stall next to us, a merchant was doing brisk business selling French wine, though it was the rustic peasant kind of no good quality. Nevertheless, these days the tide of popular sentiment ran in favor of all things French.

Having thrown off their monarchy and beheaded their king, the revolutionaries sent a new minister to the United States: Edmond-Charles Genêt. And as he made his way to Philadelphia, he'd been hailed as a hero by American crowds crying *Vive La République!*

Now I noticed women of the middling and lower sort wearing tricolor cockades. Even the better sort dressed with ostentatious republican simplicity, making me over-conscious of my embroidered neckerchief and powdered hair. And we found ourselves nearly trampled when a hawker near a sign that advertised fresh clams cried, "Get your tickets to the Civic Feast of the Citizen! Three dollars a head."

"Who would pay so much to attend?"

"I wouldn't pay half that," Johnny said with contempt. "But refusing to attend such festivities gets one labeled an *aristocrat*."

"Better an aristocrat than part of a mob."

Glancing at the Phrygian cap atop the clam vendor's head, John Quincy murmured, "We should be careful what we say in public, Mother. We have Jacobins enough on this side of the ocean to worry about."

"Are you afraid to lose clients?"

"I'm afraid to lose my head!"

We laughed darkly, for such was the spirit of the times. Despite the violence in France, my countrymen took her struggle as proof our revolution was spreading, elevating the lot of the common man, extending the blessings of liberty, and breaking chains of tyranny around the globe.

But Nabby's letters from London told a different tale. "Shiploads of poor, distressed, penniless priests and other victims from France are daily landing upon this island, carrying tales of massacres, arrests, summary trials, and executions."

One such refugee was the Vicomte de Noailles, who gave Nabby the news of Lafayette's imprisonment and the persecution of his family.

What had been unleashed seemed less like liberty and more like anarchy. More worrisome was that the French were no longer content to war amongst themselves. The revolutionaries had declared war against Great Britain. And knowing my daughter might well be caught in the conflict, I couldn't rest easy until she returned home again.

But the war between Britain and Revolutionary France did not confine itself to the other side of the ocean. Soon it had the United States in the crosshairs.

PRESIDENT WASHINGTON DECLARED neutrality, forbidding Americans to take any part in a conflict.

John believed it to be the only prudent course to avoid being devoured by Scylla on one side or dragged down by Charybdis on the other. And certainly the proclamation of neutrality was welcomed by merchants, who didn't want trade disrupted by another war.

But the general citizenry was *outraged* at what they took as a betrayal of both our allies and our principles. The French had helped us against the British during our darkest hour; many believed we ought to help them in return. It was an understandable position, but I was appalled at the way newspapers like the *Aurora* egged on the rioting that erupted in our own cities over it.

The whole world had gone mad.

So I was relieved the day a magnificent carriage pulled up to our gate and out stepped my daughter in an elaborate periwinkle robe à l'anglaise and wide-brimmed hat festooned with yellow ribbons, blue tail feathers, and an ostrich plume.

Goodness, what a sight. It was as if an English noblewoman had fallen from the sky, and her husband with her, in a silk-embroidered waistcoat, sporting a diamond-tipped cane, his cravat fussily tied and fastened with a jeweled pin.

Why, not even Alexander Hamilton dressed like this. But my son-in-law, as I was soon to learn, could well afford it, having returned from London with a *fortune*.

After hugging my grandsons close, I kissed my daughter and congratulated her on what a fine lady she made. Embarrassed, Nabby whispered, "Mama, I should like to get out of this finery before the neighbors think I've gotten above myself. But Colonel Smith *insisted* . . ."

"On his first meeting here with your friends and relations, no doubt he wished to make an impression." Of course, he could hardly fail to, with the team of sleek horses pulling that gilded carriage.

But how could I begrudge my son-in-law his triumph? After toiling so long in government obscurity, he'd somehow become wealthy.

He wasn't keen to share details but did boast of his forthcoming plans. In the comfort of my dining room—which thankfully no longer bore any marks of Royall Tyler's neglect—Nabby's husband explained, "I'm buying land in western New York to divide and sell to settlers. And, of course, I'll be building your daughter a new house."

A new house! How excited I was for her.

I only wished Nabby seemed half so excited. Later, alone with my daughter in the parlor, I poked at the logs with the fireplace tongs. "Is it your natural reserve, my dear, or are you somehow unhappy with your newfound prosperity?"

Nabby winced. "You didn't raise me to live in luxury. Even wearing silks in foreign courts, we economized."

I teased her; I couldn't help it. "Well, I'm sorry to have imbued you with too much Puritan sentiment. The Bible *does* say there's a time to rejoice, and after all you've suffered, I think this is the time."

Knowing I was referring to the loss of her baby son, Nabby lowered her eyes. "Does the grief for a child ever go away?"

"Never. But you find a way to survive it, just as people survive the other tragedies of the world."

Nabby took a deep breath at that. "Mama, the tragedies of the world creep ever closer. We left such a scene in Europe as you would *not* believe . . ."

The hour was too late to say more. She'd save it for morning when John Quincy came from Boston to accompany us to the Sunday meeting and take supper after.

I was so happy to see them reunited. Though Nabby doted on all her brothers, her relationship with John Quincy was deeper. Both were old enough to remember the war. Both remembered our time together in England and France. And knowing John Quincy would understand the pain she felt over it, she reported, "All is swept away in France now. Lafayette is in a dungeon, and I've heard from refugees that his wife is under house arrest."

My heart ached to hear this news of our friends. I could all too well remember the kindness of the Lafayettes, and I could not countenance the morals of any person who might harm them.

Meanwhile, John Quincy wanted to know, "What of Americans there? Our ambassador, Gouverneur Morris?"

Nabby's hand trembled as she stirred sugar into her tea. "The French complain that we Americans do not step forward in their cause the way they stepped forward in ours. Not one American officer has joined them, nor do they hear a word of comfort. And our ambassador, Mr. Morris, refuses to pay what we owe from the war, so they won't permit him to quit Paris."

"But of course it must be paid," broke in Nabby's husband, who had, until now, listened quietly. "We *did* borrow the money and are honor bound."

"But who must we pay?" asked John Quincy. "We borrowed it from a king. We cannot know who the sovereign authority of France is now. It seems to change every day."

My eldest son had given the matter much thought. Simple lawyer he might still be, but since his essays as Publicola, he'd been writing more, his words circulating even in England, reaching the eyes of the prime minister there. He was getting a reputation as a fine political thinker, but his sister wanted to know, "What does Papa say? What about Mr. Jefferson?"

I snorted. "That last question we do *not* want answered. For on this matter, the opinions of Thomas Jefferson do much mischief."

"How so?" Nabby asked.

Either Jefferson had changed much during his years in the administration, or perhaps we hadn't understood how radical his philosophy had always been. Whilst offering wise counsel in many matters of our government, he seemed always to be distressed by the shape of it.

Indeed, despite the adoption of a Bill of Rights, I believe he'd begun to fear that with our Constitution, we'd merely replaced one form of tyranny with another. Our factions became opposing political parties. The president's party—the Federalists. And the Jacobin-loving Democratic-Republicans founded by another Virginian—little James Madison, who was always in Jefferson's shadow.

All this deeply distressed my husband, and his relationship with Jefferson suffered for it. But not wishing to distress my daughter, I merely said, "Secretary Jefferson still defends the French Revolution, and this has emboldened the citizenry of Philadelphia to riot."

I didn't tell her that John reported Washington being hanged in effigy—*Washington*! Or that crowds wore pins and earrings of the guillotine. Or that her father was quite sure that the government of the United States was saved from the rioters only because yellow fever emptied the city.

ARRIVING HOME AFTER the outbreak that autumn, my husband announced, "Well, I escaped the pestilence. And the fighting between Hamilton and Jefferson, too, which is a pestilence of its own."

"How long can it go on between them?" I asked, for the battles of the two men in the cabinet had spilled out into the press with enormous venom. "I fear they're going to destroy each other."

John sighed. "Whenever I speak to either of them, it is plain their quarrels have evolved into a mutual and personal dislike. And here I am, still caught in the middle between them."

"I doubt that," I said, helping him out of his greatcoat. "You have an opinion about which of them is right, and which of them is wrong."

John didn't want to admit it. "Hamilton *is* an ambitious upstart. How many times did we sit with him at some dinner party, listening to the man vapor about his administration like some young girl over her brilliants and trinkets?"

I had, indeed, suffered through many a party where the

sparkling-eyed Hamilton, a man of small stature but large presence, maneuvered every conversation to his own glory. And it'd always pained me to see the way his lovely young wife, Eliza, sat by his side gazing up at him with a nearly religious awe. I loved my good man, too. But I was long past blind adoration. In Eliza Hamilton's place, I would've cautioned my husband against arrogance and hoped she was doing the same.

"The problem is that I *like* Jefferson," John confessed. "But these days, in almost every political matter, Hamilton is right, and Jefferson is wrong."

I smirked, filling a basin of water for him to clean himself of dust from the road. "Likability should hardly be the test in politics if we mean to have good governance."

"Well, there is little I can do about it either way. Truly, I ought to resign this useless post."

I thought so, too, but knew his vanity wouldn't allow it. I believed all the men in Washington's administration to be entirely too stubborn and ambitious to give way. Which was why it surprised me when John reported, "Jefferson tells me he'll resign. He'll retire to Monticello to spend his days in rural amusements and philosophical meditations. At least until the president dies or resigns, when I suppose Jefferson fancies the people will plead with him to take the reins of the state and conduct it forty years in piety and peace. Amen."

"Sarcasm is an unattractive trait."

"To the contrary, my dear, my sarcasm is one of the things you love best about me. For I say all the sarcastic things you think, but your better nature will not permit you to say."

I laughed, but my smile soon faded. "I'd love you even better if you'd carried our children back from New York to escape any pestilence there."

"Charles says he's too busy and Nabby wouldn't come so soon again after their recent visit. In any case, her husband is so proud of his wealth that he'd not let her go without a coach and four, and such Monarchical Trumpery I must have nothing to do with."

I grinned. "Colonel Smith was once too poor. Now too rich?"

Grumbling, John admitted, "Truthfully, I wish my own sons

had a bit of his cleverness in securing a fortune. I do believe Colonel Smith is helping to tutor Charles in that direction. But he must stop boasting of his wealth. Especially now that I have some idea that he's dealing with the French, who hope to have him use his influence in collecting outstanding war debt."

Well, this was a tangled web best left alone.

At least our own financial footing was steady, and when I told him as much, John said, "Then I'll be content if my boys are plodders like their father. Can you imagine if I'd put all my energies into farming and practice of the law, instead of public service? I'd be wealthier than John Hancock."

I almost laughed, because he had little idea of how he made money. "Speaking of our boys, how does Charles do?"

Taking up the washrag, he said, "Charles is fat, handsome, happy, and doing well in business."

"*But?*" I asked, for I sensed hesitation.

"It'd be better if Charles spent less time with girls," my husband said, vigorously scrubbing his face. "For that matter, better if all my boys spent less time with girls. All form easy crushes and none are situated to start a family. So, time spent with girls is nothing gained." He caught my expression in the looking glass. "Pardon me! Disciple of Wollstonecraft!"

"*Pupil*," I said, archly, for I had been reading Mary Wollstonecraft's *A Vindication of the Rights of Woman* and learning much from it. "You say there is nothing gained from spending time with ladies? I demand that you admit Eden was tasteless till an Eve was there."

"Probably so," he said.

"When you're sick of the treachery of your own sex, you seek comfort and consolation in the gentleness and tenderness of mine."

"All right, my dear."

I wasn't finished. "Moreover, these nurturing qualities of my sex are beneficial to the human race."

John snapped the cloth playfully. "You may rest your case, barrister. You've carried the argument. You've become a good lawyer."

I straightened my cap with smug satisfaction. "I should think so. It *is* the family profession after all."

I WAS WRONG to say that law was the family profession. As it turned out, it was diplomacy that called with a siren's song to the *brace of Adamses*. For in May of the following year, whilst his father was back in Pennsylvania, our eldest son rode so fast and hard to our gate that his horse was left frothing and lathered.

Of all my boys, John Quincy seldom allowed himself an obvious enthusiasm, so I nearly wilted with fear when he burst into the garden where I was tending my budding rosebushes. "What's wrong?"

My son shook his head, as if he didn't know where to begin, marching back and forth in the spring mud. "I've had word from Papa and the secretary of state."

He pulled from his coat a packet of official letters, his hand shaking. I saw the signature of Secretary of State Edmund Randolph—for Thomas Jefferson had resigned the position at the start of the year, to which my husband had sniped, *Good riddance of bad ware.*

Now my son explained, "I've been appointed resident minister to the Netherlands."

So thunderstruck was I that I nearly dropped my shears. "Appointed?"

"By President Washington," my son panted, still winded from his long hard ride. "But I had no notion of this—not the slightest inkling!"

He showed me the other letters, holding them so that my dirtied garden gloves would not mar the wax seals. And I divined upon an impressive fact he neglected to mention. "Unanimously confirmed! My dear boy, what an honor. And you knew nothing?"

"How should I know anything? I didn't seek the post. Apparently, Washington read some essay I'd written and decided I was his man. Father swears he didn't seek it for me, though he advises I should accept. And now I'm obligated to go." For the first time I realized that Johnny's frenzy wasn't entirely excitement. "I wish I could've been consulted. In fact, I wish this appointment had not been made at all."

"Why wouldn't you wish to accept?" I asked, vaguely worried about a young girl I'd heard about who may have caught my son's fancy in Boston.

But my poor dutiful son met my eyes with fear. "Mother, I'm only twenty-six years old. Neither my years, experience, reputation, nor talents could possibly entitle me to an office of so much respectability."

It was a trial not to smile at his unwarranted self-doubts. But I managed it, removing my gardening gloves, letting them fall to the dirt, and taking my son's hands in mine.

"John Quincy Adams." I used his full name so he'd know how earnestly I meant what I'd say next. "We devoted you to the public at a very young age accompanying your father to embassies abroad. There you spent nearly a *decade* studying diplomacy and the various languages of Europe. Just how many Americans do you think have your breadth of experience?"

He didn't answer—for it may have shaken him a little. Instead, he lowered his head. "Then you want me to go, too?"

No. I didn't *want* him to go. He had, in these past few years, been a godsend. From helping plant trees, hauling seaweed to fertilize the fields, bringing supplies from Boston, to taking his father's place at the hearth for late-night discussions—we'd both strived to make up for all the years we had spent apart.

Alone amongst my sons, I couldn't think of one instance in his whole life when Johnny had ever given me embarrassment or regret. And I was loath to send him again across a war-torn sea, for Revolutionary France—having now killed both her king *and* queen—was at war not only with itself, but also with all Europe.

But I'd always hoped that my eldest boy was meant for great things. How else but destiny to explain that he'd now serve as diplomat in the very same embassy his father had established in Holland years ago?

Despite my selfish longing for him to stay, I mustered the strength to tell him, "Painful as the separation will be, I will derive satisfaction from knowing you'll be eminently useful to your country. So, yes. You should accept. You should go."

My son removed his hat, ran a hand through his sweat-soaked dark hair, then turned his face to the sky, as if petitioning the heavens. "I want Tommy to go with me. He cannot always be left behind, the only son of John Adams never to see Europe. I'll need a secretary I can trust, and I can have none better than my own little brother."

No, I wanted to say. In truth, I wanted to shout it. It'd transport me back to those days of having to worry for the lives of *two* sons on the sea. But I knew that Tommy—so often overlooked, so often an afterthought—would be made happier by this opportunity than he had ever been in his life.

And so it was on a September morning bright and fair, that I straightened my spine and watched another ship leave bearing away from me two of my children, part of my heart gone with them.

Chapter Thirty-Six

NEW YORK CITY
New York
Spring 1795

WHAT IS THE proper way to address John Quincy?" I asked my husband from the writing table in Nabby's parlor. "I have been addressing my letters to JQA Minister Resident, but has he the title of Excellency?"

John looked up from an ornate armchair where he was sipping our son-in-law's best wine, for we'd come to visit our children in New York and were now staying as guests in Colonel Smith's lavish new lodgings. "Best keep it: John Quincy Adams, Esq., Resident Minister of the United States. Otherwise, if that letter falls into the wrong hands, the Jacobins will say we're conveying noble titles on our son."

In this benighted age, it was sound advice, so I nodded, continuing to scribble. Then John said, "Tell the boys that never was a father more satisfied, or gratified, than I've been since they went abroad."

I smiled and wrote it at the bottom of the page. Then John said, "Tell Johnny that I have no language to express the pleasure he's given to the president with his clear, comprehensive, and masterly accounts of the politics in Europe."

That, too, I wrote into the margin, fanning the letter dry to fold into its envelope.

"Tell him—"

"John, I'm sure Nabby can provide more paper on which you can write your own letter."

"Bah, I've lost the habit of writing from weak eyes and trembling hand. I'm an old man."

"You're not an old man," I said.

"Older than you, my pretty child bride . . ."

I raised an accusing brow. "So you *did* learn to flatter like a courtier in Europe."

"Yet, never will I have so silver a tongue as our Charles. It's unseemly the way he makes girls giggle."

Lowering my voice so the family downstairs would not overhear, I asked, "Did you see what I saw between the crystal glasses and candlesticks at Colonel Smith's table tonight?"

"Nabby cringing at yet another course of pheasant being brought to the table?" John asked.

"No, *Charles.* He started to sample some of that pricey Madeira until Colonel Smith's sister gave him a look, and our son withdrew his hand from the decanter, meek as a child."

"Which sister?" John asked. "The one betrothed to a Frenchman, the pupil of Wollstonecraft, or the wallflower?"

"Sally." When he stared at me blankly, I allowed, "The wallflower."

John scratched absently at his chin. "You think Charles is sweet on Sally Smith?"

"All I know is that Nabby said her sister-in-law has been a great comfort to Charles."

"I hope he hasn't given her a hold on him."

The next day John continued on to Philadelphia to discharge his duties as vice president for the sixth consecutive year. The debate that raged there would be the same as everywhere else in the country, where effigies of poor John Jay were being burned up and down the coastline in sufficient quantity to guide ships into harbors.

The British were once again destroying our commerce. And because we could ill afford another war with anyone, diplomacy was our only hope. So John Jay had been sent to negotiate and returned with a treaty Americans found too humiliating to accept.

John presided over the Senate as they made up their minds about whether to swallow these humiliations, while I spent time with my new little granddaughter, the flame-haired Caroline, just born in the new year.

The birth hadn't gone so easily for Nabby this time, and her sickness was made worse when the wretched apothecary gave to her the wrong medicine. Still, she looked on the bright side. "I cannot complain. My head is still attached."

We went not a week without hearing about the beheading of a friend or acquaintance in France. "Adrienne Lafayette's mother, sister, and grandmother have been beheaded," said my daughter, mournfully. "And poor Adrienne is sure to meet the same fate."

If I were Catholic I'd have made a sign of the cross to ward off this fate. Instead, I put a hand to my forehead, having dreaded this news. It pained me to think of our friend, not much older than my own daughter, in such peril. And with nothing we could do for her!

To distract us from this glum talk, Nabby's husband suggested an afternoon jaunt in the countryside.

"I'm still recovering my strength," Nabby said by way of excusing herself. "But you should go, Mother. Colonel Smith is eager to show you his new property. It would mean so much to us."

Given the heat of the sun, I didn't relish leaving the shade of the house, but to make her happy, off I went with my son-in-law, the foul scents of the city giving way to the earthier scents of nature as his gilded carriage carried us away. We made our way on bumpy roads lined with wildflowers, and I heard the axes of workers clearing the land long before we stepped out into the tall grasses. Helping me down, Colonel Smith swept an arm over the view of his meadow, which stretched in green splendor to the silt-rich river where gulls soared above frothy swells.

Without feigning the slightest enthusiasm, I said, "It's beautiful. *Absolutely* beautiful."

"I paid only five thousand pounds for it," Colonel Smith said, unfurling sketches upon a felled tree for me to examine. "I'll build the new house here. The portico will have this very view of the water. Like Washington always described the view of the Potomac from his manse. Your Nabby shall be mistress of her very own Mount Vernon."

Though still modest by the standards of castles in Europe, his plans were impressive for the Americas. But I saw that a great many tools, furnishings, and other supplies would need to be imported. "You don't fear that much of what you need to build this house will end up seized?"

Britain was again sinking or capturing our trading ships on the high seas, keeping the cargo for booty, kidnapping our soldiers, and forcing them to fight in the Royal Navy.

But Colonel Smith assured me, "Once the Jay Treaty with Britain is ratified, all will be well."

I wasn't so certain. "The treaty is very unpopular. Nabby said a brawl broke out about it yesterday in the Tontine Coffee House."

Smith chuckled ruefully. "It did. I was there."

"Then, how can you be sure of the treaty's ratification? You seem to know more than the vice president has told me."

I shouldn't have been surprised. My son-in-law ran in connected circles these days. Upon the death of the Baron von Steuben, Colonel Smith had been elected president over his fellow veterans in the Society of the Cincinnati. And now he said, "I've been chosen to chair a public meeting about it tomorrow. Hamilton told me the treaty will be ratified, and if *he* says something like that, we may rely upon it."

I couldn't argue that. Like Thomas Jefferson, Alexander Hamilton had resigned his cabinet post. But he still had tremendous influence—enough to still be thought a political puppet master.

"Besides," Colonel Smith assured me, "I have two sleek privateer ships of my own now to slip past the British with the supplies I need, and trade goods aplenty. Money shall not be an object."

LIKE ALL PROMINENT young men in the city, my son Charles meant to attend the public meeting about the Jay Treaty and agreed to let me accompany him. But on the walk there, my son decided to confess, "I've formed an attachment to Sally Smith and I want her for my wife."

Charles was twenty-five now, by all accounts a rising lawyer with a good head for business. His easy charm with men and women alike was another skill he put to good use. He made friends quickly and without prejudice, dining one night with Hamilton and the Federalists, the next night sharing brandy with Senator Aaron Burr and the Democratic-Republicans.

My bonny Charles might not be resident minister to the Nether-lands, but he had a grand future ahead of him if he could only establish himself a few years more before marriage.

Forestalling this objection, my middle son said, "Mother, please don't tell me I must wait years to have the object of my heart."

"Not *years*," I said, as if I truly had any say in the matter. Even John wouldn't forbid it. "But at least a little longer. At least until the world is more certain."

That was an answer my boy could not abide. "I'm going to marry Sally as soon as possible, because the world has never been certain a day since I was born."

To that, I had no argument. Especially not given the scene that unfolded that afternoon. A huge crowd turned out, packed so tightly it made us all prey for pickpockets. Banding together, angry dockworkers in sweat-stained shirts shouted *Vive la Révolution* and sunburned farmers in homespun railed about British abuses.

"Damn John Jay!"

"Damn anybody who won't damn John Jay!"

An innkeeper in a leather apron groused about the noise disturb-ing his customers, but he was paid no heed by this group, or the other—the cluster of Wall Street's monied men, in powdered wigs, brightly colored embroidered waistcoats, and clean white hose.

They shouted back things like: "Do you want war with our best trading partner, you fools?"

While Charles shielded me from the sun with his umbrella, I exchanged a little wave with Mrs. Hamilton, who had come out in her best straw bonnet, accompanied by her own boy. And, of course, Hamilton himself was not far off, climbing onto a stoop to harangue the crowd.

I looked up to see Colonel Smith take his place as chairman of this meeting on the balcony behind the wrought iron balustrade, acknowledging Mr. Livingston, who wished to speak.

That's when Hamilton shouted, "By what right does anyone speak before me?"

Oh, for heaven's sake.

He was no longer secretary of the treasury. Yet, he seemed to expect people to treat him with the deference due government officials. Must he give the Jacobins amongst us an excuse to think our party was an enemy of equality?

From the balcony, my fair-minded son-in-law took a quick vote of concerned parties, and a large majority wanted Mr. Livingston to speak first. But the unfortunate man couldn't get out a sentence without being hooted down by Hamilton and his cronies.

"*Order*," my son-in-law called as chairman, bringing down a gavel upon the table. But this, too, was drowned out by the shouts of our own faction until, in exasperation, Smith barked like the military commander he'd been. "*Mr. Hamilton*, you are out of order!"

I suppose I'll never know when precisely it was that Hamilton turned against us, but the look of vainglorious fury he shot up at my son-in-law made my blood run cold—why I saw the very *devil* in his eyes.

Then, like a madman possessed, Hamilton continued to taunt the crowd with admittedly superior arguments and cutting wit. But the people hadn't come to be told what to think about the Jay Treaty. And they responded much like they had all those years ago when pressured to buy the East India Company's tea.

Forming into little mobs, the citizenry burned copies of the treaty and flung the flaming pages into New York Harbor. And when Hamilton tried to shame them for it, they pelted him with bricks.

As the pelting stones rained from the sky, Charles tugged at my elbow. "Mother, as entertaining as this has been, we ought to retreat."

"But Colonel Smith—"

"Nabby's husband can handle himself in scenes of violence," Charles said, his grip tightening.

As he dragged me off, I searched the crowd in vain for sight of Eliza Hamilton, hoping to help get her to safety. Though, if anything happened to her, she'd have her husband to blame.

By God, I couldn't count all the times I had accused John of vanity, but Hamilton had not even a *speck* of diplomacy in his blood.

Chapter Thirty-Seven

JOHN WAS HOME in the summer, digging up stones to build a wall between our garden and the new road. And while I sorted a basket of apples, choosing some for baking and some for the cider press, I watched him work himself into a lather, muttering with each stone he hefted.

"Careful, John," I warned, because he'd recently got himself so agitated that he tripped over a wheelbarrow and hurt his shin. "We don't need a catastrophe."

"*Another* catastrophe, you mean," he snapped.

Just as swiftly as Nabby's husband had met with great fortune, so did he meet with complete financial ruin. His ships seized. His properties in foreclosure. His furnishings, carriages, artwork, and expensive wine were all to be auctioned off.

There'd be no more talk of building another Mount Vernon for our daughter. It was a miracle he did not land in debtor's prison.

Nabby pleaded with us not to worry that they'd be without a roof over their heads, as her husband retained some small property in East Chester. But worry we did . . .

It was of no comfort that our son-in-law wasn't the only one in dire straits. He'd been caught up in a spiraling financial crisis that threatened to collapse the whole economy. Despite ratifying the Jay Treaty, international business was contracting. Shops, trades, and businesses of all kinds shuttered in our port cities.

Many men were ruined. But those men weren't the vice president's son-in-law on the eve of the most fateful election our new nation had ever had.

It had been a foregone conclusion that George Washington would be re-elected to a third term, and that my husband would be asked to continue as vice president.

So, truly, no thunderclap could've resounded with more force than Washington's announcement that he intended to retire from office.

I thought all America ought to be in mourning to lose the leadership of a man with such profound wisdom and modesty. Washington had resigned covered with glory and crowned with laurels as the father of our nation, which would place him in the archives of time with the greatest heroes and benefactors to mankind.

But oh, what a mess he left behind.

And with my husband as *the heir apparent*.

John was now past sixty years of age. The responsibility of the presidency, at this stage in life, would surely kill him. He ought to have been greatly agitated on that score. Indeed, he ought to have removed his name from consideration. But I couldn't bring myself to advise that he do it.

In the weeks that followed, as the electioneering began in earnest, my husband said very little, and his agitation gave way to a preternatural calm. Instead of muttering over stones, John cheerfully informed me, "The next president could just as easily be Jefferson, Pinckney, or Jay."

I snorted, knowing it would not be Jay.

I was suspicious of my husband's sudden mildness. Daily, newspapers like the *Aurora* condemned John as an infernal monarchist who'd become king and tyrant if given the reins of power. And newspapers like the *Gazette of the United States* condemned Jefferson as an atheist. As for Pinckney, they condemned him as being Hamilton's puppet.

"You don't worry on that score?" I asked John one afternoon while he was digging in the garden.

"I worry about very little here on the peace of my farm. In fact, I should like to call this place Peacefield."

Peacefield? Really! Since when had he become a philosopher? "John, how long our home, or our country, shall be peaceful relies in great measure upon the next president."

John took up a clump of dirt in his hands. "Oh, I daresay whoever shall be chosen will not do us any harm. Not even if it is me."

I narrowed my eyes, not trusting this coolness of temper. At night, when he should've been writing letters to his colleagues to help swing the election, I found him scribbling inane things in his diary, such as, *It looks like rain.*

Whilst *I* scoured the gazettes for news from every corner about the fate of the nation, my husband mowed bushes. He whistled to himself while plowing the meadow. He hummed while washing casks and making compost with seaweed. And in the evenings, he cheerfully soaked his feet while reading Cicero's discourse on civic virtue.

John's uncharacteristic equanimity was maddening! And one night, I pulled that volume of Cicero right out of his hands and said so.

Laughing, John explained, "There's no benefit to fretting about whether I'll be elected to the presidency. The vote shall assuredly be close—a miserable, meager triumph to either party. I'm not ambitious for it."

Or so he was trying to convince himself.

"Oh, you *want* it," I accused.

My husband toweled his feet dry. "As you must want it for me, or you'd have pleaded with me to bow out of the contest."

"It's only that I fear for someone else to win! But I also fear for *you.* We both know the toll the presidency took upon Washington. You're not much younger."

Taking light umbrage, John pulled me into his lap, as if to prove he was a much younger man. "Nevertheless, I think a man had better wear than rust. Abigail, if called to the presidency, I'd brave it because I have only a few years of life left and they cannot be better bestowed than upon the country in defense of which we've jeopardized all from the start."

Chapter Thirty-Eight

BRISTOL
Pennsylvania
May 1797

W HY DOES THE carriage stop?" I called to the driver. "Have we damaged a wheel?"

"No, madam," the driver shouted back. "The wheel is fine."

Everything had gone wrong in my efforts to reach my husband in Philadelphia. So I wouldn't have been surprised if the driver said the muddy clay road was impassable, or one of the horses was ailing, or perhaps it was a highwayman and I ought to fear for my life. Any explanation seemed more plausible than the truth. "It's the presidential coach up ahead."

The presidential coach? I leaned out the window, craning my neck to catch a glimpse around the bend. There it was—a magnificent vehicle with brass fittings and a gilded seal—pulled by livery-clad black horses adorned with plumes in red, white, and blue.

I fought back continued disbelief, even as my husband's stately carriage pulled closer and I heard John's voice boom over the clatter of hooves. "You there, do you carry Mrs. Adams?"

"I do, Mr. President, sir," said the driver with a great sense of decorum.

But I had none. In a fit of exuberance unfitting for my age and station in life, I threw the door open and kicked the step down. "John!"

Abandoning baggage, I ran to him like a woman half my age, climbing up to take my seat by his side. My husband's cheeks colored as I threw my arms around his neck and cried, "Oh, John! Or shall I call you Mr. President? Please tell me this is a happy meeting and not a sad one."

He grinned. "A happy occasion indeed. I simply couldn't wait one more moment, so I set out to fetch you myself."

We held each other's faces, contemplating the changes. We'd only been a few months apart this time, but we were, in some sense, now obliged to be new people.

My husband as president and me as first lady.

Interrupting our conjugal reverie, one of John's beautiful horses threw her plumed head back and gave me a welcoming nicker. "Meet Cleopatra," John said. "My new favorite mare. I thought you might approve of her if I named her after a female politician such as yourself, Madame La Presidante."

He was teasing, and I took his bait. "Well, history does say that the queens who have reigned for any length of time have been celebrated for excellent governors."

John smirked. "Is that so?"

"You know it is. But as reigning is so much out of fashion, my ambition is to reign only in the heart of my husband. That is my throne, and there I aspire to be absolute."

"So you are, madam. So you are."

I smiled with satisfaction. "What is the name of the other horse?"

"Caesar, of course. Cleopatra's consort."

I laughed, vastly amused. "You play a dangerous game, sir. The risk you run naming your horses after monarchs and tyrants, adorning them in plumes. I thought you foreswore all signs of extravagance!"

"Can a man not make an exception in retrieving his wife in fine style, plumes and all?"

I wouldn't complain of it, especially since our reunion was an unexpectedly romantic interlude.

We dined at a little tavern overlooking the Delaware River. And enjoying a generous helping of braised rabbit over early spring greens, I said, "You must be quite pleased with yourself, Mr. President. To be chosen as the first of men by your countrymen."

"But only by three votes," John muttered.

"Oh, you curmudgeon! You *won*, didn't you?"

John downed his glass of beer. "No thanks to certain friends and relations. Do you know that my cousin Samuel campaigned for Jefferson?"

I did know it and had hoped John did not. "Sam is a habitual contrarian. Besides, you'd have won by much more were it not for Hamilton pushing his own candidate. Beware that spare Cassius!"

"Trust that I will keep my distance from Hamilton and any other man who is lean and hungry with ambition."

"Like your vice president?" I asked, archly.

But John was in a gracious mood toward our old friend. "Oh, Jefferson and I should go on affectionately together and all will be well."

"What makes you think so?"

"Before the votes were counted, he said that if there should be a tie, he wanted Congress to throw the presidency to me as I'd always been senior to him in public life."

"Did he?" I asked, pleasantly surprised.

"He also let it be known that he wouldn't serve as vice president under any man but me."

That warmed my heart. "Well, though he is so mistaken in politics, I don't think him an insincere or corruptible man. My friendship for him is unshaken, and I'll do my best to bring harmony in the capital."

John's expression became a little wistful. "It would've given me pleasure to have had you present at my inauguration, which was the most affecting and overpowering scene of my life."

"I *am* sorry," I said, wishing I'd come sooner, despite all that prevented me.

John confessed, "I couldn't sleep the night before and feared that I might faint in presence of all the world."

"But you didn't," I said, taking his hand in mine. "You gave all the world an example of a worthy leader; I read it in the papers."

Once we'd dined and continued to Philadelphia in my husband's fine coach, our discussion turned to our children. And John sighed. "Poor Nabby. When I saw her on the way to Philadelphia, she was surviving well enough in a little farmhouse—your lessons in frugal housewifery serve her well. But her husband absented himself. And now he isn't answering my letters. Too embarrassed, I take it. So he should be, after squandering such a fortune."

"He's not answering *anyone's* letters," I said softly. "For disappearing into the wilderness helps keep his creditors away."

John grimaced. "He cannot run from them forever. He has a wife and children to provide for."

When I was silent, my husband's head snapped up. "You don't think he's abandoned them, do you?"

With my hands tightly clasped in my lap, I admitted, "I don't know. Nabby is too fiercely loyal to wonder. But Charles believes we have reason to despair."

Several emotions crossed my husband's face as he contemplated his daughter being left by herself to raise three children. Fury, guilt for having once left me in similar difficulty, then denial. "I was told Colonel Smith was in western New York trying to sell off his properties there. It's still the frontier. Perhaps it's not easy to get letters home."

"Perhaps."

John blew out a breath. "Well, you should've brought Nabby and the grandchildren to live with us in the president's house."

"I tried, but she won't come. She said she'd be too humiliated to appear in outdated dresses and explain her husband's financial ruin. She doesn't want to be an embarrassment to you in Philadelphia."

"Fie on that! But if she won't come to us, she should live with Charles. His townhome is a modest place, and he must feel burdened with a new baby of his own, but there's room."

The truth could be put off no longer. With my thumbs worrying over one another, I broke the bad news. "Charles also lost a great deal of money in the economic panic, John."

My husband's jaw clenched, but he took it in stride. "Well, these are hard times. It's what I had in mind when I gave each of the boys two thousand dollars to help them make their way in the world. He'll have to be frugal, but he can at least draw on the interest."

"It's gone. Lost in his attempts to keep Nabby's husband out of debtor's prison."

John's hands clenched in surprise and then dismay. *"Damn it."*

How quickly I leaped to defend my boy. "Charles was trying to help. Both his sister and his wife were pleading with him on Colonel Smith's behalf. And you know what a tender heart he has."

"He's a tenderhearted fool!"

My husband was already so angry, I might as well tell him the rest. "John Quincy's money is at risk, too."

"Now how the devil did *Johnny's* money get caught up in this with him all the way across an ocean?"

"He entrusted his savings to Charles to invest. Now it is likely gone, and Charles is sick about it. Truly, I've never seen our sunny boy in such a state of despondency."

I didn't exaggerate. Having passed through New York on the way to Philadelphia, I'd stopped to see Charles and could still feel the wet tears my son wept on my shoulder. To have failed his wife, his child, his sister, and his brother this way was a crushing blow to our middle son.

But now John said, "Curse that boy for dragging Johnny down with him."

"It's *William Stephens Smith* who has dragged three of our children down with him."

My husband showed his teeth, but it wasn't a smile. "Well, as it happens, I'm the president, so if Smith doesn't return to make matters right, I'll send federal marshals to dispatch him."

It was a father's rage speaking. He wouldn't actually do it—at least I didn't think he would. I let my husband vent in the coach, hoping he'd be in better temper by the time we reached the president's house.

I reminded my husband that we still enjoyed good fortune. None of our children were beheaded, imprisoned, or likely to starve. Money troubles they had aplenty, but money troubles could be solved in time. And we were able to help them, so we ought to thank God for our blessings.

We arrived at sunset, whale oil lamps glowing on Market Street, and stepped out before the redbrick home I thought of as belonging to the Washingtons.

The house was all but vacant, the furniture having been so battered over the past few years it needed to be discarded.

I felt melancholy to know that the Washingtons had long since departed for Virginia and that I might never see either of those wonderful people again. But I could still smell the scent of Martha's lilacs and roses in the garden as they wafted to us on the evening's breeze—a lingering reminder of that great lady in whose footsteps I'd now have to tread.

That night, in the privacy of the president's canopied bed, John embraced me, whispering, "While I've been here I thought of you, dreamed of you, and longed to be with you again. I hate speeches, messages, proclamations, levees, and drawing rooms. I hate to speak to a thousand people to whom I have actually nothing to say."

"Yet all this you can do, *if* you put your mind to it."

"All this I can do, *if* my Abigail is at my side."

"I'll be at your side," I vowed. "But I fear I have not the patience, prudence, and discretion sufficient to fill Martha's place. I'm used to a freedom of sentiment. I know not how to look at every word before I utter it, and impose a silence upon myself when I long to talk."

"A woman *can* be silent, when she will," John teased. "But in truth, I can do nothing without you, and I've never wanted your advice more in my life. Assist me with your counsel and console me with your conversation. Do not leave me alone so long again."

It hadn't been so very long this time, but I gloried at the feel of his fingers twined with mine. "I suppose that no man, even if he is sixty years of age, ought to live more than three months away from his family."

John pulled back to feign a glare. "Madam, how dare you hint or lisp a word about sixty years of age? I will soon convince you that I am not above forty!"

I was too mature now to blush at such a remark. Instead, I said quite shamelessly, "You've always been a very good lawyer, John. So by whatever proofs you deem necessary, I'm ready and willing to be convinced."

MY FIRST ORDER of business as Lady Washington's successor was to establish orderly levees or I should be overrun entirely. For on my very first entertainment I received thirty-two ladies, and nearly as many gentlemen, in an under-furnished house, without enough chairs for a drawing room!

To get anything done between visits, I'd have to rise at five in the morning, breakfast at eight, tend to family affairs until eleven, then dress to receive company the rest of the day.

In trying to know how to conduct myself, I remembered the Court of St. James. *Dear God.* I, too, was going to have to ask vapid questions such as *Did you take a walk today, madam?* and *How do you like your house?*

It was said in society that my husband and I did not have the innate aristocratic dignity of the Washingtons. That was meant for a compliment. As it happened, my preference to *mingle* with the ladies was taken for good conduct in the first lady of a republic.

And because, in his portly old age, my husband wanted nothing more than to slump into a comfortable chair, smoke his cigars, and sip his brandy with the guests by a fire—he was said to be *convivial.*

An unexpected triumph for both of us.

This did not forestall all criticism, of course. I'd expected to be vilified with my whole family when I came into this situation. And I might have borne it with better grace were it not for the godless French faction amongst us, led in Congress by the little Virginian James Madison.

We had it on the authority of our son, the foreign minister, that the French government intended to go to war with the United States for our alleged fecklessness in paying our debts and failing to support their revolution. Their great expectation was founded upon the hope of our internal disunion—a hope encouraged by Americans who associated with the ruling men in France. And amongst them, we must now count Thomas Jefferson.

We knew this because a letter he wrote to a neighbor had been indiscreetly shared and then published in a French newspaper. Our once bosom friend denounced us as aristocrats, accusing my husband and the Federalist party of being "timid men who prefer the calm of despotism to the boisterous sea of liberty."

While Jefferson plainly regretted the exposure, he didn't deny having written it. And this time, it was an undeniable insult.

That *boisterous sea of liberty* he praised in France had not been kind to the men who actually fought for freedom. Admiral d'Estaing beheaded. Rochambeau arrested. Lafayette still rotting in prison—his wife and daughters having narrowly escaped the guillotine only through American influence.

How could Jefferson possibly countenance it?

"Does he even write an apology?" I asked John.

My husband's mouth flattened to a grim line and I decided not to press the matter. After all, the job of the president was arduous, perplexing, and hazardous. It was little wonder Washington retired from it.

John was sweating over a speech to Congress, and I gave my help eagerly. "You must emphasize that while both the British *and* the French now seize and harass American ships, only the French are refusing to receive a new ambassador from us."

John scribbled, contemplatively. "At this point, I am unsure who else to send."

"Send John Quincy," I said, though I shivered to contemplate sending my son to a place where the guillotine reigned. "They cannot refuse him. You need an ambassador in France, and there's none better than your son."

My husband slumped with a sigh. "But what does that look like for a ruler of a country to send his own son to negotiate? It looks like nepotism at best and monarchy at worse."

I didn't want to admit that he was right.

War with France might come anyway, which is why he intended to tell Congress, "Without some means of protection against a foreign enemy, national dishonor is unavoidable."

We needed a navy.

We needed an army, too, for as the French marched out to conquer Europe, the saber they rattled was very frightening indeed.

"Will the vice president support you?" I asked.

John snorted. "Jefferson will say that his role is merely to preside over the Senate, not to guide it. And for this I am grateful. For if he spoke his true feelings, he might still favor the French."

I couldn't understand Thomas Jefferson. However high-minded the French Revolution was when it started, it had devolved into a cycle of beatings, beheadings, and reigns of terror that begot new reigns of terror. France had become a dangerous Leviathan. But somehow our old friend couldn't see it, even now that the Leviathan was bent on devouring us, too.

IT FELL TO me to plan the forthcoming Independence Day celebration. And in that I was likely to come up short. I'd have to entertain not only all of Congress but also the city gentlemen, governor, officers, and companies. The house couldn't hold everyone, so some would have to be placed at long tables in the yard to be served cake, punch, and wine.

It would cost at least five hundred dollars, and it was an expense we couldn't avoid, for the Washingtons always made a splendid celebration of it. But of course, Washington was a very wealthy man.

I reminded myself that we were wealthy in other ways when a portrait arrived from overseas. It was painted by Mr. Copley in London, and the nameplate read MINISTER JOHN QUINCY ADAMS. When the servants unwrapped it, I gasped to see our eldest rendered so beautifully.

"Oh, how distinguished he looks!"

It'd been years since we'd seen John Quincy as he traversed Europe with his little brother in tow. He wrote that he now intended to take a wife—an Englishwoman named Louisa Catherine. Though he wanted no delay, we still hoped he'd reconsider.

John said, "It pains me to think we'll miss the wedding."

We hung the portrait of John Quincy above the mantel to inspirit us, though we feared our guests would accuse us of grooming him as a princeling.

As the summer heat rose, so, too, did tensions with France, now ruled by a *directoire* of five in which Napoleon Bonaparte was the dominant leader. Every day we anticipated that a vessel might arrive with a formal declaration of war. And our people wondered if President John Adams was capable of leading through such dark days.

Naturally, we both fretted about the forthcoming holiday—wondering how our more frugal version would be received. It'd be the country's twenty-first Independence Day, and with a wary eye over the sea, many worried it'd be our last.

On the day in question, Philadelphia was a bake oven. I stood on the dais in pearls and a pale gown underneath the chandelier where Mrs. Washington once stood, sweating so much I feared I'd melt into a puddle. Then I could stand the empty formality of it no longer, and plunged into the crowd.

Our country, which was now comprised of sixteen states, needed to unite under threats of war. And the holiday ought to have pulled us together. But I noticed Federalist ladies shunning Democratic-Republican ladies. And though I wished to do the same, I set a good example, pulling Mrs. Gallatin into the court circle, paying her much attention.

It galled me, because her husband had become our avowed foe in Congress. But the gossip at the party—from what snippets I overheard—was far less about my husband's failings and more about the notorious scandal involving Alexander Hamilton.

"Do you believe the accusations?" Mrs. Gallatin asked. "That Mr. Hamilton embezzled money from the treasury?"

"Certainly not," I said.

Hamilton was too vain and prideful about his financial system to steal from it.

But there was another accusation, less sinister but more sordid— that Hamilton had betrayed his wife with a base harlot and made himself vulnerable to blackmail. And according to my children in New York, Hamilton's infidelities were amongst the worst-kept secrets in that city. Why Nabby said he even panted after his own sister-in-law!

Oh, my heart bled for Eliza Hamilton, remembering the way she had always gazed so adoringly at her husband. I couldn't possibly add to her humiliation by crediting the words of Mr. Callender—the shady immigrant muckraker—who brought the scandal into public light.

Besides, as Hamilton was part of our Federalist faction, it felt disloyal for me to say anything against him to Mrs. Gallatin, the wife of a man who bore us no goodwill.

So instead, I ushered Mrs. Gallatin back to her husband, who was then conferring with Senator Burr. Gallatin was still complaining about the Jay Treaty while Burr, in silver-buckled shoes and every inch the rake, drank punch.

I mistrusted both men—suspecting at least Burr of being on the French payroll.

But before I could say anything to either, a certain social buzz vibrated around the room, and I turned to see it was the hum of adoration that now seemed to accompany Vice President Jefferson wherever he went.

Jefferson made his way to me amidst admiring toasts and hands that reached to greet him, his popularity undiminished by our troubles with France.

When finally he reached me, I gave a wave of acknowledgment with my feathered fan. "Vice President Jefferson."

"Mrs. Adams," he said, and like the diplomat he once was, he swept a bow so low that the hat in his hand nearly touched the crimson carpet. "I must congratulate you. What a lovely affair you've put together."

"How kind of you to say!"

I had learned to be diplomatic, too.

With the old familiar smile, Jefferson confided, "I think it does you much credit as the new first lady in our republic that you converse liberally with guests rather than presiding over the crowd from a dais with royal detachment."

Remembering that he had called us aristocrats, I quite nearly said, *"How relieved I am to have your approbation!"*

Instead, I said, "I feel too silly standing upon a dais by myself without a second lady to attend to me."

At this, the vice president winced. And not having intended to raise the subject of his widowhood as if his wife's death was an inconvenience to me, I quickly added, "I would so welcome your daughters at my side during such gatherings. You know how fond I am of Patsy and Polly."

I was able to say this much with honesty.

And I believe Jefferson spoke honestly when he said, "As they are both fond of you. Polly is soon to be wed and I hope she will join us next year."

"I shall rejoice on that happy occasion."

I was polite. Jefferson was polite.

We were all so *very* polite on the occasion of our nation's birth.

But inside, I seethed.

For Jefferson would not stand beside my husband against France. And now I didn't even want him to. We'd been loath to give Jefferson up as a friend, but no matter how wise and scientific as he was a philosopher and as a politician, I now believed him to be a vain child easily flattered and duped by the faction of zealots who fawned over him.

And this was never more evident than when Jefferson—and not the man who had *actually* been elected to the presidency— was toasted as the Man of the People.

Party factions were tearing our young nation apart and it fell to my husband to hold this union together, alone if must be. Well, I resolved he wouldn't be alone. He'd have me. I didn't know how much I could help by charming ladies in the parlor or smiling at hypocrites like Jefferson. But for John and for the country, I was willing to do this and much more.

Chapter Thirty-Nine

EAST CHESTER
New York
October 1797

THE BANKRUPTED COLONEL Smith had been gone a year while my daughter soldiered on alone. To ease her burdens, we had food sent from Quincy. We'd also taken our grandsons and paid for their schooling in New Hampshire, with my recently widowed and remarried sister Elizabeth watching over them. But with only two-year-old Caroline for company, Nabby had been too much alone. So we decided to pay her a brief visit in New York.

She'd come to greet us in her best dress, saying she otherwise had very little occasion to wear it.

"Doesn't Charles visit?" John asked.

"Oh, yes. Charles, Sally, and their two little girls," Nabby rushed to say. "Charles is so kind to me, Papa. Always helping to repair things. The fence. The leak in the roof. A rotted floorboard on the stairs. I don't know how I'd have survived without him."

It had been a hard and lonely year for our daughter. And a difficult one for the country. Fortunately, there was some good news. First, that propertied freedmen and women in New Jersey would be able to vote. Second, that our youngest son would soon return from Europe.

Though Tommy had been an excellent secretary for John Quincy, he'd been away for more than three years and without his own profession for longer than that. I suspected his impending return also might have to do with not wishing to be always in his eldest brother's shadow, or to play the part of an interloper. For John Quincy had married his English sweetheart. And I was happy to deliver this news to Nabby as we walked up the sloping drive and into her modest two-story house with its gabled attic.

"This Louisa Catherine must be a remarkable woman indeed, to have won Johnny's heart," Nabby said.

I nodded without reminding her that all her brothers fell in love easily.

"You've learned of the release of the Marquis de Lafayette and his family?" John asked, a little prideful, since our American diplomatic corps had applied pressure to bring it about.

"Praise God," Nabby said, leading us into her sunny but sparsely furnished parlor.

I could see that our girl had done her best to make the place hospitable. She'd knitted throws to cover threadbare spots on the chairs. A lace cloth disguised the crate that now served as a table. And everything was freshly scrubbed. Still, Nabby was apologetic. "I wish it were more fitting to serve as a place for state business while *the president* is in residence."

"It's more than fitting," John reassured her. "And I'll get far more done here than in Philadelphia."

Thereupon he kissed Nabby's forehead, then her hair, then her forehead again. "You mustn't worry, my treasure. Come back to Philadelphia with us. We'll make sure you see only the people you wish to see, and we'll take care of you there."

At that, our daughter finally let us see the crack in her brave facade. Sobbing with relief against her father's neck, she confessed how deeply depressed she'd been. "But seeing my parents again has restored me. Your kindness has given me hope."

"You'll be restored to even greater happiness in Philadelphia," I said. "Say that you'll come. You and Caroline. She can eat her fill of plum pudding, and your smiling countenance at the breakfast table will give your father a respite from the cares of the presidency."

Our daughter worried at her lip. "I never want to be a burden to you, Papa."

"That you could never be," he said.

To our great relief, Nabby consented to come with us. And

when we finally went up to bed, she had the look of a woman who'd get her first good night's sleep in a long while.

Of course, I also noticed that John checked the newly repaired stair, and I hissed, "Don't you dare criticize Charlie's workmanship when we see him. He's a lawyer, not a carpenter."

"He also drinks too much if the rumors are true."

I held tight to the banister. "What rumors?"

John refused to say more until he'd nudged me into the small bedroom, closing the door behind us. "I've had a report today of Charles I don't like. To begin with, he spends time with Hamilton—a man completely disgraced."

The accusation that Hamilton had misappropriated funds as treasury secretary was an ongoing scandal. Especially since Alexander Hamilton defended himself by writing a pamphlet exposing his own adulterous affair. Reading it had confirmed every wicked thing ever suspected about the man—and left me feeling dreadfully sorry for his wife.

Still, I couldn't blame Charles for offering comfort to an old mentor. "John, we once apprenticed Charles to Hamilton. We wouldn't wish him to be cruel to an old master who is now mired in shame and humiliation."

John scoffed. "Hamilton is incapable of shame. My worry is for Charles. They say he's gambling to win back the money he's lost—and that he's a drunk."

I gasped at the latter. "Surely you don't believe it."

"I didn't believe it when I heard he ran naked through Harvard yard, either. But here we are."

I took my index finger and poked his arm. "That was a childish lark nearly a decade ago!"

"Ouch! Be careful woman . . ."

"Charles is a hardworking family man now. You've been *so* hard on him. Not harder on him than he's been on himself, but certainly harder on him than the man who caused his financial trouble to begin with."

John lowered his voice, presumably so that Nabby wouldn't overhear. "Well, *that* man may have my daughter's hand in marriage but, praise God, does not have my blood flowing through his veins."

I was sure that John would soften once he saw his son in the flesh. None of us had ever had the heart to resist Charlie's dimpled smile. But the next morning the captain of the light horse that was to accompany us to the city broke the bad news. "I'm sorry, Mr. President. But there is yellow fever in New York."

We couldn't visit Charles, nor could he come to us. And as for Philadelphia, we were unable to go there either. "The outbreak is worse in Philadelphia than in New York. In fact, it might be worse than four years ago."

That outbreak had killed 10 percent of the city, so we'd have to abandon the capital until the first winter's frost, which, for some reason the physicians could not divine, drove the illness away.

Thus, we stayed with Nabby that autumn.

John found it entirely agreeable to conduct the business of the nation from our daughter's cramped kitchen, with its cookware hanging from the ceiling, while our nearly three-year-old granddaughter, Caroline, banged upon a jug with a wooden spoon.

Messengers for the president swept in and out with word of France's march of victories in Europe.

Then a message came for Nabby from her husband.

Gulping air, she sank down in relief. "Colonel Smith says he'll be home soon. He says he's written many letters to me that must've gone missing. Here, look, Mama. An address where I can claim some funds."

This news positively brought her back to life, which is why I studiously avoided my husband's gaze, because I knew he was skeptical.

I rode out with Nabby the next day to the address provided. Unfortunately, the man from whom she was to receive this money was gone—if he'd ever existed.

But Nabby was still brimming with good cheer. "It's the fate of women in our family to wait on letters and packages and to be disappointed. But I'll muster the fortitude of my dear Mama when Papa was away all those years."

Your father was a different sort of man, I wanted to say. *On a very different mission.*

But I merely smiled, praying my son-in-law was only a fool with money and not, in fact, another duplicitous scoundrel in our lives. For now, Nabby determined to stay here alone, convinced her husband would return to her at any moment.

Eventually, the frost came, the epidemics abated, and we were obliged to return to Philadelphia without her.

There we found Congress so set against one another that an actual brawl broke out on the floor when Democratic-Republican Matthew Lyon spit in the face of Federalist Roger Griswold, who responded by beating him with a cane.

Could guillotines be far behind?

Though I'd never confess it, I began to wonder if the enterprise of the so-called *United* States was doomed. How long would northern and southern states rub along together when oil and water were not more contrary in their natures? Then again, perhaps we *shouldn't* hold together. There were certainly days I wished to be rid of the whole pack of southern slavers.

"But if we divided," John warned, "we'd be easy prey for other nations. We must *make* the union hold."

How much better for us if my husband's cabinet agreed! Instead, they each found a way to fan the flames of faction. They were all holdovers from Washington's administration—Pickering, Wolcott, McHenry.

All Hamilton's creatures.

They were a hindrance rather than a help to their president, who felt increasingly embattled and isolated, turning more often to me for advice and support.

Now John was bundled up in blankets by the fire, writing another speech to Congress, while I coaxed him to drink a hot chamomile tisane with lemon and honey to ease his cold. And though he'd asked to see the newspapers, I kept them from him— for he didn't need to be further sickened.

One paper had referred to him as "blind, bald, crippled, toothless Adams."

Thomas Paine wrote, "Some people talk of impeaching John Adams, but I am for softer measures. I would keep him to make fun of."

There were worse things printed, many of which I thought deeply disloyal, given the state of our country. And the next day, when my husband's old colleague Dr. Rush stopped by to check on the president's health and recount their glory days from the revolution, I said, "I think there ought to be a law against printing such things!"

"If Philadelphians are turning against President Adams, it is only because of impatience," Dr. Rush said, knowing we'd been waiting half a year for news from the envoys John sent to France. "They will change their tune."

I hoped he was right, though I could never seem to warm to Philadelphia. I found the place odiferous, crowded with disagreeable people, and the climate unpleasant regardless of the season.

I wished very much not to be in this city. In truth, I longed for home. So when I wasn't about the business of being the president's lady, I distracted myself with plans to remodel the house back in Quincy.

I wanted a dairy room for our milk and cheese. An outhouse in more privacy from the residence, too. The interior must be painted—dining room, parlor, bedchamber, and all. The stairway, in particular, I hoped would be a cheery yellow.

But these plans I kept secret from John, so I tucked the bills into an envelope when my husband burst into my parlor.

"Outrage from France," he cried, waving dispatches that he wasn't sure he ought to show me. "In truth, my dear, I fear to show *anyone* these missives."

"It cannot be that bad," I said, pulling a woolen shawl around my shoulders. "The French haven't harmed our envoys, have they?"

"Worse," he said.

I couldn't imagine what might be *worse* until I finally wheedled the truth out of my husband. "Our emissaries met with French agents, code-named X, Y, and Z. To avoid war, these French agents demanded three things. First, we must loan them millions of dollars. Next, I must apologize for the speech I made in taking office. And finally, we must pay the French foreign minister a personal bribe."

John sputtered a furious laugh.

But I was nearly struck dumb. "Is it perhaps . . . a matter of practicality . . . like when we paid the Barbary pirates?"

John didn't like being reminded of *that* one bit. "That was a different time and a trifling adversary capable only of harassing us, not destroying us. Now we have a duty to defend ourselves. And I won't cringe from war if war it must be."

How my chest swelled with pride in my good strong man, who was made of oak instead of willow. He might be torn up by the roots—but in defense of his country he'd never bend.

It wasn't until a month later, in April, that John finally shared the full contents of the messages with Congress, and a wave of anti-French sentiment swept over America. Where people had once rioted to support our old ally, they now burned their cockades, poured French wine into the gutter, and glared suspiciously at French immigrants, wondering who amongst them came for asylum, and who came to undermine us.

It would be war, then. And in preparation, government officials flooded the president's house, striding through our halls in muddy boots, clustering in grave conversation behind my potted plants, and arguing while perched upon the sofas like crows on a fence.

Everyone wanted to speak to the president, *urgently.*

Ten, twenty of them went in and out, asking direction on matters large and small. Dispatches arrived by courier with requests for money, signatures, pardons, or authority. It went on and on.

I did my best to guard the gates, and in so doing, I realized that things were finally going my husband's way. Congress authorized a navy for our defense. A provisional army would be recruited, too. But who would command it? I heard whispers in every corner of the president's house.

"Washington must come out of retirement—"

"—too old—"

"Knox, then—"

"—too round—"

"What about Hamilton?"

I knew what John would say about *that* even before he snapped, "It will be Hamilton over my dead body! I'd rather appoint Colonel Smith."

"That isn't a terrible idea, John," I said.

"I wasn't being sarcastic, *Madame Presidante,*" John said, adjusting a pillow to support his aching back. "Colonel Smith is on the list."

Perhaps it wasn't my place to advise, yet I said, "Whatever the faults of our son-in-law, he's respected by his fellow war veterans. He's a seasoned professional soldier with fighting experience. More than Hamilton. Much more."

"But how would it look?" John asked, even more sensitive than usual on this point, because the papers were accusing us of having profited in some way by sending our eldest son to Europe as a diplomat.

Well, I'd already taken it upon myself to write a shaming letter to *that* newspaperman and was in no mood to suffer venal fools. "Nominate Colonel Smith and find out."

I believed it would be in the interest of the nation to have a man lead our military who had fought and bled in the revolution. Better Colonel Smith than a philanderer like Hamilton, whose single claim to battlefield glory was taking a redoubt at Yorktown.

But I could not deny that a part of me suggested it because I hoped it would restore my daughter's husband to a place of honor and prosperity, so that she could be happy. And I thought we might get away with it because my husband was now hailed a hero in the streets of Philadelphia—and even in the theater, where a delightful presidential march was played in his honor.

We were still humming the tune when we returned from the theater, both of us a little damp from the rain and drying off by the fire. Alas, our momentary contentment was interrupted by a servant from the kitchen, fretfully wiping his hands on an apron. "Please forgive the interruption, Mr. President. It is only that—well, two young women came to the back entrance." A long pause followed. "They said they must deliver something to you. Normally, I'd shoo them away but . . ."

"Good God, man," John said. "Spit it out or send them up."

The two young women came before us, one shaking as she held out a water-stained piece of paper. John took it, squinted at it in the candlelight, then, unable to remember where he put his spectacles, he handed it to me.

"It looks like an anonymous letter," I said, seeing no obvious signature or seal.

"Where was it found?" John asked.

One of the young ladies said, "We were walking past the house, Mr. President. It was at the edge of the gutter. When we read it, we didn't know what to do except show it to you."

I spread the page on the table and brought the candle near, blood running cold as I read aloud.

> Certain French people in this city are conspiring to set fire to the city and massacre the inhabitants on the 9th day of May. I was in league with them until I understood their true villainy. Signed, a real though heretofore misguided American.

Quite alarmed, I asked, "Can this be true?"

My husband was already waving it off. "My dear patriotic ladies, thank you for bringing this to our attention, but you mustn't take fright. This is only an incendiary letter meant to alarm and distress us. It's all shadow and mist."

When we were alone again, my gaze cut to John. "How can you know it isn't a real conspiracy?"

"Because I've seen more credible threats," John said, lighting a cigar as he shrugged out of his damp coat. "Threats delivered through credible messengers, not left in a ditch."

However, when a letter with similar details was sent ten days later to an associate, we began to take it seriously. A guard was placed at our door, and wearing the black cockade that Washington favored during the revolution, some of our best men fanned out through the city to investigate.

The fear spreading through the city seemed to support the argument for the new Alien and Sedition Acts proposed by Congress. "You must sign and enact them," I told my husband, finding him at his worktable, those proposed laws spread out before him.

John hadn't asked for these measures, which empowered him to expel any foreigner he deemed dangerous. Now he was scowling down at the pages. "Well, I daresay Secretary of State Pickering, that blackguard, is salivating over the idea that he can use this to kick every Frenchman out of Philadelphia."

"Pickering isn't the president," I argued. "It's for the purpose of defending ourselves against enemy agents, that is all. You wouldn't abuse it."

"God willing, I won't be the *only* president this country will ever have. Will you trust the others?"

"If you don't sign it, you may be the *last* president this country ever has. Emissaries of France are hidden amongst us, and if something isn't done about them, this city—indeed, this whole country—may burn."

In response to that, John lit another cigar—despite my having told him this new habit was harming his health. "Even people on our side say the Sedition Act is particularly odious. Unconstitutional, even. I had an earful this afternoon from John Marshall. I told him I considered these acts to be war measures only—never to be used in peacetime—but he believed it made no difference."

John Marshall had been one of the envoys we sent to France. The Virginia statesman had been a valuable ally ever since. We trusted him implicitly, so it was sobering to hear this from John, who added, "And you don't even want to know what the vice president has to say."

"You're right that I don't," I said with an indelicate snort. "As if we ought to put any stock in Thomas Jefferson's opinions . . ."

"Jefferson is a rival, but he holds much influence, and some wisdom, still. He says these laws will be a blot on my reputation for all time, not to mention a blot on the history of our country."

"Oh, he has a flair for the dramatic. And as usual, he's more worried about philosophy than reality."

John sighed. "He believes it deeply, Abigail. He says he won't remain present in his post as vice president to oversee the passage of what he deems to be tyrannical laws. He's packing up and returning to Monticello."

"*Good*," I said, hoping Jefferson's departure would give us some peace. After all, John had grown thin in recent days. Pale, too. Lacking for exercise and fresh air. Only one lovely jaunt had I persuaded him to take into the countryside, where we gorged ourselves on strawberries.

He'd feel better once he signed the bills, and I rejoiced when he finally relented. I rejoiced again when the most seditious newspaperman—Benjamin Franklin Bache—was arrested and charged under these new laws.

For years now, as the publisher of the *Aurora*, Dr. Franklin's grandson had been the chief criminal amongst the newspapermen, forging and then printing letters that purported to incriminate Washington, as well as my husband and my son.

Bache was a base liar who had endangered the whole country, so I felt quite satisfied by his arrest.

However, John Marshall thought it a terrible precedent. "Sir, libel laws would've made the scoundrel pay for lies just as easily, and without abridging the rights of the free press!"

"We are at *war*, Mr. Marshall," I argued.

"None that has been declared, madam," he shot back, seemingly puzzled as to why my husband allowed me to remain in the room. "And nowhere in the Constitution does it say that war suspends our rights. Indeed, not one state would've ratified it if it had."

Seeing John pinch the bridge of his nose, I asked, "Why *don't* we have a formal declaration of war? The French are already waging one against us. They've meddled in our elections and threatened our diplomats. They've seized *hundreds* of our ships and imprisoned our citizens without cause."

I didn't see the point of fighting only a quasi-war, or a half-war as John called it. The war was, in my opinion, absolutely inevitable. But the diplomat inside my husband still insisted there was room to negotiate. "I'm going to send another emissary."

"And be *mocked* for it here and abroad," I insisted.

"Out," John said, pointing at the door. "Both of you, go. You both have better things to do."

For one thing, I needed to plan another Independence Day celebration, but it would be quite different from the first. Oh, there would be my excellent plum cake for the ladies. Rum punch for the gentlemen, too. But we were on a war footing now—the clash of armies on the other side of the ocean too loud to ignore.

So here in Philadelphia, four hundred young men, all in uniform, and sixty grenadiers would march in review for the president. On the grand day, to these young men willing to defend our equally young nation, I presented cockades with a small silver eagle. And their commander said, "Mrs. Adams, with your permission, we will call them *Abigails*."

Flattered, I said, "I hope you do. For I want every soldier who fights for the United States to know he is a chivalrous knight of liberty and has the special blessing—not merely of the president's lady, but of a mother who loves her country and all the young men in it."

They straightened, shoulders squared as if they heard the praise of their own mothers in my words. Truly, many were young enough to be my sons. And realizing it, mist gathered at the corners of my eyes, because I knew that if any of them were to fall in war, I would mourn them as such.

I would feel the loss in my own breast.

Some congressman took my emotion for mere display, whispering the backhanded compliment that I was *as complete a politician as any lady in the old French court.*

But he could whisper all he liked, for the soldiers knew the purity of my heart.

A Federalist friend later met me with a toast. "Well done, Mrs. Adams. With the soldiers and in convincing your husband to sign the Alien and Sedition Acts. You ought to be autocratrix of the United States."

"I don't know why you abuse me so," I said, fanning myself to cover my pride. "I've always been for *equality* of the sexes, as my husband can attest."

Chapter Forty

QUINCY
Massachusetts
Summer 1798

M Y TRIUMPHS IN Philadelphia soon gave way to mortal peril. For on the journey home for the summer, I was overcome with the sensation that my entire body was afire.

"Stop the horses," I said. "I need a bed."

Twice in four hours I pleaded with John to stop at any house where I could undress completely and lie down. I thought it was the sun that oppressed me. But not all the water in the world could make me cool.

And now, back in Quincy, delirious with fever, I knew it was not the sun. At my bedside, Dr. Tufts said, "It may be yellow fever."

"Dear God," someone said. Was it Nabby? We must've taken her home with us—but I couldn't remember. "Philadelphia is raging with it again, but I was sure they'd left in time."

Hadn't we left in time?

My mind was a whirl of heat and confusion. My head throbbed and my gums ached whilst a strange taste of iron coated my tongue. Was it blood?

In the painful days that followed, I didn't understand much but fully apprehended that I'd never been so sick. Not even with dysentery.

Nabby helped to feed and wash me during the day. John sat up with me at night, talking incessantly.

What I said to him I'm not entirely sure, though I remember pleading for him to leave and spare himself contagion. I told him

I'd rather perish than suffer the guilt of my loved ones sacrificing their lives for me the way my mother did.

But my loved ones refused to go.

While I tossed and turned in a stupor, I sometimes overheard Phoebe and my sister Mary praying over me. I heard Dr. Tufts talking low and serious. And I overheard John, utterly distraught, say my destiny was precarious. "And mine in consequence of it."

While I lay tangled in the veil that separated life from death, the business of the country went on. My husband asked Washington to come out of retirement to lead the army, though everyone knew he was too old to take the field. And the former president agreed on one condition—he wanted Alexander Hamilton for his right-hand man with the rank of Inspector General.

Say no, I tried to say. *Washington is no longer the president, John. You are. You must have your own men.*

But I only managed a groan whilst John raged about it. "If I consent to the appointment of Hamilton, I should consider it the most irresponsible action of my life and the most difficult to justify. His talents I respect; his character—I leave—"

"A man who has broken the most solemn private vow will betray the public trust," I murmured, but my words came out slurred.

"Let Mama sleep," Nabby insisted, settling beside my head a sachet of lavender.

In the end, John's cabinet prevailed upon him to let Washington have his way. Hamilton would be second in command by rank but leader of the army in reality. And one of the first ways Hamilton used his influence was to ensure that our son-in-law could have no important role.

On a rare day when I felt well enough to sit up and take tea, Nabby explained that Colonel Smith would command a brigade— no more—and would suffer the indignity of reporting to men who had been his equals or inferiors.

"Papa thinks he'd do better to preserve his pride and refuse the appointment, but my husband cannot, for he is able-bodied and feels he cannot refuse to serve the country in a time of war and still call himself a patriot."

How she still defended him, despite his long, shameful absence!

Still, why Hamilton insisted on humiliating Colonel Smith this way was a mystery. Perhaps it really *was* because my son-in-law ruled him out of order all those years ago during the debates over the Jay Treaty. Or perhaps it was that Hamilton didn't wish for the president of the United States to have his own son-in-law as eyes and ears in the military.

Of course, the official excuse was that our son-in-law could not be trusted in a significant leadership role because he'd gone bankrupt and had yet to repay all his creditors. But Hamilton was fast friends with many men who'd been ruined in the speculation bubble, so I doubted that could be true.

But I could advise very little from my dying bed as my illness lingered, week after week. Thousands were dying in Philadelphia, from whence we came. Among the victims, several of our servants at the president's house and the publisher of the *Aurora*, who perished whilst out on bail before his trial under the Sedition Act. Which caused us as much opprobrium throughout the country as it saved us.

When Dr. Tufts next came to care for me, I choked out, "I want to write letters of farewell to my children."

"Don't surrender, Abigail," he said, dosing me with willow bark and quinine.

I noticed that the years had been relatively kind to Cotton Tufts. Or perhaps because he'd always cut an odd appearance, the years did him no harm. At sixty-four years, his mouth was an even more grim gash, but I'd known him so long that I saw nothing but benevolence on his visage.

He'd been not only my business partner, and our financial manager, but a kindly uncle watching over my sisters and me. I realized now how long I'd taken him for granted and reached for his hand.

With my throat painfully dry from misuse, I said, "You once teased that I called you Cousin Cotton when vexed, and Uncle Tufts when not. But in truth, I flatter myself to call you uncle as I would be honored to be the niece of so kind and generous a man. And though I can never adequately thank you for your many kindnesses to me, I hope you will accept my heartfelt gratitude and esteem."

"I should thank *you*," he said, smiling as if touched by my words. "For you've made my life infinitely more interesting than it would've been without you. But I wish you were not now presenting me with such a curious medical challenge."

"I fear it *is* my time," I whispered.

"I don't think so. We're of good Puritan stock. We die hard." With that, he produced a candied orange from his pocket and offered it to me as if I were still a girl. "Sit up now, take a tiny bite. You'll feel better."

I didn't want to sit up. Nor did I want to take a bite. Yet, with great difficulty, I did as I was bid.

"You mustn't sink under this," the good doctor said. "For one thing, you must recover to see all the renovations I made to the house on your behalf—including that beautiful yellow paint you wanted."

Realizing that I must've been carried up the stairway with its new yellow paint without remembering it, I murmured, "I meant to surprise John. Was he well pleased?"

"Someone had already spoiled the surprise for him, don't you remember? In any case, the president is delighted and wondered how you afforded it."

"Did you tell him?" I asked.

"I told him only enough to satisfy his curiosity without revealing the growth of your pin money. It's still our secret, my dear. Now drink this dose of Peruvian bark or we'll both end up taking that secret to the grave."

It wasn't until early November that I was able to leave my bed. Even then, I needed help down the stairs. More than ten weeks I'd lain at death's doorstep with friends and family ministering to me.

Meanwhile, John had refused to leave, despite being needed in Philadelphia. On the morning I was finally strong enough to breakfast with him, I said, "If I'd died and you'd lost the war to France because you refused to leave my side, I'd have haunted you from the next world."

"There's my Portia returned to me," John said, helping to ease me into an armchair. "But as it happens, there may be no war."

John explained that circumstances in Europe had changed. France now wanted peace. The evidence was convincingly laid before us from abroad by our own son Minister John Quincy Adams.

"Hamilton and his High Federalists itch for war," John said. "But I wish to take this chance at peace. Great would be the guilt of an unnecessary war."

I was, myself, more of the same mind with the so-called *High Federalists*, but said, "Then you must go swiftly to Philadelphia. Take Nabby with you to serve as hostess in my place if she'll go. And I'll follow when I'm strong enough."

I was still his Portia indeed.

IT WAS NOW lonely at Peacefield. Thanksgiving was usually a day of festivity when the family circle met together, even though apart the rest of the year. But this year, no husband dignified my board. No children added gladness to it. No grandchildren to smile, eyes all a-sparkle for minced pie. Not even my sisters or Uncle Tufts could join me. But I perceived many public and private causes to give thanks for, so I hoped my heart was not ungrateful.

Especially since I could spend the day with Phoebe, the only surviving parent I had.

We shared in the bounties of providence together with Mr. Abdee and my servants. And after we supped, Phoebe clapped her hands together and insisted on a sleigh ride. "Fresh air dispels gloom."

I agreed, so I let Mr. Abdee help us both into the sleigh. He drove it while Phoebe and I sat together, enlivened by talk of Reverend Wibird's most recent sermon, thanking God that New York was soon to abolish slavery.

"The first good news in a while," I said.

"May it not be the last," Phoebe said, offering a brief prayer for the deliverance of all those in bondage.

At length, she asked, "I thought your boy Tommy was coming home? I'm mighty eager to hear his tales from Europe."

Like me, Phoebe had a fascination with places she'd never seen. Perhaps that's where I'd come by my own wanderlust—though by now, I considered it quite quenched. "His not coming yet has depressed me, and reflections respecting our other children pain me daily."

Phoebe nodded knowingly. "Your poor Nabby."

I sighed. "Yes. For Nabby I feel most keenly; because she's innocent of the cause of her misfortunes. I hope better days are reserved for her, though at present the prospect is dark and I wonder what I could've done to avoid it."

"If you did everything intending for the best," Phoebe said, "then I think you've no cause for regret. What remains to us of life, we must expect to have checkered with good and evil. It's God's will, so let us rejoice in one and patiently endure the other as becomes those who have a better hope and brighter prospects beyond the grave."

There was a great deal of wisdom in her words. So much so that I'd repeat them to others. But I pointed out, "President Adams disputes that God takes an active hand in the world, you know. He says it is superstition. And he vexes me by keeping his religion and politics separate, in these times, of all times."

"Perhaps that accounts for his irritable nature," Phoebe offered.

I couldn't argue. Shaking my head, I admitted, "He's wroth with our married children. He thinks even John Quincy is foolish and blind because our eldest son thought he was marrying an heiress when he took an Englishwoman for his bride. But on the morning of the wedding feast, he was informed the dowry he was promised was forfeit and that his father-in-law had lost his entire fortune. Too late for Johnny to change his mind about the wedding even if he wanted to."

Phoebe winced. "Did he want to?"

"My son is too much a gentleman to admit it if he did. Now he's in financial straits thanks to that mistake and to his brother's mismanagement of his money."

Phoebe seemed less troubled by this news than expected. "You needn't worry about John Quincy. That boy will always make it out right. It's *Charlie* you need to worry for. His shame of losing his brother's money will sink him."

She'd seen the note I received from Charles in which he said, "I've not enjoyed one moment's comfort for upwards of two years, my sleep has been disturbed, and my waking hours embittered."

Now Phoebe said, "You raised good-hearted children in a wicked world."

Well, I didn't know how to fight against the wickedness of the world. But there *was* something I could do to guard against the slings and arrows that threatened my family. I could create a fortress, right here in Quincy. So that winter, as I recovered from the ailment that nearly killed me, I oversaw additions to our farm: a carriage house and a barn. I also built onto the house a larger salon, and an even bigger library upstairs for my husband and his sons, who might one day find it necessary to return home to practice law.

With my investments, I'd make of our home a place that could shield our family. I'd make Peacefield live up to its name as our sanctuary against what may come.

Chapter Forty-One

W HEN I HEARD the carriage approach, I wanted to run to the door. Instead, I stopped by the mirror near the door to fluff the curls of my graying hair, and to pinch color into my cheeks.

"Is it the president's coach?" I asked the servants.

I was eager to see not only John but also my youngest son, finally returned from his diplomatic mission in Europe. Before anyone could answer, Thomas burst into the door bearing a basket of flowers, fruits, and other delicacies he'd collected throughout his travels.

"Tommy!" I exclaimed, trying to find some way to wrap my arms around him without disturbing the packages. "Oh, Tommy, Tommy, Tommy . . ."

My youngest boy put the basket down and embraced me. *Five years.* Five years he'd been gone. He was a man of twenty-six now, with broader shoulders than either of his brothers. And oh, how solidly comforting he was in the flesh.

"I want to hear everything, my dear boy," I said. "Absolutely *everything*. About your journeys and adventures, and especially about your brother!"

Thomas laughed. "Let me go back and help get the president down from his coach first."

By the time the two of them were inside throwing off dusty cloaks and muddy boots, I had a table of refreshments ready with hot syllabub, peach brandy, nuts, cheeses, and maple buttered bread.

When John had finished kissing me, he threw himself into his armchair with a slice of buttered bread. "My dear," he said, wiping a crumb from his lips and staring about the place with wonder. "I daresay you've doubled the size of this house whilst I was gone."

He was not far wrong. "Meanwhile, you've delivered a master stroke of policy, Mr. President!"

"You're the only one to think so," John grumbled.

For upon announcing that he planned to send another commission of diplomats to France, my husband's warmongering cabinet had roared at him in impotent anger.

Our political enemies, including the vile pamphleteer James Callender, a Jefferson supporter, spat that John was a "repulsive pedant." Some of our staunchest allies also accused John of having a foul heart and a base mind. One even said he hoped my husband met with a fatal accident on his way home.

John almost took perverse pleasure in this.

And with a little astonishment, Thomas reported, "They're saying the president would never have done it 'if the old woman was in Philadelphia to stop him.'"

I laughed, not knowing whether to be flattered or offended. "Saucy of them to presume, since *the old lady* approves. Regardless of whether war is inevitable, this puts to the test French sincerity when they say they want peace."

Though it was a different tune than the song I'd sung before, John nodded in appreciation. "And upon *them* the responsibility now rests in the eyes of all the world."

I pulled my chair closer to his, thinking through this statesmanship as more became apparent to me. "Your decision to send diplomats to France also may delay the directory from sending a French minister *here*. Which is not desirable, lest they stir up our populace in riot."

John lifted his glass in toast to my logic.

"Pray am I a good politician?"

His countenance was serious. "That you are, my dear. Certainly wiser than those hotheads in my cabinet."

"If *I* were in your cabinet, I'd say we should always hold a sword in one hand and olive branch in the other."

Thomas smirked. "Mother, everyone thinks you *are* the president's cabinet."

I laughed. "I've never had the influence ascribed to me."

Tommy threw a few nuts into the air and caught them in his mouth. "You have more."

Swiping the dish of nuts from him until he could eat like a civilized person, I cried, "And here I thought we sent you to Europe to gain sophistication!"

John pretended not to hear and gobbled his bread. Tommy just grinned. And I liked the look of him, my baby boy. He was dark like me and compact of stature, but his looks and build were all his father. His sturdiness, too. I couldn't stop reaching for his hand to reassure myself that he was finally home.

"What will you do now, Tommy?" I asked.

"I was thinking of starting a law practice in Philadelphia, for I wouldn't like to compete with my own brothers. When Johnny returns with his wife, they're sure to settle in Boston. And with Charlie so prominent in New York, only Philadelphia is left to make a name for myself."

Ugh, *Philadelphia*. I didn't like to think of my boy settling in that Jacobin-infested city. But John Quincy had already written with a cheeky warning that Tommy must be allowed to make his own decisions and that I mustn't give him too much advice.

That night my husband retired early, exhausted and complaining of tooth pain. But I stayed up, peppering my son with questions. How were our surviving French friends? How did he enjoy Holland, Britain, Portugal, and Prussia? And especially what was Johnny's wife like, this English rose, Louisa Catherine?

We conversed until I could keep my eyes open no longer and finally padded up the stairs to join my husband in slumber.

Then I startled to find him still awake.

"What ails you?" I asked, for I could tell at once from my husband's expression that something weighed heavily upon him. "Your tooth?"

He shook his head. "We saw Charles in New York on the way home. We found him drunk in the middle of the day in his office."

I blinked, stunned and upset all at once. "But Tommy said nothing of it."

"Tommy believes his brother's excuses. That he just had too much to drink with clients in a tavern. But Charlie's wife tells me a different tale. One of frequent drunkenness and dissipation."

My hands went to my cheeks. From Nabby, the loyal sister, I heard only of how Charles helped on her farm. Never a word leaked from her pen or passed her lips that Charles was sinking into dissipation. Perhaps I'd raised my children to be *too* loyal to one another . . .

"The gambling is worse, too," John said. "I've been sending him a little money, here and there, to keep him afloat. He's lost it all."

I didn't dare admit that I, too, had been slipping Charles money. It was meant to feed his two little daughters, our precious granddaughters. It wasn't to be spent on liquor, cards, and dice.

While I reeled, John said, "I remonstrated with him. I reminded Charles that he has a family. That his actions will determine their happiness, and that his actions reflect on his parents, too. What does a nation think when the president's son behaves like a wastrel?"

"What did he say to that?"

"He promised he'd stop, but I put no stock in it."

How many times did my brother swear he'd stop drinking? Sometimes he did. But always the bottle seduced him in the end . . .

Now I sank down onto the side of the bed, head hung low, wondering what we could do.

"Happy Washington to be childless!" John barked. "My children give me more pain than all my enemies."

Now my head snapped up. "Oh, you go too far. Your children suffered all their lives under the burden of their father's public service. Now Charles may have stumbled, but Nabby, John Quincy, and Thomas have been nothing but dutiful. How could you wish any of them weren't born?"

I said this with savage anger, and John had the grace to appear ashamed. "I'm sorry. I didn't mean it."

I was not appeased. "You *should* be sorry to have said such a terrible thing. I do not consider George Washington to be at all a happier man because he has no children. If he has none to give him pain, he has none to give him pleasure either. And a man of your age, president or not, ought to remember it. Because this nation will *never* love you as much as your family does."

Chagrined, my husband stubbed out his cigar—which, in any case, he ought not be smoking in the bedroom to begin with. And now I was doubly vexed because I needed to open a window to dispel the smoke. As I flung it open and let in the evening breeze, John came up behind me, almost meekly. "You're right, my dear. I've lost my senses in Philadelphia. It's good that I'm home for a few months to remember myself on the farm, and to get your good counsel."

"Indeed," I said, stiffly.

As it happened, it was to be a relatively pleasant and restorative interlude at Peacefield, where we reacquainted ourselves with our youngest son. Tommy wasn't a witty entertainer like Charles. Nor was he interested in debating philosophy with his father the way John Quincy always did. No, our youngest was a plain, hardworking man.

He mowed, sawed, manured, picked apples, pressed cider, and otherwise put his strong back into the prosperity of our farm. Meanwhile, his father put his energies toward the presidency without all the interruptions of the capital.

John could dash off instructions and commands as easily from Quincy as he could in Philadelphia, I was certain. And I wished it could always be this way.

In truth, Peacefield did wonders for our health and happiness. Nevertheless, Congress would soon be in session. So, after a respite of seven months, it was time to gird our loins and return to the nation's capital.

Chapter Forty-Two

"MR. PRESIDENT," JOHN Marshall said, gravely. "I regret to inform you that George Washington is dead."

We had only just arrived at the president's house, where my husband took up his duties, and I took up mine in what would assuredly be a grim term. For with Washington's passing, every countenance was covered with gloom.

"I shall die," Washington is reported to have said from his bed at Mount Vernon. "But death has no terrors for me."

Remembering our former president and all he had meant to the country, I could scarcely collect myself. Though the survival of the nation had never *truly* rested upon Washington's breath alone, it had often felt like it did. And I didn't blame citizens for being frightened about a future without him.

But now every lady in the capital looked to me to set a mourning tradition for the republic, and I was hesitant to do so. "Whatever length I choose will either be thought too disrespectful by the Federalists, or too monarchical by the Democratic-Republicans."

My husband *almost* laughed at my complaint. "I am familiar with that dilemma . . ."

A state memorial service must be held for Washington. We'd have to set a precedent in this, too, about how the United States should say farewell to her presidents. Important personages were coming from all over the country to take part, some of whom might expect lodgings with us in the president's house.

But we didn't expect our daughter-in-law to appear at the doorstep with our two granddaughters in tow.

Charlie's wife was dressed all in black, but her pinched expression was not public grief for Washington. In the privacy of the parlor where we served tea and closed the doors against the curiosity of the servants, she said, "I've left Charles."

"*Left* him?" I asked, blinking. "Oh, Sally . . ."

John narrowed his eyes. "What's he done now?"

Sally sat as stiffly as possible, squeezing her hands between her knees to contain her anger. "I cannot live with a drunkard, a gambler, and *an adulterer*, too."

The shock was such that I sat down, hard. "Why would you suspect—"

"Charles was found at a brothel," she said.

This news was mortifying. I was *literally* mortified into silence. How could I have raised a son who could betray his wife?

Meanwhile, John shot out of his chair. "I pity you, Sally. I grieve with you for the husband who must be dead to you now. And I mourn for a son who is a mere rake. A beast! He's no son of mine any longer. *I renounce him.*"

"*John,*" I said upon a gasp.

In answer to which my husband held up his fist and slammed it down on the table. "I renounce him!"

At that moment, a servant knocked timidly upon the door to announce that the secretary of war needed the president urgently.

Somehow John collected himself and strode out.

Meanwhile, I was left with Sally, wanting to die of shame. My daughter-in-law was waiting to know whether I, too, would declare that Charles was no son of mine. But I couldn't do it, not even as crushed with disappointment as I was.

Charlie's good looks had become a curse, not only because of the temptations they drew to him, but also because he was used to relying on those looks and dimpled charm. When looks and charm couldn't solve real problems, like debt or failure, perhaps he had no other tools at his disposal but drinking and dissipation.

No, no. I refused to excuse him. Or myself for not having raised a better man. My heart bled for his wife and daughters at every pore.

"There's no hope of reconciliation?" I asked.

"None," Sally said.

Wincing to think of my daughter-in-law in the same position in which my brother left his wife, I asked, "What will you do?"

"Take in washing. Or become a housekeeper."

"We won't let it come to that." We owed her support, since it was our son who caused this breach. Also, my husband was up for re-election soon, and there would be political ramifications if it was learned that John Adams let his own daughter-in-law resort to being a washerwoman.

"You think I'm wrong to leave Charles," Sally accused. "But, madam, with such an upright man for a husband, you cannot imagine what you'd do in my place."

Oh, but I *had* imagined it once. When John was so long in France that I feared he'd taken a mistress, it nearly shattered me. My mind now retreated to that long-ago day when Phoebe had so starkly reminded me of how few choices I had. *If he has taken a mistress, do not imagine you'll ever benefit by taking the slightest notice of it.*

Well, Sally had taken notice. Yet not much had changed for women since then. It's why, I suppose, Eliza Hamilton hadn't sued for a divorce, even though she had proof of adultery in a published confession by her own husband.

I should be proud that my daughter-in-law's dignity forbade her from meekly allowing Charles to humiliate her. The trouble was, she'd pay for that dignity. Indeed, it was likely to cost her all future happiness.

"My son is wrong, and I'll beg him to reform and seek some way to earn your forgiveness. I'll speak to him after the term's end on our way back from Philadelphia."

I prayed this might be long enough for Sally's anger to burn out and for my son to come to his senses. But that night, I told John, "Whatever happens, we cannot let Charlie's wife or children starve."

John nodded. "Beyond that, I never wish to hear his name again."

Perhaps John, too, would calm with time. For now, he retreated into the work of the country, urging me to do the same. And amongst our most important duties was the funeral for George Washington.

"What will we wear?" John asked.

"It will be cold—your black coat might suffice," I said. "But I'll need a black cape and muff. We must look decent and suitably dressed, but not too becoming, as the world's eyes will be upon us."

Thus, John and I stood together in the cold on the day after Christmas as the chief state mourners. A sixteen-cannon salute was given along the parade route with a riderless horse and an empty bier. Citizens lining the way wept openly. The eulogy called Washington "First in war, first in peace and first in the hearts of his countrymen."

Though my husband would later feel frustration at forever being compared to George Washington and found wanting, John did not bristle at this. On the day of the funeral, President John Adams was more than willing to give his predecessor his due.

As the eulogy reached its conclusion, I thought it was perhaps a blessing that Washington was taken before he reached the age that bodily decay and imbecility effaced from memory his brilliant days. Washington would always be remembered as the father of his country. His glory was secure.

Now others would try to rise up in the emanations of that glory—including, especially, Alexander Hamilton. "He thinks he's the *heir*," John complained that night. "But Hamilton has not the greatness of spirit to be president. He does not care for *all* American citizens without regard to party. He's only the High Pontiff of Federalism."

There'd been a recent confrontation between the two men in Trenton, and John was still enraged by it. "Imagine my surprise to be set upon suddenly, when, without invitation or summons, in strides Hamilton. Without so much as a *by your leave*."

We all knew that a general ought to wait with his troops until he was summoned by the president. Nevertheless, my husband explained, "He'd come to remonstrate against the idea of peace with France. War, war, *war* is what he demanded. And his vehemence wrought the little man up to such a degree of heat, and with such agitation, that I really pitied him instead of being displeased."

I doubted that last part very much, since John was *still* displeased. "Never before in my life had I heard a man talk like such a fool!" he fumed. "That insolent coxcomb has fixed his eye on the highest station in America and hates everyone who stands in his way."

Well, John Adams was standing in the way. And my husband wouldn't be easy to move. "I must disband Hamilton's army. If I don't, he'll defy my orders. And I'll end up having to raise a *second* army to stop Hamilton from invading Florida or South America or some other place."

My husband didn't ask for my advice in this, but I questioned his course of action anyway. "Isn't it a little mad to disband the army when we aren't *entirely* sure that the danger of war with France has passed? We may still need that army against Bonaparte."

John's nostrils flared. He knew that the French Revolution was over; that Napoleon Bonaparte was now France's tyrannical dictator on the march. Yet he said, "Without Washington to keep General Hamilton on a leash, I believe he's the more immediate danger to *this* republic. Either Hamilton is stark raving mad, or I am."

Chapter Forty-Three

SCOTCH PLAINS
New Jersey
May 1800

FTER ALL THAT blood spilled in their revolution, the French had merely traded a king for a different sort of tyrant. And I feared the United States might meet the same fate if my husband was not re-elected to the presidency. Accordingly, I was more willing to take on public functions. Even those slightly unusual for me . . .

Arriving at the military encampment, I was both apprehensive and eager to stand in the president's stead in saying farewell to the provisional army. Together with Nabby, I searched for Colonel Smith's lodgings—a log house on a yard muddied from the rain. Still, for Nabby, it was as if the sun burst forth when we found it.

She ran to her husband, so proud to see him in uniform. For so long now, he'd been lost to her, if not in body, then in soul. But now Colonel Smith seemed himself again in the army, even with a lower rank than he'd earned.

My son-in-law was a born officer and justly gratified by what he'd accomplished with his men—some of whom stopped by to thank him for forming them into soldiers. Some even wept to know they'd be parted from him.

All this added to Nabby's happiness as she set about preparing a little camp dinner out of army rations. Pork stew with corn cakes to be washed down with a whiskey flip she frothed with an iron from the fire.

As we dined at the little wooden table, my son-in-law said, "I'm sorry to know the army must be disbanded. Does it not seem wiser to maintain it in case negotiations with France bear no fruit?"

"Congress doesn't wish to keep up the expense of an army," I said, which was a fact I could admit without revealing my husband's true fears that the army would be misused. "How do the soldiers take it?"

"They like it not but submit with good grace."

"And you, sir?" I asked, trying to forget the way he'd left my daughter alone for so long. "What will you do now without your soldier's pay?"

In answer, the colonel stared at the table forlornly. "I haven't the savings to go back into any kind of business that might return me to wealth. I'll have to turn yeomen farmer on my lands in western New York."

It was a sensible plan, though I dreaded it for Nabby. She'd live a hardscrabble life as a farmer's wife on the frontier. A life more isolated than mine had ever been. Nevertheless, it filled me with pride to see my daughter put on a face of good cheer. "It'll be another adventure for our family! I'm only sorry we'll be far from you, Mama."

We'll never see her, I thought, miserably. Why must my family always be so scattered? But I, too, put on a happy face, saying that of course they were always welcome at Peacefield whenever they wished.

Blowing delicately on her stew, Nabby said, "I wish Papa had come to inspect the troops himself, but perhaps it's for the better. Because as of late, I'm not sure it's safe for the president and General Hamilton to be in the same spot."

I raised a brow. "Are we certain it's entirely safe for General Hamilton to be in the same spot with *me?*"

They both laughed.

I was well acquainted with Hamilton and his bravado, of course. I'd seen him work as a lawyer mentoring my son Charles. I'd watched him command the machinery of government as secretary of the treasury. I'd even seen him try to move public opinion as a prominent citizen of New York. But it was another thing altogether to see the pomp and circumstance the next morning when he marched with an attendant drumbeat onto the muddy field in his exquisitely tailored uniform, gold buttons glinting.

What a little cock-sparrow general he made.

Still, from my place in the reviewing stand, I took genuine pleasure in the pageantry of horse and soldier as they came into formation. I liked watching this smartly uniformed and well-trained soldiery execute their maneuvers with bayonets flashing.

I was quite proud of them and asked permission to address the troops. When Hamilton granted it with a nod, I told those assembled, "The president regrets he couldn't be here to see your accomplishments. You've performed wonderfully today, as I know you would whenever called upon to defend your nation. I admire you all, and you've done great honor to your officers and to yourselves."

How warmed I was by their cheers.

"God bless the President's Lady, a patriot brave and true!"

"Three cheers for the First Lady!"

"Huzzah! Huzzah! Huzzah!"

With great ceremony, General Hamilton dismissed the troops. And when the last had filed away, he asked, "Will you honor me by sharing breakfast, Mrs. Adams?"

"Gladly, sir. I can imagine nothing more agreeable."

A lie, of course. I knew Hamilton did not want to breakfast with me. And I wanted even less to breakfast with him. Nevertheless, form must be observed, and a tent had already been erected for us under a nearby tree.

We sat before a spread of tea, coffee, cakes, biscuits, apple butter, and boiled eggs. And I was the first to speak. "I must ask after your dear wife. How is Mrs. Hamilton?"

"She's very well. The best of wives and best of women."

She would have to be, I thought. *To put up with all you've put her through . . .*

Then Hamilton leaned toward me. "My wife recently served some excellent confections to my friend, the former secretary of war. I may tell you, in confidence of course, that James McHenry thinks himself much abused by your husband. And he also believes the disbanding of this army to be sheer madness."

Surprised that Hamilton was willing to raise these subjects with me, I stiffened. "If that's what he thinks, then it's not a surprise that he offered his resignation."

"President Adams *told* him to resign," Hamilton said. "Didn't you know?"

Of course I knew. I was the one to recommend that McHenry be dismissed because the rift between my husband and his cabinet was ever widening. He couldn't trust them. And I'd said so in no uncertain terms. It'd all come to a head in a furious meeting in which John shouted at them. I'd have preferred it happened quietly and with dignity, but I couldn't blame the president for venting his spleen after he'd tolerated disrespect for so long.

Now, I stabbed my knife into the apple butter with more force than necessary and said, "It's the president's prerogative to have men of his choice in his cabinet."

"Perhaps so," Hamilton replied. "But it isn't his prerogative to slander me in the process. I'm told that in his altercation with Mr. McHenry, the president spoke several slurs against me, calling me a bastard and a foreigner."

No doubt John called him worse than that, yet I feigned a lady's delicacy. "Is this subject quite fit for our breakfast, sir?"

Hamilton cracked his egg, ignoring my protest. "I should be sorry to see it become an affair of honor. I assume the pressures of the presidency sometimes elicit unwise words."

I blinked. Was he issuing a threat to duel the president of the United States? Maybe he *was* mad . . .

Pointedly, I said, "General Hamilton, I should think you would happily let the matter pass. After all, we all sometimes say—or even do—things we might later regret."

Had he not been foolish enough to print a pamphlet confessing his torrid affair? Surely he regretted that!

Yet he didn't flinch against my veiled barb but only smiled thinly. "I know you wield great influence with the president. I hope you'll use it to prevent him from standing for a second term."

I'd been about to bite into my biscuit, but now I put it down again. "Why would I?"

"Because if we make peace with France, madam, we will have guillotines on these shores."

"I think it much more likely if we make war with them."

Hamilton's grip tightened around his cup. "Do you know that we had an opportunity to strengthen ourselves against the French or any other enemy by liberating the Spanish colonies? We had a chance to expand this nation, which President Adams has *thrown away* by disbanding my army."

It wasn't *his* army, and the fact he was willing to refer to it as such confirmed my husband's instincts. "Do you mean we had the opportunity to *liberate* the Spanish colonies the way Bonaparte is trying to *liberate* Egypt by way of invasion and conquest?"

Hamilton didn't dignify me with an answer. "Your husband prefers to live as Farmer John in Peacefield, does he not? I'm sure you prefer him there, as well. So have him retire and let someone else better able prevail in the election."

"Someone better able?" I asked, probingly. Surely he didn't think that he could be elected. Even Hamilton must know an infamous adulterer couldn't be chosen to lead this nation . . .

"Yes, someone," Hamilton replied. "Someone more suited to the presidency. Someone more willing to block the political rise of that raving Jacobin, Thomas Jefferson."

My spine straightened, and it was not for Jefferson's sake. "The president is more able and suited to his role than any other man I know. He has no intention of removing himself for re-election. And I won't suggest it to him."

"Then you ought to warn him, Mrs. Adams. Because I do not intend to sit idly by. I *will* use my influence to encourage another candidate."

"That would split the vote," I said, now furious. "It would risk throwing the election to the man you've just called a raving Jacobin. No, I don't think you'll take that risk. Not if you believe what you say."

"Then you do not know me very well, madam."

"Nor do you know me very well, sir, if you think this conversation will persuade me to do anything other than tell my husband that you're looking to install a puppet in the presidency, so he must stand for re-election and he must *win*."

We finished our breakfast in silence.

Then I rose and returned to my son-in-law's cabin, where I promised Nabby that I'd try to convince her father to find some appointment for Colonel Smith.

I didn't care if the Senate would call it nepotism.

Our son-in-law had been loyal, dutiful, and humble in the face of Hamilton's humiliations. Far from being advantaged as the president's son-in-law, he'd been held back because of it. And no more would I allow us to buckle under the insincere and disingenuous criticisms of ambitious madmen.

Chapter Forty-Four

NEW YORK CITY
New York
May 1800

I'D GROWN ACCUSTOMED to warm welcomes as the president's lady. People passing me on the street always touched their hats. So why did I feel a decided chill as I walked the streets of New York City?

It was a Federalist stronghold, but it was Hamilton's city, and I ought not forget that.

I hadn't warned Charles I was coming. I simply walked into his cluttered law office, where dust gathered in the corners of smudged windows, books spilled from every shelf, and an inkpot had overturned onto the pine floor.

At the sound of the bell pull on the door, my son looked up from his desk and tears instantly sprang to his eyes. "*Mother . . .*"

Tears sprang to my eyes, too, because I scarcely recognized him! Liquor had made my handsome cherub into a *ruin*. His once dewy complexion was dry as paper. Spider veins crawled over his nose and cheeks. Darkness encircled his eyes. And when we embraced, I felt nothing but skin and bones. Which is why I couldn't help but say, "Oh, Charles, you look so *unwell*."

"I'm working hard on a case," he said. Given the pages sprawled on his desk, I saw this was the truth. Even if not the whole truth. Straightening his cravat, Charles said, "I'm expected at court soon. If I'd known you were coming—"

"You would have absented yourself," I accused.

He hung his head. "I've wanted to see you. But Father . . ."

His father wouldn't reply to his letters. Wouldn't even hear mention of him. There was much we needed to discuss. Yet my son's glance darted down to his pocket watch. "Mama, I truly am due in court."

"Then I'll go with you."

"No, *please*. I'll come see you tonight."

His word was still good, at least in that. He came that evening. And I asked, "Charles, what's happened to you?"

He shrugged, staring down at his hands, which were splayed on the table. "I *have* tried to stop drinking. But I couldn't sleep for the shaking, which meant I couldn't work. It only got better when I gave in. So I gave in."

Remembering my brother's fate, I said, "You must give it up. For honor, for reputation, for your family. You must give up the bottle, the women, the gambling—or whatever other means by which you've blackened your good name."

"The drinking habit is too rooted."

I couldn't accept that. "Think of what you're doing to your wife!"

"Do you mean the woman who abandoned me at the lowest moment of my life and ran to tell tales to my father?"

"How can you blame her?" I asked.

He had no answer. Instead, he said, "When we met, Sally thought she saw in me someone important. Now that Papa's presidency is imperiled, she's eager to divorce."

Oh, the contempt that dripped from his voice . . .

"Charles, if you persist in these attitudes, you'll lose everything. *Everything*."

"Haven't I already lost everything? All I've ever really had of my father was his name. Now he's renounced me."

Though I could feel my frustrations with him boil up in my blood, I willed myself to calm. "My dear prodigal son, change your circumstances and he could forgive you. He'd say *my son was lost but now he's found!*"

To that, Charles gave me the saddest smile I ever saw. "That's your idea of who you married. I wish I didn't have to rip that illusion from your tender heart."

"*Charles*," I snapped. "Your father is the president of the United States. He has more cares upon his shoulders than you dare imagine. And you've added to them. Your father will come see you when the election is over—"

My son snorted. "*The election.*"

"Yes, the election. Have you no care for your country's future?"

"I have too much care. I still socialize with those in Hamilton's circles. I collect information that might be useful to my father— that is, if he would read my letters. But Papa has a softer heart for Thomas Jefferson than he could ever have for his children."

"Absurd. What are you raving about?"

"It's what they say in this city!"

Charles pulled from his satchel a pamphlet entitled *Letter from Alexander Hamilton, Concerning the Public Conduct and Character of John Adams, Esq. President of the United States.* "This is General Hamilton's broadside against Father. Page after page of attacks. T'would be sedition if the laws truly applied equally to everyone."

I snatched the pamphlet from him, and one line in particular caught my eye: "Not denying to Mr. Adams patriotism and integrity, and even talents of a certain kind, there are great and intrinsic defects in his character, which unfit him for the office of chief magistrate."

So Hamilton truly *was* willing to split the Federalist vote. "He's out of his senses to print this."

"It's worse," Charles said. "Hamilton's lackeys are spreading the rumor that Father is no true Federalist. That he has come to terms with Mr. Jefferson in a corrupt political deal to eject all Federalists from power."

Oh, this was too much. "By spreading these lies, they're all but *ensuring* Jefferson will be elected, and I almost wish it for them."

Charles's smile turned wry. "I see your heart is also soft still for Jefferson. Yet, hardened against me. Will you renounce me, too?"

I blew out a frustrated breath. I wanted to reassure Charles that I loved him and always would, for that much was true. I wanted to cry that he was still my beautiful baby boy. But that was a lie. For I could only think of the ugliness that would come of the dissipation of this miserable man whom I could no longer consider my son. Or at least, I should not consider him so.

At my silence, Charles's bravado collapsed. He sank from his chair to his knees, wrapped his arms around my waist, and murmured, "I'm sorry. I shouldn't have said that. I never meant to hurt anyone. Ever. Except myself."

"Well, you've done that, my boy," I said, stroking his hair, knowing that if he couldn't reform, it would embitter every moment left to me in life.

I had to try to save him.

"Good habits take time to build," I finally said. "If you can stay away from the bottle for the entire summer, I'll prevail upon your father to permit a visit to Peacefield. He'll see you restored to yourself. And if your wife and children see you sober and chastened, it may yet save your marriage."

Charles nodded his head, pressing his cheek against my bosom. And I kissed the top of his head praying God might grant him strength.

"So you saw him," John snarled when we were reunited at Peacefield. I'd already written about it, so he had no cause to be surprised, but now he flung it at me like an accusation. "You saw Charles."

I'd come to his study with a glass of milk to settle his stomach, and now I set it down on his desk. "You never forbade it."

Not that it would've stopped me if he had.

The president reached for his milk. "Did the reprobate justify himself?"

"No."

"Then what did you speak about?"

"We spoke about your re-election, for one thing."

John made a sound of disgust. "And?"

"In truth, in New York I heard so many lies that I'm disgusted with the world. And the majority of its inhabitants do not appear worth the trouble and pains it costs to save them from destruction."

It was something John would've said. Probably something he *had* said a dozen times before. But hearing it from me, he looked pained. "Do you mean lies from Charles or about the election?"

"The latter," I said.

"Well, if the treaty of peace with France arrives before the voting, people will see through these lies and I'll be vindicated and win re-election."

"Then pray the treaty arrives soon."

The grandchildren were all with us for the summer. Nabby's boys and my granddaughters Caroline, Susanna, and Abbe. Hooligans running up and down the stairs and making mischief in the garden. Their mothers were with us, too. Sally was as dutiful a daughter-in-law as we could wish, though she was sometimes cool to me.

When Nabby and I took a long walk, I asked her if she knew why.

"Sally loves Charles, Mama, but they've both said unforgivable things to one another. Yet she knows you'd have her reconciled to him . . ."

"Well, that depends entirely upon your brother. I wouldn't try to force it upon her."

Together Nabby and I walked and walked until we found ourselves outside our old saltbox house, where we stopped to visit Phoebe. And there I made the mistake of repeating that I was in an ill humor and so disgusted with people that I wasn't sure they were worth saving.

Phoebe sucked her teeth. "That's an uncharitable sentiment. Especially coming from a girl I raised, who has become the lady all Americans look up to."

That shamed me. But in defense of myself, I murmured, "Well, not *all* Americans."

Phoebe's husband piped up to say, "You leave Mrs. Adams be. In truth, you'd do better to be less charitable to people, Phoebe. I'll do anything to support *you*, but not the vagrants you feed and house. I'm sorry, Mrs. Adams. I try to keep her in line . . ."

But Phoebe was now too old, it seemed, to worry about the opinion of a husband.

"You've got no compassion," she told him.

"I've got good sense," Mr. Abdee argued, for Phoebe was constitutionally incapable of turning away needy strangers. All the town knew of it. Whenever a man got a servant girl in trouble, he dumped that girl on Phoebe's doorstep.

"People *are* taking advantage," I said.

She was also too old now, it seemed, to worry about my opinion either. "If you've come to scold me about doing my Christian duty, it'll fall on deaf ears. You can put me out on the street if you please."

"Mama would *never* do that," Nabby said.

"I wouldn't," I insisted. "Of course I wouldn't."

There was, it seemed, a great deal I couldn't control anymore. Not even in my own sphere. I couldn't make Charles stop drinking, though I feared it would kill him. I couldn't make Sally reconcile with him, though failing to would impoverish her. I couldn't make John Quincy come home from Europe, no matter how much I missed him. I couldn't make Phoebe stop offering sanctuary to strangers in my old home. And I couldn't convince voters that my husband was a better, wiser, more worthy president than they could ever know . . .

Chapter Forty-Five

EAST CHESTER
New York
Autumn 1800

I N THE YEARS of my husband's presidency, we'd established a pattern. Every autumn, John would set out for the capital, and I'd follow to play my role as first lady when the weather was most auspicious.

I always stopped on the way to visit our children in New York. But this year was different because Sally and Nabby and the grandchildren traveled with me. And after dropping them at Colonel Smith's home in East Chester, I'd be traveling south on unknown roads to our new capital, on the Potomac.

Traveling with children—even beloved grandchildren—was arduous, so upon our arrival at Colonel Smith's farm, I was so weary that I went directly upstairs and fell asleep.

At sunrise I was awakened by an ashen-faced Nabby.

Blinking away dreams, I asked, "Has bad news come from France?"

"No," she said, trying to hurry me out of bed. "We must take the first ferry to see Charles."

I lifted my hands in a helpless gesture. "What more can I say to that boy? He had only to refrain from drinking for one summer and he couldn't even do that."

"He's in a wretched state, Mama," Nabby said. "Desperately sick. Sally has gone to nurse him."

Charles must be very sick indeed if his estranged wife rushed to his bedside. I paused, wondering if word should be sent to my husband, but Nabby mistook my hesitation for reluctance. "*Mother*, whatever Charles has done, mercy is the Lord's command."

She was quite right, and we set out for the ferry straightaway. In the city, we found Charles sprawled weak upon a narrow sickbed at a friend's cramped and inhospitable town house—for Charles had been evicted from his own lodgings.

My son was bloated and swollen, hacking up phlegm. The doctor took us into the hall. "Mrs. Adams, your son has a distressing cough, dropsy, and an ailment of the liver brought on by too much drink."

I shook my head in dismay. "I told him he must stop drinking."

"He did," the doctor said. "He cut himself off completely. But as I've seen before in cases such as these, there is a point at which the damage already done is past recovery. The seizures, malnourishment, and insomnia—they leave a patient, especially one without tender loving care—vulnerable to other ailments, like this cough."

A breath hissed out of me as I tried to make sense of this. "What can be done for him?"

"Rest, nourishment, and good nursing can make him comfortable and may extend his life."

I was so distressed that I put my hand on the wall for balance. But Nabby's spine went so straight it looked apt to snap. "How far along is my brother's ailment, Doctor?"

Under my daughter's scrutiny, the doctor's confidence seemed to falter. "I cannot say. Medical science is not exact. The cough may be reversed. The functioning of his liver is apt to be permanently compromised."

How I wished for my good Uncle Tufts to explain it all!

But this doctor only made ready to take his leave. "Mrs. Adams, please convey my regrets to the president. And please tell him that I'm voting for him. No matter what General Hamilton says."

As the doctor went out, I began to pace. Nabby stared off into the mid-distance. And Sally wordlessly returned to my son's side to make him comfortable. She brought him a bowl of boiling water so he could inhale the steam. She gave him sips of an herbal tisane. And she replaced the bandages from his bloodletting until at last Charles wanted no more, and in a lucid moment, he whispered, "Enough, sweetheart. You've done enough for me. How truly I love you. And how sorry I am for all the ways in which I've hurt you."

His words to her were tender, and I could see he meant them. Yet Sally did not return his words of love. "I'll come back to tend you in the morning," she said. "Once I've rested."

Nabby then took over nursing duties. She gave Charles small sips of tea with honey. She adjusted his pillows so he could be more upright. Then she said, "I'm taking you home with me in the morning, Charlie. You, Sally, and the girls. You'll be more comfortable in East Chester, where you've rested your head so many times before."

His eyes lit up and fixed upon his sister, as if she were his guardian angel. "Colonel Smith will have me in his home?"

"Eagerly," she promised, without even the blush for the lie it must've been. "We're taking you home to heal."

How eager Colonel Smith could *truly* be to take in the man who'd saved him from debtor's prison but dishonored his sister, I couldn't guess. But given the urgency with which Nabby left to make the arrangements, I doubted she'd give her husband a say in the matter. Nabby had always been the mildest of my children, but I'd seen my own iron in her spine before.

And it was evident in her every mannerism now.

When she left me with Charles, he reached for my hand. His hand was clammy and frighteningly swollen. Still, I took it and kissed it gently.

When he spoke it was only a rasp. "I was afraid you wouldn't come. I was afraid that like Papa, you'd say I was no son of yours."

I had *thought* it in my angrier moments. As a stern parson's daughter, I convinced myself that I'd rather my children die than fall into sin or disgrace. I'd believed it, too, like an utter fool. Now, faced with the real possibility of losing my boy, there was no hardness in my heart at all. "Charles, you're always and forever my son, and it pains me to see you suffering this way."

Another cough wracked his whole body before he made his sad admission. "It's my own fault. Many people have said so. It seems there was no hope for me from the moment my lips first touched a bottle in Spain."

In Spain. Where he'd been left to fend for himself so his father could play the role of diplomat in foreign courts. Then we left him at Harvard, where more temptations abounded. The guilt rose up in my throat until I nearly suffocated of it. I didn't know what to say, except to press my lips to his hand again and again, professing love.

"I love you, too," he whispered. "And Nabby and Tommy and John Quincy. I hoped I could tell him in person how much I regret the money lost. I only ever wanted to serve him. Knowing I disappointed him has poisoned me more surely than any liquor. Nabby promised to tell him if I do not recover."

"You'll tell him yourself," I said. "You'll recover and Johnny will come home and you can make your peace."

But there was no guarantee of that.

"Rest," I said, softly. "Rest, my dear boy."

Alas, he was too agitated. Manic even. He began talking of legal cases he needed to attend. He asked for his books. How he couldn't realize how *truly* ill he was, I didn't know.

A few hours later, he was wracked with pain and said, "I wish to plead my father's forgiveness. To tell him that I'm a penitent man. Will he come to me? Would you go to him and convince him to come? After the election, of course. I know he has the election. But after that."

I tried to calm him with a cool cloth on his wrists. "I'd rather stay with you and help make you well. But I'll send word to him."

"He ignores letters," Charles said, a frantic edge to his words. "But he cannot ignore you for long, not when you're with him. Once the election is over . . ."

With that, exhaustion overtook him again, and my son drifted off murmuring, "It's all right. If my earthly father won't forgive me, I'll try to earn forgiveness of my heavenly father." A smile so beatific passed over his face that I could almost see the cherub of days long past. "Do not despair of me, Mother."

The next morning, we had him carried by ferry to East Chester, where the bedroom was made up for him. "Charles needs to be with family," Nabby said. "And I mean to see that he wants for nothing until he recovers."

"That's a balm to a mother's heart," I told her, tears in my eyes as my bags were loaded back onto the carriage. I feared to leave, but I'd promised Charles that I'd go to my husband and convince him to visit.

Nabby took my hands. "Tell Papa that we're all praying for his re-election."

But I did *not* pray for John's re-election.

Instead, with every turn of the carriage wheels, I used my prayers for my son.

Chapter Forty-Six

WASHINGTON CITY
District of Columbia
December 1800

I COUGHED, EYES STINGING. "So this is to be the president's house . . ."

To more quickly dry the plaster in the newly constructed residence, fires burned in every chamber. John was wreathed in a haze of smoke where he worked. A desk had not yet been located in these cavernous halls so John was making do with a table.

Rising to help remove my cloak, John asked, "What do you think?"

"I'm not sure yet. But from the carriage, the city looks quite a wilderness."

"Yes, I'm afraid our Federal City is, at present, a *city* in name only, but that will change!"

I saw that a portrait of Washington hung upon the wall looking down on our enterprises and I wondered what he'd think of the shambling state of the new capital, which bore his name. Washington City boasted of only a few houses scattered over a space of ten miles. Tree stumps dotted the landscape as far as the eye could see, and enslaved men worked to haul the wood away. In truth, the miserable effects of slavery were visible everywhere.

I thought about Jefferson's Monticello plantation. We'd all been assured he was a kind and gentle master—but as Phoebe would say, *still, he was a master.*

Yet people were casting votes for him, calling him *The Man of the People!*

No, that wasn't quite true, was it? It wasn't *people* who were casting votes. It was men. Propertied white men. They understood themselves to be free and equal in the eyes of God. But ask them to extend that principle . . .

Oh, I had little love for the French Revolution, but at least in France, women had been in the vanguard. Black people, too. In our own revolution, the runaway slave Crispus Attucks had been one of the first to fall to a redcoat bullet at the Boston Massacre. How might he feel, now, to walk around this city, seeing his brethren half fed, destitute of clothing, forced to labor whilst the owner walked about idle and called himself a *true republican*?

As workers continued to plaster around me, I said, "Well, at least the president's house is a proper castle with a lovely view of the river."

"Let me show you my favorite room," John said, leading me upstairs to an oval-shaped chamber with red furniture.

"It will be handsome when completed," I allowed.

"Yes," John said, fingers on the windowpane, as if he could imagine the new city coming alive. "I pray heaven to bestow the best of blessings on this house and all that shall hereafter inhabit it. May none but honest and wise men ever rule under this roof."

"Only men?" I asked.

John cracked an indulgent smile, which I took for my opening to say, "*I* pray that whoever lives in this house after us are good mothers and fathers over the nation, and to their *own* children, too."

John's smile gave way to a scowl because he knew the turn of my mind. "I don't want to talk about Charles."

"He's sick. You must see him after the election. You must forgive him. He was always a soft boy, and perhaps you blamed him for it—"

"To the contrary, I delighted in him as a boy. I loved him too much. It's the man that *disgusts* me."

"He's a flawed man, but no man's enemy but his own. That must count for something."

John was quiet, staring out the window, and I sensed my words were reaching him.

But infuriatingly, at that very moment, John Marshall interrupted with a dispatch for the president. And off he went.

Later, when I was downstairs dusting our gilt-edged, floral porcelain dinner service for whatever occasion it might be needed in this still-unfinished house, I asked, "Is it France? Is there a peace treaty yet?"

"No," John said, tossing aside a report from a friend about the election that had begun in October, stretching into December. "It's South Carolina. The votes aren't going my way."

To lose South Carolina would be a blow. It might be the nail in the coffin of my husband's presidency. I did not know what to say.

John explained, "Jefferson's acolyte, Mr. Madison, is the political mastermind in the South." Then he said, darkly, "I wonder if that little man is behind the rumor that when we were in London, I asked Pinckney to procure four harlots for us to share between us."

I gasped. "No one could believe that."

"Well, I swear on my honor, if it's true, then Pinckney kept all four and cheated me of my two!"

"*John*," I said, snapping the dusting cloth at him.

His dark mood grew darker still. "The Alien and Sedition Acts give my opponents much to complain of. But I've not deported one foreigner. Not one!"

Yet there *had* been prosecutions for sedition. The most justified case was against the journalist James Callender, who had first exposed Alexander Hamilton's affair. More recently, Callender wrote that my husband was a deranged hermaphrodite who planned to crown himself king. Callender was convicted and sentenced to nine months, every bit of which I believed he deserved.

I was less confident about the arrest of Congressman Matthew Lyon, who was charged for saying that my husband had a thirst for ridiculous pomp.

His enraged constituents re-elected him from prison.

Now John complained, "I didn't ask for these prosecutions, but I'm paying for them."

"If the Federalists remain united, you can defeat Jefferson easily."

But John was now very grim about his chances. "Well, to be relieved of this office will be a respite for me. I'm old, old, very old. And never shall be very well—certainly not while in this office. For the drudgery of it is too much for my years and strength. Perhaps it's best to let Jefferson try."

"We cannot know the outcome yet."

John snorted. "I will make my peace with it. I can be content with no other inscription on my gravestone than 'Here lies John Adams who took upon himself the Responsibility of the Peace with France in the Year 1800.'"

I did not believe that would content him. It would not be enough for him, even if he achieved it. Not for my proud, talented husband, who had dedicated the better part of his adult life to his country. But on the day the electors were to meet, we already knew that we'd lost.

Hamilton had split the Federalist vote. The Democratic-Republicans would be victorious.

John was crushed. We both were. And yet, the pain of losing the presidency was positively eclipsed for me by the most tragic letter of my life.

Charles has died, Nabby wrote.

He hadn't lived a fortnight since I left him. My boy, my little cherub . . .

John and I both stood thunderstruck by the news, as if a gorgon had turned us to stone. My husband cracked first, grabbing the letter from my stiff hands to read again, as if it simply could not be true.

I went cold all over, breathless, a stranger in my own skin. But then came a storm of John's rage and tears, all of which lashed against my stony silence.

I just stood there, unmoving, as my husband sobbed into the crumpled letter in his hands.

I remained silent. Terribly silent. Silent as a distant star.

John took this for rebuke, and perhaps it was.

"Abigail," he said, clasping my rigid arms, gripping me too hard. "If I'd known he was dying . . ."

I only stiffened in his grasp.

John swore, "I'd have done all I could to help him!"

I said nothing.

John gave me a little shake. "You know I loved him. Despite all. I would've forgiven him. I vow it."

Still I was silent.

"Say something," John finally pleaded. "Say something, *any-thing*, my dearest friend."

I knew I was frightening him. I was frightening myself. I'd never been silent a day in my life, but now I understood the retreat into the mind that so often called to my daughter. Silence was my only refuge from this *agony* of grief. And so, despite my husband's tempest of emotion, I simply turned and walked away.

I roamed the presidential mansion from unfinished room to unfinished room, like a ghost. Why had I left Charles? Hadn't I feared his death was imminent?

I should've listened to my mother's instinct. Now my child was dead, and I'd never see his dimpled smile again. Never caress his beloved face. Never hold him in my arms again. It was too much to bear.

John finally found me in some unfinished room—I know not which. "Is there something I can do for you?"

Staring out at the rain, I didn't reply.

"Abigail, however hard you think my heart might be, I wish you could remember that Charles was once the delight of my eyes and a darling of my heart."

I shook my head to deny it, and John forced me to look at him. "I would've died for him if that would've relieved him from his faults as well as his disease. I would've willingly laid down my life to save him. As I would lay my life down now to spare you the pain I see in your eyes."

I believed him. Or at least, I chose to believe him, because if I didn't, I'd go mad. But I still had little to say. "I'm afflicted with a loss of voice," I claimed, my throat tight and raw with such an immense torment of spirit that I couldn't swallow it down. "A cough from the plaster dust, as everything is under construction."

He knew it was a lie but let me be.

I didn't come to bed that night.

I did not sleep. Instead, I donned a black dress of mourning, realizing that what funeral arrangements must be made, Nabby would make. We would get to New York too late to see Charles buried.

"*Rest*," everyone advised.

But I would rather dash my head against the newly plastered walls of this place. Instead, stumbling with exhaustion, I busied myself with marketing, which could only be done in Georgetown, the filthiest hole one ever did see. There was nowhere clean to dry the laundry, so I hung it up in the East Room by myself, refusing assistance. I wanted to work myself to the bone. To make myself so weary that I could, in desperation, consent to lie down beside my husband.

The next day, John looked encouraged to see me emerge where he labored with his writing. Like a man testing the ice, he asked, "Do you wish to advise me on this speech?"

"I do not." After all, what did a speech matter? My husband had lost the electoral college and the presidency. I had no desire to help write a speech for such an ungrateful nation.

Four years of the presidency gone to waste.

Why stop there? More than twenty years of sacrifice and public service gone to waste. Everything that John and I had loved and hoped for our entire lives was likely to collapse into bloody anarchy just as in France, where political faction after faction cut off each other's heads.

I believed there was still some decency in Thomas Jefferson. That he wouldn't give us over to a mob to be hauled up on a guillotine. But I couldn't seem to care either way because my beloved Charles was cut down in the bloom of life . . .

The tender remembrance of what Charles once was rose before me, when I wished to forget. I wanted to draw a veil over all that wrung my heart.

What I needed most was distraction, and into that breach, when I needed her most, came Martha Washington with an invitation to visit her at Mount Vernon.

We were the only women in the world who knew what it was to serve as the lady of first rank in an American republic. And given that Jefferson was a bachelor, we were likely the only two who would know it for at least four years more. Perhaps as a mother who had also known griefs, Martha could comfort me in a way John could not.

So I started out for Mount Vernon alone.

MOUNT VERNON WAS situated upon a rising ground where a cold winter's wind attempted to strip the few red and yellowed leaves still clinging to the trees. It was an isolated spot, without another house or neighbor nearer than nine miles. But many enslaved persons went about their business among outbuildings in a state of funereal gloom.

As I stepped out of the carriage and onto the drive, the grand lady of the house came to meet me. And I nearly curtseyed to her before remembering that our roles were changed. For I was now the president's lady, and she was not. "Thank you for the invitation, Mrs. Washington."

"My dear friend," Martha said, clasping my hands with sympathy.

Like me, Martha was in mourning.

What a miserable pair we might've been, but the embrace of the only other woman in the world who understood my torn feelings in such a moment was a solace beyond measure.

Martha led me inside the mansion, and I was surprised to find the rooms small and low. The greatest ornament about the long-fabled place was a piazza with a fine view of the river at the bottom of the lawn.

I knew it must require a great deal of money to beautify and cultivate the grounds—but it was now going to decay. And Martha was apologetic. "They were beautiful once. Unfortunately, we can no longer afford to maintain it with my husband gone. I can scarcely provide for my family, some three hundred souls."

Three hundred souls? Not her family, surely, unless she included the enslaved in this number. Harsh judgments must've flashed across my expression, for once we were alone, bundled against the cold in quiet conversation, she said, "One hundred and fifty persons here are to be liberated soon. You must count that a good thing."

"I count freedom a very good thing indeed."

She paused. "President Washington granted our servants their freedom in his will. Some wish for it, but others have begged me to retain them."

Having so long opposed slavery, I didn't believe such pleas could be genuine. "Why should that be?"

"Because men with wives and children who have never seen an acre beyond this farm are about to quit it and go adrift into the world without house, home, or friend. It frightens them. Still, what else can I do?"

She explained that Washington specified in his will that those he held in bondage would go free *after the death of his wife*, thereby inadvertently putting her life in danger. "How could I ever feel safe in the hands of those who have been told it is in their best interest to get rid of me? My lawyer advised it's better to free them now."

"Indeed," I said, the complications of her situation only confirming the evils of slavery.

I wished I could do something to help these people—a wish that helped me make sense of my feelings about my husband's loss of the presidency.

"There is the humiliation of it, of course. To be turned out," I confessed when the conversation turned to politics. "Then, of course, there is the loss of salary. But, I can say truly and from my heart, that the most mortifying circumstance upon my retirement from public life will be that my power of doing good for my fellow creatures will be diminished."

"You still have the will and the want?" Martha asked.

"I am as surprised as you to realize I do."

"Then I'm sorrier than ever that Jefferson is to ascend to the presidency. Indeed, I consider it the greatest misfortune our nation has ever experienced."

Martha, too, had reason to be bitter about Jefferson. He'd absented himself from Washington's funeral. But much worse, he'd accused Washington of being a monarchist. This, Martha Washington had never been able to forgive. And I would not persuade her that she should.

"Do you mind if we go in?" Martha finally asked. "Your New England constitution is sturdier than mine against the chill."

"Not sturdy enough," I said, following her indoors. "The older I get the more difficult it is to endure cold."

"Everything becomes more difficult," Martha said, leading me to a table where warmed cider awaited us. "Thinking back on loved ones who have passed, I grow ever more eager for a reunion with them in heaven."

With similar pangs, I said, "As I approach that reward myself, I am solaced by my faith. I cannot imagine how those without religion meet the challenges of age."

"To faith and friendship, then," Martha replied, raising her cup in toast.

I toasted her in return.

After that, we enjoyed a warm respite together, reminiscing about days long past, and otherwise soaking up one another's company—for both of us knew, given age and distance, that we two who had been the presidents' ladies would never see one another again . . .

Chapter Forty-Seven

I RETURNED FROM MOUNT Vernon with a puppy and would not be parted with her. "If you love me, John, you must love my dog."

"As long as she doesn't piddle on the country's red velvet sofa," John said, poring over his papers, for he still had many duties to attend to before his successor took the helm. "Don't let her up there next to you."

"I can scarcely convince a dog named Juno that she ought not be allowed on the furniture. She thinks she rules Olympus."

He didn't smile. Not even slyly. He was still grieving over Charles and brooding about the election. "Two hundred and fifty votes. A nation of five million people, and I lost by only two hundred and fifty votes."

"Probably because most of those five million cannot vote."

My husband sighed. "Perhaps I'd have lost by more if they could. I should've been a shoemaker."

"Shoemakers don't forge peace treaties," I said, for my husband's diplomatic gambit had finally paid off.

We'd lost the election, in part, because my husband cut the warmongering Hamilton off at the knees by securing a peace treaty. It had finally arrived.

John had secured a true and lasting peace.

There would be no war with France.

"If this news had only come a little sooner," he said.

I nodded, knowing what preyed on his mind. "You would've

won re-election. You'd have won easily, even with Hamilton's meddling."

John's jaw tightened, bitterly, so I reminded him of another bitter truth that might remedy the first. "Of course, you'd have also won re-election if you'd taken our country to war."

"Thereby leading my country to ruin."

My smile was pained. "Yes. You saved the country rather than yourself."

He said he would've died for Charles if it would have saved him. Well, he hadn't been able to save his own son, but he *did* save the sons of his country. "It was a noble sacrifice. You may be content with that."

"And are you content with it?"

The legacy of his administration was his—but I knew I could claim a large part of it, for both good and ill. And while I'd have liked to see it end in glory and gratitude, I had, in the end, always been willing to love my country more than it loved me.

One term was enough. Especially given all that was accomplished in furthering the strength and longevity of the nation. We were leaving it at peace, without scandal or corruption, and with its coffers full.

"I have few regrets," I told my husband. "At my age and with my bodily infirmities I shall be happier at Quincy. If I didn't rise to prominence with dignity, I can at least fall that way, which is the more difficult task."

John rubbed his chin. "There are still a few more things to do and I hope to do them well."

He had federal jobs to fill and judges to appoint. He was already making a list of them for me to review. So I said, "Give Colonel Smith an appointment." John sighed, but I didn't care about his objections. "Are you really going to let Nabby be banished to the frontier?"

"You know I can't give family members a job."

"Why not? Will it hurt your re-election chances?"

John barked a grim laugh at that. Then he laughed again, a real laugh, and I joined him in it. My dark jest had loosed a torrent inside us and made us laugh like lunatics.

When I could finally speak, I said, "I wouldn't ask if he were unqualified. Our son-in-law wants to serve his country. And if you weren't his father-in-law he'd already have an honorable position in this government."

My husband knew that to be true.

And so the appointment was made.

Our son-in-law would be federal surveyor and inspector of the port in New York. It wasn't the military post that he dreamed of, but it came with a handsome salary and opportunity enough for him to pay his debts and restore his reputation. It would also allow Nabby and her children to live together under one roof in a modest but comfortable home, with money left over to send our grandsons to college.

It was, to my mind, an easy choice.

The appointment of a new chief justice of the Supreme Court was, on the other hand, a more difficult one. John Jay refused to take it up—he'd had quite enough of glowing effigies in his life—so my husband turned to John Marshall.

We couldn't know then what a consequential appointment it would be, but we felt well satisfied by it. And we continued to make the best appointments we could to the very last moment, because the business of the government must go on. And it might be some time before we had a new president.

This was because, by some twist of fate, the electors had inadvertently cast an equal number of votes for Thomas Jefferson and his colleague on the Democratic-Republican ticket, Aaron Burr. It was precisely the kind of vexing constitutional problem that Hamilton tried to avoid all those years ago while undermining votes for my husband.

Now we didn't know which man would end up being president, and John was almost amused. "The ironic justice of it! Thanks to Hamilton's scheming, the two men—the very two men—in all the world that Hamilton is most jealous of will now be placed above him in one capacity or another."

We again shared in the peculiar pleasure of dark amusement until I said, "Burr surely knows he was never meant to be elevated to the presidency. But, of course, it would serve Mr. Jefferson right if Burr were to snatch it anyway."

John frowned. "But it wouldn't serve the country."

Sighing again, I had to admit, "No, it would not."

They were neither of them fit to shine my husband's boots, but Thomas Jefferson was the man of far better talent, reason, and character. "Can we bolster Jefferson's position somehow? Ought we try?"

"Officially, no," John said. "It must work itself out as the Constitution specifies. The president has no part in it. But I think Jefferson ought to prevail. It's the will of the people. So if we wish to leave the republic with dignity, perhaps you can be especially cordial to him as a guest of honor at your New Year's levee."

Oh, the gall of having to host the man turning us out! But John had his duties still to the country, and I had mine. "Very well. I'll do it. So long as our bags are already packed and ready to leave the next morning."

"You'll go ahead of me, my dear."

"Why can't we leave the capital together?"

"Because there is no telling how long it will take Congress to break the tied vote, and you shouldn't have to suffer a winter here. Besides, I'll be occupied with various matters, the most important one being to bring Johnny home from Europe."

Oh, those were some of the sweetest words I ever heard. The best possible consolation. At last, at long last, to have our oldest son back. What we wanted most now was to put what remained of our family back together and finally be free to attend to our own affairs without public care.

"You're sure you don't want me to stay?" I asked.

"With you gone, I will delight in the shutters being thrown open at night," he teased. "When I return home I shall wish to be simply Farmer John of Peacefield and nothing more the rest of my life."

But, of course, John could never be simply anything. That night a fire broke out at the treasury building. And the president of the United States grabbed his hat, rolled up his sleeves, and joined the bucket brigade to put it out.

It was his way.

It had *always* been his way to do any good possible.

And it was my inspiration to do the same.

At the reception for the new year, I received Jefferson with exaggerated warmth, as if his victory was inevitable. He seemed both surprised and made happy by it. "Mrs. Adams, it is always a delight to be in your company."

I wished I could say the same. Still, I kept up the cheerful charade with meaningless pleasantries until Jefferson said, "I don't suppose you know what the Congress might do about the tie vote . . ."

"I don't know. But Our Lord said *they know not what they do.* And I've heard a clergyman preach that when people do not know what to do, they should take great care that they do not do—they know not what."

Jefferson laughed at my wordplay. "Mrs. Adams, I truly appreciate your everlasting good humor."

It isn't for you, I wanted to say. I was doing it to help ensure a peaceful transfer of power and the continuity of a benign government. Soon we'd have to walk into the dining room together and put on a show of unity in front of officials from both parties.

Then I never wanted to see him again.

But Jefferson said, "In case I don't have another opportunity to say so before your journey home, if it should lay in my power to serve you or your family, nothing would give me more pleasure."

This was more than I expected, but I was no longer so easily charmed. Nevertheless, I thanked him and plastered a smile upon my face, entering the dining room on the vice president's arm—which was the last and most difficult act of my public life.

Part Four

Chapter Forty-Eight

QUINCY
Massachusetts
September 1802

FARMER JOHN LOOKED quite well, I thought, as he gathered up the last of the beans and the onions. On the morrow, he'd take the grandchildren apple picking in our orchard, as it was cidering season and I was of a mind to bake a pie.

In the two years since leaving the presidency, we'd thrown ourselves into the soft rural pleasures of farm and family.

Nabby was returned to respectability in New York, thanks to her husband's position as port inspector. Tommy had quit his law practice to help tend our farms. Charlie's widow and her children were living with us, too. And having returned from Europe with his English wife and children, John Quincy was now a Massachusetts state senator living in Boston, near enough to visit every weekend.

We counted ourselves lucky that President Jefferson's administration kept a leash on the radicals, and no one had yet lost their heads to the guillotine.

Politics was none of our concern now.

Let our whole world be only our neighbors and our farm. Let us lose ourselves in the hayfields. Let us lose ourselves in the garden. In the full bloom of the pear, the apple, the plum, and the peach. For envy nipped not their buds, calumny destroyed not their fruits, nor did ingratitude tarnish their colors.

But into our Garden of Eden, news did sometimes slither . . .

"Have you heard?—"

"—President Jefferson's scandal—"

"Fathered a child on an enslaved girl!"

The talk came up around the fire after supper, following a Sabbath meeting. Poor Reverend Wibird having passed away, the preaching was done by Reverend Whitney, who went on so long that the children were put into a near stupor and went up early to bed.

Naturally, John and I didn't believe the accusations against Jefferson and were appalled to see them taken up in Federalist newspapers with glee.

But Tommy laughed at the profane cartoons being printed of Jefferson as a lecherous rooster. And our eldest son, John Quincy—who had taken on a mantle of gravitas—*did* believe the worst of the new president. "It is my opinion that the sin of slavery corrupts the soul of everyone it touches. Jefferson is not immune."

"Oh, my boy," John replied, having carried his dish of apple pie from the table to the comfort of one of my French upholstered chairs. "You can believe nothing that wretch James Callender says in the newspapers. I would not convict a dog of killing a sheep if that man was the witness."

I felt the same way, though I took at least a little satisfaction in Jefferson finally suffering the same abuse that he thought we ought to suffer in silence. "I daresay President Jefferson wishes he did not pardon Callender for sedition now!"

Still, I couldn't help but be appalled by the perverse specificity of the newspapers that John Quincy spread out before us. The accusation was not merely that Jefferson was debauching women he purported to own. The newspapers named Sally Hemings. The so-called African Venus of Monticello.

I remembered her well—that lovely mulatto girl who had come to our house in London, slept in our bed, and accompanied us to puppet shows. "She was just a slip of a girl, scarcely older than his daughters . . ."

"Which is why I don't believe it," John said. "That Jefferson would seduce his own daughter's pretty maidservant? No. Whatever my quarrels with the man, it's a disgrace that any president must endure such slanders."

John Quincy gave a wry smile, nursing a glass of peach brandy. "You have a generous soul, Father. I suppose it's because nothing weighs upon your conscience. Here you are, in happy retirement, with the consolation of knowing you discharged all the duties of a virtuous citizen and the genuine pleasure of knowing you left the country in a safe and honorable peace without the smallest sacrifice of national honor and dignity. And you accomplished that against the advice of both your allies and your enemies."

"Prettily said, brother." Thomas took a gulp of his drink. It was his fifth of the night, and I looked at him askance. "It seems that over in Europe, Johnny traded his once fine head of hair for eloquence."

"A deal with the devil," John Quincy said ruefully, touching his balding pate and taking the ribbing in good stead. "Pray tell, what did *you* trade away to keep your mop of curls, brother?"

"What little sense of refinement I had," Tommy replied. "For it seems to me that if our father had been less virtuous, he'd still be president."

I thought Thomas was right.

But John Quincy grew serious. "Only the common and vulgar herd think of personal interest before public. Our father is a statesman who sacrificed his own interest to the benefit of his country."

To which my husband groused, "And you see how *that's* rewarded!"

Fortunately, John Quincy knew how to keep his father from too much bitterness. "But Mama tells me that from the earliest period of your political life, you've always *expected* such treatment in return for every sacrifice, and every toil, and done it anyway. So I hope you won't think more harshly of your country than she deserves."

Looking up from my knitting, I said, "Well, your mama, these days, thinks very harshly of her ungrateful country indeed."

John Quincy folded his hands in his lap. He'd always had a grave countenance, even as a boy. Now it was very grave. "I wonder how much the country can be blamed when they were lied to. And when those lies were funded by the very man who stood to gain the most power from the deception."

I wasn't willing to excuse the voters who turned my husband out of the presidency as if they were addled children. "Perhaps the public should've known better than to put stock into the election lies of an adulterous schemer like Hamilton."

"I'm not speaking of Hamilton," said John Quincy. "It pains me to deliver this news. But I ought to be the one to tell you." We all leaned forward in curiosity as he explained, "There's a reason Callender is printing these accusations about Jefferson. And it isn't because the newspaperman has changed sides from Democratic-Republican to Federalist. It's because he's avenging himself on the very man who encouraged him and likely paid him to print all those lies about you, Father."

My husband inched to the edge of his chair. "What do you mean?"

"It was Jefferson," said our oldest son. "Behind all those newspaper attacks when we were on the verge of war with France . . ."

Tommy let out a long whistle at this revelation. "Your own vice president, egging on sedition!"

My husband shot up, shaking his head in vehement denial. "Is there proof?"

John Quincy shrugged. "Circumstantial. Jefferson gave the newspaperman a pardon and fifty dollars after he was released. But he refused to give him a government appointment, and so now the wretch is retaliating."

My husband paced, nearly toppling one of my hand-embroidered fire screens. "What does Jefferson say against these charges?"

"Nothing," John Quincy replied. "Which is wise."

"It's beneath the notice of a president," my husband agreed. "I wish that I'd noticed less. But I never wrote a line against my political enemies nor contributed one farthing to a writer to do it for me."

We all knew this was true. Yet my husband's natural fair-mindedness came to play. "No, I cannot believe it. Jefferson's charities to this scoundrel are a disgrace, but his refusal to give Callender a political post is evidence of virtue rather than corruption."

Reluctantly, I agreed. Though, later, as we readied for bed, I realized that against my will, something had stuck to the back of my mind. John had remembered Sally Hemings as a *pretty maidservant*.

Yes, the young Sally had been pretty. And even my husband had noticed. *Pretty, poised, personable Sally . . .*

I shook away the thought. "Perhaps President Jefferson will learn a well-deserved lesson from this humiliation, but I cannot wish it upon his poor daughters."

Patsy and Polly—who were both grown now—must each be mortified. My heart went out to them. To have to *think*, even for one moment, that their father was capable of such immorality.

They might just die with shame.

As I brushed my hair for bed I said, "I can only shudder to think of how our children would feel if they ever read such a thing about *their* father."

John whirled upon me. "Abigail, I swear by the Almighty, whatever is printed, my children will never have just cause for such humiliation for even one moment."

He stood before me, hands on his hips, his nightcap askew, and I could almost laugh at myself for my youthful fears. Whatever my husband's faults—and I could name plenty—he was an honest and upright man. He'd *always* been that. And I was grateful that in the evening of our lives our love remained, leaving me curious about what was yet to come of it.

Chapter Forty-Nine

QUINCY
Massachusetts
Spring 1804

MY RASPBERRY BUSHES and strawberry vines were likely to bear a fine crop, I thought, dusting mud from my gardening gloves. In the far-off field, my granddaughters were feeding the geese. And John was carting a load of salt hay because Tommy had gone off somewhere without a word, as he was prone to do more and more these days.

"He's too busy courting to tend to his chores," John had complained. That was true. But I'd also heard from my sisters that Tommy was frequenting taverns—a thing I'd warned him no man in our family ought to risk.

Nevertheless, my mood was fine. For in the year past we had the pride and joy of seeing our son John Quincy Adams elected to the United States Senate on the Federalist slate.

"Ah, there he will exact revenge for his father's political downfall," many said. But to the frustration of his fellow Federalists—and his mother, too—our boy had shown a remarkable independent streak. He even went so far as to back President Jefferson in his bid to purchase Louisiana.

"Curse the stripling," some angry Federalist wrote of my son's refusal to tow the party line. "How he apes his sire!"

Like his father, my son took an almost perverse pleasure in acting contrary to the desires of his party. John heartily approved, living vicariously, it seemed, through our son's political career. And whenever we were melancholy about how the country had discarded us, John Quincy would say, "Father, neither your fame nor your honor will suffer by the result. Posterity will show that you were the man, not of any party, but of the whole nation."

Of course, posterity might need a little help on that score—and John needed more to do with his mind than fodder cattle, potter in the garden, and plant a potato yard lest, he said, "ennui rain upon me in buckets."

So, with my help and encouragement, John had begun writing his own history. And on an afternoon when we took a gentle horse ride together on the seashore, I attempted to jog my husband's memory about certain things he meant to write down.

Unfortunately, present matters intruded.

"I cannot understand John Quincy's political support of Jefferson's decisions," I said. "I don't recall any provision in the Constitution that empowers the federal government to buy Louisiana. And isn't Jefferson always crowing about how dangerous the powers of the government might be if enlarged?"

My husband chuckled. "Well, Jefferson can either preserve his ideological purity or adopt the more reasonable point of view that the Constitution empowers us to make treaties that ensure the general welfare of generations of Americans by doubling the size of the nation. Johnny is right to support it, though it will be unpopular here when people find out the cost."

"Whatever the right thing is to do will always be unpopular with our ungrateful countrymen," I said.

It was the kind of thing my husband used to say, but lately the misanthrope had changed his tune. "My dear, I still love the people of America and believe them to be incapable of ingratitude. It's as John Quincy said. They've been deceived. It's the duty of somebody to undeceive them."

Not my duty, I thought. I'd mothered the country enough. For what years I had left to me, I wanted to steer clear of anything that brought Jefferson to mind. But then, in May, we heard the news . . .

JOHN FOUND ME in bed in the middle of the day, huddled beneath a quilt, blinking tears away. "What's happened, Abigail?"

With a voice that seemed to echo from afar, I said, "The president's daughter has died."

John sank to the edge of the bed. "Which daughter?"

"The youngest," I said, remembering darling Polly, and how we'd come to love her in London. "Mrs. Eppes was her married name. She died in childbed."

John released a sorrowful breath. "A heavy blow for Jefferson."

And a heavy blow for me, too, since this news brought back every tear of grief I had suppressed for my Charles, and now I couldn't help but sob into my pillow. "The heaviest for a parent to endure!"

I felt anew all my regrets that I hadn't been with Charles when he died. All my resentments that we might've been more forgiving with that child. And a malaise encircled me that I couldn't shake.

I remembered how, when I learned that Charles had died, I'd wandered the president's house, my soul in agony. I wondered if Jefferson was doing the same now.

My mind searched back. Had he expressed sympathy for the loss of our son? I think he must have. For whatever else he was, Jefferson was a diplomat—a man of decorum. I thought I remembered now his condolence before the dinner party into which I walked on his arm. In the fog of grief in our last days in Washington City, I had simply forgotten.

Or perhaps I was misremembering now, only because my heart yearned for kindness and kinship.

In the days that followed, I tried to distract myself with household chores but couldn't put the poor doomed Polly Jefferson out of my mind. Kneading bread. Sweeping floors. Canning fruit. None of it gave me respite. I kept remembering that darling girl stuffing cakes into her mouth at my table or clapping at puppet shows or clinging to my skirts.

To my irritation, I supposed there was a little corner of my heart where Jefferson once sat as a friend whom I esteemed and loved, from whence I found it hard wholly to discard him. So I gave up to temptation and picked up my quill pen.

When was the last time I wrote Jefferson? I could not remember. Much had passed between us since that made it difficult to write. Still, I tried.

Sir,

It has been some time since I conceived of any event in this life which could make me feel sympathy with you. But I know how closely entwined around a parent's heart are those chords which bind parent to child, and when snapped asunder, how agonizing the pain. I, too, have tasted the bitter cup. That you may derive comfort from a firm belief in God is the ardent wish of she who once took pleasure in calling herself your friend.

I shouldn't send this letter. At the very least, I should show it to John before opening a discourse with the new president of the United States. But I'd raised no issue of politics. It was right and good to extend condolences amidst another person's grief.

And sending it made me feel better.

At least until June, when came Jefferson's reply.

Now I didn't know what to do with myself.

Escaping the heat of the day, I went into the house to read it alone. And I was gratified by the tender and warm words Jefferson returned to me.

Dear Madam,

I can assure you my daughter always asked whether I had heard lately of you, and how you did. In giving you this assurance I perform a sacred duty for her and am thankful for the occasion furnished to express my regret that a line of separation has arisen between us. The friendship with which you honored me has ever been valued and fully reciprocated.

If I'd stopped reading there, it would've been a balm for old wounds. Unfortunately, Jefferson's letter went on in that fine politician's script, flowing from his pen in eloquent hypocrisy.

I will only say that I considered Mr. Adams' midnight appointments as personally unkind. They were my most ardent political enemies. After brooding over it, and not always resisting the expression of it, I forgave it cordially and returned to the same state of esteem and respect for him which had so long subsisted.

I blinked. He *forgave* it? Well, we hadn't asked his forgiveness. Nor was I conscious of anything we'd ever done for which we'd need his forgiveness.

The nerve of the man!

Now I wished to march straight out into the fields where my husband was supervising our farm help and show him this infuriating exchange. But, of course, I'd begun it without his knowledge. And my anger was too hot to wait upon anyone else's advice.

Again, I took up my pen.

Sir, you have been pleased to enter upon some subjects which demand a reply.

I reminded him that the Constitution gave to a president the authority to make appointments right up to the end. That President Washington had done exactly the same. We'd filled vacancies with men we believed would be faithful to the Constitution and the government. Men who would resign from their duties if political differences embarrassed the new president.

Moreover, we couldn't have filled those posts with a motive of *personal* unkindness, for at the time we didn't even know if Jefferson would be president or the tie vote would be broken in favor of Aaron Burr.

I wrote all this swiftly, in a fury. Then I decided that since Jefferson was of a mind to vent his spleen, so would I, for we had grievances aplenty.

I pointed out that he'd rewarded the newspaperman James Callender for printing libels against us—the very same serpent who bit him with the Sally Hemings scandal. That's how badly he miscalculated the man's character.

My anger having been given full expression, I felt it important that he not think he jousted with my husband. I wanted him to know it was me.

This letter is written in confidence. No eye but my own has seen it.

I did not anticipate a reply. Then again, I'd poked him with a zeal that many would say was unladylike. His pride might not tolerate that. As indeed, *pride* was the byword by which all our political enemies now seemed to destroy themselves.

I'd scarcely posted this letter when my husband stumbled into the kitchen as if someone had struck him between the eyes with a hammer. "Hamilton is dead."

This I could not credit unless it be of some venereal disease. And yet, John explained that at a place called Weehawken, Hamilton had fought a duel with Vice President Burr, to whom he would not apologize for some disparaging remark or other.

I wouldn't cry for Hamilton, though I could almost admire his inability to apologize and retreat from a fight though it cost him his life.

Meanwhile, John pulled his hat from his head, dazed. "He died with Burr's pistol bullet buried in his spinal marrow. They say he died a penitent. Well, I have forgiven my arch enemy, but I do not forget his villainy."

"Nor do I."

"Still," John said, terribly disturbed, "we ought to write a note of condolence to his wife. Whatever her husband's faults, Mrs. Hamilton was ever a saintly figure."

It was true that I remembered Eliza Hamilton fondly. We'd passed many hours together at Martha Washington's levees in the earliest days of the republic. And truly, I did feel for her to lose her husband—especially knowing she had young children to raise now, on her own.

So how was I to explain to John that I'd already sent a note of condolence to another political foe, only to have it explode into a war of words that still continued?

In his latest letter to me, Jefferson said he didn't free Callender as a reward for spreading lies about my husband. But rather, he considered the Alien and Sedition Acts to be a tyrannical abuse of power, completely unconstitutional, and therefore he issued a general pardon to all.

Burn his letter, I thought. It wasn't my place to argue. Just burn his letter and all the others and be done with this man. But how does any American banish the president of the United States from one's life?

It couldn't be done. Or, at least, I couldn't do it.

As it happened, Alexander Hamilton wasn't the only one unable to retreat from a fight.

Taking up my pen again I said that if Jefferson wanted to talk about *tyranny*, I was happy to oblige. The sedition prosecutions were the work of the legislature, and the justice system, with prosecutors and judges and juries. Yet, Jefferson, on his own say-so alone, had issued pardons to the convicts.

Who was the tyrant, then?

If a chief magistrate can by his will alone annul a law with pardons, where is the difference between a republican and a despotic government?

Jefferson replied with another lengthy justification of his actions, which only inflamed my contempt. So I took up my pen one final time to express my fear that he was going to wreck the country.

Absolutely seething, I added,

I will not further intrude upon your time, but close this correspondence with my sincere wishes that you may be directed to that path which may terminate in the prosperity and happiness of the people over whom you are placed.

BY THE TIME my temper cooled, I wondered if I'd conducted this correspondence in some fit of absolute insanity. I wanted to destroy it all but couldn't make up my mind to do it. So when John

Quincy came for an autumnal visit without his English wife—whose constitution was ill suited to farm life—I confided all.

Eyes wide behind his new spectacles, John Quincy said, "You'd better tell Father."

I groaned with mortification. "That wasn't what I'd hoped you'd say."

"Jefferson is careless with his letters," my son reminded me. "They've been intercepted and printed to embarrass him at least twice before. This debate between the two of you would prove irresistible to the press. Is that how you want Father to learn of it?"

I felt the blood drain from my face at *that* possibility while my son pressed his argument. "The exposure of these letters will not help me in my political career, I can tell you that. And in any case, people will assume that my father wrote these letters; they'll never believe you capable of carrying on a debate with President Jefferson."

"I've been debating politics for more than forty years," I snapped. I'd matched wits with men, in and out of my husband's administration, but John Quincy was probably right that the public wouldn't believe it; women in our country hadn't come that far.

In fact, the widowed Mr. Jefferson didn't even have a lady to preside over Washington City to give further example of our capabilities in political circles. He'd had to borrow his eldest daughter to be his hostess. Or, on occasion, Mrs. Madison. And neither of those ladies opined on politics as readily as I did—though I'd heard that Dolley Madison was shrewder in political matters than people realized.

I considered Johnny's advice, and as the weather turned cold, I took pleasure in having our oldest at home again, even if only for a visit. My husband also took joy in it, relishing their debates by the fire. John loved to talk about the farm with Tommy, but our eldest son alone fed him with the political banter upon which he still thrived.

Proudly, John told me, "In Congress, John Quincy is making a strenuous effort to prevent the spread of slavery into the new states and territories. Certain threats have been made against him, but he pays them no mind."

I tried not to show how that frightened me. "Well, at least here at Peacefield, he can think clearly without the cries of violent slavers outside his office windows. We must invite him to stay longer."

Unfortunately, John Quincy declined our invitation. "My wife and boys await me at home." He knew I couldn't protest against that, but he promised, "I'll be back soon enough."

"I'll write you in the meantime," John said. "Or, at least, have your mother or Tommy write for me. My hands always ache these days."

While studiously avoiding my gaze, John Quincy said, "Father, *please* be careful what you write. Both political parties hate me virulently for my independence. And these are still dangerous times."

This warning was more for me, I knew, and it made me all the more conscious of my guilt of exchanging compromising political letters with President Jefferson.

But John was in the dark about that and puffed that barrel chest of his. "My boy, twenty political times as dangerous as these have I weathered, and I'm alive and hearty yet. I'll write as I please. If the peepers violate public faith and get stung by a wasp in the folds of the paper, let them have the smart for their reward."

Our son liked that answer, I could tell. "Nevertheless, we're not *entirely* past the time of guillotines."

My husband chuckled with bravado. "Should that come to pass, I should think it an honor to go with you to the scaffold."

I wasn't amused. I wanted no more talk of death and danger, so I pressed some of my knitting into our boy's hands. "Socks for my grandsons to keep their feet warm this winter."

John Quincy took them in grateful farewell, then kissed my cheek to whisper, "*You must tell Father.*"

Later that night, I found my husband rummaging through old trunks for diaries and notebooks. These days he was always looking for scraps of paper to verify what he was writing in his history.

Alas, I had more urgent reading for him now.

Wordlessly I handed him Jefferson's letters, and copies of mine to him. Oh, how I cringed to think of what John might make of it.

Curiously, my husband found his spectacles, lifted one of the letters to the light, and narrowed his eyes. "*Abigail . . .*"

"Keep reading."

An hour later, when the candle was halfway gone, he looked up again, and this time his voice was harsher, and accusatory. "*Abigail.*"

"I know," I said, rubbing at my face. "I *know.*"

John stared at me as if I'd grown two heads. "I am sensible that your love compels you to defend me, but the *recklessness* of it in this political hour."

"Didn't you just tell Johnny that you've weathered twenty political storms just as dangerous? Well, I've weathered them, too. I, too, struggled to make a place where I could write as I please."

With a jaw clenched so tight I feared it might fracture, John collected all the letters into a pile. Then he got up—though it was the wee hours of the morning now—and scribbled upon a note for his files. "The whole of this correspondence was begun and conducted without my knowledge or suspicion. Last evening and this morning at the desire of Mrs. Adams, I read the whole. I have no remarks to make upon it at this time and in this place."

Chapter Fifty

QUINCY
Massachusetts
Summer 1807

ALL SHOULD'VE BEEN quiet in our retirement. But thanks to our son-in-law, we couldn't enjoy it in peace. I will never understand why Colonel Smith couldn't simply be *content* in the government position we'd secured for him. Why he couldn't have simply enjoyed his renewed prosperity, buying Nabby new dresses, attending meetings of the Society of the Cincinnati, and swanning about New York with his jeweled cane and modest political influence.

He and Nabby spent six years rebuilding their lives and fortune in New York City, only for him to now throw it away on another mad scheme.

As it happened, Colonel Smith had used his own money to outfit a mission of private soldiers intent upon liberating Venezuela from Spain. He had even allowed our oldest grandson to withdraw from his studies at Columbia to fight as a soldier of fortune in this plan. Our grandson Willy had been nursed on tales of the revolution, so we couldn't be entirely surprised that he got caught up in his father's ill-considered adventure.

But Colonel Smith was a government official. And his actions reflected upon the president.

"Jefferson fired him from his post and ordered his arrest," John Quincy reported. "And though I did my best to intervene on his behalf, I must tell you as a senator of these United States, Jefferson had little choice *but* to arrest him lest Spain consider this an act of war."

Hearing this, my enraged husband shouted, "It would've been better if, instead of our grandson, it was his fool of a father on that ship to Venezuela and we'd be glad if he sank down into the ocean with it!"

It was a terrible thing to say. I was glad Nabby wasn't present to hear it, for it would've added to her heartbreak. Our daughter stood loyally by the man she'd vowed to God to love, and I admired her for it.

But I couldn't help but silently agree that her husband was cursed.

At least Colonel Smith had the good sense to send Nabby to us in Peacefield so that she wouldn't have to endure the scandal of the trial. And we comforted her as the drama played out, month after month.

Thanks to Johnny's legal advice, Colonel Smith was acquitted, but, as my eldest son explained, "There was no point in jailing him. He is thoroughly ruined. His public career is done, and his place in society forfeit. Now he really *will* have to try his hand at farming on the frontier."

How my heart ached for Nabby; we'd tried to save her from this fate, but there was no help for it.

Fortunately, after nearly being captured by the Spanish, our grandson returned home safe to us, chastened by his misadventures on the high seas. "We *did* reach Venezuela, Grandmama. But it didn't seem as if they wanted to be liberated. There were no pamphleteers spreading the spirit of freedom. No Sons of Liberty meeting in taverns. No militias drilling in anticipation of a fight."

My poor grandson. He'd perhaps imagined revolution to be a more unified affair than the long, ugly, and uninspiring slog from boys being shot in the snow to the country in which Thomas Jefferson had been re-elected to a second term in office.

"All glory to the Man of the People," John muttered when the results of Jefferson's re-election came in. "And a continual pox on the House of Adams."

We'd been so occupied with family woes that we had somehow not yet read the history of the revolution published by Mercy Otis Warren. Friends and family had hinted grimly that we wouldn't like what she'd written. Nevertheless, we were still shocked when we finally cracked open the pages.

"What in the *devil* have I ever done to Mrs. Warren?" John demanded to know.

He was back at his stone wall with tools, trying to repair the winter damages where the edifice was falling away. And as he violently split a rock, he asked, "How have I merited such unjust treatment from a lady about whom I've never uttered an unkind word?"

I didn't know how to answer him, for I, too, had been thunderstruck by Mercy's accusation that my husband had been corrupted by his time in Europe.

"*Corrupted!*" John brought a hammer down on a chisel to break another stone. "Well, who sent me to Europe? If I was corrupted there, perhaps I ought to sue the public for damages."

"John," I warned softly, for he was so red in the face I feared he might huff and puff his way into the grave.

"She writes that I was for monarchy—this woman who was our *friend*. By what evidence does she purport to know this? Have either of us ever said or written anything to her of the kind?"

"Of course not."

Mercy had written but two letters to me in ten years, and both contained political barbs aimed at my husband. As a result, I was more apt now to give credence to what my sister said about Mrs. Warren's pettiness. "She's still nursing a grudge that we wouldn't find her husband or sons public employment."

"Then who is the corrupt one?" John asked.

I made no defense of my old friend. Indeed, I'd begun to question my judgment of people altogether. To be betrayed by one intimate friend was no reflection upon a person. But to be continually betrayed by old friends spoke to a pattern of credulous naïveté.

Like my husband, I felt the effects of time chipping away at our bodies and legacy. We'd been out of the public eye for years, and what we'd accomplished was increasingly mischaracterized or forgotten. I, too, wanted to do something about it. To shore up the truth, break up the lies, and patch the holes in the stories now being told of a nation I'd helped mother into being.

"The history of our revolution will be one continued lie from one end to the other," John groused. "The essence of the whole will be that Dr. Franklin's electrical rod smote the earth and out sprang General Washington."

"Don't forget Jefferson," I sniped, which broke the tension and made John laugh.

"Yes, Jefferson. They'll surely carve his face somewhere in the pantheon. Whereas *John Adams* will only appear in some dusty old tome with an asterisk."

"Then why won't you finish your autobiography?" I asked, because he'd been scribbling and tossing drafts into the fire for years. "Set the record straight!"

"No one will read it. And if they did, they won't believe it. They'll say 'the envy of this John Adams could not bear the truth of his insignificance.'"

I was sorry that Mercy's book had upset him so.

It had upset me, too.

But at present we had enough to do to keep our family from ruin. When I went back into the house, Nabby was tying Willy's cravat so he'd look smart in applying for a position at the school here in Quincy.

"From sailor to schoolhouse," Nabby said.

Having sworn off adventuring, my grandson said he was ready to take up employment as a teacher. Yet, I feared he lacked the stern discipline required to manage rowdy children.

"Don't forget your spectacles," I warned as we pushed him out the door. "They'll make you look older and wiser than you are."

My grandson laughed. "Grandfather already humbled me this morning. Now I go off with a double dose. I'll see you at dinner!"

Dinner was, as always, to be at one o'clock. John Quincy was coming from Boston with his wife and children. Which meant that we'd need extra pies for the occasion. Having sent my granddaughters to gather berries, I now picked over the baskets on the porch, scowling whenever I found a berry that was underripe.

Meanwhile, my husband—having exhausted himself of his rage while working on the stone wall—collapsed into a porch chair with a newspaper. "It seems in this eternal war between

England and France, our country is still but a squeaky mouse being batted about by two cats."

"No doubt your son, the senator, will have something to say about that tonight," I said sourly, for our oldest boy continued to show an irritating willingness to side with President Jefferson on matters of state.

"There are whispers of an embargo," John said.

I gave an indelicate snort. "An embargo would be the most foolish, destructive policy possible, so naturally Jefferson will pursue it."

"I think the proposed embargo is a bit cowardly," John said, closing his eyes against the sun. "But an interesting experiment to prevent war with Britain. In any case, I'm determined to support Jefferson in this as far as my conscience and honor will allow."

Not that Jefferson would care or appreciate it.

John might still be capable of fair-mindedness, but *I* could hold a grudge. And when it came to President Jefferson, I held it fast.

I retreated to the kitchen to bake my pies. I was particular about the crust, having perfected Phoebe's old recipe. There was an art of mixing the dough—one I didn't trust anyone else to master. Which meant I insisted on doing it myself, even though my arthritic hands took twice as long with every task.

"Why won't you let me help, Mama?" Nabby asked.

"Because I'm set in my ways. And I should do things myself whilst I'm still able."

"I think it's because you fear I'll scorch the crusts," she accused. "Which is why you only let me make the Indian pudding. And even then, you fear I'll bake another spoon into it—which wasn't my fault."

One of the grandchildren had dropped the spoon in while she wasn't looking, and we all had a good laugh when it was discovered. Given all the trials of her family, it had amazed me that Nabby *could* laugh. So I encouraged it by continuing the playful quarrel until John poked his head into the kitchen to chide me. "Wife, your uncontrollable attachment to the superintendence of every part of this household truly vexes me."

"You don't want to vex Papa, do you?" Nabby asked, but when

she saw my sidelong glance she sighed. "I'll go make myself useful by helping Sally pull out an extra table for tonight."

Upon Nabby's exit, John playfully tugged me away from the pastry dough by my apron strings.

"John, I have flour on my hands!"

"So you do," he replied, refusing to release me. "You'll save yourself much trouble if you let our daughters and granddaughters take more responsibility in the household, you know."

I sighed, because I knew it was true. "But they won't get the crust right."

"And the boys never manure the cornfield to my liking. But I've learned that sometimes it is more important for the work to get done than to get it done *your way.*"

He was right to tease me, of course, because my insistence that I could do everything better than anyone in my family ensured that I was therefore punished for my own vanity and conceit.

"Abigail," he said, "Come out riding with me on this fair day."

I groaned, confessing, "It is more and more difficult to ride, these days."

"Which is why we must keep at it. Given how few minutes either of us has left to live, I want to spend them together, so leave the pies to Nabby. She'll need the practice, as she will soon be a farmer's wife again."

Colonel Smith and his brothers were now building houses together in what was being called Smith's Valley in western New York. And Nabby was resigned to her fate. *It'll be better to start fresh*, Nabby had said. *Better for us to leave society behind for a plow. In truth, I'll henceforth teach my children that they're better off eating locusts or sawdust than chasing patriotic ideals.*

She was bitter, and I couldn't blame her.

The least I could do was trust her with pastry.

That night, as we passed Nabby's perfectly crisped pies round the crowded dining room, I was struck by the most affecting realization.

There, sitting safely between his mother and his grandfather, was our beloved twenty-year-old grandson, Willy, who had appointed himself master of cutting slices. Near to him sat his sister, twelve-year-old Caroline, waiting eagerly for her portion. Charlie's orphaned daughters—ten-year-old Susanna and eight-year-old Abbe—childishly whispered to their mother behind cupped hands.

At the other end of the table presided John Quincy and his pregnant wife, Louisa, who scolded their plump boys—six-year-old George and four-year-old John-John—for snapping napkins at each other. Meanwhile, to give his own wife a respite, Thomas bounced his restless toddler upon one knee.

"All my children," I said, overcome with a sense of well-being that had eluded me for some time. We had all three of our surviving children and all but one of our grandchildren gathered here tonight at Peacefield.

The only one missing was Nabby's seventeen-year-old Jack Smith, who, to the relief of his grandfather, was finishing his studies at Columbia.

Through all the privations of war, the sacrifices, and separations, John and I had still somehow forged this family. Brothers and sisters and cousins and nieces and nephews who all cherished one another. And despite all the turmoil and disappointments of political life, perhaps the Lord might yet grant us time to build our family into something that might endure. Could we devote ourselves now to preserving this private legacy—and could it be enough?

Chapter Fifty-One

BOSTON
Massachusetts
March 1809

TIME MARCHED ON for our family.

John and I suffered the slow torments of age—new aches and pains, senses dimming, and memory fading. But our love for our children sustained us.

Tommy took over much of the management of our farms. Nabby sent letters from the western New York frontier, where she and Colonel Smith were building a life in the wilderness with fellow settlers and the remaining members of the Oneida Nation still residing there. Meanwhile, having lost his Senate seat over his support for Jefferson's embargo, John Quincy was now making his living in Boston as a gentleman lawyer and Harvard's Professor of Rhetoric and Oratory.

We visited him as often as our good health would allow. On this particular visit, as our chaise rolled through the still-slushy streets, my husband was filled with nostalgia. "Do you remember when the children were little, toddling about in our our Boston town house?"

"I remember." If I closed my eyes, I could see Nabby in braids, fighting off sleep whilst insisting she was too old for naps. Johnny stacking blocks. Little Suky clutching her silver rattle. Charlie with his little fists curled under his chin, sleeping like an angel. Tommy still a gleam in his father's eye . . .

Tasting the familiar brine on the air, I said, "The ocean remains the same, but much else has changed in the forty years since we first lived here."

Gone were the days when redcoats drilled in the streets. The king's emblems had been stripped away. The damage from the war repaired. New homes now rose up next to the old, made of brick instead of wood to prevent fires. The Green Dragon Tavern was still open, but these days people met at the new and elegant Exchange Coffee House.

Fashion had certainly changed. Gentlemen strolled in black top hats instead of tricorns. Ladies wore wide-brimmed bonnets instead of mobcaps. We heard more variety of voices in passing, too. From the street corners, lady shopkeepers openly hawked warm bread and hot toddies. On the widened cobblestone streets, Irish dockworkers rolled casks of rum and barrels of fish. Haitian washerwomen in colorful head cloths rushed past carrying sacks of laundry.

Time had marched on not only for us, and for Boston, but for the country, too.

Following Washington's example, Jefferson had resigned after two terms, leaving a terrible mess for his successor, James Madison. The British were still preying upon us. And our new president—like the three who had come before him—was trying to exhaust every option for peace.

"Boston Gazette!" cried a newsboy splashing through puddles alongside us, trying to sell his paper. *"Federalists say Madison is too weak for war!"*

"Poor devil," John grumbled. "Now it's Madison's turn upon the rack."

I thought he was remarkably sympathetic to Madison, considering that the small-statured Virginian had once been a formidable foe. But perhaps there would always be an unspoken kinship among those who held our highest office.

Those few who understood the weight of it.

John Quincy was waiting for us at his law office, where several clerks did brisk business. Our oldest son could be well-satisfied with the life he led now, taking on clients, lecturing at the university, teaching his little boys, and making of himself a dutiful son on the Sabbath at our supper table.

And I could be well satisfied for him—for though it was natural for me to have ambitions for my sons, it was also natural to want him close.

But he was restless. Like me and his father both, John Quincy missed the fray of public life. We all *said* that family could be enough, but none of us could quit the newspapers. And all of us were grateful that John Quincy still made trips to Washington City to argue before the Supreme Court, because he always returned with intelligence that made us feel as if we were still a part of the political world.

"I have much news to impart," John Quincy said. "Important news, though it can wait till tomorrow after we settle you into the guest room."

"A hint at least, Johnny," my husband said.

And his son obeyed. "I was there to see the electors cast their votes for the new president."

"I was surprised it was Madison," I replied. "I expected George Clinton or James Monroe, both of whom I'm told are more dynamic."

My son smiled. "Oh, Madison is a wilier politician than most suspect."

I remembered at the start of our government, when every idea Madison proposed seemed to me a bad one. But he *had* founded the Democratic-Republican party, which was still ascendant, while Federalists foundered in disarray.

"Madison is a deep thinker," said John Quincy. "A coalition builder. Besides, he was secretary of state, which positioned him as the heir apparent."

My husband waggled his brows. "I heard some wanted to put *you* forward for the vice presidency, my boy."

To that, our son only said, "Let my feelings not be sported with by *those* electioneering intrigues. What the country needs right now is smooth sailing into a new administration."

We dined that night at John Quincy's house, and our little grandsons crowded around the table shouting, "Grandmama! Grandpapa!"

We made gifts to the little ones of molasses candies. I also presented a basket of seed cakes and apple butter to John Quincy's

English wife, Louisa Catherine—a woman to whom I had tried to warm without ever quite achieving it.

It wasn't entirely her fault. With the pallor of a corpse, and a whisper of a voice, Louisa simply tended to fade into the wallpaper during garrulous Adams family gatherings. And I thought her delicacy and somewhat romantic notions made for an ill match with my austere and practical son. Still, she was the mother of my grandchildren, and for that alone I could hold her in high esteem.

I was also grateful that my English daughter-in-law was always sweet to Charlie's fatherless daughters.

We'd sent twelve-year-old Susanna and ten-year-old Abbe to Boston for dancing lessons, and now the girls demonstrated how properly their aunt Louisa had taught them to curtsey.

Charlie's girls were fair-haired, dimpled, and blessed with his good looks. That should secure them ample choice for husbands when the time came. Provided, of course, that they had good *heads*, as well.

But I wasn't encouraged on that score when, over supper, our conversation turned to the latest headlines and my granddaughter Susanna asked, "Must we *always* talk about the newspapers?"

"*Susanna*," I scolded. Unlike most families, we didn't have a rule that children mustn't speak until spoken to. But we did have a rule that we wouldn't countenance blockheads. "It won't hurt you to pay attention to the newspapers, my dear girl."

My granddaughter made a pained face. "But I hate politics."

My husband chuckled, hand over his heart, as if mortally wounded. "Hate politics, child? How can you bear the name Adams and say so?"

"It's so very dull," Susanna whined.

At hearing that, I nearly dropped my spoon onto my daughter-in-law's altogether too fussy china plates. "*Dull?* When your native country is so continuously threatened by foreign powers, and disagreements about slavery, you cannot be a descendant from the spirit of '76 and be indifferent to what is passing."

"I would only be frustrated if I took an interest," Susanna said. "Because what could *I* do about any of it as a girl?"

I wished to say that as a citizen of this republic she had a duty and responsibility to give her attention to its cares. But despite my entreaties all those years ago to *remember the ladies*, we'd been forgotten. Worse than forgotten, in truth. For those few women who had been allowed to vote in our country had *just* been stripped of that right two years ago. Knowing this ought to have given me pause in hectoring my granddaughters about patriotism.

Then again, to love one's country when that country did not love you in return might as well have been our family motto.

Later, when I tucked my granddaughter into bed, she asked, "Am I likely to find a husband who would look to me to read newspapers and advise him the way Grandpapa looks to you?"

I took her question seriously, thinking about all the men I knew. Some *did* value and recognize the intelligence of their wives. But not even my own sons gave their wives all the consideration they were due. So it was with a deep sigh of disappointment that I admitted, "No, child, you're not likely to find a husband like your grandfather. But you must look for one anyway."

The next morning, before the children were awake, John Quincy delivered the important news he'd been waiting to share.

And in shock, I cried, "No, no! You mustn't go."

My son pulled his chair closer, intent that I should look into his eyes. "Mother, this is what I was *made* for. These past years since losing my seat in the Senate, I've severely felt my own defects, and the want of experience in business. It's diplomacy that I know well. And it is what I am wanted for."

It turned out that his trip to Washington City hadn't merely been to argue a case before the Supreme Court or to watch electors cast their votes. He'd gone on to enjoy a private meeting with the new president, who intended to appoint my son as minister to the Court of Tsar Alexander.

"It is a great political reward," John Quincy said. "And it may one day lead to higher office."

"How wrong you are, my boy. You are a political rival and he is sending you into exile. Russia, again! He might as well banish you to the *moon*. You need not accept this appointment. Nay, you *must* not accept it."

I expected John to agree.

Rarely had we been so happy and content as these past three years with Johnny nearby to enliven our society and keep our minds agile. I couldn't bear the thought of parting with my son yet again.

But my husband said, "Johnny, I cannot think of a man more qualified for the post."

While I rounded on my husband with confusion, our son said, "You raised me a firm patriot. If my country calls, I owe her a duty."

"You've already done your duty," I argued. "You've already spent nearly *fourteen years* in Europe, not to mention your years of service in the Senate."

Our son laced his fingers together in his lap. "President Madison believes another war with Great Britain cannot be avoided, and that we'll need Russia for an ally. He flatters me to say I'm the only one who might achieve an alliance. But I might well be."

"A terrible thing to be a man of so much importance," John teased, beaming with pride.

I was neither amused nor willing to let pride in our son overcome good sense. "What of your wife? You cannot *possibly* take Louisa Catherine. She'd never survive the ruthless winter of the Russian tundra. Neither can you leave her behind to manage your boys and farms. She hasn't the aptitude."

It'd been so difficult for me to manage when my husband was abroad. It would be impossible for a fine English lady like Louisa Catherine. But John Quincy waved this concern away. "Tommy can manage my farms. My wife will join me in Russia, of course. I will keep her alive even in winter. So please give your blessing, Mother."

He was serious. Sitting there, hands laced in his lap, his dark eyes revealed a stubborn resolve. Well, I could be stubborn, too. "I cannot give my blessing to this."

"*Abigail*," my husband said, reaching for my hand.

I snatched it away. "No. I cannot, *will not*, give my consent, much less my blessing, to yet another painful separation."

My son did not need my consent and I embarrassed myself by suggesting that he did. But I was now too overwrought to moderate my emotions or my tone in any way.

John Quincy's expression softened, but he would not change

his mind. "I could wish to please my parents and have their blessing. But my duty, I must do. It is a law far above that of my mere wishes."

I FELT SO angry and helpless that I could scarcely speak a word on our return to Peacefield. I strode into the house with the energy of a woman half my age and slammed the door behind me.

It wasn't until I saw John sitting alone on the porch, smoking his cigar, that I confronted him. "How could you encourage John Quincy when you know very well that if he goes to Russia, we will never live long enough to see him again?"

Only then did I see tears glistening in the corners of my husband's eyes. "One never knows. We *may* yet meet again."

I shook my head, sinking into a rocking chair with true grief welling inside me. "You've seen seventy-three years and mine will soon number sixty-five. Hopes are but the whispers of winds against that hard reality."

John inhaled, then blew out a long slow breath. "Abigail, there is no office on earth I would accept if it tore me from Johnny's company. But we mustn't be ruled by selfish motive."

To which I snapped, "Oh, you're *entirely* selfish in encouraging this! You want your son to be a great man."

"What's wrong with that?"

"He's already a great man," I argued. "He's a distinguished public servant, a warm father, a loving husband, and a dutiful son. That should be enough. He doesn't need to follow in your footsteps, leaving behind his farm, his business, and his children the way you did, no matter the harm."

"What harm did I do my children?" John asked with irritation, letting ashes fall where I would later have to sweep them up. "I gave them a free country in which to live. What they do with that freedom is up to them."

It was a powerful argument—though my heart refused to hear it. "Can you really so easily take your last leave of him? Because I believe it will kill me. Don't pretend that Johnny isn't one of the strongest ligaments that still hold us to this earth."

"Good God, woman. To give him up will crack my heart in two and take years off what remains of my life. Is that what you want to hear? Because it's true. I don't know that I'll live a year, a month, or even an hour after he boards that ship for Russia. But it's his *choice*. This is the whole of everything we sacrificed for."

I knew he was right. Perhaps that is why I turned into his shoulder and sobbed. Or perhaps it was because I had already buried three children, and this would be like burying a fourth. And to lose John Quincy, our golden child . . .

In the end, there was nothing for it but to submit, though it made me feel numb and lifeless.

In the days that followed, when I sat down to my correspondence, I felt as though I couldn't write a paragraph worth penning. My fire was out, my wit decayed, my fancy sunk. All before me seemed grim.

To console me, John said, "At least we'll have Johnny's boys with us. That *is* something."

Little George was nearly eight, and his brother John-John was only five. Those precious little faces would surely give me better remembrance of their father than the portrait that still hung over our mantel.

To prepare my mind for the inevitable heartbreak of John Quincy's departure, I attended his farewell lecture at Harvard. Though it wasn't customary to admit ladies, I wasn't alone on this occasion; the chapel was crowded with both men and women in every aisle. Yet I felt as if my son were speaking to me alone when he said, "Let us remember the pleasant hours we have trod together. The only regret with which the remembrance of you can ever be associated is that which I now experience in bidding you farewell."

Neither could I remember another moment of regret with my John Quincy. The brave boy who climbed a hill with me to watch a battle. The young man who greeted us in London and dazzled us with the sights. The dutiful son who had given us so much comfort in our old age . . .

On the day my son and his wife were to depart for Saint Petersburg, I couldn't master my grief. All I wanted was to throw myself upon my knees and beg my son to stay. So I couldn't risk seeing them off, lest I lose all my dignity and sully theirs. Instead, I penned a farewell note to my boy, giving him the blessing he'd asked for.

My heart is with you, my prayers and blessing attend you. God bless, preserve and prosper you, my dearest, beloved son.

Chapter Fifty-Two

QUINCY
Massachusetts
March 1811

I DREAMED OF RUSSIA.

In that faraway land of ice, the Winter Palace rose up in gilded splendor, bathing the magnificent square in a pale golden glow. I saw the bronze equestrian statue of Peter the Great mounted atop his rearing steed, facing the bridge of boats crossing the Neva River and its granite-sided quay. I heard the jingling sleighs, the laughter of fur-bundled children sledding down the ice hills, and the clip-clop of horses drawing magnificent carriages past numerous whirligigs and swings.

That is how vivid a picture John Quincy painted for me in his letters—letters that I treasured, though they took an *unbearably* long time to reach us.

Still, I lived for the thick packets my son sent with detailed descriptions of opulent court life.

Just as preciously longed for was Nabby's familiar script, detailing her frontier travails making lye soap, or restoring their log cabin after the flooding of the river left mud on the floors and dampness upon the firewood.

I missed her desperately and looked forward to her visit, though not its cause. For my daughter wrote that she'd discovered a lump in her breast, and better care for it could be sought here with us in Boston than in the wilderness of New York.

"They don't think it cancerous, do they?" Tommy asked upon hearing the news.

"They don't think so," I said to reassure him and my husband both. "But Colonel Smith thinks it might be best to bring it to the surface."

"Is he a doctor now?" John snapped.

"He might have some battlefield experience with wounds and other ailments," Tommy said, patiently.

Of our children, Tommy was the last who still remained near to us. Though, as a married man of thirty-eight years, with children of his own, he wanted to be out from under his father's roof. So when Phoebe's husband died and she was unable to live by herself in the old saltbox in Braintree, Tommy leaped at the opportunity to move there and look after her.

The move had been good for him. He was now serving as a judge on the Massachusetts General Court while holding office in Quincy as both town treasurer and supervisor of schools. And having impressed people with that good service, he'd recently been appointed by the governor to help mediate some violence in Lincoln County over land rights.

At learning this, John teased, "My sons the diplomats. Johnny drew Russia and you drew Lincoln County—both frigid tundras overrun by drunk barbarians."

"John," I warned.

But my husband was altogether too amused with himself. "Pshaw! While John Quincy negotiates treaties in the ornate halls of Saint Petersburg, Tommy will be slogging through mud, judging whether a farmer's blueberry bush has grown on the wrong side of the property line. It's just the same but with less caviar."

"*John,*" I said again.

Tommy laughed the way he always laughed when teased. He loved and revered his older brother. He rarely showed jealousy, pettiness, or resentment for Johnny's success. But I'd started to notice the flash of pain in Tommy's eyes when he allowed John to make sport of him by way of comparison. The same pain I'd seen when he was just a boy, crying that his father didn't love him as much as his siblings. And I wished my husband would be more sensitive to it!

Thankfully, Nabby would soon be with us. She'd always had a softening influence on her father and bolstered the confidence of her brothers. Our spirits would all be lifted when gathered together.

AT SEVENTY-SEVEN YEARS old, Uncle Tufts was enjoying a dignified retirement and no longer made house calls. The best of his doctoring days were behind him. But for me, he'd grabbed his old doctor's bag and had a servant carry him by carriage to Quincy straightaway.

"We're so grateful for your coming," I said, helping him shuffle into the entryway.

Straightening his old spine, he asked, "Nabby is upstairs?"

I nodded, for though my daughter had arrived for a visit *looking* in perfectly good health, I was alarmed by the reddened, misshapened sight of her breast when she revealed it to me.

The doctors she'd consulted near her home on the frontier advised her that because the lump was movable, it could not be cancerous. But when I confided this to Dr. Tufts, he did not agree and came swiftly to examine her—as indelicate a matter as that was between kin.

Upstairs we found Nabby seated at the edge of the bed, forcing a smile. "Am I too old now for the comfort of candied oranges, Dr. Tufts?"

"For you, my dear, I brought a pocket full."

Touched, I said, "I'll leave you both to it."

Quietly, I closed the door, shooed away curious grandchildren, and joined my husband where he paced by the fire. Other fathers might've shied away from the indelicacy of a woman's ailment, but John wanted to know everything. "Is it cancer? Must it come to the surface?"

"The doctor has just arrived, John. Let him do his work."

When Uncle Tufts finally came back downstairs, his report was grim. "I cannot be entirely sure if it is cancer without cutting, but my years of experience lead me to believe we must remove the breast to save her life."

The breath hissed out of me, and I dropped down hard upon the settee. "Is there no other way? Surely there must be some medicine. Nabby mentioned the possibility of arsenic pills . . ."

"I've read about that," he said. "Benjamin Rush mentions it in one of his volumes, but I know too little about it."

"I've already written to Dr. Rush," John said, offering that man's reply for our doctor's perusal. "He says internal medicines won't help. Like you, he believes only surgery can save her."

I caught a glimpse of the letter, which read, in part, "Let there be no delay in flying to the knife. If she waits it may be too late."

Dear frail Cotton Tufts was apologetic when he spoke. "I'm now too old and blind to perform the surgery, but I'll find the finest surgeon in Boston if Nabby consents."

I groaned, pressing my palms to my eyes, wondering how we could possibly break this news to our daughter.

In the end, John couldn't bear to tell her.

The task was left to me.

"My darling," I said, softly, as if she were a very little girl and not a mother of three. "Your life is at stake."

"But no guarantee can be made that surgery will save me," Nabby replied. "How can I submit to such a painful trial knowing that I might lose my life anyway?"

I gripped her hand and pulled it against my heart, tracing the little scar where I'd persuaded her to let a doctor cut her once before. "You must take the risk. Just as with the smallpox inoculation all those years ago. Please do this for the husband and children you love. And for the parents who have loved you every moment since you came into this world."

THE SURGERY WOULD not wait for Colonel Smith to arrive. And Nabby said stoically, "It's better this way. If I live through it, then my husband will be spared seeing this done to me. If I die, then he'll only suffer the grief of my passing without the agony of witnessing my mutilation."

But I would not be spared, for I had promised my daughter to be with her every moment. And I saw to the preparations for Nabby's surgery myself, piling her bed high with pillows, collecting every spare scrap of cloth for bandaging, throwing back the drapery, and amassing candles upon every surface to help the surgeon see.

Then I cleared a large table for the instruments.

I tried not to shudder as I pushed the reclining chair in which my daughter would be strapped nearer to the fire so they could cauterize the wound with a burning iron.

I shuddered, wondering how John and I could possibly bear witness to this. But I couldn't let our child face it alone. Just as I had promised her as a child, I would be with her, whatever might come.

"You're in the best possible hands," I told her as we made ready, brushing her beautiful auburn hair before giving it over to Sally to pin up away from her neck. "The surgeon will rid you of this illness and you'll see your own children grow old."

It's what I needed to believe as I helped her pick a dress to wear—one she could spare, since it would no doubt be stained with blood. But Nabby insisted upon her best church dress. "I must be garbed properly in case I'm soon to meet the Lord."

The doctor, his son, and assistants arrived in their frock coats and cravats, unpacking the needle-sharp fork, the glinting slicing knives, and grim-looking iron cauterizing spatula.

Seeing them, I was all atremble as I led my girl to the chair where she was to be bound. One of the doctor's assistants knelt to tighten and fasten a belt around each of my daughter's ankles. Another at each knee. Her waist and right arm. Only the left arm would remain free so it could be lifted to give access to the blade.

I watched them bind her with such mounting horror that when the doctor's assistant finally reached to unfasten Nabby's gown, I snapped, "*No.*"

Everyone turned to look at me—even Nabby—and at shame for my weakness, I made an excuse. "My daughter's virtue quails under this unwanted familiarity. Please let me undress her."

The doctor and his assistants withdrew a few paces, and I stepped toward Nabby, forcing an encouraging smile. Gently—so gently!—I removed the modest muslin fichu from round her neck. I kissed her head, then worked the delicate buttons at the back of her gown with its cheerful pattern of rosebuds and sprigs. A pattern I knew I would never look upon again without the memory of this monstrous moment.

At long last, I bared her breast and shoulder. And if Nabby's glassy eyes were any indication, already the laudanum was working on her.

I only wished it to work faster.

The surgeon said, "Forgive me, Mrs. Smith, but I must straddle your knees to get the best position for cutting."

His demeanor was as professional as possible. Nevertheless, the sight of a man climbing atop his daughter caused John's jaw to clench, and his hand to close hard over mine.

While an assistant held Nabby's left arm up and pressed her shoulder to the chair, I only saw a flash of metal as the surgeon quickly thrust the sharp fork into the flesh of my daughter's breast. Perhaps it was the swiftness with which he stabbed her, but she didn't cry out.

It was only when he lifted the speared breast on this fork to saw it off that Nabby grimaced—her legs straining in her desire to escape the knife. As blood began to flow, my mind was unwillingly thrown back to when she was a little girl, offering her arm to the doctor to cut for inoculation. I remembered the way she bit her lip, the way she tugged at her lace cuff, and the way she'd so bravely winced at the pain.

It is *like inoculation*, I repeated to myself. *It will save her life.*

But there was so much more blood as they severed her flesh, amputating the breast. So much blood that it tinged the air with iron.

Pain constricted in my own breast as I prayed, *God*, let me take this from Nabby. I would take it onto myself gladly!

Yet, all the while, Nabby was silent.

Though her teeth began to chatter through lips now tinged with blue.

It felt an *eternity* before the breast—tumor and all—was finally severed and thrown into a waiting basin with a horrifying wet slap.

In truth, it had been speedily done, and I swallowed a gasp of relief, knowing they now only needed to close the wound and dress it. But as the gore-spattered doctor investigated the flesh, he said, "The tumor has extended into the lymph nodes. I have to keep cutting."

No, no, no.

The mother in me wished to fly at this surgeon and wrestle his instruments away. Only John's hand gripping mine kept me still. How I wished they had bound me to the chair instead of my child.

As the surgeon razored away her flesh, I quaked. For glistening ruby in the light, blood now flowed in such quantity it looked as if someone had tipped a barrel of claret wine. It soaked the surgeon and Nabby both. It soaked the chair and the sheets on the floor beneath them.

I couldn't stand this macabre scene anymore, but neither could I swoon or avert my eyes. For Nabby's gaze met mine and held it.

"Brave girl," I whispered, willing my strength into her. "That's my brave girl."

At last, the surgeon reached for the hot iron to cauterize the wound. He pressed it down on my child with a hiss and spit, sending smoke into the air that smelled like charred flesh.

Not once, not twice, but *four* times did that iron brand her. And as Nabby groaned and twisted her head in agony, I twisted my own head, burying my face in John's shoulder.

When I could finally look again, I saw Nabby sagging with pain and exhaustion, her hair now hanging in sweat-soaked ringlets.

She had never screamed—not once. The heroine had endured it all with such fortitude that the doctors all proclaimed her the most stoic patient they had ever encountered. Not one cry—not even one *word*—had escaped my silent Nabby.

Nor did it now that all was over.

"It is all gone," the surgeon said, wiping his bloody hands with one of my dish towels. "The morbid substance is totally eradicated and nothing left but flesh perfectly sound. A complete success."

My knees now finally surrendered, and John and Sally had to hold me steady at the elbows lest I sink to the floor.

Meanwhile, an assistant freed Nabby from the chair upon which she'd been tortured.

It was left to Sally to tend to her now, stripping from Nabby the ruined dress, sponging her clean, helping her into fresh bedclothes, and taking charge of the laudanum doses that might allow her some rest.

The first night was the worst.

Though Nabby endured it with little complaint, the pain was too obviously brutal. Her daughter, Caroline, sat with her, making certain to adjust pillows or fetch water or relieve her in any way possible.

And this comforted me. The love of family would get my daughter through this—a sentiment I felt more keenly when, a few days later, Colonel Smith arrived on a Sunday morning, and the family reunion was nearly complete.

"She didn't wait," he said, blinking. He had, I think, half expected her to change her mind by the time he arrived. That the ordeal was already finished left him enormously relieved.

"She's up and walking a little," I told him. "Just from her chamber to mine and back. She's able to sit up most of the day. The wound has closed. Her arm, kept in a sling, she's forbidden to use. And though she is weak, I believe seeing you will revive her spirits."

That it did, for Colonel Smith was still handsome and dashing in his way. And he was gentle with my Nabby. If she worried he might think her mutilated, he put her mind at ease by repeating how beautiful she was. And she smiled a lovely smile before drifting back to sleep.

I was grateful for that. I'd long mourned that Nabby's once-brilliant marriage prospects had landed her with a man of neither good fortune nor good sense. But he *did* love her faithfully, and he was kind. Not every woman was so fortunate in marriage as that.

Chapter Fifty-Three

QUINCY
Massachusetts
March 1812

PEACEFIELD WAS NOW like a comfortable old shoe: still of good service but showing the signs of wear—for our large family had lived, quarreled, and cared for each other nearly a quarter of a century within its walls.

The cheerful yellow paint was so faded that it was now better papered over. Our Turkey carpets, so often beaten of dust, had certainly seen better days. And my once polished wood panels now boasted dents and finger smudges of so many grandchildren running about.

But to have a house filled with children's laughter was always a comfort to me. A recompense for the indignities of old age. Which is why I was so stricken by John Quincy's latest letter from Russia.

"He wants us to send his boys to live with Thomas," I said, numbly.

My husband's head snapped up from his book. "For what reason?"

"For their education."

Swiping the spectacles from his nose and throwing them down with a clatter, John said, "We were good enough teachers for him, so why not our grandsons? Does he think me so addled that I've forgot my arithmetic?"

I glanced out the foggy windows at John Quincy's boys playing with sticks and ball on the gravel path. Weedy George—soon to turn eleven—had inherited John Quincy's serious turn of mind, whereas eight-year-old John-John was a rough-and-tumble little fellow like his uncle Tommy at that age. And if I squinted, I could almost imagine myself a young mother again with my boys home with me, hearty and hale, their futures yet to be written.

Now I read from our son's letter. "The boys are coming of an age when they must learn much for which there are no schools. They have in their Uncle Tommy a manly example."

With Britain still menacing us, John Quincy wanted his boys instructed in the use of firearms. He wanted them both capable with muskets and pistols. He'd written, "In every thing of this kind I know there is danger; but it is a world of danger in which we live, and I want my boys to be familiar as soon as possible with its face, that they may be better guarded against it."

My husband's temper cooled a bit hearing this. "Whether here in Quincy or there in Braintree, Tommy can still teach them to shoot and ride."

Perhaps if their uncle Tommy could manage to stay upon his horse, was my unbidden thought.

Having lost a little infant daughter to the whooping cough, our youngest son had taken solace in a bottle. He struggled with what he said were the *blue devils* of depression. And he had recently taken a terrible drunken fall from his horse, injuring his leg so badly it was feared he might not walk again.

But none of this did John Quincy know.

And neither did my husband wish to acknowledge it. But the painful subject could no longer be avoided. "They cannot live with Tommy. They'd be no safer with him than they would've been with Charles at the end."

John's eyes bulged and filled with denial. "Tommy is a good farmer. A respected judge. He's having a hard time of it now, but he'll recover himself. He's steady."

This was how I knew John was terrified. He'd been stern and judgmental with Charles, and we'd lost him. Now my husband seemed to think that if we indulged and denied the disease, we wouldn't lose a second son to it, and I desperately hoped the same.

So, I pretended to accept Tommy's fall was a mere accident. And I didn't raise the matter of whiskey when, in a hunting incident not long after, he nearly shot a neighbor.

But neither would I allow Johnny's boys to go live with their uncle Thomas.

John Quincy simply couldn't judge the situation from Russia.

And despite what he'd written about guns and manly pursuits, they needed actual schooling with *books*.

Perhaps they were too cosseted here. We did pet and pamper them, lavishing all the affection upon them that we could not lavish upon their father. So, I chose to interpret John Quincy's words liberally and send Johnny's boys to study in New Hampshire under the watchful gaze of my sister Elizabeth.

My sister had re-married after being widowed, and her new husband, the Reverend Peabody, was an enlightened educator who taught boys and girls at his academy. Johnny's boys could learn much there, and if he didn't like it, he could return from Russia to fetch them himself.

Our grandsons went off before Sunday dinner, at which their uncle Tommy's fork lay untouched, sauce congealing next to the ham on his plate. I noticed he'd passed over most of the food, tasting only a spoonful of oyster stew, making little crumbs of the crusty bread in his fist. "Johnny wanted them to live with me."

This utterance silenced the table, and with my stomach in knots, I hastened to make excuse. "But you're so often absent. The raising of those boys would fall on your poor wife, and she has children enough to tend."

Tommy tossed his napkin onto the table and slid back in his chair. "I'm thirty-nine years old. The state of Massachusetts has seen fit to make me chief justice of the Circuit Court of Common Pleas for the Southern Circuit. But my *mother*—"

"Your *mother*," my husband interrupted, attempting to avert the imminent clash. Pointing his fork in Tommy's direction, he continued, "Your mother has watched over you and your siblings with benevolence all your life. That is what your mother has done."

This answer didn't appease our youngest son, whose voice quavered in asking, "Did it occur to either of you that I, too, was sent off to board with Aunt Elizabeth when my parents were absent? Might you have asked me what I thought of the experience?"

At that, our son's wife, Ann, reached for his clenched fist, covering it with her own gentle hand. Glancing at the children, Ann let her voice fall to a whisper. "Perhaps we can discuss this after dinner."

There were, after all, gathered around us various family members, including my wide-eyed grandchildren. So, Tommy held his peace, his fists clenched, his brow furrowed, and his eyes burning with unspoken emotions.

After the plum pudding was served, the children went to play, and the servants cleared their plates. Then Tommy raised the subject again, his voice firmer than before. "You've little idea what it was like to be a child with scarcely a memory of one's parents to sustain you. To be shown pictures and told to love and worship these absent figures as if they were deities."

"Thomas, be careful where you tread," John warned, knife suspended in air as if ready to fence.

But our son didn't cower before his father's displeasure; he squared his shoulders and put both hands on the table. "You have little idea what it's like not knowing whether your absent parents would care, or even believe you, if you sent word of what it was like to live under the roof of Reverend Shaw. To live in fear of his strap—and of the fist he drove into Aunt Elizabeth's ribs and belly when he thought we weren't watching."

I startled to hear this. Truly, I startled, halfway out of my chair, my lips parted in dismay. Of course I'd known my sister feared her first husband's temper. But she'd never detailed the violence Tommy described. And jaw still agape, I sputtered, "Why did you never tell us this before?"

Tommy folded his strong arms. "Why did you never ask?"

My husband and I both fell utterly silent with mortification. Into that silence Tommy continued, "Shall I tell you who did ask? Johnny. My brother knows what we suffered, even under the eye of a loving aunt. Which is why he preferred to have the boys with me."

All but stammering, my husband finally said, "But—but—but Reverend Shaw is long dead now, and Reverend Peabody is a different sort of man."

Tommy stood and shoved his chair into place. "Pray you are right. Because I will not be held to account for this decision."

Reverend Shaw, I thought bitterly. I'd never liked that man. I'd tried to dissuade my sister from marrying him. And I'd been *right*! Yet, I'd delivered my boys into that man's hands for their education. What had they suffered there?

Given Tommy's explosive emotions, I feared to ask. Not only for what it might say of his depressions but also for the questions it raised about Charles. I'd asked myself a thousand times if—given a different childhood—our middle son would've lived.

I did not like the answer now suggested to me.

I followed Tommy into the hall, heart hammering as I reached to clutch his arm. "Did Reverend Shaw hurt you?"

My son's back stiffened. "I've said all I'm going to say about it."

Oh, my children, and their infuriating silences!

Words felt too insignificant for the weight of sentiment I wished to convey, but still I must speak them. "Tommy, I wish I'd known."

My son's pained sigh crossed the distance between us. And when he leaned to kiss my cheek in farewell, with lips gone cold and dry, he smelled of whiskey and sorrow.

That night, I sat down to pen a letter to John Quincy, advising him to come home. "A father and a mother may be too long absent from their children."

And if he would not come home, I now thought it best to send his boys to him in Russia.

Chapter Fifty-Four

QUINCY
Massachusetts
Summer 1812

T HESE DAYS I used a magnifying glass to sort the mail for neither John nor I could see well anymore. I squinted over each missive. Still, I'd know Thomas Jefferson's penmanship anywhere . . .

When I realized that John wasn't surprised to receive a letter from our old nemesis, I flapped the note accusingly. "You're writing to Jefferson?"

John shrugged like a child caught with his finger in the plum pudding. "Now that we're both retired from the arena, what harm can a correspondence do?"

With both hands on my hips, I stood aghast. "How can you forget the ways in which that man schemed against you and your presidency and your place in posterity?"

"Yet, *you* wrote a passel of letters to him behind my back, as I recall . . ."

I pressed my lips together, guilty as charged. In the end, all I could say was "I don't see why you'd repeat my folly."

With a sly side-glance, my husband asked, "Aren't you corresponding with Mrs. Warren again? Surely you recall how much pain *she* caused me and my place in posterity. With less cause, I might add."

I was, in fact, guilty of that, too.

Mercy had sent a kind note asking after Nabby's surgery, and I hadn't been able to snub her. I was overjoyed that the surgery had been a success, and beyond grateful that my daughter was well enough to return to her husband on his farm in New York. But I was lonelier without Nabby. And then, of course, there was the loneliness of growing old. A narrowing of one's social circle as ancient friends and loved ones passed away.

In recent years, I'd lost my beloved sister Mary. Her husband, Mr. Cranch, had passed, too. Phoebe was sick and dying. Uncle Tufts was not long for this world. And perhaps that's why I was willing to exchange pleasantries with Mercy Otis Warren. "But *Jefferson!*"

"I know who he is. Warts and all."

"Oh, no one on earth knows Jefferson truly. He's always been a riddle worthy of the sphinx."

"Enough." John waved me off. "We're too advanced in life now to leave grudges between us and the grave. Or to deny ourselves any remaining pleasure in life. Despite all, I love Jefferson and I've always loved Jefferson. I cannot explain it, but it is true."

I certainly couldn't explain it. But there was no denying that the Sage of Monticello had a talent for hurting those who loved him, while making his victims love him still.

Perhaps that's why he'd done so well in politics.

I was determined to hold my grudge to the grave, but the important thing, I supposed, was that John was writing again. Tremors still marred his pen, but he threw himself into a renewed correspondence with Jefferson. It solaced him and sharpened his mind to correspond with one of only three men living who knew what it was to be the president of the United States.

I could not begrudge him that.

While John took to his desk making peace with an old foe, it seemed that some fights would never end.

Not for two consecutive years in the past forty had the British refrained from committing some violent outrage upon us. Whether shooting at us, seizing our ships, kidnapping our soldiers, refusing to honor our treaties, or destroying our commerce, they never ceased in their attacks. Four presidents had tried everything—from neutrality to trade agreements to boycotts and embargoes.

Now Congress had finally declared war. A Second War of Independence, they called it, and I fretted to think my grandsons might take up arms. For now, a new generation would have to fight for our freedoms, and if such fights could never be won, then each generation must fight anew.

As American men began joining militias and mustering to fend off British invasion again, Phoebe was fighting a different kind of war. The war we all fought against time.

Her memory had stuttered. She needed help dressing herself; she no longer remembered to eat. Some days she stood by the window, having fallen mute, deaf, and dumb to all around her.

I came every morning with porridge, milk puddings, and other soft foods Phoebe could still chew. And every morning, she'd say, "It's been so long since I've seen you, Miss Abby. Where are you coming back from now, Honey?"

"Just over the hill," I said.

Phoebe shook her head. "I told my husband just yesterday that you've been to Paris, London, Philadelphia, and every place in the world."

She didn't remember that she had been widowed. And I knew better than to remind her and put her in grief anew. Instead, I squeezed her hand, and she squeezed mine in return.

"I've still got the lace handkerchief you sent me," Phoebe said, pulling a dirtied old cloth from between her bosoms. "The one from Paris."

I was touched to know her disordered mind still treasured it.

"When will I see you again?" Phoebe asked.

"Tomorrow morning," I promised.

I was sixty-eight years old—too old and infirm myself to stay with her overnight. Neither could I bear to leave her alone. Thankfully, my granddaughters, nieces, and daughter-in-law took shifts with her at night.

It took two of them at a time to manage her because she needed help getting up from bed at night.

"Your granddaughters are kind girls," Phoebe said. "Tender-hearted, like their father. But too pious, if there could be such a thing."

Charlie's daughters were never to be found without their prayer books. They thought the Bible itself would fend off the dissipation that had carried off their father, and I was not keen to disabuse them of that notion. But I had learned that prayer alone seldom fended off evil.

Phoebe gripped my hand harder. "I wanted to see freedom before I passed. Freedom for all."

"I wanted that, too," I said, knowing that slavery was, in the South, more entrenched than ever and expanding into new states. And as for women, it sometimes felt as if we were back to where we started without having accomplished anything at all.

"It's been so long since I've seen you, Miss Abby. Where are you coming back from now?"

"Just over the hill," I said, tears brimming.

"When will I see you again?"

"Tomorrow morning, my dear Phoebe."

That I loved her, I always knew. That I respected her was something I only came to know later. That I venerated her as a mother I did not know until this long and painful parting.

I was with Phoebe when she passed, my pale fingers twined with her dark ones. By then, she no longer knew how to dress, how to eat, or even how to swallow. She had forgotten me, forgotten her husband, forgotten herself, forgotten all but the Lord, whose name she whispered with her last breath.

Phoebe had every reason to resent my sisters and me for the sins of our father holding her in bondage. For the way we benefited from her labors and felt entitled to her affections. We were grown women when she finally achieved her freedom, and she might have abandoned all ties to us without a backward glance. Especially when, as much as we loved her, we never did treat her with the true equality she deserved. And that was a shame that would weigh upon me the rest of my life. Alas, there was yet more pain in store.

Chapter Fifty-Five

QUINCY
Massachusetts
Summer 1813

M Y HEART BROKE when the carriage door opened to reveal my poor daughter—emaciated and worn down with pain, her once lustrous hair now dull and brittle. For the cancer had returned—worse than before—and if I'd harbored hopes that more surgeries might save her, they were extinguished now.

This time my beloved daughter had come home to die.

As her son lifted her from the carriage, her arm dangled weak and pale, for she had survived a courageous, nearly impossible journey of more than three hundred miles in agonizing pain. We settled her upstairs, where, despite the summer's heat, she shivered under three quilts. Her children and I sat beside her, my thumbs worrying over her bony fingers until Nabby roused herself from the opium.

Her eyelids heavy, her breathing slow and calm, she took one look at my shattered expression and said, "It's all right, Mama."

No, I thought, denying what my eyes clearly saw—that despite seeing her through the trials of a brutal surgery, the Lord had now seen fit to let cancer eat her alive. How could she say that anything was right about this?

But as my insides flailed in view of the chasm of heartbreak before me, Nabby's blue eyes were serene. "I am perfectly sensible to my situation. Grateful for the life I've led. For the love I've given and received. For the children bestowed upon me. I'm reconciled to my end."

Well, I was not reconciled to it!

I shook my head so hard I hurt my own neck, wishing away this tragedy. I wanted to scream and howl at the injustice of it.

Not my Nabby. Not my precious girl. Not the young girl who had been my closest companion in those long days of the war without John. Not the young woman so full of life who had married the man of her heart. Not the mother who had already suffered torments no one should ever be called to endure.

It took all my strength to simply hold her hand and offer comfort and calm. But her eyes *pleaded* with me to be calm. "Mama, I want to choose my own hymnal for my funeral, but I'm too tired to hold the book. Will you turn the pages for me?"

I nodded, one of the few times in my life I was unable to speak. So dark were my thoughts about an unmerciful God that I feared to hold the hymn book lest it singe my fingertips. Nevertheless, I held the hymn book for her in my own shaking, age-spotted hands and let her choose "Longing for Heaven."

She spoke of other final arrangements with a contentment and gentleness meant to ease the pain of all those who loved her.

I admired this strength in my daughter. A strength I had not often recognized for its silence, but which had always been present from the days she ran to fetch help when I had dysentery, to the way she endured bankruptcy, abandonment, and disgrace. And through it all, she'd protected her family to the very end. Even to the point that when, to everyone's surprise, Colonel Smith had been elected to congress, she insisted he remain in Washington City until he was satisfied that he had done his duty for the war effort. It cost her the comfort of her dearest friend whilst she lay dying, but her chief concern was for her husband's honor.

While we awaited his imminent arrival, we all tended her. Sally took charge of the medications. Tommy helped write letters for his sister to those she wished to say farewell. Nabby's children read to her from books when she had the strength to listen. And the other grandchildren made themselves quiet in the house so that Nabby could rest.

I sat with my daughter during the day, but it was my husband who kept her company in the worst, most agonizing hours of the night. Despite his arthritic knees, he went up and down the stairs with trays of milk toast, stewed peaches, snipped roses from the garden, or little books of verse—anything to cheer or distract her from the pain.

One evening, when we went to her together with an old bundle of letters from our time together in Paris, Nabby was too tired to read them, but her gaze lingered on the lace that bound them. "What extraordinary parents I have," she said, eyes soft and dewy. "I hope I have been in my life a source of comfort to you, if not pride."

My husband looked away, a knot bobbing in his throat. He had to clear it before he could speak. "No child could be more so . . ."

A wilting smile passed over Nabby's lips. Then, spent of energy, she closed her eyes. "I dined on warships," she said, dreamily. "I saw London. I saw Paris. I danced at balls with ministers of state. I fell in love. Had beautiful children. My father was the President of the United States. And my mother . . . oh, how God blessed me to have such a life and *such a mother*."

It was too much. I stood rigid, overwhelmed by her grace. Then I fled.

In the hall, I pressed my forehead against the door, trembling with my efforts not to wail. I cursed myself for my weakness when my daughter was so courageous, but I could not contain myself and gasped with wet sobs for the grief of what was soon to come.

In the end, our daughter died clasped in her husband's tearful embrace, surrounded by her family. She'd smiled through the agonies to spare our hearts, then cheerfully surrendered her life to her Maker.

At the funeral, the well-meaning reverend reminded me that Nabby was partaking of that immortality brought by him who endured the cross and went before to prepare a place for her. So, I could resign her into the hands of that being who gave her to me and had the best right to take her.

But it was the worst affliction of my life.

I will never recover from this, I thought. Oh, I might still float through existence in this aging body. But I'd never wish for life's continuance.

It was Nabby who had first made me a mother. She had thus,

in some sense, defined my adult life as much as my marriage to John. Now I scarcely knew myself.

With Nabby, all my daughters were dead and gone, buried in the soil of a country that did not value them, and lost to a world that never deserved them.

My husband, too, seemed lost.

One evening I found him sitting on the bottom stair, head in his hands. Instinctively, I sat beside him, and he turned to my shoulder and sobbed. "I keep thinking I must go up to bring her a tray of supper, only to remember she's gone. Our baby girl, our precious jewel. She's gone, forever."

It was the way of nature that, in old age, one begins to lose everything acquired in life. We lose friends, family, hair, teeth, the ability to see and hear. Everything goes, and every day, we grow less attached to that which makes life worth living.

But it is unnatural to bury a child, and we had buried four.

IN THE MISERABLE year after my daughter's death, meetings where sermons and psalms had so often sustained me now felt a hollow exercise. Our prayers—whether for our country or for our family—had been coldly and brutally refused.

Our punishment, perhaps, for thinking ourselves creatures of free will. For having the temerity to believe that our good works, that our choices—moral or otherwise—might justify an earthly reward.

In the end, maybe the Calvinists were right that we were merely puppets upon God's stage, preordained to succeed or suffer only at the whims of our Divine Creator.

These thoughts burned a hole in my heart.

So, when I went to the First Parish Church it was not for the scripture, but to visit the sepulcher where Nabby was buried.

I planted flowers and herbs and shrubbery, speaking to my daughter as if she could still hear me. I told her of the progress of my garden, of her father's aches and pains, and of her son, who was now defending New York's harbor against the British as an officer in the 2nd Battalion, 11th Regiment of Artillery, State Militia.

But I didn't tell her how poorly the war went for us.

We'd lost the Battle of Queenston Heights on the Niagara. The British were blockading the Chesapeake Bay. And as I knelt by Nabby's grave and dug in the dirt, I knew full well that redcoats had landed in Maryland and were now marching on our capital.

If I weren't so miserable and defeated, I'd have laughed at the perversity of it. If the British conquered us again, it would mean the final unraveling of all John and I had dedicated our lives to.

I could find no purpose to it.

No purpose to the entirety of my life, for I was no mother anymore. God had taken my children, one by one. First little Susanna, then the daughter who died before I could name her. Then Charles and Nabby. Thomas behaved as a distant stranger now, always drunk. And John Quincy was a world away . . .

By death, drink, or distance, they were all gone.

And perhaps now we'd lose the country, too.

It was all, everything, falling to pieces.

Chapter Fifty-Six

QUINCY
Massachusetts
September 1814

I AM QUIET NEXT to my husband in the carriage, still absorbing the news. With Washington burning as John has reported to me, my fears are all realized. The British mean to put an end to the United States of America, and they are winning.

Would it have been better, I wonder, never to have known the blessings of liberty than to have enjoyed it and then have it ravished from us?

I don't know the answer.

I only know that with no children, and no country, and every sacrifice for naught, I cannot think of a reason to go on.

Like me, John is also silent as we return to Peacefield, for I know his mind is as filled with dark ruminations as my own. When we reach our gate, we find friends, neighbors, servants, relations—all gathered to exchange bits of what they've heard.

"President Madison narrowly escaped the British—"

"—they found his dinner still hot on the table—"

"They say Mrs. Madison was a great patriot that day!"

Allegedly, in the chaos of the attack, before she would flee, the president's wife rescued crucial government papers, stuffing them into trunks while directing the doorkeeper and the gardener to cut down the painting of George Washington so it would not fall into British hands.

Someone asks, "Where is President Madison now?"

"In hiding, they say," John replies. "The army is cowering and the capital laid waste."

I feel so sick at heart I want to climb into bed, cover my head, and never awaken from my slumber. But somehow duty still resides in me like a bad habit. And though I am a very old woman now, I remember that I, too, was once the lady of first rank in this republic.

It behooves me to show some of Mrs. Madison's fortitude, so to our nervous and frightened neighbors, I say, "Washington was a city in name only—an embryo in the wilderness, inhabited largely by enslaved people who cannot be expected to defend it. The British will not find our other cities so easily taken."

I don't know if this is true, but it isn't my place to drag others down with me into the depths of gloom. There is *still* some remnant of my upbringing, some iron at the core of me, that keeps my back straight.

John predicts that the British will next attack Baltimore, but if *I* were to give the dastardly villains advice, I'd tell them to try Boston. For here in Massachusetts, Federalists have been braying that we should secede from the union. These remnants of Hamilton's faction would happily surrender to the British, for they want no more of this unholy union with slave states.

But John believes *union* is all that can save us from becoming the hewers of wood and drawers of water for our British masters. I don't know if I agree. I only know that it is all out of my aged hands. I can offer a stiff upper lip, but young men on the battlefield will decide our future.

Yet, even knowing my own grandson is in the fight, in this desperate hour, the destiny of men is not what occupies my thoughts.

I have decided that if everything else is to collapse, at least *I* will remember the ladies.

IN THE DAYS that follow, with the nation's fate hanging by a thread, I am occupied at my desk with a magnifying glass, scribbling with pained hands now stained by ink. My fingers hurt in every joint, and my penmanship is pitiful. But still I keep writing, scratching out lines, and tossing whole pages into the crackling fire to begin anew.

I burn the candle down without stopping for meals. Nor do

I eat much when trays are brought to me. And John becomes distressed. Hobbling into the room with the latest dispatches, my husband leans on his cane to inform me, "The tide of the war may be turning . . ."

I'm unwilling to believe it. "We always said that during the revolution. Yet it dragged on eight years."

John glances at my writing table where I've covered my scribblings. "What are you up to, Abigail?"

I've no intention of endangering my enterprise by speaking of it prematurely, so I say, "You'll know soon enough."

But he's not content to leave me to my writing. My mysterious and manic behavior drives him mad. And every hour he intrudes upon my work with the excuse of *news*.

Eventually, I close the door.

When that doesn't stop him, I lock it.

Through the keyhole, he shouts, "Abigail, I have news!"

He's like one of the grandchildren pestering at me for attention, but I cannot simply send him outside to play. "Unless you've come to tell me that we've sunk the British Isles, I don't wish to hear it."

"We've won a battle," he says.

In spite of myself, I unlock the door.

"In Lake Champlain," John says, flapping the dispatch in my face with pride. "*My navy* . . ."

Oh, he was once mocked for his insistence upon a navy, but now it might be our salvation, and his chest swells as if he'd been the admiral of the flagship.

"Baltimore!" John crows, flapping another dispatch that neither of us can read without squinting. "The British attacked Fort McHenry. Bombarded our soldiers for twenty-five hours. We drove them off!"

I have to sit down again to digest this.

It is good news. Monumental news.

It is, in fact, a *miracle*.

But my battered heart doesn't trust it. I read the dispatches for myself, my eyes already strained and weary, but now wet, too, with the possibility that all might not be lost.

My desperate mind tells me this is decisive—this must mean the end of the war. Our enemies may have burned our capital but they will leave, yet again, with ashes in their mouths, and these United States will remain free!

Hope sparks a fire in my breast, giving me the final inspiration I need to finish what may be the most telling act of my life. And the next morning dawns brighter than any in recent memory.

I join my husband in the parlor amongst the Louis XV sofa and chairs, the four-seat ottoman, the tiny end tables, and the other souvenirs of our time in Europe now gone shabby with age. Wrapped in a shawl, I carry a rolled document that John eyes suspiciously as he dabs apple butter upon a biscuit.

With one hand, I struggle to pull down the sash of the open window to block the autumn chill. And John grouses, "Now we must close windows during the day as well as night?"

"We're too old to let such cold into the house."

"But I like the earthy scents of our orchard," he says, taking a ferocious bite of his biscuit. And when he finishes chewing, he glints me a mischievous smile. "Besides, I'm not cold at all. I'm warmed from within by the knowledge of today's anniversary. Happy day of jubilee, Mrs. Adorable! Or did you forget?"

"I did not forget." Despite all the despair of recent days, I cannot help but smile. And clutching his arm for balance, I lower into the chair beside him. Then I kiss his beloved cheek, thumbing away a bit of apple butter from the wrinkled corner of his lips. "Fifty years of marriage to my good man, finding our way through love, war, politics, and revolution. Only to wind up back where we started."

"Not *quite* where we started." John nods at the window to encompass our orchard, our farms, our lovely house.

"You are in an unusually pleasant mood," I accuse, still clutching my rolled-up paper.

And John's smile is nearly smug. "How can I be otherwise when I am in the company of my beloved wife, and our star-spangled banner yet waves?"

"You think we've won the war then . . ."

"I think it a draw, but we'll call it victory and be glad."

The faint stirrings of long-absent faith warm my breast. "*Praise*

God," I say and mean it earnestly for the first time in a very long time. "Can it be that Providence has saved the United States?"

John is thoughtful. "No. We may make ourselves popular by boasting that Americans are the chosen people, exceptional by nature and worthy of God's special notice. But it will be flattery and delusion. If this republic survives, it will always be because we saved it ourselves."

"Yet here we are in a state of turmoil and distress, in suspense of knowing whether the liberty of the country is truly secure."

He takes my hand, brushing a kiss across the knuckles. "We've lived nearly all our fifty years of marriage in a state of turmoil and distress. So why should today be any different?"

I surprise myself with a laugh that bubbles up from my chest. The first laugh I can remember in a very long time. "You speak the truth. For I daresay that if we have ever had a dull or untroubled year, I cannot remember it."

"Nevertheless, we have both lived with a determination to suck the marrow out of whatever joys might still remain between us and the grave."

That was true until this last year. I am painfully aware that old age gallops upon us with rapid strides, and there are matters between us I must, at long last, resolve.

"I've a gift for you to mark the occasion of our anniversary," I say, reaching into a pocket to pull forth a fob for his gold pocket watch.

It has a pendant similar to the one he gifted me before leaving for France. And squinting to examine it in the light, John seems quite moved. He blinks several times, clutching my gift to his heart, his expression filled with adoration.

At last, his gaze drops to the fob, and he fiddles with the chain, sheepish. "Now I feel a doddering fool for I've no gift of equal value for you. I meant to surprise you with a sumptuous feast, fearing you'd scold me if I gifted you with anything grander."

"As it happens," I say, mustering my courage, "there *is* a gift I want from you. And it will be far grander, and more expensive, than any gift you've ever given me."

"Now you frighten me," John says.

"This is my Last Will and Testament," I say, unrolling the paper to show him.

"*Abigail*," he whispers with what sounds like dismay. "None of this, now. I didn't think you, of all people, would surrender."

"This isn't surrender," I say, slightly affronted. "When the lengthening shadows admonish us of approaching night, it must reconcile us to our destiny. Thus, my twilight hours ought to affirm who I am, who I have been, and what legacy I leave."

"Explain," John says.

I pull my shawl tighter round my shoulders, less to guard me from the cold than from the potential for disappointment. "By law in this country that you fathered, I own nothing. I *am* nothing other than Mrs. John Adams."

His chest sinks, curling inward, as if taking a blow. "Is that so inconsiderable a thing to be?"

"No, my dearest. It is the pride of my life. I do not regret that upon our marriage vows, we became one. Nor that I have toiled beside you for fifty years of marriage, running with you every risk of ruin. But I am not your equal unless you acknowledge it to be so."

He doesn't bristle, as he might've in the old days. Instead, he reaches for his spectacles to read what I've written.

His silence weighs heavy and is too oppressive for me to bear. So I say, "I turn to you for justice where the law denies it. To you, my husband, my partner, my dearest friend—the man most apt to recognize my rights as a citizen. Important amongst them the right to do as I please with monies earned by my own industry."

John finally gives up reading the document. He hands it to me to read for him. I know he long ago surmised that I amassed a fortune; I also know he doesn't like to think about the grubby business of money. But he's no fool. It hasn't escaped his notice that I always find the funds we need. He simply decided not to ask the details, until now.

Steeling himself, he asks, "How much?"

When I tell him, his eyes widen, as if they might pop from his skull. Then he asks, "What is it that you want to do with it?"

"I want to give it to our granddaughters. Our daughters-in-law. My nieces. Our women servants. My lady friends and widowed neighbors. I want to give it to *women*. And I want them to have a right to it."

"But how—"

I cut him off with an upraised hand, because I dare not let him muster a legal argument against me. Not until he has heard me out. "You were a formidable lawyer, John. So, you must help me accomplish it somehow." Predicting one possible objection, I promise, "I will do our male heirs no injustice. I know you'll provide for them of your farm and the lands in Vermont. But I want to provide for the women."

John shakes his head a bit, attempting levity. "What a peculiar fancy."

"It's no fancy. I asked you once to remember the ladies and you laughed at me, John. You *laughed*."

Well, he does not dare laugh now.

He winces, which emboldens me to continue. "John, you may no longer be in a position to make our laws fair to my sex, but you can be fair to *me*."

Furrows deepen in his brow. He blows out a breath then holds his hand out to me, asking to see the paper again. I give it to him, and let him stare, though I wager he is only buying time to think.

If his eyes can make it all out, he'll see I've accounted for everything. Clothing, bed linens, jewelry, and furniture. Even my shares in local bridges. And then, of course, the larger sums I've hidden away.

How consternated John looks. His lips twist, he grunts, and I sense a storm brewing. So, I hasten to explain. "I want my Last Will to say something. To mean something. And yet, you look so vexed that I fear you may deny me, and then I shall not be held to account for my heart."

"My dearest friend," John begins. "The only thing that vexes me is that this document supposes you will die before me—a thought I cannot bear."

"You will do it then? You'll do this for me?"

John nods slowly, solemnly. "I will find a way. Your will, Abigail, will be done. Whether I breathe yet or no. I gladly make you this vow and will keep it with the same fidelity as the one I made at the altar fifty years ago."

Never in happiness or grief have I ever felt so untethered, my spirit cut loose. Entirely overcome, I cover my mouth with both hands. I fear I will cry. I fear I will laugh. I fear I will do both at the same time. "Oh, John . . ."

He draws me into the circle of arms once strong enough to carry me to bed, now trembling with age around my shoulders. And I fall into his embrace, my home and my haven.

Against my ear, he rasps, "But you are mistaken in one thing, my lovely Portia."

Wetting his neckcloth with grateful tears, I look up into his eyes to ask, "About what am I mistaken?"

John chuckles, the warmth of his breath caressing my face. "You said this would be an expensive gift. But the love and happiness shining in your eyes recompenses me so lavishly I am in *your* debt."

"I am yours," I say, because it is true love between us then after all. He has allowed it to be. "I am, wholly, and *freely*, yours whatever comes."

John kisses me tenderly and smooths my hair. "Whatever comes, they will say that of *all* the decisions President John Adams made in his life, none was more brilliant or consequential than marrying you."

Epilogue

QUINCY
Massachusetts
Summer 1817

WHAT GOOD LONG letter is complete without a postscript? Like so many of the missives I wrote or cherished to receive, it seems my story, too, will close with a tender trailing note.

Here I am still alive at the age of seventy-two. And John at eighty-one. My thinning hair is *entirely* white, and what few hairs he has left are white, too. We are stooped. Our steps are slow and shaky. John naps often by the fire, and I am never to be found without my shawl, even in summer.

Except for today, when I am warmed with an inner *conflagration* of joy.

At long last, my son is returning to me. And when John Quincy steps out of the carriage at our gate, I feel light-headed, nearly faltering to see his beloved face—a face I believed I'd never see again.

It has been so long since last I beheld him. And as he comes into my arms, I weep. "Eight years! Eight long years . . ." I clutch him tight as pride and gratitude fill the ancient vessel of my person to the brim. "My darling boy."

John Quincy is now a man of fifty, the roundness of his face all his father. Those penetrating eyes still all mine. And he holds me tight, as if he knows I'm close to a swoon.

Now John reaches to share in our embrace. I remember when my husband's voice boomed through a courtroom, but now his voice is a thin reed. "My son! Johnny, my son, my child . . ."

What a reunion it is, with tears and laughter. Our grandsons all but dance with excitement. Even their stiff English mother, Louisa Catherine, beams with happiness, looping her arm in mine to help me back up onto the porch.

Once we are seated in our rockers, I follow John Quincy's gaze as it sweeps over Peacefield and its weather-beaten shutters, overgrown hedges, and the stone wall in bad need of repair. After so long abroad, he's taking it in. His country, his state, his family, and what will one day be his house.

John and I are both embarrassed that in our old age we can no longer maintain it to our liking. "I'm afraid that like its owners, Peacefield has gone to decay. But not the less ready or willing to welcome and accommodate you until, like a bird of passage, you again take flight."

Like his father, I believe he is destined for greatness, our son.

After a loss of more than twenty thousand American and British soldiers, John Quincy Adams ended our Second War of American Independence by negotiating the peace treaty at Ghent. And for his reward, our son was recalled home, having been nominated and *unanimously* confirmed as President Monroe's secretary of state.

The country will soon claim him, but for this month's respite, he will be all ours.

Johnny, his wife, and his children stay a month with us. And we savor every moment. The butter on our toast tastes sweeter every breakfast we share together. The fire glows brighter at night as we listen to all the news from Europe that is fit to share. And there is even a lessening of our griefs as we share an accounting of the family.

Having abandoned his wife after a drunken quarrel, Tommy's whereabouts are not known to us. My sister Elizabeth, Uncle Tufts, and Colonel Smith are all gone to their graves. John Quincy and his wife, too, share their pain of having lost a little daughter while abroad.

There is too much loss to make sense of.

But there have been gains, as well.

I tell my son the news of his nieces and nephews. How Nabby's daughter, Caroline, made us great-grandparents, having forged a brilliant marriage match with the wealthy Mr. John DeWindt, a businessman and investor in the new Erie Railroad along the Hudson River. Nabby's son Willy also has a daughter now, albeit in circumstances far less financially secure. His brother, Jack, is yet childless but earning good money. And both of Charlie's daughters have married well.

The seeds John and I sowed have multiplied. And whilst I know I won't live to see how each will bloom, I take great satisfaction to witness them take root.

I want to keep Johnny with us forever, but as the month stretches on, I sense that he is tarrying. That he dreads to take up his place in Washington City.

"I must get my boys established at Harvard first," he says. "And I must have advice from my father on how I shall proceed as secretary of state."

He lingers with John in the study for hours.

But not all nights are for his father.

Tonight, I find him at the fire, his brow furrowed as he waits for me. And I know something weighs upon his mind. John Quincy has always been a prodigious thinker—more so, even, than my husband, I suspect. I am sure he feels the enormity of his new office. Like his father before him, he will be shaping the future of the nation. It need not be said it is firm tradition now that the position of the secretary of state leads to the presidency.

"John Quincy Adams," I say, reaching for his hand in reassurance. "I know you doubt yourself at times. But I remind you yet again that there is no one better qualified. You personally witnessed the opening scenes of the revolution not far from where we now sit. You've traveled the world, contending with international intriguers in more countries than many of your fellow citizens even know exist. You mustn't allow worries about what the future holds, because there's no one in this entire country better prepared to help America meet that future."

My son smiles without looking at me, his fingers lacing affectionately with mine. "I'm less worried for the future of the country than I am for my parents."

Surprised, I ask, "What worries you?"

"Upstairs just now, my father told me that in all the vicissitudes of his fortunes, through all the good and evil of the world, in all his struggles, and in all his sorrows that the help and encouragement of his wife was his never-failing support, without which he'd never have survived."

I flush as these words linger in my mind with pleasure. "Does not Louisa Catherine do the same for you?"

I ought not have asked it, for my daughter-in-law struggles at times with my son's emotional reserve. But time seems to have sanded the edges of their relationship, dulling the misunderstandings and sharpening the shared sense of purpose. So, I'm relieved to hear him say, "Indeed, she does. She's the delight and pride of my life."

"Then what troubles you?"

"It is that *you*, Mother, have been the hub of the wheel in this family. And if I take my wife and children to Washington—if we leave you again—I fear you'll sink under it, as I'm told you did when Nabby . . ."

He trails off, staring into the fire, suddenly unable to express himself, as if he's eloquent in all the languages of the world but that of emotion.

Lowering his head into his hands, he asks, "How can I leave you again, knowing all that I owe you? Knowing that you've been more to me than a mother, that all that I am is what you have made me?"

My son's words fill me with the sweetest pain—love and pride swelling to burst. "I'm honored to know you think so. But I did *not* make you all that you are. You're what I made you, what your father made you, and what *you* made of yourself thereafter."

His throat bobs under my scrutiny until I realize what I must promise him. "I won't sink in parting from you this time. I shall soar."

"Soar?" His expression turns wry. "Have I overstayed my welcome?"

"Never," I say, pulling his hand to my lips to kiss. "I am greedy for your company, but you're no longer a world away in snowy Russia. I shall have the nameless satisfactions of knowing that you're within reach. And that you carry all my hopes and dreams within you."

I press my lips to the top of his head, marveling at the fine mind held within it, and the even greater heart below. Like the country he will serve, he has such a great capacity to do good in the world. And there is no sacrifice of my life I regret to have helped make it so.

After all, a mother can never know if her children or country will survive. She cannot know if her struggles and sacrifices to defend them will ever be known or appreciated. She cannot guarantee that teachings she gives or the faith she cherishes in them from infancy will take root. Nevertheless, she must create, defend, guide, and put her faith in what she loves. For the Lord has given us this one life to sow goodness for mankind, even if we don't live long enough to partake of that harvest.

It is all for a purpose. None of it for naught.

Not a single moment for naught.

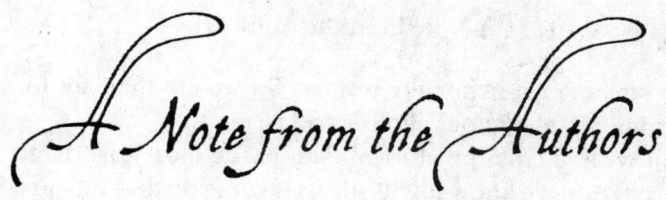

A Note from the Authors

ABIGAIL ADAMS DIED of typhoid fever on October 28, 1818, three days after her fifty-fourth wedding anniversary and a little more than a year after her son John Quincy Adams took his place in Washington as secretary of state.

As she lay dying, the doctors, perhaps fearing agitation, forbade her to speak or be spoken to. But Abigail had never been a woman to be silenced.

To her husband, who was so upset to see her suffering that he expressed a wish that he could lie down beside her and die, too, she said, "Do not grieve, my friend, my dearest friend. I am ready to go."

Though bereft without her, John adjusted to Abigail's death as if it were just one more of their many long absences from one another. John Adams lived almost another eight years, famously dying on July 4, 1826, the fiftieth anniversary of the Declaration of Independence. Newspapers reported his last words to be "Thomas Jefferson still survives"; in truth, the Virginian had preceded him in death by five hours.

While the Adamses' lives and legacies were deeply entwined, they were also distinct.

Abigail is certainly the most influential of the early founding mothers. She was the wife of one president, the mother of another president, and advisor to both. But the legacy for which she is best remembered is her own—a lifelong advocacy for women.

Thus, even though we knew that in writing this book we would be walking in the shadow of Laura Linney's superlative performance in HBO's John Adams miniseries, we thought Abigail deserved to have her own story told.

But of course, in any work of historical fiction, clues must be ferreted out, theories must be adopted, and liberties must be taken to create a streamlined fictional narrative. So we are thankful for this opportunity to clarify our choices and changes.

To begin with, as in all historical fiction, the most surprising parts are true. And we know it will surprise some readers to learn that Abigail Adams was an ardent and consistent champion for women.

Now, we have noticed that certain historians stumble over themselves to reassure us that our most influential founding mother was not, in fact, a feminist as we would understand the word today. Certainly, the terminology of feminism as a named movement did not exist before the nineteenth century. But the ideas—and the activism—began long before that, much of it taking place in Abigail's time. And if a feminist is a person who advocates for women on the basis of their equality as human beings, we believe she qualifies.

For example, it is claimed that in Abigail Adams's famous "Remember the Ladies" letter, she only "jests" about female rebellion. And yet, in that very same jest—if it was a jest at all—she spelled out the moral principle that no person—man or woman, enslaved or free—could be morally bound by laws they have no voice in.

Moreover, she reacted to John's dismissive reply with disappointment, complaining to Mercy Otis Warren and asking her to join her in a petition to the government. Far from dropping the subject, Abigail repeatedly raised women's issues in her letters to her husband and others.

She spoke approvingly of New Jersey giving some women the right to vote—a right later taken away. And more than once did she mention that she would vote if she could.

Movingly, she pointed out the miracle of female patriotism given the injustice of women being excluded from government and public accolades.

She called herself a pupil of Mary Wollstonecraft, the proto-feminist who argued for the equality of women as moral beings. And Abigail championed women's education again and again—not merely as an acknowledgment of female intellectual abilities, but specifically in the context of a healthy republic.

It is worth noting that when one of John's associates joked that

Abigail ought to be autocratrix of the United States, she wrote back that she did not know why he abused her so, as she was only ever for equality.

This is remarkable when you remember that at the start of the revolution, it wasn't clear that all free men, much less women, would have a vote in this still fantasized about new nation. So we cannot dismiss her thoughts and her efforts on behalf of women as being too modest when judged against the context of her times.

The truth is that since girlhood, Abigail struggled against the limitations put upon her as a woman. She took on nontraditional roles in marriage, money, and motherhood. And she frequently circumvented laws that oppressed her, while attempting to ease the oppression for other women, too. She did this more than any other American founding mother. So it seems to us a patently absurd semantic argument to say that an otherwise socially conservative woman who prized spirituality, social order, and security should not be considered a feminist because she didn't burn a bra that had not yet been invented.

As we said, the most astonishing things in this novel are true. For example, during the Battles of Lexington and Concord, seventy-eight-year-old farmer Samuel Whittemore really did kill three British soldiers before being bayoneted and shot in the face—and thanks to the help of Dr. Tufts, lived to tell the tale until the age of ninety-six.

Though it may seem like a comical fictional device, the confusion between John Adams and Samuel Adams was very real, and created a number of sticky situations during the revolution. Whether it was the misdelivery of tea or a misdelivered letter, it not only happened but sometimes had political consequences besides.

Moreover, Abigail's charitable nature was not an invention for this book; while she was certainly a frugal New Englander who otherwise kept a tight fist on her coin purse, she was also well known for giving money and foodstuffs to her neighbors, particularly widows and mothers, and especially at Christmastime. In fact, these neighbors came to be so reliant upon her generosity that she called them her pensioners.

Another remarkable but true fact is that though both women were active throughout the revolution, Abigail did not cross paths with Martha Washington during the siege of Boston. Though Martha visited George Washington's war camp in Cambridge, the two women did not meet until 1789 in New York upon Abigail assuming her role as the wife of the vice president.

More wild history that was not our invention: Abigail really did receive letters from James Lovell that would have been considered scandalously flirtatious; Vice President Burr really did shoot and kill Alexander Hamilton; Jefferson's daughter Polly really did stay with the Adamses in London; Abigail really did carry on a secret correspondence with Jefferson after Polly's death. Charles Adams did, in fact, socialize with Alexander Hamilton and his associates in New York, reporting back political intelligence to his father. And yet, that same father renounced him when he suffered from alcoholism.

Lastly, the barbarous mastectomy undertaken by Abigail's daughter Nabby, without modern anesthesia, is both ghastly and true, right down to the detail of her not crying out. Nabby was a stoic from childhood—to her parents, puzzling in her reserve—and that she lost her battle to cancer is also regrettably true.

But, of course, many things had to be simplified or condensed to streamline the story. For example, the Adams family lived in at least three houses in Boston, including one on Cold Lane, one on Brattle Street, and one on Queen's Street (later Court Street). We have mentioned only one to cause the least confusion. Additionally, not all those killed during the Boston Massacre died immediately, but we pretended as much for brevity. And we tried to be ambiguous about the Battle of Bunker Hill, which actually took place on Breed's Hill.

The Sons of Liberty were originally called the Loyal Nine, but we decided to stick with the term most familiar to the reader. We also referred to variolation as inoculation because that is not only most familiar to the reader but also what people called the procedure at the time. The term *first lady* as we know it today was really popularized by Dolley Madison. In Abigail's time, she was more frequently called the "president's lady." However, this distinction did not seem important, so we used the latter term occasionally to denote what Abigail truly did feel and express about the role she played in the nation. A final example of this is when Abigail refers to "the shot heard round the world" to describe the Battles of Lexington and Concord. This phrase wasn't popularized until at least 1837, when Ralph Waldo Emerson wrote his famous poem "Concord Hymn," but the power of the phrase and the reader's familiarity with it argued for its inclusion.

While we try not to put our characters where they wouldn't or couldn't have been, we occasionally let them know things either more quickly or more slowly than they would have learned them. For example, it appears that John Adams did not stay long enough out of doors to know that Governor Hutchinson ordered the arrest of the British soldiers who fired on the crowd in what would become known as the Boston Massacre, but it was efficient to have him have heard about this immediately. Yet, when it came to the confrontation between John Adams and Alexander Hamilton that happened in Trenton, New Jersey, Abigail wasn't there and didn't see it, so we didn't have John tell her about it until they were in Philadelphia, though he wrote of it to her long before then. Perhaps a more important example is that John Adams and Abigail Adams traveled to Philadelphia separately in the autumn of 1799. John learned of Charles's drunkenness first and renounced him, leaving a letter for Abigail. But we decided to move this whole sequence into December of 1799 because it was easier to dramatize the emotions of the situation if John and Abigail were together.

Whenever possible, we streamlined travel so the reader is spared having to see the to-ing and fro-ing. One instance of this is that Washington's request to see Abigail despite his lying down sick actually happened upon her second visit to the president's house, but we combined them for the sake of brevity. In the autumn of 1778, Abigail Adams twice dined with Admiral d'Estaing. At the earlier occasion, it appears the Marquis de Lafayette was present. At the second, more sumptuous occasion on board his flagship, Lafayette appears to have already left Boston for winter quarters with Washington. We chose to conflate the events because they were similar in nature. (It's unclear if Nabby

Adams was present either time, but given her age, it seemed to us quite likely.)

And for the sake of narrative flow, we also made small changes to the timeline. For example, James Lovell actually made his Boston Massacre commemorative speech in 1771 but since we skipped over that year, we put the speech where we thought it fit best, though it pained us to supplant Joseph Warren's speech of 1775. Abigail asked John for pins earlier than this novel posits, but we didn't want to interrupt the war drama of early 1775 with domestic concerns. Another example is that Abigail's mother died of dysentery slightly before Abigail's servant girl Patty died, but we reversed this for dramatic impact. Abigail didn't find out about John becoming the president of the Board of War until May of 1776, but we put it slightly earlier for brevity. We decided to postpone the Cranches' move to Braintree until it made dramatic sense, but that necessitated moving the New Year's Day meeting with James Lovell in 1777 to the parsonage in Weymouth instead of the Cranch residence, where it actually took place. In fact, much of 1777 is slightly out of sequence—Tommy's accident, Abigail's stillbirth, and the capture of her brother—to make the events flow sensibly by topic.

Abigail's father died in September of 1783 but we moved it later so we could lead the chapter with victory in the war. Nabby and her husband did not leave for Wimpole Street until June 30, but we wanted to condense as much as possible. John was protesting British impressment of sailors as of 1787, but we posited it a little earlier. And of course, the British insults against American independence at this time were far worse than the impressment of soldiers, but it was the most straightforwardly horrible thing they were doing, so we used it as the sole example for the sake of simplicity.

Sometimes it was better to just leave things unsaid. For example, despite John's eviction of the truculent Mr. Hayden, it actually took Abigail three tedious years to get him off the property. We decided that the reader did not have to suffer that tedium alongside Abigail.

Of course, our most serious simplification is that when John Adams first crossed the ocean en route to France in 1778, he took with him his eldest son, John Quincy Adams. He returned briefly to America in August of the next year, at which point he took both his eldest son, John Quincy Adams, and his middle son, Charles Adams, with him back to France. We chose to combine both these trips for the sake of brevity. But one extremely unfortunate side effect of combining the trips is that it forced us to skip over what Abigail's husband actually did during the brief time that he was home—and that is write the Massachusetts state constitution. It is the oldest written constitution still functioning in the world, and a model to democratic governments everywhere.

The largest omissions in this book are the people we left out of it. And the most consequential of these people is Abigail's niece Louisa Smith. While we mention that Abigail committed to help support her brother's abandoned and ultimately orphaned children, we did not explain that Abigail actually took her niece Louisa in. Louisa would live with the Adamses most of her life, and was, in fact, the recipient of Abigail's largest bequest in her will.

But because few traces of Louisa remain—what she thought, what she felt, and who she was as a person—we thought it best not to introduce another character into the book for whom we would have to invent an entire inner life.

We also don't give much attention to the family of John Adams, despite the fact that Abigail lived next door to them in Braintree and spent many years caring for her elderly mother-in-law. To include John's family would have meant exploring his complicated relationship with his mother and his brother Peter, with whom we found only one extant letter, rather frosty in nature. We felt that we had enough of Abigail's family to deal with, and this was her story, so we left John's family in the background.

Another regrettable omission is the Baron von Steuben—the colorful Prussian revolutionary hero who was a mentor to both Colonel William Stephens Smith and Charles Adams. We would have loved to explore the influence he had upon the young men who caused Abigail the greatest grief, but she was not privy to the details.

And in any case, we were mindful of not making the book longer than it needed to be.

For that same reason, we omitted Abigail's faithful and dedicated servants Esther Field and John Briesler, both of whom accompanied her to Europe. Sadly, this meant that we could not include a character-revealing story about Abigail when Esther confessed to being pregnant and tearfully begged her forgiveness. Rather than harshly judge the young woman or dismiss her for the scandal, Abigail fretted about Esther's health, quickly securing medical care and making wedding arrangements for Esther to marry John Briesler, the father of her child.

Another thing we were sorry not to have an opportunity to include is that John Adams dined with Haiti's lead emissary, making him the first man of African descent to be the dinner guest of an American president. This distressed Jefferson, who, fearing slave revolts, hoped that Adams would not give assistance to Haiti.

Abigail's Vermont land purchases never amounted to much. And in 1803, the Adamses lost their savings in a bank collapse. John Quincy Adams had advised his parents to invest in this bank, and when it collapsed, he bought their land and gave them a life tenancy in it, so they could recoup what they'd lost. He also sold his house in Boston and moved back to Quincy to help support them. We regretted having to leave this out of the narrative because it shows how close the relationship was between these parents and their oldest son.

Finally, there were a great many interesting happenings we did not delve into, such as when Vice President Burr was charged with treason. The Adamses assuredly had opinions about this and a great many other things, but we tried to keep the focus on Abigail's direct sphere.

Then we come to our speculations and educated guesses. Whether Abigail divined upon a plan to sell goods and start a mercantile business on her own, or if this idea was suggested to her by Cotton Tufts, is not known. But as the buying of land and selling of pins seemed to be all her idea, we think it likely that the mercantile business was her idea, too.

John's position vis-à-vis the Sons of Liberty was an interesting puzzle. Some historians claim he never officially joined. Others say he was listed as a member. His own diary says he met with them near the Liberty Tree. So we decided upon some ambiguity there.

It's also interesting to note that John's cocounsel in the Boston Massacre trial was Colonel Quincy's son Josiah, while the prosecutor was his Tory son Samuel. Because of this, one almost suspects the trial to be a bit of theater.

Though celebrated historians say that the Adams family was not present in Boston by the time of the Tea Party, Abigail's biographer Woody Holton implies she was home alone in Boston that winter night. We think Holton is correct and that John was out riding the circuit the night in question. One reason we think so is that John's letter from the day after the Tea Party is written from Boston and he mentions Abigail sending her compliments.

Holton's biography also claims the famed romantic pendant was given to Abigail in 1778. Others say John gave it to her upon his brief return from France in 1779. Since we omitted that trip, we accepted the former interpretation.

There were reports that John Adams was captured at sea in his crossing to France, as attested to by a letter from Samuel Cooper to Adams in July of 1778. But whether these reports were in the newspaper is not known. Since similar reports of Franklin's assassination did appear in the newspaper, we decided it was likely.

Mercy Otis Warren did rather mysteriously stop writing to Abigail, long before the formal trouble erupted between them, which left us to speculate why.

And it is unclear what ailment John Adams suffered in Holland. Some say malaria, some say scurvy, but given the length and severity of the illness, and the local prevalence, we thought malaria the more likely.

Another instance of unsolvable mystery surrounded the two letters that Nabby showed her mother about Royall Tyler. We don't know the identity of the second author. We decided to use Nabby's brother as a source, though in truth, the Adamses did not know of John Quincy's arrival in America for quite some time.

Some natural liberties were also taken in this novel. For example, though Patty was a real servant girl who died of dysentery in Abigail's home, we entirely invented the widowed Mrs. Copeland to be her mother.

We have no evidence that soldiers ever tried to search Abigail's house in Boston with or without a writ, but we wanted to demonstrate what sorts of abuses were happening that aggravated the colonists.

John Adams indicated that he faced some blowback for taking on the case of the Boston Massacre. We think it was not too severe a blowback, because he was subsequently elected to congress, but he says he did lose business, and that the stress and strain and public scrutiny of it all took a deep toll on him, so we invented the rotted eggs and flaming horse manure.

Additionally, Henry Knox's testimony is listed amongst the affidavits in "A Short Narrative of the Horrid Massacre in Boston" published in 1770. But he does not appear in John Adams's notes for the first twenty defense witnesses. Nevertheless, Knox is a famous witness to these events and went on to be secretary of war, so we included him.

James Otis Jr. was probably too mentally ill to have been at the Green Dragon Tavern in 1773 with the other Sons of Liberty, but we put him there anyway because he deserved to be part of that story.

Because of the nature of intelligence work, we don't know what specific consequences flowed from Abigail's passing on of information during the revolution, but John indicated it was very useful, so we implied that Abigail's intelligence work impacted the attack on a lighthouse.

The sequence of disastrous letters between Abigail and John when he was in France has been slightly massaged for a clearer narrative arc. But we quote from those letters liberally, as they were shockingly hurtful.

Though we did not exaggerate Abigail's financial acumen, we did exaggerate her husband's disinterest in money matters because his correspondence gives the impression he paid more attention to the fiscal situation of the country. But we do not want the reader to leave with the idea that the historic John Adams was wholly ignorant or entirely disengaged from his personal finances. Very occasionally, we let Abigail do something actively instead of receiving news passively to keep the story engaging.

For example, it was actually Abigail's uncle who sent a rider with a dispatch that Charles was in Spain, but we sent her to Boston to find out for herself that Charles and his guardian had disembarked from the *South Carolina* because the captain was after booty and the passengers just wanted to go home. Charles and his guardian made their way to Bilbao to take another ship home.

While there are scant records about the Thanksgiving food riot at Harvard, it is probable that only Charles was involved. But we included both boys because it streamlined the narrative about Abigail's worries for both her sons and their future.

With regard to Phoebe's husband, Mr. Abdee, he died sometime before 1798. She was remarried at least one more time. But to keep the cast list from expanding, we let Mr. Abdee live on for some years longer than he did. Phoebe had moved to a different Adams property by 1811, but we just had Tommy move in with her.

We presented Abigail Adams as being adamantly opposed to slavery, which is historically true. In fact, she sometimes expressed that the difficulties the country endured might be some form of divine retribution for the sin of slavery. We also portrayed her as having a meaningful and loving relationship with the enslaved servant Phoebe, which is also true. We know that Abigail wrote often of her distrust and dislike of slavers and the slave states. That she hired and paid her Black workers. She often praised them. And she seems to have been both fair and generous to people of other races.

But she could also be horrifically patronizing. And she did harbor prejudices, which she acknowledged. Her letters are peppered with the occasional racial stereotype, and she readily confessed her absolute discomfort with seeing the mixed-race relationship in *Othello*.

Moreover, though Abigail Adams writes very little about Sally Hemings, she wrote just enough to hint at how much she disapproved. She considered Sally a servant girl, and having employed many serving girls herself, she directed most of her attention to Polly. But we chose to have her be friendly with both girls here to show both her humanity as well as her anger at Jefferson later in life when the Hemings scandal broke.

When, precisely, Abigail Adams developed her opposition to slavery is unknown to us. We only know that Abigail benefited from the labor of enslaved people as a girl and young woman, but she and her husband never trafficked in slavery and wrote against it.

That she remained close enough to Phoebe Abdee to host her wedding and give over her house into the woman's care made us think that Abigail probably developed this aversion to slavery in childhood, that it developed because of her affection for Phoebe, and so we fictionalized her confrontations with her father about it accordingly. What we do know is that Abigail did consider Phoebe to be a second mother, and that she cared for her as such when she was dying.

In conclusion, we invite the reader to recognize the relevance of this story to today's struggles in the United States. We've presented a fair and honest assessment of the founders' justifications for rebellion and their hopes and dreams for this country, drawing wherever possible from their own writings at the time. Though we modernized the language detailing the list of accusations against the king in the Declaration of Independence, we accurately listed the concerns the founders had about the state of society and human rights. This book is being published upon the 250th anniversary of the Declaration, and therefore we think it essential for all Americans to give extra thought to our founding documents, the men who wrote them, and their continued meaning and relevance to American society today. To learn more, please visit DrayKamoie.com, StephanieDray.com, or LauraKamoie.com.

Acknowledgments

THIS NOVEL WAS written under the most extremely trying circumstances of our careers, when after a panoply of health challenges, Laura was diagnosed with breast cancer in the summer of 2024, followed by a double mastectomy that autumn and a stroke that winter.

We are so grateful for her recovery and for all the people who helped her survive.

We are also grateful for those who helped Stephanie bring this book to fruition when Laura was unable. Our heroic critique partners Kate Quinn, Lea Nolan, and Sheila Accongio all leaped into action, reading on very short notice, often just as parts of the book were still being scribbled. Our editor, Tessa Woodward, was always there for advice and guidance during these harrowing times.

We also had help from the well-respected Revolutionary War author Lars Hedbor, who gave advice on handling some tricky early American politics. Fellow Abigail Adams author Jodi Daynard offered both some research help and encouragement. And the fascinating and multitalented Carol Cohen brought her expertise as a reenactor to bear in consulting on this novel. We are grateful for all the help we received in fact-checking and consultation, but any mistakes are ours alone.

Along the way, we were helped by our assistants, Lisa Christi and Franci Neill, without whom the wheels would have come completely off the bus.

We're also indebted to our hero agent, Kevan Lyon, and grateful for the unending patience of Amanda Bergeron. Not to mention the National Archives, where the letters of the founders are preserved and digitized at Founders.Archives.gov. We are often stunned by the generosity and kindness of our favorite librarians and booksellers, including Jan Boston, Trisha Shively, and Melody Wukitch.

We also want to acknowledge the creative inspiration of HBO's miniseries *John Adams*, starring Laura Linney as Abigail Adams. We knew we could never outshine her, but she helped light the way. Biographies consulted include *Abigail Adams: A Life* by Woody Holton, *Dear Abigail* by Diane Jacobs, *John Adams* by David McCullough, and *A Woman's Dilemma* by Rosemarie Zagarri. Specific credit goes to Irving Stone's *Those Who Love*, which speculated upon Abigail's differing way of referring to Cotton Tufts as Uncle or Cousin depending on her mood. That idea was not original to us.

Finally, we wish to thank our husbands and loving families, who supported us both during the rough times.

About the Authors

STEPHANIE DRAY is a *New York Times, Wall Street Journal,* and *USA Today* bestselling author of historical women's fiction. Her award-winning work has been translated into many languages and tops lists for the most anticipated reads of the year. She lives near the nation's capital with her husband, her history books, her fluffy Ragdoll cat, and an endless parade of foster kittens. Visit StephanieDray.com for more.

LAURA KAMOIE is a *New York Times, Wall Street Journal,* and *USA Today* bestselling author of historical women's fiction. She has a doctoral degree in early American history from the College of William and Mary and held the position of associate professor of history at the U.S. Naval Academy before transitioning to a full-time writing career, penning more than forty novels in multiple genres. She lives in Annapolis, Maryland, with her husband, two daughters, and a distinguished gentleman of a German Shepherd, Schuyler. Visit LauraKamoie.com for more.